TOWER AND GRAVE

MEGAN O'RUSSELL

Ink Worlds Press

Visit our website at www.MeganORussell.com

Tower and Grave

Cover Art by Sleepy Fox Studio (https://www.sleepyfoxstudio.net/)

Editing by Christopher Russell

Interior Design by Christopher Russell

Printed in the United States of America

For the ones who have braved the darkness.
You are more than the scars you bear.

White Mountains
Royal Palace
Map Mast Palace
Barrens
Barrens Bay
Arion Sea
Ilara
Frason's Glenn
Harane
Ian Lioche
Ian Mithe
ILBREA
Ian Ayres
Ruthir Mountain
Mountain Road
Southern Citadel
T E
Pamerane

N
Spice Trail
Spice Trail
Mountain Road
EASTERN MOUNTAINS
WYRAIN
Spios
Golden Sea
JUNGLESS TERRITORIES
Acalia
The Horn

TOWER AND GRAVE

PART I

1

ENA

The fading of the sun warned me to stop, but the heat of the stone in my hand begged me to keep pressing onward, climbing farther into the eastern mountains. Weaving between shadows, I searched for the haven promised by the bit of magic resting on my palm.

Fallen leaves rustled on the forest floor as all the little animals fled into their dens for the night. Safe, warm, home.

Climbing a tree and finding a place to perch as I waited out the dark was the only safety I'd had in days. I could forage for food, I could find water, but the only shelter I could offer the child I carried lured me back into a world of ghosts and legends.

The babe squirmed in my belly as though he too could feel the growing heat of the little black stone as the tingle of foreign magic grew up my arm. For the child, I would keep climbing. For him, I would face the darkness of a life I thought I'd left behind forever.

I ignored my body's pleas for rest and scrambled to the top of another rise.

As the sun abandoned me, the heat of the stone faded.

I shut my eyes, swallowing my need to shout.

"You're all right, little one." I pressed my hand to my belly, trying to douse my rage with the need to comfort the child. "Magic was never meant to be simple for people like us. Even when magic longs to protect you, its power will draw you down dark and twisted paths."

An owl hooted his agreement as I turned south, cutting along the side of the slope.

The heat of the stone burned again, hotter and brighter, though the stone itself stayed the same shining black it had been when a stranger on a ship had tempted me with a thin shred of hope.

I made myself believe the man didn't know how painful hope can be.

Jumping into the Arion Sea had been simple. Fleeing the paun ship bound for Ian Ayres was the only path the gods had left me.

Climbing the cliffs on the shore, crossing the miles upon miles of open space between the sea and the forest of the eastern mountains, climbing slope after slope following the whims of a chivving stone—all those trials had been simple, childish tests of a person's will to live.

But I had given up my life three times, lost everything I loved and was and forced myself to trudge onward.

If the gods remade me a fourth time, there wouldn't be enough left of me to keep fighting to endure.

The child kicked and squirmed, pressing up into my lungs.

"I know, little one. I'll see you to safety."

The heat from the stone sharpened, the tingle reaching all the way into my chest.

"There are places where myths and magic rule. Beautiful places that have never been tainted by the evil of the Guilds. You'll be far away from the paun and the Lady Sorcerer, and I won't ever let them find you."

The heat twisted in my chest, pulling me onward.

I climbed the slope to a ridgeline just above the trees. The silver sheen of the moonlight bathed my rocky path.

Sense told me to go back down the slope, stay near the trees where I'd have a chance of climbing their branches out of reach of any beast that might catch my scent, but the pull of the magic had gotten too strong.

Hours passed as I followed that ridge. The magic lost its patience, pulling me south as though the mountain herself had driven a hook into my chest and would drag me as she pleased, even if it ripped my ribs from my body.

The child and the mountain worked their will on my lungs, making it hard to breathe as the ridge pitched down then up again with a slope I had to use my hands to climb.

The forest reclaimed the mountain as my path leveled out.

I shielded my belly as I forced my way through a thick stand of trees. The branches clawed at the tattered remains of my finely made dress, catching the frail cloth that hadn't been made to survive outside the luxury the paun were too foolish to understand they enjoyed.

I sucked air in through my teeth as a branch snapped across my cheek, ripping deep enough to draw blood. Holding my palm to the wound, I fought through the last few trees that tore at my hair and scratched my arms.

I kicked my way into a clearing and took two steps before I realized I wasn't breathing.

I pressed my bloody palm to my chest. The painful pull of magic dragging me forward had vanished. The stone in my hand had gone cold.

I watched the stone tumble from my palm. It landed on the ground, settling beside the dirt-stained rocks that had never been touched by magic.

At the far edge of the clearing, a boulder lay nestled into the slope of the mountain. No moss or lichen had dared mar the face of the stone.

Heat brimmed in my eyes as I forced myself to drag in air. Pain clenched the front of my throat.

"For you, little one," I whispered to the babe still fussing in my womb. "I'll face any ghost for you."

I banished the tears that threatened to spill down my cheeks and leaned against a tree to untie my dirt-caked boots. The chill of the ground beneath my bare feet sent bumps all over my skin before I'd even unfastened my skirt. I didn't bother trying to keep the blood from my cheek off the fabric as I pulled my shift over my head.

An awful, weak fear clawed at the back of my neck as I stood naked in the moonlight. Not from shyness at exposing my body to the stones and shadows, but for leaving the child so exposed, unmistakably growing inside me. No amount of lies or layers of fabric could hide the life the Guilds had condemned me for carrying.

I closed my eyes and clasped the black stone pendant that hung around my neck.

The wind whipped around me as though all the ghosts of the eastern mountains had come to whisk my fear away.

I let my heart still.

"Thank you," I whispered into the wind.

I took off the pendant and laid it on top of my clothes. A barren hollow carved into my chest as I turned away from the pendant to face the boulder.

Holding my arms out and my palms up, I slowly crossed the clearing, listening for the shink of a sword clearing its scabbard or the swish of a stone aiming to pierce my heart.

The forest stayed quiet and unnaturally still.

I pushed my grief away, plucking out the memories I couldn't bear, forcing them into the darkest places of my mind where the flames of my rage could hide them beneath a shroud just thick enough to allow me to face the bloody path the gods had laid out for me.

"I am Ena Ryeland." I offered my name to the night. "I am a Black Blood sworn to the Duwead Clan. Named Solcha by the children beloved by the mountain."

The wind stilled.

"I've come seeking sanctuary for the child I carry, and aid in my fight against the Guilds."

I stopped in front of the boulder.

"The mountain guided me through her darkness. The mountain claimed me as her own. Stone magic led me here. Do not turn me away."

Crack.

A sliver of blue light sliced through the boulder as the Black Bloods welcomed Solcha home.

2

ADRIAL

"Please, sir."

The pleading words pressed against Adrial's clouded mind, but they weren't strong enough for him to properly hear.

"You've got to eat, sir. Just a few more bites."

A sharp, stinging pain pierced the fog but didn't break it. And when the pain ebbed, the fog thickened.

He was grateful.

"They'll take you away, sir."

Cold dragged across Adrial's face.

"There's already talk of it. You've got to eat, or you'll be sent to the healers. There's even whispers of you being sent to the Sorcerers Tower."

A flare of anger singed away the edges of the fog.

"Please, sir." The voice rattled in Adrial's ear as the cold rubbed his hand. "After all they've done, you can't let those beasts take you away."

A new pain, heavy and brutal, pressed down on Adrial's chest.

"It's not what she'd want, sir."

Adrial snatched his hand away from the cold.

The movement stole more of the precious fog.

"You know I'm right, sir."

The cold clamped around his other hand.

"If Ena were here—"

Adrial smacked the cold away.

The sharp clang of metal on stone shocked his mind back to the unrelenting brutality of the moment.

Taddy stood beside Adrial, his eyes swollen, his pale face marred by the patchy red of recent tears. The apprentice knelt, righting the metal bowl and wringing out the cloth in his hands before mopping up the water Adrial couldn't bring himself to feel guilty for spilling.

"You can't argue against it, sir," Taddy said. "Ena hates the Sorcerers Guild and the Healers Guild."

"Hated." A horrible pain curled through Adrial's chest. "Ena is dead."

Tears brimmed in Taddy's eyes. "I know."

"My wife is dead. The baby is dead."

"Sir—"

"Drowned in the Arion Sea." The words broke in his throat. He begged the blessed fog to return, but the room didn't disappear.

The wardrobe where her clothes still hung. The bed where she'd slept beside him.

"It should be me. I should have been the one to die." The pain sliced into a deeper, more painful place in his chest than he'd ever known existed.

"Dudia has never shown such mercy, sir," Taddy said. "We're not allowed to trade one life for another. The sea took Ena, and you're still alive. You can't trade places."

"Then leave me be. Let them lock me up or whip me. There's no torture they can offer that's any worse than this. I wish there were. I failed her. I failed my wife. I deserve every pain the Guilds can offer."

"You don't, sir." Taddy set the bowl on the table and shoved the stopper back into the bottle of stinging ointment.

Adrial should have refused to let anyone clean the wounds the whipping had carved into his back.

Let the wounds fester. Let their rot end his wretched life.

"Ena didn't die because of you, sir." Taddy poured broth into a mug. "If everything they're saying is true—"

"Don't. Don't you dare—"

"—it was the Guild Lords who condemned you that caused all this pain." Taddy raised his voice, speaking over Adrial. "They wanted to punish you and plucked a chivving reason straight out of their asses, and I didn't come up with that wording, sir, I got it right from Scribe Tammin. Ena let them put her on that ship to Ian Ayres to protect you. She saved your life, and now you're tossing it away like yesterday's sheep shit."

"Taddy—"

"You curling up in your room and letting grief devour your mind while you refuse to eat dishonors the sacrifice she made to keep you alive, and I cared too much for Ena to let that happen," Taddy shouted. "Find a new apprentice if you like, but until you do, I'm going to keep stomping into your rooms and trying to make you survive, because it's what Ena would have wanted."

Taddy panted as the red that had devoured his face deepened.

"If I died protecting someone that someone else had tried to murder, I'd be chivving angry beyond all reason if the person I'd protected gave up on living instead of fighting the people who tried to have the person I'd protected killed in the first place." Taddy held the mug out to Adrial. "You're already living a tragedy, Head Scribe. Are you going to be the hero or another chivving victim?"

"I'm not a hero, Taddy. I couldn't protect Ena. I couldn't protect..." Adrial swallowed the painful, spiked knot in his throat. "Her baby will never be born because of me."

"Because of the monsters who condemned you. Lady Gwell,

Lady Byrd, Map Maker Traim, even the King. They wanted you dead. They were going to whip you to death. Why?"

"I spoke against them. I meddled. I peered into shadows they thought they'd washed away."

"If whatever is hiding in the shadows is worth killing the Head Scribe of Ilbrea for, I'd wager my apprenticeship Ena would want you to keep digging and prodding and meddling." Taddy took Adrial's hand, wrapping Adrial's fingers around the mug. "You can't bring Ena back, sir, but you can make sure her death has meaning."

"And if I fail her again?"

"They already took your wife and your child, sir," Taddy said. "There's nothing left for you to lose."

3

———

KAI

Kai tucked his tongue between his teeth and rammed his heels against the packed dirt floor as he willed himself not to scream. He took a deep breath through his nose. The pain in his side flared, shooting spikes from his ribs to his ass then straight up to his throat. The taste of blood filled his mouth as his teeth cut into his tongue.

"Again." Lewis crossed his arms, glaring down at Kai.

"Papa, he's had enough," Valia said.

"Again," Lewis ordered.

Kai winked at Valia and took another deep breath, allowing a fresh wave of pain to claim his body. Spots danced in his vision.

"Every bit of me goes against it." Lewis's frown twisted to a comical level.

"If he can't, he can't." Landon stood from his seat on the ladder that led from the cellar to the alley above.

Kai swallowed the blood in his mouth. "I'm fine. I can stand. I can walk."

"There's not a bit of me that believes that's all you'd be doing," Lewis said.

"Smart man." Drew kept his gaze fixed on the worn wooden planks of the wall opposite his bed, not bothering to mask his refusal to look in Kai's direction.

"Of all the ways to die, letting a broken rib skewer my lung is not on my preferred list. You've explained the dangers, and"—Kai held up a hand before Lewis could interrupt—"I did listen to the warnings. Even if I wanted to do something foolish, I've a chivving broken hand keeping me from fighting."

"I can keep an eye on him," Landon said.

"I don't think you can," Drew said.

"Helping to plan, that's all it is," Kai said. "I'm to walk across the city. Go into a different hole under the streets and talk. Maybe not even talk. I might only nod while I listen to other people talk."

"He's right there," Landon said.

"The greatest danger I'll be facing is the tenuous balance between frustration and boredom," Kai said.

Lewis dragged his hands over his thinning gray hair. "He's only to be aboveground long enough to get to the tunnels. He's not to be anywhere a person might even think of needing a weapon."

"So, I should leave Ilara?" Kai said.

Lewis redoubled his glare. "No carrying heavy loads, and if the pain gets worse, someone's to come and fetch me. Not in an hour. Not after the meeting. Immediately."

"Anything else?" Landon said.

"Yes." Lewis stepped closer to Landon. "If he dies from this foolishness, no one is to blame me. Two getches arrive in my cellar bloodied up and flirting with Death, and I manage to save them both. I'll not allow my excellent twork to be questioned because a chivving fool wouldn't let himself heal and got himself killed by not following my orders."

"I will sing your praises to everyone in the underground." Kai stood, moving gingerly enough he only paid with a moderate surge of pain in his side. "While not sharing your name or where you are, of course." He pulled on the clean, dark shirt Landon had brought for him. "I will tell tales of the ghost healer of Ilara, whose great gifts seem granted by the gods."

"That's quite enough," Lewis said.

"Are you sure? I've plenty more praises to offer." Kai slid on his boots, feeling foolish as he wriggled his feet into place instead of stomping them in.

"Just go," Lewis said. "And try not to need my help again anytime soon."

"As you wish." Kai gave Lewis a nod and Valia a grin.

"Come, Papa." Valia took her father's arm. "We should go upstairs."

"Where I can sit and worry over fools in a proper chair." Lewis stepped in front of his daughter, pulling aside the bit of wall that blocked off the tunnel leading up into the illegal healer's home.

As she stepped into the tunnel, Valia turned and gave Kai a sly smile, glancing between him and Drew before closing the wall behind her.

Kai looked around the dull brown cellar, searching for inspiration. The two cots he and Drew had been stuck in for far too long didn't spark any genius. Neither did Lewis's shelves of healing supplies or the crooked table and worse-off chair.

"Landon," Kai said, "be a friend and stand by the ladder pretending you're deaf."

Landon sighed and shook his head, but still went back to the ladder. He faced the rungs and pressed his fingers to his ears.

"Look, I'm sorry." Kai stepped closer to Drew's bed. "I don't want to leave you in this sad burrow. If I thought it wouldn't kill you, I'd carry you back to the tunnels with me."

"Carrying me would kill *you*."

"It wouldn't be the worst way to go."

The creases on Drew's still-bruised brow deepened.

"As soon as whatever planning I'm being called to help with is done, I'll ask to come right back." Kai sat on the edge of Drew's bed, careful not to let the bed wobble. He laid his hand right beside Drew's, leaving his palm up as a pathetic peace offering. "The last thing I want is to abandon you."

"I'm not a child sulking over a lack of company," Drew said. "We almost died."

"I know."

"We're both still healing."

"I know that, too."

"If you go up there and get yourself into a mess, there's chiv all I can do to save you." Drew finally met Kai's gaze. "I can barely stand. I couldn't even limp after you shouting for you to be careful."

"I have to be careful. I couldn't even throw a proper punch. I can't get in a fight."

"We both know you'll find a way."

"I promise you, on my honor as a sailor, I will not go looking for trouble."

"You draw trouble to you like feral cats to a fish."

"Then I will walk away from the trouble as quickly as my poor healing body will allow." Kai gave his most charming smile. "Besides my general want for survival, if I have a chance at…" The words pressed against Kai's throat, but he couldn't make himself speak them.

Drew shifted his hand forward just far enough for his fingers to lay across Kai's.

"I've got too chivving much to live for," Kai said. "So you stay here and heal up. I'll be back as soon as I can."

Kai studied Drew for a moment, memorizing the worried creases at the corners of his eyes, then stood.

"You're forgetting something." Drew winced as he reached into his pants pocket.

"Careful."

"I've got it." Drew held out the silver token. "This goes back to you."

"Drew—"

"You saved my life dragging me here." Drew pressed the token into Kai's hand. "And from what you've promised, I'll be healed enough to earn it back next time you need saving."

Kai bent over, ignoring the pain in his ribs as he kissed Drew's hand. "Rest. I'll lure you back into the mayhem soon enough."

A tiny pinch twisted in Kai's chest as he let go of Drew's hand and went to the ladder.

He tapped Landon on the shoulder.

"After me then," Landon said, as though he hadn't been pretending not to exist a moment before. "Let me lower the stone, too. Don't want you mucking yourself up before you've even made it to the street."

Landon climbed up the ladder and pushed on the wide stone at the top, grunting from the weight of it. Holding the stone an inch above its place in the ground, he stared out into the darkness, the trembling of his arms growing worse every moment. He grunted again as he lifted the stone up and out of the way, clearing their path to the alley above.

Landon crawled through the hole, then reached down for Kai.

Kai looked to Drew, but Drew had settled himself back onto his pillows, his face hidden by their worn fabric.

Gritting his teeth against the inevitable pain, Kai reached up and took Landon's hand, using Landon's grip for extra balance as he climbed the ladder and took the first breath of fresh air he'd had since the night he and Drew had almost died at the sorcerers' hands.

The stench of piss and rot tainted the scent of the sea, but no smoke hung heavy in the air, no rancid stink of sulfur reminding all in Ilara the price of inciting the sorcerers' wrath.

Landon waited until Kai had stepped clear of the hole and

steadied himself against one of the houses flanking the alley before kneeling to move the stone back into place, erasing the hideaway where Drew would be stuck for only the gods knew how long.

Landon turned to Kai. Even in the shadows, Landon's pursed lips were unmistakable.

"Are you sure you're up for this?" Landon whispered. "I didn't want to ask in front of nursemaid Lewis and have you locked belowground until Winter's End, and I didn't want to interrupt whatever you and Drew were spatting—I mean—discussing as..." Landon wrinkled his nose and shook his head. "Well, as good friends. I suppose what I mean is, far be it from me to tell a man what he's capable of, especially in front of slitches who are trying to tell him he can't.

"But I'd also be a slitch for not asking. There are patrols on the streets. We're not going to be able to take our time getting back to the tunnels. I don't want the blood of a good man on my hands because I didn't give him a chance to say that if I made him run, he'd be running right into Death's embrace."

"Thank you, Landon." Kai clapped Landon on the shoulder, as though that might prove his health. "I'm up to running if it comes to it. Running might actually help with some of the soreness. I've never been good at sitting still."

"Then my conscience is clear." Landon turned and headed toward the far side of the alley, keeping to a pace that allowed Kai to breathe without spiking the pain in his ribs from problematic to sight-stealing.

Landon paused when they reached the road, searching the street, then studying the roofs of the surrounding houses, before crossing toward the next alley. He quickened his pace for the few moments he was in the open but didn't run. He kept his chin tucked as though he were hiding his face, making him seem more like a husband trying to sneak home without anyone finding out where he'd stashed his lover than a man looking for a fight.

Kai chose a different approach, matching Landon's pace, but keeping his chin up and letting a smile light his face, portraying a man who wanted the world to know he'd just had a spine-melting roll with a gorgeous getch and couldn't wait for someone to ask him what he was so happy about.

The next alley smelled of piss, shit, and dead rat.

Kai watched the ground, trying to step around the worst of the foulness, which managed to distract him until the next street crossing.

Landon followed the same pattern—searching the street and roofs before crossing like a man desperate not to be seen.

Kai plastered a stupid grin on his face like he'd just left the one who'd stolen his heart.

Don't blur lies and truth, Mara whispered. *At least not in your own head. Happiness is too precious to be whittled away by pride or fear.*

Chivving sodden cact of a chivving cowardly slitch. Kai's smile faltered. He settled for a roguish smirk.

A kiss on the hand. That's how he'd left Drew. With a chivving kiss on the hand like he was slinking away from a lusty tavern maid.

Drew deserves more.

Whether or not Drew wanted more from Kai was a question that weighed heavy in Kai's lungs, adding to the pain of his injuries.

But Drew had had his skull bashed in. The poor man had been bleeding from his head when he'd mentioned, briefly at that, that he might in fact want more from Kai than the friendship that had kept them both alive through so many horrors.

Kai tipped his head down as he crossed the next street.

And—*and* Drew's mind had been sluggish since he'd barely dodged Death. The poor man spent half his time with pain driving through his head and the other half sleeping.

Pressing a man for the truth of the words he'd spoken while

wounded, when he still couldn't walk well enough to climb the ladder out of the cellar and escape, was a level of cruelty to which Kai refused to stoop.

But he should have done better than chivving kissing Drew's hand. He could have kissed his forehead, or cheek…

Or lips.

Before the end of the next alley, Landon stopped short.

Kai knocked into his back, gasping at the pain that shot through his lungs.

Landon held up his hand, silencing Kai, then waved for him to retreat.

Kai backed away, instinctively grabbing for the knife at his hip. His broken hand throbbed. He drew the blade with his uninjured hand, trying not to feel like a chivving failure for forgetting to move his chivving blade to a place where he might actually be able to quickly grab it if his life were threatened.

Landon sidled back through the alley, his head swiveling from the street they'd come from to the street he didn't want to cross.

Kai followed his movement but couldn't catch sight of whatever had spooked Landon.

When they reached the end of the alley, Landon cut around Kai, retaking the lead as he hurried south, away from every entrance to the tunnels Kai had ever used.

Prickles of fear climbed Kai's spine as they kept to the open street, passing from the houses of the well-employed common folk to the shacks the worst off in Ilara called home.

Swaths of buildings had been destroyed. Most seemed to have been taken by fire. The anger that distracted Kai from his pain screamed that the damage had been done by the Sorcerers Guild, but the violence seizing the city wasn't that simple.

When did Ilara fall so low?

Landon finally cut into an alley between a wooden house with warped walls and a tannery. He stopped in the middle of the alley and leaned against the tannery wall, gesturing for Kai to join him.

Kai stayed upright, breathing as steadily as his ribs would allow to catch up on the air he'd lost through movement and anger. He studied the ground and walls around them, looking for whatever marked the alley as special enough for Landon to lead him there.

Landon looked up to the sky, squinting at the stars peeping through the clouds.

Keep moving. We need to keep moving.

A minute ticked by. Then another.

Kai's lungs caught up on air.

Still, Landon waited.

The echo of a faraway scream drifted into the alley.

Landon took Kai's arm, stopping him from running toward the sound.

Another scream came before a flurry of shouts.

Landon nodded to himself and dragged Kai toward the far end of the alley. He cut north, going back the way they'd come but one street over, keeping to a quicker, near-running pace that tested Kai's lungs.

Flames clawed up into the sky.

Landon cut through two alleys, then farther north on the road.

The sound of the screams changed, rising to a terrified, soul-penetrating pitch.

Over one alley, up one street. Three more alleys, a longer stretch out in the open.

The screaming stopped, but the flames continued to grow.

Through an alley, south a street. Another alley and farther south. Along a garden wall, then north to one of the stables where wealthy merchants boarded their horses.

Landon slowed as he looped behind the stables, taking time to check each window that overlooked the street, making sure no one was watching before stopping beside a shoulder-high garden wall.

"Can you make it over?" Landon looked from the wall to Kai.

"Sure," Kai whispered. "Give me a boost, and I think I can manage it without disobeying Lewis's edicts."

Landon nodded and bent over, linking his fingers together to make a step for Kai.

May the gods watch over this poor slitch.

Kai planted his good hand on top of the wall and stepped up into Landon's hands. He exhaled, willing his body to ignore the pain as he twisted his hip onto the wall, leaving him sideways with his legs dangling over the street.

I'm an embarrassment to myself.

Stifling his gasp of pain, he swiveled his legs over the garden.

I'm bearing the punishment for every boast I've ever made.

He leaned sideways, trying to lower his feet to the ground, gagging as pain flew through his body. He pushed away from the wall, choosing falling over putting more weight on his broken ribs.

A jolt of pain flashed white through his vision as his feet hit the ground and he stumbled, landing face first in a bush.

Chivving, steaming, sodden shafts of godsforsaken, tormented slitches.

A hand gripped Kai under his good arm, hoisting him back to his feet.

The price for regaining a shred of his dignity was another jolt of pain from his ribs.

Landon stepped in front of Kai and met his gaze, as though asking if Kai would rather curl up and die where he stood or keep plodding on and make Death wait a bit longer.

Kai waved Landon on with his good hand.

Landon nodded and slid back into the gap between the bushes and the wall. He cut around the edge of the garden, his gaze darting from the windows of the well-built merchant's home to the empty garden, not pausing until they'd reached the far side of the house.

He gestured for Kai to kneel behind the bushes then turned to face the wall. He ran his fingers along the mortar between the stones.

Kai watched his movements, squinting to see what Landon might be searching for.

A bit of cracked mortar, not fully fallen away, but crumbled enough to loosen the stone it should have held fast.

Landon pulled out his knife and worked the tip in below the loose stone until the rock fell into his hand. A hint of a smile lit Landon's face as he reached into the gap and pulled out a rusted key. Winking at Kai, Landon shoved the stone back in place.

Again, Kai followed as Landon crept along the wall, not stopping until they'd come level with a patch of wilting, pink-bloomed bushes growing right up against the house. Landon peered over the wall into the garden of the neighboring house, then checked each of the windows in the house they faced.

Landon leaned close to Kai. "Stay low and wait for my signal."

He bolted toward the decaying bushes without bothering to tell Kai what the signal might be.

I'm going to be caught by a gardener and killed with a rake.

Kai knelt beside the wall, using his good hand to shove aside enough branches to watch the place where Landon had disappeared.

Of all the undignified ways I've thought I might die, this could be the worst.

A laugh flickered in Kai's chest as even he couldn't believe his own lie.

Landon's hand appeared above the pink-flowered bushes, waving Kai over.

Ah. The signal.

Gripping his knife, Kai ran across the lawn and into the flower bushes.

A hand wrapped around Kai's arm, yanking him back.

He couldn't stifle his yelp as he fell to his knees.

"Shh." Landon glared at Kai, still gripping his arm.

Kai swallowed the bile in his mouth. "Sorry."

Landon pointed not even a foot ahead of Kai where a set of steep steps led into the ground.

Flattening his lips into a straight line, Kai gave Landon a nod of thanks.

Landon chivving winked again and climbed down into the chivving hole.

Defending the Guilds by hiding in a chivving bush.

A bottle of frie, that would lift Kai's spirits. Or a hot bath. Or a chance to properly speak to—

"Come on," Landon whispered from below.

Accepting that his ribs may never stop throbbing, Kai went down the stairs and into a dull brown room that, except for not having Drew, was of the same make as Lewis's cellar.

Landon knelt beneath a table along the back wall, huffing as he yanked on something. "Lower the doors if you can."

Kai stepped back up onto the stairs, carefully lowering the cellar doors one at a time, keeping as much weight away from his injuries as the godsforsaken doors would allow.

Instinct shocked sparks of awareness through Kai as he lowered the second door and total darkness devoured the cellar.

"This way," Landon said.

A crack and a hiss came before a candle flickered to life beneath the table.

Landon knelt beside a hole in the wall just large enough for a man to crawl through.

"Only a few hundred feet before you'll be able to stand." Landon set the joined planks he'd pried from the wall aside. "After that, it's only four tunnels, two trapdoors, a slight run back up on the streets, and one more passage until we're there."

"Perfect." Kai tucked his knife back into its sheath.

"After you, then." Landon scooted aside. "You've got to crawl backward after pulling the planks into place, and I wouldn't want to put your hand through that."

"Your thoughtfulness is uncanny." Kai dropped to his knees and began crawling forward, shoving the pain of his body away, hiding it beneath the deeper ache of churning through all the things he should have said to Drew.

4

ALLORA

The pounding rain spattered against the wide windows of Allora's parlor, each drop seeming to mock her failed hope that the storm might keep the newly allowed stream of visitors from begging for her ear.

Brannon, or those working on Brannon's orders, had remade the late Queen's parlor for Allora's use, carefully crafting the space for the comfort of her guests. A fire crackled in the wide, white marble fireplace. Well-placed tables sat nestled between the bevy of chairs, allowing the palace servants to discreetly feed the horde. The windows offered an impressive view of the palace grounds. The lights in the parlor cast a gentle glow on the gold and white couch where Allora sat, lending the gold of her dress an ethereal softness.

Any hostess in Ilara would be thrilled to have such a well-appointed place to entertain, but Allora couldn't deny the need scratching at the back of her mind, begging her to abandon propriety and hide in a secluded corner where not even her guards could find her.

Don't be a petulant child. You are the Queen. It is your duty to greet the people.

She adjusted her necklace, making sure the jewels pointed to the crease between her breasts as the parlor door opened.

Gillien stepped back into the room, snapping the door shut behind her. "If all the women in the hall are telling the truth, you have several closest friends and confidants waiting to see the much-adored Queen."

Lightning split the sky, solidifying the storm's mockery of her useless wish for the biddies of Ilara to find other entertainment.

"You can send them all away." Gillien stepped around the arc of chairs meant for visitors to stand right in front of Allora. "I can assure you the King wouldn't mind."

"Is it my husband who wouldn't mind or the Sorcerers Guild?" Allora lifted her glass of chamb from the tea tray where it sat beside the teacup she hadn't bothered to fill.

Gillien's pleasant smile didn't falter. "Both. The King wishes his wife to be happy and comfortable in the palace. If being invaded by false friends agitates you as much as it seems, there is no reason to indulge the driveling horde."

"And the Sorcerers Guild?" Allora set her glass of chamb aside. "Why would the Lady Sorcerer have me refuse my guests?"

"Would you prefer the complete truth or a politically colored lie?"

"Tell me both and I'll choose which I prefer."

"As you wish, Your Majesty. There are people in the city who would very much like to see you dead."

An uncomfortable worry sank in Allora's stomach. "What have I done to earn their hatred?"

"Married the King." Gillien sat beside Allora, not reacting when Allora slid over, placing herself as far from the sorcerer as the couch allowed. "I hope you don't find this to be too insulting, but the dissidents care more about hurting the King than taking your life."

"I find no insult in the people of Ilara not having a reason to loathe me in particular."

"Very wise." Gillien gave Allora a proud smile that set Allora's teeth on edge as she bit back the words she longed to scream. "But whatever the reason the rebels wish you harm, the fewer people who have access to you, the safer you'll be. Protecting the King's bride is of great concern to the Sorcerers Guild."

"Isolation as protection. The grand life of a queen." Allora poured herself more chamb. "And your other reason?"

"Giving the people access to you, even if it's only members of the Guilds and the most elite of the merchants, brings the risk of your gaining more favor with the people than you already have. The Queen should be loved by all in Ilbrea, but never more loved than the King. The King and the Sorcerers Guild also prefer you not be tainted by those outside the palace."

"Tainted? Is the city now being ravaged by illness as well as violence?"

"The illness the commoners face is not a concern."

"The commoners are ill? Why wasn't I told?"

"The petty happenings in the city are not your troubles to face." Gillien stood and crossed to the tea tray. "You are a good and caring person, Allora. And, as Queen, the people should see you as mother to all."

"It is my duty."

Gillien took Allora's glass, pouring chamb all the way up to the rim, but keeping the glass out of Allora's reach. "It is a grand illusion. The Queen should be seen as caring, generous, and maternal, but the work behind that image is done by others. Allowing the troubles that plague Ilara to taint your spirits would not be beneficial to the King or Ilbrea.

"Worry and stress must be avoided if you are to protect Ilbrea in a way only *you* can—by ensuring our country will have a ruler fit to lead the next generation and continue King Brannon's legacy of prosperity and peace. You will only ever be involved with the drudgery of ruling a country enough to sign your name on letters or, once peace has been restored, to smile prettily when faced with the public."

"And what would you have me do when I'm not signing or smiling?"

"Pleasure the King."

Heat rushed to Allora's face. "It is not your place—"

"Don't be petulant." Gillien cut across. "You are to keep the King well-pleasured and content. Bear his children, build a happy home."

"I cannot build a home that could be destroyed at the sorcerers' whim!" Allora leapt to her feet.

"Ah ah ah." Gillien waved her hand.

A rush of air surged down Allora's throat, choking her.

"Walls are thin in this part of the palace," Gillien said.

Allora shut her eyes and took in a shaky breath, trying not to scream as the image of a black-stone room knocked all other thoughts aside.

"This is the kind of upset we must strive to prevent," Gillien said.

"You want me to live isolated in a pretty, gilded illusion." The heat of angry tears pressed against Allora's eyelids.

"It's not an illusion, sweet Allora."

Allora flinched, opening her eyes as Gillien took her shoulder, still holding the glass of chamb just out of Allora's reach.

"You have been granted the privilege of leading a protected life," Gillien said.

"A pretty prison doesn't make you less trapped."

"You insult those who struggle by complaining of your privilege."

"I insult my people if I ignore their pain to be the King's placid bride. I will not sit on a shelf until the King calls for his plaything. I want to know everything that might upset me. Illness among the poor, rebels wanting me dead, every whisper of malcontent in the city, I insist on being told."

"That is neither healthy nor necessary," Gillien said. "A calm woman hosts a productive womb."

Allora stepped close to Gillien, daring to whisper in the sorcerer's ear. "Nothing can be worse than knowing the horror your Guild has buried beneath my feet. I will never be placid or calm while you can destroy my home."

"Do not test us, Allora. The sparrow cannot battle the storm."

"What storm?" Allora snatched her glass from Gillien, letting chamb slosh onto the sorcerer's purple robes. She took a sip. The bubbles joined the nerves dancing in Allora's stomach. "I am the placid wife of the King. I live to lie back and accept my husband's seed. I know nothing of storms." She smiled as she set her cup on the tray. "Send all the guests in."

"Is that truly the choice you wish to make?" The wet spots disappeared from Gillien's robes.

"They've already made their way here through the rain." Allora settled herself on the couch, carefully smoothing her skirt, allowing the fine fabric to be properly admired. "Tossing the guests back out into the storm would be rude at best."

"Very well, Your Majesty." Gillien gave a proper bow before going to the door. The buzz in the hall stopped as she stepped out to face the horde of women. "The Queen will see you now."

Allora straightened her shoulders, taking comfort in the familiar act of giving welcoming smiles to those she barely knew.

"Your Majesty." The women filtered into the room, each taking their turn to greet the Queen before silently struggling to claim a chair as close to Allora as possible without being seen as pushing someone older or higher-stationed from a better seat.

Allora waited until the gaggle had settled into their places before speaking. "It's so lovely to see all of you. Thank you for venturing through the storm."

"It's only a drizzle, Your Majesty." A woman, with the bottom six inches of her skirt soaked in mud, gave a pleasing smile. "The carriage ride to the palace was quite refreshing."

"I hope the roads weren't too full of muck," Allora said.

The wet-skirted woman gave a laugh that held an edge of panic. "Of course not, Your Majesty. The streets in Ilara are the best to be found."

"Such devotion to your home." Allora reached behind, pulling the discreetly placed cord that would summon the servants to deliver tea to her sopping guests. "Tell me of the city."

"The city is well, Your Majesty," a woman in the red robes of the Healers Guild said.

"I had heard there was an illness sweeping through the unguilded," Allora said.

"Nothing to fuss over." The healer's smile grew a bit too pinched at the corners.

"Your Guild is successfully caring for the sick?" Allora asked.

A panel in the wall opened, allowing three maids carrying trays to enter.

A few of the women stared at the panel as though they'd never known of the servants' passages hidden within the palace walls.

"The Healers Guild has been successfully caring for its charges," the healer said.

"Despite the troubles in the city?" Allora kept her gaze fixed on the healer as the maids laid out the trays of cakes and steaming pots of tea.

"Troubles in the city?" One of the merchant women glanced toward Gillien, who stood beside Allora's couch. "I haven't...the grapes for chamb have grown very well this year."

"Grapes." Allora gave a gentle laugh. "Surely there is something more interesting than grapes happening in the city. I'm kept in the palace for ease of my protection. And"—she leaned toward the women—"as much as I dearly love Princess Illia, and I promise her wedding will be the grandest affair Ilbrea has ever seen, I do long to talk of something that isn't her gown for the wedding, the climate of Wyrain, or the depth of Prince Dagon's devotion to his future bride."

"Princess Illia's met Prince Dagon?" One of the women froze with a bit of cake halfway to her mouth.

"Not yet. But they've exchanged wonderful letters." Allora sighed. "Dudia has truly blessed the pair."

"How wonderful," the cake woman said.

"Now come, tell me news of the city," Allora said. "Surely there's been an engagement or fresh feud since I married the King."

"The Zellys and the Winthrops have begun competing for customers," a merchant in a yellow dress said. "Very civilly, of course."

"There must be something better than that," Allora said.

"I'm not—" The merchant who'd spoken of grapes glanced toward Gillien again. "There is a scandal that's taken over everyone's chatter, but I don't think it's a subject fit for the Queen."

"Then best not to speak of it," Gillien said.

The woman's face paled.

"Nonsense, Gillien." Allora patted the couch for Gillien to sit beside her. "This is not a formal affair."

"It is a bit shocking, Your Majesty," the healer said.

"All the better," Allora said. "My life in the palace is perfect and peaceful. A bit of a shock will be good for me."

"Your Majesty doesn't need to be upset," Gillien said.

Allora looked to the sorcerer. "Sit, Gillien. Give yourself a moment to enjoy the whispers of the city."

Gillien held Allora's gaze for a moment, then finally sat, perching on the very edge of the couch.

"Well," the grape woman said with breathless excitement, "it is a torrid scandal."

"The best kind," the woman in yellow said.

"The head scribe's wife was shipped to Ian Ayres," the grape woman said.

"You must be mistaken," Allora said.

"I'm not." Excitement gleamed in the grape woman's eyes.

"The head scribe's wife was shipped off to Ian Ayres for being a common whore! She was carrying another man's child when the head scribe married her. Such a shame."

"Don't pity that petal whore," the healer said. "I know the healer who examined her. The girl knew she was pregnant when she married the head scribe, and she did it anyway. After dragging the head scribe into her mess, she deserved much worse than the death she got."

"Death?" Cold seeped into Allora's chest.

"Jumped off the ship to Ian Ayres and drowned herself," another woman said. "Couldn't bear to face the price of her mistakes. After dragging a well-respected man of the Guilds into her torrid mess, I hope the rotta felt properly ashamed before dying."

"A foul creature like that is incapable of feeling shame," the healer said.

"Ena." Allora laid her hands in her lap, waiting for the woman's gleeful tone to meld with the reality of her words. "Her name was Ena. She married Adrial."

"Did you know her?" The healer leaned forward.

"You didn't tell me." Allora's voice stayed steady. "Adrial's wife is dead, and you didn't tell me."

"Calm yourself, Your Majesty," Gillien said.

"Do not tell me to be calm." Allora's hands started to shake.

"The decision not to bother you with such unseemly—"

"The decision?" Allora stood, rounding on Gillien. "Who decided? How long have you kept this from me?"

"There was no reason to tell you. The King agreed it would only cause undue worry." Gillien reached for Allora's hand.

"Do not touch me, sorcerer." Allora stormed around the couch and slammed her hand against the panel the maids had entered through.

The panel opened without a click.

The panel snapped shut.

"Your Majesty," Gillien said. "You're upset. Perhaps you should lie down."

"Open this door, now." Allora kept her back to the sorcerer. "You may prefer secrets, but I assure you I have no qualms in screaming the things that need to be said in front of these women."

The panel popped open.

"Do not follow me, sorcerer," Allora said. "Hearing your footsteps tapping along behind me would destroy my placid calm."

Allora stepped into the passage, yanking the panel shut behind her.

She pressed her hand to her mouth as she fought to swallow a sob.

Adrial. Her sweet Adrial. His wife. His child.

Gone.

A furious scream tore from her throat.

Down the poorly lit passage, a shadow skittered away.

Swiping the tears from her cheeks, Allora stormed down the corridor, ignoring the shadows of frightened servants fleeing around corners to avoid their Queen's wrath.

The path to Brannon's study wasn't long enough for her to choose all the things she wanted to shout at the King.

Villain. Captor. Liar.

She slammed open the panel that led into his study, a childish wish for him to fall from his seat in fear flitting through her mind.

His absence deprived her of that petty satisfaction.

A half-eaten plate of food and empty teacup were the only signs of his recent departure.

Allora looked to the door to the throne room.

She could throw open the door and scream for all to hear. Make a worse scene than she had in her parlor.

You're smarter than they know, Allora, Mara's voice whispered in her mind. *Don't give them a reason to demean you.*

Allora snatched a napkin from the table and dried her tears, making sure she could feign composure before opening the door and stepping into the throne room.

5

ALLORA

The usual array of merchants and Guilded waited in the throne room, all of them staring at Brannon's seat on the dais, all of them eager for their chance to bend the King's ear.

The guards along the back wall looked to Allora as she stepped out of Brannon's study, but none of them tried to stop her as she approached the King.

My husband.

Disgust swept through her stomach.

Brannon's hand hung over the arm of the high-backed throne, which hid the rest of his body. He fidgeted, rubbing his thumb along the tips of his fingers, warning Allora of his mood even before she reached the front of the dais, stepping between him and a man in sailor blue.

"My love." Brannon's face brightened as though he were truly happy to see her.

Allora took a breath, waiting for a hint of sympathy or caring to scratch away a bit of her rage.

Brannon reached for her hand.

The only thing Allora felt was a desperate need to scratch the King's eyes out.

"What a wonderful surprise." Brannon stood and came to the edge of the dais, still holding his hand out to Allora.

"Wonderful indeed." Allora stepped close enough for him to touch her.

Giving up on taking her hand, Brannon laid his hands on her shoulders and kissed the top of her head.

"Send them away, Brannon," Allora whispered.

"I wish I could." He trailed his fingers up her neck and across her lips.

She turned her head just enough to free her face from his touch. "Send them away now, or they will all leave the palace knowing what an uncaring beast you are."

"Allora." Brannon furrowed his brow.

"Your Majesty"—Allora raised her voice for everyone in the throne room to hear—"I hate to interrupt what is surely important business—"

"Allora," Brannon hushed.

"But my heart has just been broken by terrible news. My dearest friend lost his wife and child." Allora held the King's gaze. "Such a horrific tragedy surely warrants the attention of my loving husband."

Brannon stayed silent for a moment, as though testing her recklessness, waiting for her to crumble and slink away to hide her embarrassment at having inconvenienced the King.

Allora didn't flinch.

He pursed his lips before stepping away from her to address the room.

"My apologies," Brannon said, "but you will all have to come back another day. The Queen has just received dreadful news."

A flutter of murmurs rolled through the crowd.

Allora turned to face the people, her people. "Your prompt departure is greatly appreciated. Guards, see them out. Your services are no longer desired in this room." She turned back to her husband, making sure the wretch didn't flee.

"Your Majesty." A guard stepped forward and bowed to Brannon.

"Wait outside," Brannon said. "The shock of loss is a private affair."

"Yes, Your Majesty." The guard bowed again.

Allora kept her gaze pinned on Brannon's falsely sympathetic face as the sound of the guards' boots faded away and the throne room doors closed with a soft thump.

"Why didn't you tell me?" Allora's anger pinched in her throat, changing the pitch of her words.

"Allora, calm yourself. Take a breath and tell me what's happened." Brannon touched her cheek.

"You know very well what's happened." Allora batted his hand away. "Adrial's wife is dead, and you kept it from me."

"There was no need to upset you, my dearest."

"No need? Adrial is my friend. You are my husband. How could you hide this from me?"

"I hid nothing from you."

"You knew, and you didn't tell me!"

"Did the head scribe tell you?" Brannon stepped off the dais. "If he truly is your friend, did he write you a letter declaring his shame?"

"What shame?"

"Your head scribe's wife leapt off the ship to Ian Ayres."

"How dare you repeat such a vicious rumor!" Allora's shout bounced around the room.

"It is the truth, my dear." Brannon reached for her again.

"No." Allora stepped away. "Ena and Adrial were married. She couldn't have been on a ship to Ian Ayres."

"I assure you she was."

"That's impossible."

"The lurid details of the matter aren't your concern."

"Ena's death is very much my concern."

Brannon glanced to the door of his study.

"Will you run from me, husband?" Allora said. "Have you behaved so badly you can't face me?"

"I have done nothing wrong." Anger crisped Brannon's voice. "Any blame for this salacious situation comes from the mistakes of the head scribe and his whoring wife."

"Don't you dare insult Ena's memory."

"That the truth is distasteful cannot be blamed on me." Brannon stepped closer, glaring down at Allora with anger in his teal eyes. "The head scribe married a common woman who was already carrying a child."

"But he *married her*, Brannon."

"The law is clear—"

"The law?"

"The punishment for marrying a woman already carrying a child is whipping."

"They whipped Adrial?" The room swayed.

Brannon took Allora's arms, holding her steady. "His punishment had been chosen. But the common woman confessed before the full sentence had been carried out."

"Confessed what?" Allora looked up at Brannon. "She'd shared a bed with the man she loved before they'd married? She was already carrying Adrial's child in her womb before their wedding ceremony? For this, you'll steal a woman from her husband?"

Something like genuine sympathy pinched the corners of Brannon's eyes. "The child wasn't the head scribe's."

"That is a wretched lie."

"I heard her confession myself. The child she carried was not the head scribe's."

"No. You misunderstood." Allora backed away, breaking free from Brannon's grip. "Adrial loves her. Ena is his wife. He is the father of her child."

"Adrial Ayres was cuckolded by a commoner. A vile woman deceived your friend, using him to claw her way into Guilded society." Brannon held his arms out to her. "The head scribe's wife brought him great shame. She betrayed him, humiliated him, and left him a broken man. Getting that whore and her unborn bastard out of Ilara was the kindest thing that could have happened to the poor man."

"But he loved her." A faint screaming sliced through Allora's thoughts, growing louder every heartbeat.

"Love makes fools of the wisest men."

"But he married her. He had a wife…and a child." Allora fixed her gaze on the faint pattern in the marble floor, forcing the room to hold still without Brannon's support. "He was so happy."

"He was deceived, my sweet. The pain the poor head scribe felt, his screams as she confessed, it was a terrible thing to behold."

"Adrial was there?" Her body went numb. She couldn't feel Brannon's hands as he gripped her arms. "You watched him scream?"

"It's a sight I won't soon forget. I've never witnessed a man suffer such grief. He may mourn her now, but once his mind has cleared, he'll be grateful not to be raising another man's bastard."

The floor stilled. The horrible scream tearing through Allora's mind fell silent.

Tears rolled down her cheeks as she looked up at the man she had pledged her life to. "You're a fool. An evil slitch of a fool."

"Allor—"

"Are you incapable of understanding a good man's heart?" She shoved Brannon away. "When you watched Adrial lose everything he loved, did he scream in shock at the truth of the child his wife carried, or in pain that you stole the woman and child he loved away?"

"The child wasn't his."

"They were his family!" Allora's breath caught in her throat as her shout thundered around the throne room. "I know Adrial.

He's not the fool you paint him to be. If Ena truly was carrying another man's child, Adrial knew. He knew and chose to love them and protect them anyway. He never would have tossed Ena or her child aside. He loved his wife and the child they would share with a larger heart than you could ever possess."

"A sentimental man's feelings have nothing to do with the truth or the laws of Ilbrea."

"So King Brannon Willoc takes the head scribe's wife and condemns her to Ian Ayres? How did banishing Adrial's wife to that awful place become the business of the King? Were there no other tasks worthy of your attention? Will all those bound for Ian Ayres be brought before you, or only commoners who dare to marry well-placed Guilded?"

"Your hypocrisy is astounding, my dear." Brannon's tone dropped to a harsh whisper. "Should the laws only be ignored for your precious friend, or will you shout at me every time we send a new shipment of whores and bastards to Ian Ayres? Is there a list of which women my Queen deems worthy of salvation?"

"I am a selfish beast, and I know it." Anger stemmed the stream of Allora's tears. "I only fought to have Kai's ship found because I loved Kai. I am disgusted beyond redemption because you condemned Adrial's wife to Ian Ayres. He barely survived that demon's island, and you sent his wife there. You sent the child he loved to be born in that terrible place."

"On a ship with other women who faced the same fate. But those women and their babes don't deserve your pity. You only care for the whore who fooled your friend into making her the future Lady of the Scribes Guild."

"I am not a good enough person to feel the terror and pain of all those Ian Ayres has destroyed. I am not strong enough to bear counting how many women before Ena have chosen death above giving birth on that accursed island. But I know Adrial. He would have loved that child as he loved his wife. The child would not have been born out of wedlock and left to starve on the streets. There was no need for all this pain, Brannon."

"The enforcement of Ilbrea's laws is not for you to decide."

"You're right." Allora stepped out of Brannon's reach. "It is the great King of Ilbrea's duty to rule our country. But you are the King and my husband, Brannon. Why would my husband allow this to happen to my friend?"

"Your friend broke the law."

"You're the King! You could have protected Adrial. You could have saved Ena."

"It wasn't possible."

"Why? Because you were afraid of a common woman marrying the Lord Scribe's heir? How cowardly must a king be to punish someone for falling in love?"

Brannon flinched. His gaze flicked toward the throne room doors.

"Or was it not your choice?" Allora said. "Did you sit idly by while the Lady Sorcerer worked her will on your people?"

"Allora, stop." Brannon lunged forward, catching Allora's wrist, holding tight enough she couldn't break free.

"Let go of me."

He jerked her closer and spoke in a low voice. "You will leave this room, find a quiet corner to cry, and never mention this again."

"I will not." Allora kept her words loud enough to be overheard.

"Do not test me." He wrapped his arm around her waist, pinning her to him. "I am your husband and your King. Do not let sympathy for your friend make you forget your place."

A laugh bubbled in Allora's throat. "Don't worry, sweet husband. The sorcerers have made my place perfectly clear. I will lie down and let you pound away on top of me. You will use me for your pleasure, and I will carry your children or face the sorcerers' wrath. I have no illusions of which monsters control the palace."

"Allor—"

"Do not try to intimidate me, Brannon. You'll humiliate yourself."

"You are my wife." He tightened his hold on her, crushing her against him. "This is my palace. Ilbrea is mine to rule."

"Such a grand façade of power. Shall I lie on the floor and lift my skirts to congratulate you?"

Brannon shoved her away.

"The floor doesn't arouse you, Your Majesty? Oh, dear." Allora tutted. "Shall you bend me over your throne?"

"Stop, Allora. Lewdness doesn't suit you."

"It is quite new to me. I suppose I'll have to try harder." Allora clapped her hands. "I know. I'll lie on the dais. Will fucking your wife on the dais complete your illusion of control?" Allora sat on the platform and raised her skirt up to her knees. "I can't unfasten my bodice without a maid, but, as your desperate pawing at my breasts vexes me and has nothing to do with conceiving a child, I'm quite relieved to leave it on."

"I will not stand your ridicule."

"My apologies, husband, you mistake my intent. I only aim to make our future quite clear." Allora didn't lower her skirt. "Expect no tenderness from me. I will allow you to writhe on top of me, a distasteful but necessary task I must endure to fulfill my duty of providing Ilbrea an heir. But any affection I may have felt for you has been destroyed."

Brannon lowered his eyes, balling his hands into tight fists. "You don't mean that. You're hurting for your friend's loss and aiming your venom at me to relieve your pain. I will accept your apology once your tantrum has ended."

"There will be no apology, husband. My heart may be selfish, but it is not fickle."

His shoulders sank, as though she might have actually

wounded the soulless beast that feigned ruling Ilbrea. "Allora. The work of a king—"

"Must be done." Allora raised her skirts higher and lay back on the dais. "Shall you plow your seed into me before you restart the work of ruling Ilbrea with an uncaring hand? There is no need for a private setting. I hardly notice your intrusion anymore."

6

***

NIKO

The pleasant buzz the frie had given Niko's body had started to fade, leaving the burning itch on his back to chip away at his thoughts.

"The winter storms won't wait for the war to end," a man, the head of the Brien's something or other, said.

"We have fought through winter before. We shall do it again." Bryana's voice didn't betray a hint of either annoyance or worry.

Niko kept his gaze fixed on the exit of the white-stone throne room, unwilling to look at the Brien Elder's face, even if her expression could offer him a hint of what the Brien clan's fate might be.

"Reinforcements should be sent now," the man said.

"Have our numbers at the front been diminished?" Bryana said.

Niko tensed his shoulders, allowing an ache to join the itching on his back.

"Continuing to maintain the siege brings us no closer to ending this war," the man said.

A nice cold breeze through the window—that might make Niko's back feel better.

But the rainstorm that covered the valley of the stronghold didn't dare let its wind disturb the demon elder's lair.

"We have no more fighters to spare," Bryana said. "The stronghold must be protected."

A new bottle of frie would take the itching away entirely.

At least for a few hours.

"Then I beg for your wisdom, Elder," the man said. "How would you have me end the siege? What should I tell the Brien fighting at the front as they spend another winter freezing in the snow, watching their fellows be picked off by the Hayes cowards?"

"Are you incapable of commanding your men?" Bryana asked.

If the snow had started to fall, Niko could just walk outside and flop onto the ground. Let the cold numb his back.

"Commanding them isn't the problem," the man said. "It's comforting them."

He could even stay in the snow. Just lie there, slowly freezing.

"Do they not believe our fight against the Hayes is necessary?" Bryana said.

"They believe in the path the mountain has laid out for our clan," the man said. "But they want to be here. The mountain led Solcha here."

Solcha.

An exhausting loathing stole the rest of the frie's dwindling comfort.

"If the stronghold needs to be protected, my men want to be here," the man said. "If the mountain leads us into battle against the Guilds, they want to fight by Solcha's side, not be left to mind the siege, huddling in misery, waiting to fall ill and die, stuck in the freezing cold until the Hayes have the courtesy to starve to death."

I can't even fight my way out of the demon's lair. Only a Death-loving fool would want to be near me in a battle against the Guilds.

"We fight the Hayes at the mountain's will. We defend our

people against the Guilds to fulfill our promise to the mountain," Bryana said. "There is no more or less worthy battle. If we are to take any meaning from Solcha's arrival, let it be the assurance of how well the mountain protects her beloved children.

"We are too closely linked to Ilbrea for the Black Bloods to ignore the threat the Guilds pose to our people. We cannot allow the Hayes to destroy the peace between clans the Black Bloods worked for generations to achieve. We fight on two fronts, but it is the same war. The Brien holding the Hayes siege are fighting by Solcha's side even if they cannot see him."

A sharp pain yanked against the center of Niko's back. He clenched his teeth, not flinching as the pain worsened.

"Solcha," Bryana said, "do you have any words of comfort to send the fighters who so bravely hold the siege?"

The pain in Niko's back shifted, changing to a more dire slicing that burned against his ribs.

"The mountain showed me many mysteries," Niko said.

The pain changed again, condensing to a point just behind his heart.

Niko made himself focus on the man.

He wore a purple uniform with fine gold embroidery on the chest. Not the clothing of a man who would soon be missing toes from suffering in the cold.

Niko stifled a gasp as the pain dug into his lungs.

"While I can't say I understand everything I saw in the great darkness below the mountain"—Niko's words ground out of his throat as he fought the need to scream—"the mountain herself protected and guided me. The mountain never let me lose hope. The Brien stand against mighty enemies, but I wouldn't have been led here if the Black Bloods were doomed.

"I have sworn to find the Brien's lost heir. Someone else will lead the fight if the Guilds come. Your men will stand against the Hayes. These are all tasks that must be done to protect the children of the mountain. None of them are more or less important.

The men you lose to the cold will have died with great honor. Make sure they know that. Make sure the ones who grieve the fallen remember them as heroes who died in service to the mountain and all Black Bloods."

The pain in Niko's back ebbed to the usual maddening, itching ache.

"Thank you, Solcha," the man bowed. "My men will find great comfort in your words."

Niko nodded to the man, not daring to shift his spine enough to bow.

"Captain Foley," Bryana said, "you have my faith. You will continue the siege. And should the tides shift, you will do whatever is necessary to protect your clan."

The man, Captain Foley, lost the faint bit of color that had been in his cheeks. "Yes, Elder. Thank you for your wisdom, Elder." Captain Foley bowed and left the throne room with nothing but a few vague words of comfort to show for having endured a meeting with the chivving Brien Elder.

The Brien guards closed the throne room doors.

"How many more?" Bryana said.

Paiman stepped forward from the other side of Bryana's throne.

Niko reaffixed his gaze to the doors, not trusting his currently almost-sober self to do anything but attack the Brien who'd dragged him out of the darkness below the mountain to play the role of the demon elder's favorite puppet.

"Captain Foley was the last who'd come to speak of the war," Paiman said. "You have four more who've requested audiences."

"The rest should be seen without Niko." Danu stepped forward, her arm brushing against Niko's as she cut around him to face Bryana.

"Solcha's presence should be felt by all," Bryana said, "not only those who serve the Brien through bloodshed."

"Niko—" Danu said.

"Solcha." Bryana spoke the false name in a maddeningly calm tone.

"*Solcha* needs to go back to his room, Aunt," Danu said.

"Has Solcha forgotten his duty to the Brien?" Bryana asked.

Niko balled his hands into tight fists, waiting for a fresh jab of pain.

"No, Aunt," Danu said. "But he has bled through the back of his shirt. Let me take him to his room to rest."

"Word of Solcha standing beside you as you greet your visitors will spread more quickly if he's not always with you, Elder," Paiman said. "If some who seek your wisdom see him and others don't, whispers will fly through the stronghold. Those who plan to seek your aid will tell everyone of their hope to be blessed with Solcha's presence. Those who don't see Solcha will bemoan their luck. Those who do will tell everyone of their audience with the Ilbrean beloved by the mountain."

"Let Solcha's presence remain elusive," Danu said. "It will add to his appeal."

"The work of an elder should not be that of images and rumors," Bryana said, "but I am not foolish enough to reject any weapon in the battles we face, even if that weapon is a well-aimed whisper."

I'm not a weapon. The words surged into Niko's throat. He shut his eyes, forcing the words back down to join the vitriol swirling in his gut.

"Take him to his room and stop the bleeding," Bryana said. "Have a coat made for him. Make sure they pad the back. The work of war cannot be stopped for one man's blood."

"Thank you, Aunt." Danu bowed and turned toward the door, not even gesturing for Niko to follow her.

Niko shifted his gaze to stare at Danu's back, narrowing his thoughts to blur everything in the world but her.

The guards flanking the throne room doors didn't exist. The

well-dressed people waiting to speak to Bryana the chivving demon elder were nothing but shadows.

The children on the stairs were mice chasing after crumbs.

The whispering women they passed on the stairs weren't midwives, they were trees rustling in the breeze.

The blue light of the lae stones in the corridors improved the illusion of isolation.

Shadows shifting through a terrible dream.

Temporary. Harmless.

Worth neither his fear nor hate.

Danu reached the door to his room first.

Niko waited until he was right behind her to stop. Her hair had been twisted up, but a few tendrils had fallen loose, shielding the nape of her neck like a thin curtain.

With a soft click, the door to Niko's room swung open.

Warm evening light peeked through the clouds, as though some cruel god were teasing him with the hope of salvation.

"In." Danu took Niko's wrist, pulling him through the door. She closed it behind him and locked it with a brush of her fingers, trapping Niko in Solcha's prison.

7

NIKO

"Why didn't you say something?"

Danu pulled Niko to one of the wooden chairs beside his table. His evening meal had already been laid out.

"Niko?" Danu grabbed his shoulders, making him sit. "Why didn't you tell me your back had started bleeding?"

"I didn't know." Niko shook her hands away and reached for the brand-new bottle of frie on the table.

"Blood is seeping through your shirt and you didn't notice?"

"The pain and itching are worse than the oozing." He pulled the stopper from the bottle and downed a blissfully burning gulp.

"Ooze?" Danu snatched the bottle away from him, spilling some of the precious elixir onto Niko's sleeve.

"I think so." Niko lifted his sleeve to his mouth and sucked the liquor from the fabric.

"Let me see it." Danu grabbed Niko's hand, yanking his sleeve from his mouth before hoisting him to his feet.

He hissed through his teeth as the force tugged at his torn skin.

"What was that?" Danu wrinkled her forehead.

"I don't like being told to sit only to be yanked out of my seat."

"You're impossible." Danu took Niko's arm, trying to turn his back to her.

He batted her hand away. "You wanted me to sit, so let me sit in peace."

"I wanted you to sit until you mentioned ooze. Now, I need to see your back."

"No." Niko squared his shoulders, steadying his stance, not allowing her to force his movement.

"The marks on your back are old enough they shouldn't be bleeding, let alone anything else. Your skin might be infected."

"Probably." Niko grabbed the bottle of frie from the table.

"That's not a thing to joke about." Danu bit her lips together, giving Niko enough time to take a long drink. "If the marks are infected, they could fester. The infection could spread."

"I'm aware."

"If the infection spreads, it could kill you." Danu held up a hand before Niko could speak. "Don't give me some chivving quip about knowing how fast an infection can seep into your blood and kill you. Turn around and show me your mark."

"No." Niko lifted the bottle back to his mouth. Danu grabbed it and tossed it aside, smashing the glass against the stone wall. "That was a cruel thing to do."

"Show me your mark, or I will call in healers and guards. The guards will strip you bare and pin you down while the healers examine you."

"I'll die before I let your chivving guards touch me." Niko stepped back, stumbling as his heel hit his chair. "Your healers, too. I'll fight them all." Panic tightened his chest. His blood pounded in his ears.

"I'm trying to help you, Niko." Danu held out her hands.

Niko sidestepped, gaining a foot between them. "I'll tear them apart. I don't care about their chivving swords. They're not touching me. No one is touching me."

"I'm sorry, Niko, all right? I'm sorry." She took a step back.

"Just take a nice breath for me. I shouldn't have threatened to bring in guards. It was wrong. I was harsher than I needed to be, and I'm sorry."

Niko stared at her hands, waiting for a weapon to appear.

"Please, Niko, forgive me."

Niko managed to make himself nod.

"Thank you." Danu lowered her hands. "But I do need to look at your back. Can I do that?"

His neck stiffened. He couldn't manage another nod.

"Please." She took a step toward him. "I'm worried about you."

"I don't want any of your chivving Brien touching me."

Danu flinched like he'd shouted. Maybe he had.

"What if it's just me, then?" Danu dared to take another step. "Only me. No one else. I promise."

Niko glanced toward the door. The quick movement cracked the wounds on his back.

"You're my friend, Niko." She reached out, brushing her fingers against his. "I'm worried about my friend. I'm afraid my friend has an infection on his back. Can you help me? Can you help me take care of my friend?" She took his hand, locking her fingers through his. "Please, Niko."

Niko swallowed, trying to push down the pain in his throat enough to let him speak. It didn't work. He squeezed Danu's hand and turned, offering her his back.

"Thank you." Danu slid her hand from Niko's grip.

The cold of her fingers brought more feeling to his back, calling the pain into sharper focus as she lifted the bottom of his shirt.

Niko gasped through his teeth as she pulled away a bit of fabric that had stuck to the wounds.

"Sorry," she whispered, but didn't stop peeling his shirt slowly up. She balled the fabric by his neck then stepped to his side, lifting the bloodstained shirt over his head and tossing it near the door to be cleaned away by the maids the next time they invaded.

She laid her hands on his shoulders, steadying him as she stepped behind to examine his back.

"Have the healers tended to you at all?" Danu asked.

"Those slitches aren't touching me."

"Niko—"

"They spent weeks patching me back together over and over so Bryana could have a fresh toy to torture every day. I'm not letting it happen again."

"Have you washed it?"

"I take my baths like a good little lad."

"I'm not in the mood for playing." Danu turned Niko around. True worry pinched a crease between her eyebrows. She took his face in her hands, daring him not to meet her gaze. "Even as large as it is, your mark should be nearly healed by now."

Niko shut his eyes, hiding the pain that flashed through his mind.

The tugging at his skin as Bryana used his mark to remind him the price of disobedience. The stabbing against his ribs, biting into the outside of his lungs as her warning to watch every word he spoke in front of the demon elder.

Don't risk the only friend you have.

"I don't know why it's still bleeding." Niko didn't open his eyes until he'd finished speaking the lie.

"If the skin got angry early on, that might've stopped the healing." The wrinkle between Danu's eyebrows deepened. "We can't let it keep going like this. It needs to be cleaned and treated with some ointment at the very least." Niko managed to back half a step away before she added, "No healers. I'll do the work myself."

"Fine." Niko shoved his fists into his pockets. "That's fine."

"Thank you." Danu brushed her thumb across his cheek, stopping at the pained wrinkles that never seemed to leave the corners of his eyes. "We'll make quick work of it."

She stepped away from him, heading toward the door.

Niko lunged forward, grabbing her hand, paying for the

movement with a sharp jab of pain along his spine. "Where are you going?"

"To call the healers, for—"

"No." Niko yanked his hand away as though she had been the one clinging to him. "You said it would just be you. You promised."

"I won't let them in the room." Danu continued slowly toward the door. "I'm just going to have them bring some things I can use on your wounds. It'll be just you and me. Is that all right?"

He made himself nod.

Danu unlocked the door and stepped halfway out into the hall. She spoke to the guards in a low voice. The hurried footsteps of one of the guards running to do Danu's bidding started thumping down the hall before she even stepped back into the room.

She locked the door behind her, then hesitated with her fingers still on the wood.

"You can leave," Niko said.

"Don't be a slitch." Danu flicked her hand through the air, as though waving away the possibility of her abandonment. "Let's get you washed up while we wait for the ointment."

"Are you telling me to strip down for a bath?" A hint of humor grazed the churning pain that had taken the place of Niko's heart and lungs.

"The basin will do." Danu wrinkled her nose at him, shooing him to the far corner where the maids refilled his washbasin every day, making sure Solcha had fresh water to scrub his precious-to-the-mountain hands and face.

Danu beat him to the washstand, grabbing a clean cloth from the pile before Niko could reach for one. "Face the window."

"Why?"

"This is probably going to hurt." She dipped the cloth into the basin. "Let the view of the valley distract you."

Niko glanced toward the door, making sure there really

weren't any guards storming into his room, before turning toward the window.

The days of rain had finally started to slow, giving Niko a clearer view of the forest and the changing hues of the leaves that had begun to lose their summer color.

A hint of blissfully cool water brushed against Niko's back just before pain shot from his shoulder blade to the inside of his ear.

"Chivving demon spawn." He arched his back, instinctively fleeing the pain. "What was that?"

"I barely touched you."

"Sheep's shit you barely touched me!" Niko started to turn around, but Danu grabbed his waist, dripping water down his hip as she held him in place.

"Cleaning this is going to hurt," Danu said.

"I've had broken bones that hurt less than this."

"The mark is infected. I'll be as gentle as I can, but the wounds have to be tended, no matter how badly it hurts."

"Your mastery of encouragement is astounding."

"Just hold still." Danu let go of him. "Take a breath and think of something else. See how many birds you can spot flying over the valley."

Niko's gasp turned into a groan as Danu went back to work.

"See, it's not so bad," she said in a soothing tone.

"Not"—the word pitched high in Niko's voice as another jab of pain sliced from his shoulder to his throat—"not the worst."

He watched the valley, trying to count the birds soaring over the trees.

The chivving birds could eat their own feathers for all he cared. He fixed his mind on the clearing in the woods where the Brien sorcerers kept themselves away from the rest of the clan.

Thinking of sorcerers brought thoughts of magic, like the kind the Brien trueborn had used when they'd carved their marks into Niko's flesh, burrowing tiny bits of stone into his skin, making sure they could kill him with the flick of a finger if Solcha ever dared disobey the Brien's chivving elder.

"Gah." He sidestepped in a vain attempt at escape.

"Hold still." Danu caught his arm, pulling him back. "I'm going to do the middle now. It looks worse than the rest, so just keep breathing."

"Lovely."

A place away from the stronghold, that's where Niko needed to be. Far from the Brien where no one could tug at the stone of his mark to make him speak like a well-trained dog.

A field. That was it.

A wide-open field where the mountains were nothing but a faraway ornament giving depth to the horizon.

Cheese, fresh-baked bread, and a bottle of chamb laid out on a soft blanket. Someone sitting beside him, their laughter catching on the breeze, lifting the joy of the morning beyond the scope of mere mortal bliss.

But the place on the blanket beside him was empty. No one to laugh. No one to distract him.

"Gah." Niko leapt forward, rounding on Danu. "Are you sure you're not stabbing me?"

Danu held up the blood-tinged cloth.

"Evil chivving cloth," Niko said.

"Yes, blame the cloth." Danu bit her lips together in a poor attempt to hide her smile. "Now turn around."

A knock on the door spared Niko from Danu's frown as he planted his feet, refusing to budge.

She set the soiled cloth on the washbasin, gave Niko what could have been an intimidating glare, and went to the door.

Niko backed into the corner, watching the door, waiting for the healers to burst into the room ready to chain him down and patch him up, preparing Bryana's puppet for the next round of torment.

"Yes, I'm sure." Danu closed the door, locking the healers out before turning to Niko, holding a little tray with two jars, a bottle, a bowl, and a cloth.

"You'd think depriving her of the chance to look after Solcha was worse than ripping out her teeth." Danu looked from Niko to the tray and back again. "Get on the bed."

"I'm sorry, what?"

"Lie on the bed."

Niko rocked back on his heels, pushing the closest he could manage to a grin onto his face. "I'm not sure now's the time."

"Face down, you flinching slitch. If you keep dodging me every time it stings, we'll never get through this."

"Seems wrong to use a perfectly good bed for such an awful purpose."

"Just do it." Danu pulled a chair beside the bed and set the tray down.

Niko paused for a moment, just long enough to try and come up with a reason to refuse besides being a chivving coward.

He had nothing.

"I supposed I've been asked to bed in worse ways." Niko lay down, placing his hands beneath his cheek.

Danu knelt on the bed beside him. "Now hold still."

"I'm lying down. I can't—gah!" Niko rolled away from her.

"Hold still." Danu grabbed his hip, forcing him back onto his stomach.

"Easy for you to say."

"I'm the one cleaning your oozing wounds. Be grateful for my help." Danu pinned his hips down and crawled over to straddle Niko just below his lower back.

"What are—" Pain swirled around Niko's spine. He pressed his face into his pillow.

"That's better. Give your pillow a good chomp."

Niko turned his head enough to speak. "Thanks."

He gritted his teeth as the pain in his back changed from the stabbing around the center of his mark to a pinching ache around the edges.

Danu finished with the water then leaned sideways, not freeing Niko as she grabbed the bottle from the tray.

"This'll sting," she said. "But then the worst will be over."

"You shouldn't have smashed the frie."

"You drove me to it." She flicked the back of his head. "Exhale and try not to squirm."

A jagged, burning spasm started in the middle of Niko's back, streaking a line of pain to the center of his ass.

"Can't you just tear the chivving skin off?" He blinked away the tears the stinging had brought to his eyes.

"Even if I could, the trueborn wouldn't have it." Danu pressed more chivving tonic onto his back. "Very few are given the honor of being marked as a servant of the Brien Cl—"

"Honor my pain-tainted ass."

"The mark you've let fester is considered a precious work of art in our clan."

"Sorry to let the art oo—" Niko's breath caught in his throat. "Ooze."

"Usually"—Danu raised her voice, speaking over Niko's groan—"a Black Blood gives their oath to one trueborn, and that trueborn draws a mark on the side of their ribs like mine. Thirteen trueborn came together to create your mark. And, once it's healed, it will be beautiful."

"There can be no beauty in it. Monsters dug their claws into my flesh. They disfigured my back. Nothing more."

Danu went still. Horribly still.

"I'm sorry. I didn't mean to insult you. The mark on your ribs is different." He reached for her, shutting his eyes as he waited for her to smack his hand away. "They didn't disfigure you."

"Bryana has done terrible things to you, Niko. I don't think any decent person could deny it."

She touched Niko's shoulder, laying her palm against his skin.

The muscles in his back relaxed as she grazed her thumb across his neck.

"I'm not sure it'll give you any comfort, and I don't know if you'll ever stop hating the mark you bear, but anyone who sees it will think it's beautiful," Danu whispered.

"Jagged lines seared into my back. Being mauled by a croilach would leave a more attractive scar."

Danu lifted her hand away from his shoulder.

"Please don't go." Niko fumbled, trying to find her hand. "I'm sorry I keep saying the wrong chivving things. It's not the clan's fault their elder is a demon. I'm a map maker. I know better than to insult regional traditions or the scars your people deem beautiful."

"Have you actually seen the mark?" Danu leaned away from Niko.

Absurdly potent panic swept through him before he realized she was reaching for the tray.

"Niko?" She picked up one of the jars.

"I can't make myself look at it, but I know where the cuts are. I felt them burned into my skin, and they haven't stopped hurting since."

"They aren't cuts or jagged lines." Danu recentered herself on Niko's lower back. "Right here"—she ran her fingers across Niko's shoulder blade—"this is the sun bringing its light to the mountains." She traced the shape of the sun, her touch leaving blissfully cool relief behind.

"This"—her fingers wove a long line across his back—"is a river."

"A river?"

"A beautiful river. Tall grass lines the rocky banks."

A soft, sweet scent reached Niko as she scooped more ointment from the jar.

"Above the river, mountains reach toward the sky." She took her time, tracing each of the peaks. "And a bird soars over the mountains."

Niko flinched as she touched the center of his back, where Bryana toyed with his flesh to torment him.

"This one's the deepest," Danu said.

Niko locked his teeth together, not allowing himself to speak.

"The bird is beautiful." She slowly trailed her fingers away from his spine, arcing up toward his shoulder blade. "Wings outstretched, a proud tilt to the head. I know you hate it, but you bearing that bird, it holds great meaning to the Black Bloods."

"Does it represent my will to flee?"

Danu finished the bird's other wing before speaking. "Solcha, the first Solcha—"

"The *real* Solcha."

"Her mark was a bird."

"I don't think I knew that."

"It's one of those things some know to be true and the rest spread as part of her legend." Danu set the jar of cooling ointment aside and picked up the other jar.

"Solcha disappeared with Bryana's daughter," Niko said. "I wonder if the real Solcha saw a chance and ran."

"I don't think so. Born to the Black Bloods or not, Solcha was one of us."

A not-unpleasant tickle fluttered across Niko's back as Danu sprinkled powder over the ointment.

"I'd run," Niko said. "If a saw a chance, even a small one, I'd run. I know I'd probably end up dead. But for even one free breath, it would be worth it."

"I wouldn't blame you, but I would mourn you." Danu took Niko's hand, lacing her fingers through his. "I don't think I could ever stop mourning you."

Everything seemed to freeze—even the rain stopped pattering against the windowpanes—as the world teetered on the tip of a blade.

Then Danu eased her hand from his, and the rain came back, and a weight settled in the middle of Niko's throat.

"We'll have to do this again tomorrow." Danu's weight disappeared from Niko's back as she got off the bed. "Keep your mark dry and let it air until you sleep." She placed the jars back on the tray. "I'll see you in the morning."

She went to the door and walked out into the hall, locking the door behind her, leaving Niko lying on the bed, still trying to find words that could pass through the knot twisting in his throat.

8

ADRIAL

No thrill of delight rose in Adrial's chest as he shifted the last of the papers to the pile Scribe Tammin was to handle. He'd spent days digging through tasks that could have been done by the scribes who worked under him, leaving those stationed just outside his door to scurry about the library searching for something to do.

Adrial ran his hands over the empty, clean desk in front of him. A perfect workspace for creating the intricate vellum that would be Princess Illia's wedding gift. A fresh stack of finely made parchment, pens…no excuse to delay the task.

"Head Scribe." Scribe Tammin stepped closer to his worktable, planting herself solidly in his line of sight, as though she'd sensed he'd forgotten she was in the room. "Shall I take the papers now?"

"Yes." Adrial lifted his hands away from the desk. "Please do. Assign the work to the other scribes as you see fit."

"Yes, sir." Tammin lifted the stack of forms and ledgers from his desk. "Is there anything else you need?"

Adrial fixed his gaze on the blank wall in front of him.

He couldn't look at his desk. The jars of ink Tammin had laid out for him sparkled in the sunlight creeping through the window.

Looking at the floor, where he and Ena had lain when she'd interrupted his work with indescribable pleasure...that might shatter the thin thread of reason he clung to.

Closing his eyes, giving in to darkness, that was the safety his soul craved.

"Head Scribe?" Tammin prompted.

"Bring in Scribe Gend," Adrial said.

"Really, sir?" Tammin said. "If it's to be the bloodletting he deserves, should I call in a maid to mop up?"

"Your presence will suffice," Adrial said. "Keep the door open so the others can hear."

"As you wish." Tammin went through the door to the office where the other scribes under Adrial's immediate command worked.

Adrial stood, leaning his weight onto his bad hip, cherishing the sharp pain that, for a slim moment, distracted him from the constant ache in the hollow where his heart and lungs should have been.

The low rumbling of tense voices came from the outer office.

Reaching into his pocket, Adrial touched the scroll Lord Gareth had marked with his seal of white wax. Such a small bit of parchment to change a man's fate.

"It wasn't an invitation." Tammin's crisp words carried to Adrial.

The gods have kept your heart beating, Ena whispered.

Adrial closed his eyes, swallowing the sob that slammed against his ribs.

A good man can't rest while monsters hunt in the shadows, scribe, Ena whispered.

"Head Scribe," Tammin said.

Adrial opened his eyes to find the hateful fiend standing in the doorway.

"Scribe Gend," Adrial said, "when I summon you to my office, I expect you to step all the way into my office."

Travers's smug grin stayed maddeningly in place as he stepped just inside the door.

Tammin shifted to Adrial's flank, pinning her glare on Travers like a dog ready to attack at her master's command.

"Scribe Gend," Adrial said, "more than once, you've offered to take on any work I find too taxing. Given the current state of Ilara, I would be remiss in my duty if I did not accept your offer."

"Head Scribe, I—"

Adrial raised a hand, cutting off Tammin's protest.

All the usual sounds from the outer office had fallen completely silent.

"Your choice is wise, Head Scribe." Travers's grin grew as he gave Adrial the smallest of bows. "Some men are born to books. Other men are born to lead."

"How dare—"

Adrial cut Tammin off again.

"Ilbrea is not made of two kinds of people, Scribe Gend. You, however, are a very specific sort of man, and those who possess your particular attributes must be carefully used when violence lurks in the shadows and grows on the streets." Adrial pulled the scroll from his pocket. "After much consideration, Lord Gareth has decided it is in the best interest of the Scribes Guild to create a new position within the library. Lord Gareth himself has chosen you to fill this position."

"The wisdom of the Lord Scribe leads us all." A putrid air of satisfaction drew back Travers's shoulders.

"The position of city scribe will be yours starting immediately," Adrial said.

A cough of disgust punctuated the growing hum of whispers from the outer office.

"The honor of your new rank has been added to your record," Adrial said.

An angry hush stopped the hum.

"It will be your duty to handle the daily requests coming in from the common folk in the city," Adrial said. "All complaints against the Guilds, any ill or injured appealing for care from the Healers Guild—"

"Head Scribe, surely there are better uses—" Travers stepped closer to Adrial.

"The library must be protected. For the safety of our Guild, a scribe of your ilk must be placed outside the library," Adrial pressed on. "You'll have a desk set up just beyond the gate. Don't worry, I've arranged for a little awning to cover your papers in case of rain."

"Head Scribe—"

Adrial raised his voice, speaking over Travers. "As you'll be meeting many common folk who are bitterly angry with the Guilds, I've also arranged for four scribes' guards to protect you at all times. Don't worry, I've chosen the guards myself. They are all fiercely loyal to the Lord Scribe."

"You are making a mockery of the Scribes Guild!" Travers shouted.

"Word of illnesses spreading through the city has come to my attention as well," Adrial said. "For the safety of all living within the library, the Lord Scribe has decided it best to house you away from the rest of the scribes' quarters to prevent any contamination you might leak into our halls. You will be housed in the stables."

The veins in Travers's neck bulged as red devoured his face. "You'll put me in your filthy rotta whore's rooms?"

"I would never allow you near Ena's rooms." Adrial kept his feet planted as Travers stepped closer still. "A horse stall has been cleared out for your use. Don't worry, I've arranged extra pay for the stable hands who will clear the bucket you've been granted to relieve yourself."

"This will never stand," Travers said.

"I assure you it will," Adrial said. "Each Guild is allowed to assign their members as their Guild Lord sees fit. Lord Gareth has assigned you as the city scribe. You will follow Lord Gareth's orders, or you will resign your place within the Scribes Guild."

"Don't—"

"By resigning your position, you would relinquish the protection of the Guilds," Adrial said. "How long do think you would survive on the streets once word spread that you sent the head scribe's common-born wife to her death? And do not doubt that word will spread. Notices will be posted all over Ilara. They will be sent to every city and village in Ilbrea."

"Saying what?" Travers sneered. "That I am a scribe who follows the laws of the Guilds?"

"Praising your work in keeping a rotta and her unborn child from infiltrating the Guilds," Adrial said. "What do you think the common folk will do to you once they've learned just how far you've gone to serve your paun masters?"

Tammin gasped.

"There are four guards waiting in the corridor." Adrial held the scroll out to Travers. "They will escort you to your desk outside the gates. Should you choose to abandon that post, I will consider it your resignation."

"You won't get away with this." Travers snatched the scroll.

"I assure you I will," Adrial said. "Whatever monster's ear you whispered in to condemn my wife will have no use for you now that your post will remove you from all contact with any person, text, or document within the library. You will not have access to any whispers, any rumors. You'll have no ears to bend. Monsters who condemn a woman and her innocent child are not the type to rescue a pawn once it is no longer useful."

Travers crumpled the scroll in his hand.

"Now, leave my office before I call your new guards to drag you away." Adrial settled back into his seat. "Be sure to bundle up as you enjoy your new desk. The wet chill of the fall can seep into a man's lungs in a deadly way if he's not careful."

Travers strode of out Adrial's office and slammed the door behind him, cracking through the wood above the handle.

A few moments of deafening silence followed before heavy footsteps pounded away and a second echoing bang rattled the door to the corridor. A burst of whispers came from the outer office.

Adrial shut his eyes as a smothering fatigue weighed on his body.

"Did Dudia spark the idea in your mind or Lord Gareth's?" Tammin asked.

"The Lord Scribe signed the scroll." Adrial forced his eyes to open and his back to straighten. "The rest doesn't matter."

"Of course it does." Tammin ran her fingers along the new cracks in the door. "There will be twelve tales of Travers's banishment flying through the library before dinner. I'd like to know which is true."

"Why?"

"My own interest. To smugly correct those who get the story wrong. To make sure there's no chance of some sorry getches painting Travers as a twisted sort of martyr."

"Lord Gareth wanted to send him south." Adrial dragged his hands down his face. His stubble had grown long enough to soften.

"The far end of the country seems like the perfect place for the getch," Tammin said.

"There are innocent common folk in the south. Ena would never have forgiven me for allowing Travers to torture them. Better to let him waste away here where I can be sure he doesn't do any more damage."

"No way to have him whipped or jailed?" Tammin furrowed her brow.

"He committed no crime. Under the Guilds' laws, he is an innocent man."

"That doesn't make him any less of a villain. It should be him who's suffering, not you."

"I deserve every torment Dudia can provide." Adrial reached for the stack of fresh parchment on his desk.

"You don't." Tammin planted her fingers on the papers, gently holding them in place.

"Please tend to the scribes in the office. From the buzz of their chatter, I doubt they've gone back to work."

"Of course not," Tammin said. "They're too busy spiraling up the whispers that will anchor the tales of Travers's exile. The scribes in the office are loyal to you. Let them chatter. It'll help tilt the rumors fully in your favor."

"Order them all to be silent." Adrial pressed his hands to his desk, willing them not to tremble. A ball of jagged guilt and loathing pressed up into his throat. "I'd order the entire library silent if I could."

"Not even the sorcerers could stop the rumors."

"Then go to the common hall and shout to all the scribes that I am a monster." Adrial snatched the parchment from under Tammin's hand, tearing two of the precious sheets. "I am the liar. I am the demon who should have been whipped to death. If any of them utter a word about Ena or the child—"

"All of them talk of Ena and the child."

"No." Adrial stood, knocking his chair backward. "They can't." A horrible pain tore through his chest, crushing the air from his lungs. "I wo—I won't let them insult her memory. I'll find a way. I'll stop them."

"Even if you could, you shouldn't." Tammin set his chair upright. "There are a few scribes who are still bitter that you debased yourself with a common wife."

"None of them knew—"

"But their grumblings are brushed aside by the grander tale

sweeping through the library. Like it or not, you're the hero in a romance that will be cherished for the ages."

"What?" An odd cold crept through Adrial's body.

"A common girl, beautiful and wild, like something from a fairy story," Tammin said. "A scribe who'd been broken by tragedy and condemned to the shadows."

He didn't fight as she guided him to sit.

"The girl had no family. On her own, she tried to survive the violence and chaos the common folk had spawned in our city. Always one step from despair until she met the scribe. They fell madly in love."

A sob punched through Adrial's lungs, but Tammin didn't stop speaking.

"The scribe wanted to marry the girl and save her from the horrors of the city, but other men coveted her beauty. They captured the girl, locking her up, hiding her from the scribe, demanding she marry one of her own kind. They told her the scribe could never want her. That he was mocking her with his promises of love. The future Lord Scribe could never love a rotta."

Adrial tried to shout through his tears, but Tammin knelt in front of him, squeezing his shoulders to silence him.

"They shattered her heart, keeping her trapped and cold and hungry until she believed their lies. Feigning pity, one of the men offered her food and warmth if she shared his bed. She was so broken she agreed, letting the man drag her into the horrible despair she thought Dudia had chosen for her.

"But the scribe never stopped looking for his love. He risked his life, scouring the city, even though he knew the men who'd taken her would easily kill him in a fight. Then the night of terror came, and the rebels set the city on fire. The scribe found the girl as they ran from the flames. The moment he saw her, he clung to her, and she knew the rotta men had lied to break her.

"She sobbed in the scribe's arms, confessing she'd taken to

another man's bed, sure she would lose the man she loved forever. Her words tore the scribe's heart from his chest, but he held her tighter as the men who had taken her found them."

A dark, bloody scene flashed through Adrial's mind. Cade and his men surrounding him. A spurt of red as Ena sliced a man's throat.

"The scribe whispered his forgiveness and undying love as he shielded the girl's body with his own. Dudia took pity on the lovers, sending soldiers to find them and kill the rotta monsters who'd so terribly abused the girl. The scribe swept the girl away to safety, and they vowed never to be parted again.

"But Dudia's pity didn't come without a price. The man who'd stolen the girl and filled her head with terrible lies had claimed her body and left a child in her womb."

The office faded from Adrial's tear-blurred eyes, leaving him on a storm-ravaged cliff, clinging to Ena as he begged her to survive.

He'd promised her safety.

He'd lied.

"The girl tried to leave, certain that this, carrying another man's child, would finally drive the scribe away forever. But lies and fire had already tried to part them. The promise of a child brought the scribe nothing but joy. He begged the girl to stay, vowing to her and Dudia that his love was strong enough to survive any storm, swearing to love the child and raise it as his own. The girl vowed her love in return, and they were married.

"But the evil of the men who had stolen her rose up from the grave, seeping into the city to breed more violence, twisting through the cracks of the library's walls to darken Ilbrea's purest glory. The terrible truth of the child's conception was discovered. Married or not, the girl was carrying a bastard. The scribe tried to sacrifice himself to protect his love and the child he called his own, but the girl wouldn't let him. She demanded to be sent to Ian Ayres to defend the scribe's honor and save his life."

Pain wrapped around Adrial's body as the memory of Ena walking away, striding toward her death, swallowed his mind.

"But the girl knew the scribe would keep fighting to trade his safety for her freedom." Tammin's words made every hurt slice deeper. "To prevent his sacrifice, the girl leapt into the Arion Sea, ending her life to protect her love."

Sobs wracked Adrial's chest.

"Only you know how closely the story follows the truth, but it's kind enough to satisfy those who knew Ena and grand enough that the tale of the heartbroken scribe will live on long after your names are forgotten." Tammin took Adrial's hands. "There is no comfort for those forced to survive such tragedy, but know that Ena's memory is protected. The tale holds no mockery of your wife or the child you claimed as your own, only sorrow for the husband and father they left behind."

Tammin kept her grip on his hands as the world swirled away into the endless darkness of grief.

9

KAI

The floor of the stale-odored burrow had been created by the gods specifically to mock Kai. The packed dirt had borne the steps of a dozen members of the underground in the last two hours, but still had enough give for Kai's pacing to wear a distinctive, ever-deepening line on the floor. Even knowing the floor's foul intentions, Kai couldn't make himself stand still.

The plan had been carefully crafted.

Kai paced another lap.

Two sets of lookouts had been watching the streets west of the docks since before dawn.

Another lap.

Cause a distraction, draw the sorcerers' focus away from the docks. A pack of drunken slitches could accomplish such an easy thing.

Lap.

But they hadn't sent drunken slitches. Members of the underground were up there right now, risking their necks.

Lap.

He should be with them. He knew the roofs of the warehouses better than anyone.

Lap.

But knowing the roofs well enough to flee shouldn't matter.

Lap.

Draw the sorcerers' attention away from the docks long enough to allow select items to be smuggled onto carefully chosen ships. Hopefully, the sorcerers would end up dead. Hopefully, the underground's people wouldn't.

Lap.

Another lap.

Another.

Something hard hit Kai on the back. He spun around.

Merial waved from her seat in the corner. She pulled another rock from her pocket. "I'll aim for your face next time if you don't hold still for one godsforsaken moment."

"Sorry." Kai balled his still-injured hand into a fist, letting the throb of pain dampen the panic that threatened to drown him.

"Sit," Merial said.

"I'm—"

"—supposed to be healing, and I'm in no mood for arguing," Merial said. "Sit. Be still. Stop annoying me."

The only other person in the room, a sallow-skinned, reedy-looking man, huffed a laugh.

"Wouldn't want to disturb anyone." Kai leaned against the wall and sank to the ground.

The reedy man sighed and tipped his head back to stare at the ceiling, as though disappointed Merial and Kai hadn't given him a distraction by starting a fight.

Kai studied the man, trying to think of something either witty or brave to say. But he didn't know the reedy man's name, and they'd spent too much time in the same room, piecing together the plot neither of them would be called upon to enact, to admit he'd never bothered to ask anyone who the man actually was.

They should be back by now. The whole thing should've been quick.

I should be there.

Something went wrong. Something had to have gone wrong.

We knew it would.

"We need to start running more supplies into the city," Merial said.

"What?" Kai said.

Merial pulled a little book and pencil from her pocket. "We should make a list of all the goods we need to keep this chivving fight against the sorcerers going."

"You want to talk about supplies now?" Kai leaned toward her, furrowing his brow.

"You're bouncing your leg, and it's giving me the strong urge to break your other hand," Merial said. "It's either maim you or distract you enough you'll stop chivving moving. Now, other than bandages, arrows, and another thousand fighters, what else do we need?"

We need Drew back.

"If we keep running through black mining powder the way we are, we'll be out soon," the reedy man said. "We need more, much more, if we want to make any true progress. I'd take some bits of metal, too."

"Metal?" Merial looked up from her notebook. "Such a useful request. Would you like a coin? A tea kettle? A crown, perhaps?"

"Doesn't matter what sort of metal," the reedy man said.

Merial glared.

The reedy man sighed again. "I'll take a bucket of rusty nails if you can find them."

"*That* I can manage," Merial said. "I can think of a few places I'd like to steal some nails from. Watch the Zellys' warehouse fall on their laxe heads."

"Tell me when the walls start to shake," the reedy man said. "Seeing the Zellys suffer has long been a dream of mine."

"What else do we need?" Merial asked.

"Food, anything for healing, weapons, the gods sweeping down from the sky to fight this chivving battle for us," Kai said.

"Food." Merial wrote the single word in her book and scowled at Kai.

"Sorry." Kai dragged his good hand over his face. "We need to go aboveground. See what's happening."

"Absolutely not," Merial said.

"We should go to Lord Nevon," Kai said.

"Lord Nevon is at the docks," the reedy man said. "He has to be visible during the attack. Make sure no one thinks to question his loyalty."

An angry, anxious energy wound around Kai's chest. "We can't just sit here."

"Can and will," Merial said. "It's a chivving terrible part of the job, but it's the role we've been given. We plan, and we wait. I know you're built to be up in the fight, and maybe next time you'll be well enough to try and get yourself killed with the others. In the meantime, you can live as Latchy and I do. Turn your mind to the next problem and keep slogging forward."

"Cheers," the reedy man, Latchy—which didn't seem like a better name than reedy—said.

"Fine." Kai leapt to his feet and, ignoring the pulse of pain in his side, went back to pacing. "We need more blankets for the people living in the tunnels. Sleeping cold can steal a man's conviction, and we can't lose fighters for lack of warmth."

"There we are," Merial said. "That is how we work on the plotting side of this mess."

"If you liked that, you're going to love my asking for tea," Kai said.

Latchy whistled. "Now he's getting greedy."

"Waking up to the choice of silty water or cheap frie will make drunks of the best of us," Kai said. "Having the option of tea lets a person cling to civility."

"Didn't expect such words of wisdom from you," Latchy said.

"A well-run ship is a well-supplied ship." Kai bowed to Latchy. "Keep moving. Go."

Kai spun toward back of the burrow.

"Go!" The shout carried through the wall. "I said *go!*"

Kai pulled his knife from his belt as a panel in the wall swiveled open. A man stumbled into the burrow, gripping his blood-soaked arm.

"We need—" The man leaned against the wall, letting Landon and the girl he half-carried enter the burrow. "I don't know what we need."

"Is anyone else coming?" Kai peered down the tunnel.

"They went the other way," Landon said. "Maybe to another entrance. Maybe to Lewis."

"They're bad enough to need Lewis?" Kai said.

"Is there anything in your arm, or are you just bleeding?" Latchy asked the man leaning against the wall.

"I think there's something in it," the man said. "A sorcerer spotted me and blasted a lark's ass of chivving rubble my way."

"Where are you hurt?" Merial helped lower the girl to the ground.

"The cuts aren't that bad." The girl pulled up the hem of her skirt. "Ended up jumping from a window. Made a mess of my knee."

Merial pursed her lips and frowned at the girl's knee, which was a nasty shade of purple and twice the size it should have been.

"I just need to rest it for a few minutes," the girl said. "I'll be fine."

"It'll need more than a few minutes," Merial said.

"Landon," Kai said. "Are you hurt?"

"Nothing frie and sleep won't fix." Landon shut the door to the tunnel.

"Wait." Kai grabbed Landon's wrist.

Landon gasped. "Watch it."

"If you think some of the party may have gone to Lewis, one of us needs to check on them," Kai said. "Make sure Lewis has everything he needs to care for them."

"I'll go." Merial smoothed the girl's hair and stood.

"I can go." Kai opened the door.

"You've been ordered to stay below until you heal." Merial glared at Kai. "If you're not allowed to go aboveground to jaunt across the city for tea with Drew, you're definitely not allowed up when the sorcerers will be out for blood. Now be a nice little lad and help care for the wounded you've got in front of you."

"Yes, ma'am." Kai stepped back, clearing Merial's path.

"And because I'm feeling generous, I'll let Drew know you pouted when you were told you couldn't risk your foolish neck to see him." Merial closed the door behind her.

"Let's get them to the bunk room," Latchy said. "You keep the bloody one on his feet, I'll carry the girl."

"If you give me a minute, I can walk," the girl said.

"Of course you can." Latchy scooped the girl into his arms with unexpected ease and carried her to the hidden door on the far side of the burrow.

"I've got it." Kai hurried over, the throbbing in his ribs a vexing reminder that Merial was right.

Digging his fingers beneath the stone façade of the door, Kai pried the panel open.

A dark corridor stretched out in front of him.

"If you're going to carry me, at least don't ram my head into the wall," the girl said as Latchy carried her into the darkness.

The man with the bleeding arm followed, waving away Kai's help, leaving Kai and Landon behind.

Wrinkling his nose against the pain of some wound Kai couldn't see, Landon pushed away from the wall, heading toward Kai.

"How bad was it?" Kai whispered.

Landon stopped in the tunnel opening. "Four of us dead. Of the survivors, I think I fared best. Fool's chivving luck, I suppose."

Kai shut his eyes, stomping down the anger building in his throat.

"We killed three sorcerers," Landon said. "Two in the first volley of arrows. Pairing archers on each target worked. Even after the arrows hit, the confusion played in our favor, took them longer to figure out where the arrows had come from. It should have gone better, but once the attack started, the sorcerers sent the soldiers out in front of them like a chivving shield. Coward slitches."

"How many soldiers fell?" Kai's words came out pinched and low.

"Don't know," Landon said. "Once we knew the sorcerers weren't going to give us a clearer attack, we sent another round of arrows, tossed some fire at them, and ran for our lives."

"Three sorcerers." Kai took a deep breath, shoving his grief beneath his anger. "How far has Ilara fallen that four of ours for three of theirs sounds like a victory?"

Landon laid his hands on Kai's shoulders.

Kai opened his eyes, grateful that no tears trailed down his cheeks.

"There are three fewer demons in the world," Landon said. "The cost was heavy, but mere men slayed monsters. Soon, the common folk will understand that sorcerers can be killed by arrows and blades, and we will swarm by the thousands to end the sorcerers' hold on Ilbrea for good.

"And, if the gods blessed us, our men on the docks succeeded and we're three hidden sails closer to protecting the sailors from the sorcerers. Don't wallow in misery to prove you're a good man. We paid a heavy price tonight, but we won, Kai. Savor that. Tomorrow will bring enough pain of its own."

10

NIKO

The unbloodied rag provided Niko the only joy he'd felt in days. He unwound the rag from the bowl of the long, wooden spoon, examining the cloth for any hint of red. But the only thing tainting the fabric was the pungent tonic he'd just smeared over his back.

He stared at the rag for a few minutes, refusing to feel foolish for taking pride in such a small, rather disgusting thing. When the pride had waned to boredom then started to sink toward anger, he pulled the jar of ointment over and smeared some on the back of the spoon.

There was no way to feign dignity in the process—using a kitchen utensil to reach the wounds on his back wasn't a tale he'd be telling over ale—but using the spoon as though he were smearing jam and his back was a large slice of bread did work. And, though it had taken days, the chivving marks had finally healed.

After applying the ointment, he leaned forward, keeping his torso at a slight angle as he sprinkled powder over his back, shaking like a sodden dog to spread the powder around.

His task finished, he set his tools back on the tray and stared at the jars for a long while. When he couldn't do that anymore, he stood and went to stare out the window, watching the storm drench the valley in a cold rain that might turn to ice at any moment.

When his feet got tired, he sat and read one of the three books the maids had brought him. After he'd spent an hour trying to read the same paragraph with his mind refusing to make sense of the words on the page, he paced beside the windows, pretending that was a new activity—entirely different from standing still and staring out the windows—that could delightfully pass the endless hours.

A stronger, or perhaps more foolish man, might have raged at being locked in his room for days. But Niko had endured torture at the hands of the Brien Elder. Boredom, however grating, could not compare to the agony of having knives slice through his flesh as magic ripped through his mind.

Niko could quietly accept imprisonment in his room. It was the gnawing worry constantly clawing at his mind that made the hours drag on.

Danu still hadn't come to see him, not since the first time she'd treated his wounds. For more than a week, Niko had been locked away without a single visit from his keeper.

Maids had come to clean his room and bring him food. A healer had tried to treat him. Niko had run the healer off. That's when he'd asked the maids for a long-handled spoon so he could care for his own wounds. The maids hadn't responded, not that they ever did, but the spoon was delivered with his next meal.

In a maddening twist he couldn't understand, Niko's attempt to please Danu by caring for his mark hadn't brought her back. Neither had his pounding on the door, demanding to see her. Or blatantly begging the maids to ask her to visit him.

Despite his best efforts to convince himself he didn't care,

Niko had thought of several reasons why Danu might have abandoned her charge.

Danu had taken genuine offense at Niko's loathing of the mark the demon elder had carved into his back. He'd insulted Black Blood tradition, and Danu hadn't forgiven him.

Or, Danu had told the Brien Elder Niko hadn't been caring for his wounds. To punish Niko, the chivving elder had forbidden Danu from seeing Niko.

Or, Danu had taken ill, and none of the chivving Brien wanted to upset Solcha by telling him the one person he truly liked in the stronghold was on her deathbed.

Or, the tide of the war with the Hayes had shifted, and Danu had been sent to the front to freeze with the other fighters as they held the line of the siege surrounding the Hayes refuge.

Or, the Guilds were storming into the mountains, and Danu had been forbidden to see Niko because Bryana knew Danu would tell Niko the Guilds were close by and Niko would make a desperate attempt to flee.

Or, the worst possibility of all, the awful thing that plagued him in his darkest moments when he couldn't find anything else to occupy his mind, he'd wounded Danu.

She was his friend. She was the only thing that had kept him breathing during his time playing Solcha for the desperate Brien.

She'd said she would miss him if he died, and he'd said…nothing. Not a single word of how losing her would rip away what little of his humanity remained. He hadn't even managed to say that facing her death would put him off his dinner.

She'd comforted him. She'd cleaned his wounds with such a tender touch. Her fingers grazing his skin. His bed holding both their weight…

He should beg the maids for another book. Or wood to carve.

Or chivving well…anything.

Dudia-wrought relief arrived when the maids brought his meal.

Lunch.

He'd only made it halfway through the day.

Chivving demon spawn and all their chivving minions.

He carved his cheese into tiny bits, trying to see just how finely his knife could cut. He made an elaborate seven-pointed star from the sliced fruit he'd been given.

Danu had said she'd miss him if he died, and he hadn't even chivving well thanked her for wiping the ooze off his chivving back.

Foolish chivving slitch.

Niko tipped his head up to stare at the stone ceiling of his room.

The stone was smooth, without any cracks or imperfections. Niko picked up his knife, running his finger along the blunt tip.

It would be difficult, if it were even possible, but if he stood on the bed, he could reach the ceiling. Carving the constellations as seen from Ilara would be an interesting challenge. He'd created star charts as an apprentice under Lord Karron, but always on paper. Stone would keep him busy for hours, maybe even days.

He pressed his fingers to the compass mark on his forearm, watching as the arrow spun to face north.

The pride he'd felt when the sorcerer had drawn the mark of the Map Makers Guild on his arm, the rush of joy the first time he'd watched the little arrow spin, and the awe of having a mark that moved—it was one of the shining moments of glory Niko had hoped to share with his grandchildren when he had them all gathered around for tales of his adventures.

One mark to cherish, one to loathe, both drawn on a man who was still locked in his chivving room.

"I'm going to go mad in here."

Niko held his breath, waiting for a voice to whisper from the shadows, *"You already have."*

No voice spoke.

Niko pulled off his boots and tossed them aside before grabbing the knife and climbing onto the bed.

If he were to use the proportions of the bed as the scale for his map while maintaining true north and using a piece of cutlery as his only tool, the angle of the star chart would pose an entertaining challenge.

He scratched the knife against the stone, carefully drawing the compass rose that would be the base of his map.

With the scratch, scratch, scratch of his knife against the stone, Niko didn't hear the thunk of the lock.

A terrified little cough came from by the door.

Niko spun toward the sound, his knife held in front of him as though it were a proper weapon.

The maid standing just inside his room gave a squeak and another cough.

"Sorry." Niko lowered his knife.

The maid made an odd noise in her throat.

"Are you all right?" He jumped off the bed.

"Ee—aai—eooo." The maid's odd noises gained vowels.

"Do you need to sit?"

The maid shook her head so violently, she nearly dropped the stack of clothes in her arms.

"Should I—" Niko flattened his lips together. "Would you like me to call for help?"

"No." The poor girl's eyes got very wide, as though she'd shocked herself by speaking. "You're to—there's umm—I mean I've been told…"

"It's all right. Take your time."

"I can't, Solcha." The girl spoke the false name with the same reverent thrill Niko had heard from so many other Brien. "I've been told to bring you these things, and to tell you—well, I suppose—tell you to hurry and get dressed. Not that I'd ever want to hurry you, but that's what I was told to say. That, and that there will be someone here to collect you soon, and I'm sorry to make it sound like an order, Solcha, but I was told that I was to tell you to be ready to leave when they came. Again, I'm sorry, Solcha. My deepest apologies."

"Nothing to be sorry for." Niko bowed to the girl, only then realizing he was bare from the waist up, which might have accounted for some of the poor girl's blushing. "Who's coming to collect me?"

"I wasn't told that, Solcha." The girl placed the clothing in Niko's hands and gave a deep bow. "Thank you for your kindness. May the mountain ever guide your steps."

The girl bolted for the door, wrenched it open, and scurried into the hall.

Someone closed the door behind her, leaving Solcha in his prison with a fresh shirt and fear clawing through his gut.

"It's only clothes, you fool." Niko tossed his old pants aside and began dressing in the new garments, not allowing himself to examine every stitch, searching for some hint of whatever horror the Brien Elder had planned for him.

Would they mark his chest, too?

Would he once again be forced to stand beside Bryana, silently accepting the pain as she tore through the skin on his back?

Would he be called to the atrium so Danu could denounce her friendship with him in front of anyone who cared to watch Niko crumble?

You're tossing yourself into a spiral, Mara whispered. *A map maker has never gotten anywhere by spinning themselves in circles.*

"You don't always have to be right," Niko muttered as he pulled on the fresh shirt.

He stopped when he reached the coat at the bottom of the stack. The seamstress had sewn a thick layer of padding into the back.

Niko ran his fingers along the extra fabric.

A way to hide the shame of Bryana tearing at his skin as though his mark were nothing more than puppet strings.

It is not your duty to hide the deeds of a monster. Mara's voice held a satisfying crispness as though, if she really were with him, she would storm up to the throne room and dare Bryana to deny the brutality of her acts.

Niko would have to stop Mara, of course. Bryana would kill Mara for her insolence. But the idea of Mara raging at Bryana brought a smile to his lips as he took the knife he'd just been using in his poor attempt to carve the ceiling and ripped through the stitching that held the padding in the coat.

He laid the rejected fabric out on the center of the table, displaying his rebellion, though he was certain whatever maid cleaned it away would have no idea what the cloth had been for, and began pacing in front of his door.

He tucked his hands into his pockets and hummed a tune he'd learned from Kai.

Niko couldn't remember all the words, only that it had been bawdy enough to make Mara blush.

In the middle of his second rendition of the song, the lock clicked. Niko kept pacing and humming, not looking at the door as it swung open.

He turned for his next pass, the words, *I thought you'd forgotten me* balanced on his lips.

A guard—not one of his normal guards, but one of the men with gold embroidery on the chest of their purple uniform—stood in Niko's doorway.

"Good afternoon." Niko gave the guard a nod, grateful his hands were still tucked in his pockets as panic curled his fingers into tight fists. "I hope wherever you're taking me doesn't require going out into this storm."

"No, Solcha." The guard bowed. "This way, please."

The guard stepped back out into the hall.

While he hadn't bothered pretending Niko had a choice in obeying, Niko did take comfort in only three guards surrounding him as he walked down the stone corridor. That, and none of the guards grabbed him, tried to drag him, or had blood stains on their hands.

Your standards have fallen sharply, Nikolas Endur.

The guards led Niko on a familiar path, up through the cliff to the throne room.

A prickle of worry grew on the back of Niko's neck as they climbed higher. The prickle brutally transformed into a vice clenching fear around his stomach as they passed through rooms with beautiful images of the mountains inlaid in the stone walls.

There weren't any screams of some poor soul being tortured or any blood smears on the floor. The mosaics hadn't been damaged by fighting.

Niko took a deep breath, trying to catch the stench of smoke tainting the air.

Nothing.

Truly nothing.

No people in the chambers that usually held the pack of Brien who lurked outside the throne room. No servants preparing the space for some fancy affair.

They hadn't passed anyone while climbing the stairs, either.

Only four guards flanked the entrance to the throne room, far fewer than Niko had ever seen before. His own guards joined their meager ranks, allowing Niko to pass through the doors alone.

Bryana sat on her white-stone throne, her gaze fixed on the doorway, something between rage and fear filling her eyes.

Dudia shield me from whatever torment may come.

Movement beside the throne caught Niko's eye.

Danu waited in her usual spot, ready to guard Solcha.

Niko met her gaze, but she didn't offer him a smile or a glare, just a shake of her head that turned his fear into a frozen terror that locked around his lungs, making him fight for every breath.

They haven't destroyed you yet.

You can keep surviving.

He took his normal place on the left side of the throne without speaking. The usual whirlwind of awful possibilities didn't tear through his mind. A faint, piercing screech consumed his thoughts instead.

A warm touch brushed against the back of his hand.

You're not allowed to die until you've apologized to Danu.

She stood right behind his shoulder. She didn't whisper any words of comfort, but having her that close…

Niko reached back, letting his pinky graze her hand. Her finger curled around his.

The thump of footsteps carried into the throne room. Danu yanked her hand away.

Bryana sat forward on her throne as though preparing for an attack.

Five people entered the throne room. The doors closed behind them, shutting out all the guards.

No one spoke.

There were three men in the group and two women.

Dressed in well-worn clothes, all five had the look of those who'd reached the end of a long journey. But four of them stood around the fifth, as though the woman in the center was to be either feared or protected.

The woman in the center held Bryana's gaze, her face calm, as though she were too foolish to fear the Brien Elder. She tipped her head and the golden gleam of the lae stones caught on her hair, brightening the effect of the hundred colors streaked through the strands.

Niko couldn't tell if time stopped or sped past as everyone waited for Bryana to speak.

"Where is she?" The Elder's whispered question filled the throne room.

"Elder Bryana," the woman with technicolor hair began.

"Where is she, Solcha?" The Elder stood.

Niko dared to glance back at Danu.

She gave a tiny nod without looking away from the woman—from Solcha.

"I'm sorry, Bryana." Solcha stepped closer to the throne. The four surrounding her mirrored her movement. "Regan is dead."

11

NIKO

The patter of the rain and soft swishing of Bryana's dress were the only sounds as the Brien Elder sank back onto her throne.

"I don't know if there's any comfort to be found," Solcha said, "but your daughter died fighting the Guilds."

"Do not mock me," Bryana said.

"I'm not," Solcha said.

"Did you even shed a tear for her death?" Bryana's voice wavered, as though the demon were capable of grieving.

"No," Solcha said. "But Regan met her end trying to protect the Black Bloods. Whatever else passed between us, I respect her devotion. She loved her people with everything she had. That's more than can be said of many."

"It's certainly more than can be said of you." The normal crisp harshness returned to Bryana's tone. "You disappeared. The mountain accepted you into her embrace, and then nothing. If you had any decency, you would have died alongside my daughter, *Solcha*."

"That's not my name," Solcha said. "How your people have twisted my life—"

"You let the Brien heir die, then dare to walk into our strong-hold," Bryana said.

"I didn't let Regan do anything." Solcha drew closer to the throne, as though she really were too chivving foolish to fear the Elder. "I don't think anyone who knew your daughter could claim to control her, not even you."

"Do not pretend—"

"And believe me, coming to the Brien for help was a depth I never thought I'd stoop to. But the gods don't always let us choose our path. The Black Bloods were born of a child sheltered and loved by the mountain." Solcha pressed her hand to the unmistakable roundness of her stomach. "I ask for shelter for the child I carry."

"Would you have me believe you carry a Black Blood child?" Bryana sneered.

"Don't." Solcha's hand shifted, rising to the black stone pendant around her neck.

"Has precious *Solcha* rolled through so many beds she can't remember the name of her child's father?"

A swallowed gasp came from behind Niko's shoulder.

"Bryana—"

"What will people whisper of the whoring *Solcha?*"

"My name is Ena, *Bryana Brien,* and you know it. Do not blame me for the myth your people invented."

"A girl protected by the mountain, given everything by the Black Bloods, disappears and comes crawling back with her bastard babe," Bryana said. "There is no name that can disguise a common whore."

"The child is claimed by my husband." A slight smile, somehow alluring and terrifying at the same time, curved Solcha's—Ena's lips. "I'm sure it's disappointing to you, but I am a married woman."

"Then make the fool shelter you."

"Pity you haven't learned not to insult an ally. I offer more to the Black Bloods than a false name to praise and a myth to cling to. I offer you the chance to finally do some good, if you're wise enough to take it."

"There is nothing—"

"My husband is the Head Scribe of Ilbrea," Ena said, "heir to the Lord Scribe."

"No, he isn't." Niko's voice bounced around the throne room before he even realized he'd spoken.

For the first time, Ena looked his way. A dangerous sort of humor danced through her eyes. "The Brien Elder has such poor information about the state of Ilara?"

"It's not poor information," Niko said.

Danu gripped his wrist, keeping him from stepping forward, but the mark on his back didn't sting with a warning from Bryana.

"I'm not sure what twisted game you're playing at, but Adrial Ayres isn't married." Niko kept his voice calm.

"Yes, he is," Ena said.

"No, he's not. He's a good man, and I will not let you drag his name into the horror of the Black Bloods." Niko gasped as pain tore through his back. "Leave Adrial out of it."

Ena stepped past the four that guarded her, keeping them from following her toward Niko with the slightest wave of her hand. She studied Niko's face, then looked down to where Danu gripped his wrist. "Who are you?"

"Nikolas Endur. Whatever you think—"

"Niko." Ena stepped away from him. "You're Niko?"

"Yes."

She studied him again, searching his face as though he might be the imposter.

"If you know my name," Niko said, "then you know how close Adrial and I—"

"You're dead. Word came from your journey."

"How did—"

"Adrial grieved for you." The dangerous gleam in her eyes brightened. "Do you have any idea the mess you started by running off with the Black Bloods?"

"Enough," Bryana said.

Another sharp jab of pain pierced the center of Niko's mark.

Ena held Niko's gaze for another moment before stepping back to face Bryana. "The Guilds are more dangerous than we ever feared. I have information, and I am willing to share it with you."

"I don't care what you're willing to do," Bryana said. "I will gladly rip whatever information I choose from your mind."

"No, you won't." Ena's smile returned. "How far have whispers of Solcha's return already spread? I've heard the twisted tale of my journey that has become so important to your people you found a new Solcha to hold my place in the Brien's hearts. Don't spout empty threats, Bryana. It's beneath you."

Danu tightened her grip on Niko's wrist.

"I am willing to let your people keep believing whatever they like about me," Ena said. "I will happily share all the information I have that could aid the Black Bloods in their fight against the Guilds. I want to see the paun drown in their own blood more than you will ever know. But you will swear upon your devotion to the mountain that when the day to burn Ilara comes, my husband will be spared."

"The Guilded deserve no mercy," Bryana said.

"He does," Ena said. "The head scribe is a good man. He's risked his life to help the common folk, and he sits with the Lord Scribe on the Guilds Council. He has information and access. You cannot underestimate his worth. His protection is all I ask in return."

Bryana looked down at her hands as though imagining the joy of spilling Guilded blood. "Your paun husband would help the Black Bloods?"

"The scribe would do anything for me and this child." Ena's

voice wavered, cracking her perfectly controlled façade. "He would tear the stars from the sky to protect me."

Bryana shifted her gaze to Ena's face. "Your husband will not be harmed by any Brien. But, if his devotion to you is as deep as you say, I expect he will still meet a violent end."

Danu drew Niko back to her as though she, like him, feared Ena might attack.

"Send word to the scribe that I'm alive. If grief devours him, he'll be of no use to anyone." Anger rolled off Ena in thick waves even as she spoke in a calm voice. "I hope you're not fool enough to let your own grief twist you into more of a beast than you were, Elder. If you don't accept my help and stand with me against the Guilds now, there will be no hope left for the Brien or any of the Black Bloods. Come to me when you've remembered who your true enemies are."

Ena turned and walked toward the door.

Niko held his breath, waiting for the stone floor to writhe up, wrapping around Ena's ankles, trapping her in place.

But the stone of the floor didn't shift as Ena shoved open the throne room doors and strode away, leaving her four companions hurrying in her wake.

One of the guards outside closed the doors behind her.

Niko couldn't convince his lungs to pull in air as he waited for the Brien Elder's rage to explode, shattering the cliff to punish Ena's arrogance.

Ena. Adrial's wife, Ena.

"Aunt." Paiman was the first to speak. "I'm so sorry."

"Your sympathy helps no one." Bryana's tone held the tense fury of a beast about to snap.

Danu shifted, easing herself between Bryana and Niko.

"Elder, if Solcha really has information—" Paiman began.

"I promise you, she does," Bryana said. "That girl drags darkness toward her. Whatever repulsive machinations lurk within the Guilds, she's found a way to tangle them around her neck. And now she's found her way into our home."

"Rumors of her return have already reached the training field." Paiman stepped around to stand in front of Bryana. "Even whispers of Solcha, the first Solcha, coming to the stronghold has brought fresh determination to the men. And that she came here, to the Brien and not any other clan, that will spread pride through the people and convince the other clans to devote more resources to our fight. Even without any information from Ilara, Solcha is an invaluable asset to the clan."

"To have her walk amongst the people." Bryana looked to Niko. Cold loathing filled her eyes. "The mountain has provided the genuine Solcha. Such a great gift should not be tainted by an unworthy paun."

"Niko is worthy," Danu said. "His bond with the Brien, especially the wounded returned from the fight, has proven valuable. To have both Solchas in the stronghold—"

"Could breed confusion among the people," Bryana said. "Two Ilbreans sheltered by the mountain, chosen by her wisdom to show the Black Bloods the dangers that lurk to the west—it allows conflicting tales. We can't have people placing one Solcha above the other."

"Then let Niko step aside," Danu said. "Let him become a true servant of the clan."

"Your precious Ilbrean swore to find my daughter," Bryana said. "My daughter is dead. His people killed her. He is no longer of use."

"Aunt, please." Danu steadied her stance. "Niko is loved by the people. If anything happened to him, they would grieve."

"Better to grieve a paun than doubt the will of the mountain," Bryana said. "Properly planned, his death could provide inspiration to the people."

"Aunt—"

"Before you order my execution"—Niko stepped out from behind Danu—"think about who she is. About who I am."

"Niko," Danu whispered.

Niko didn't look her way. He couldn't make himself let go of the demon elder's glare, not even to flinch as she tore through the skin on his back, letting a warm drop of blood run down his spine.

"I was apprenticed to Lord Karron. I lived in his house with Adrial Ayres. Adrial is family to me," Niko said. "I've never believed a breath of Solcha's story, and certainly never thought your mountain favored me by dragging me here to be tormented.

"But if that woman really is Adrial's wife, then terrifying as it is, Dudia and your mountain conspired to bring us both here. Whatever horrors lie ahead were laid out by powers far greater than any of us. Would you really risk the fate of your people by defying gods?"

12

KAI

My dearest friend Allora,

I've gotten myself into a chivving mess.

The only excuse I can offer is that Ilbrea has gone more to shit than I have.

As I write this imagined letter, I'm trapped under the false bottom of a farmer's wagon. I've been packed in with sacks of black mining powder to the point that I can't shift my hand enough to scratch the spot on my chin that's been itching for...it seems like years, so I'd wager it's been itching for an hour.

The earthy, peppery scent of the powder has invaded my nose. I think it's all I'll smell for the rest of my days.

You would have laughed at that.

I miss you, Allora. I miss our family.

There isn't enough room for any of you to cram into this godsforsaken compartment with me, and I wouldn't want you to, as a single spark could end my life in a most spectacular manner, but when I crawl free from this prison, you should be there.

You'd wrinkle your nose at the stench of the powder as you worried over me. Adrial would say something bookish about the uses of mining powder. Niko would laugh at the black smeared all over me. Mara would smack his arm and tell him to be kind, I had been very heroic. Tham would stay at the back of it all, our quiet guardian. He'd give me a nod, and I'd know it meant he was glad I was safe and proud of my work for the underground.

Then we'd all have a feast and the finest chamb and laugh and talk and all would be right with the world.

But nothing is right with the world.

We're trying to do the impossible, and the best hope we have is black powder and nails salvaged from burnt-out houses.

I was the lucky slitch chosen to fetch the powder. I wish I could say I was chosen for my excellent negotiating skills, but I think it's more that Lord Nevon didn't want to hand a bag of coin to anyone else. The amount he gave me was more than most in the underground would ever have carried in their lives.

We are a band of desperate people, hiding in the shadows, fighting what often seems a doomed war.

I don't think I could condemn any of my fellows for taking the coin, fleeing Ilara, and saving their own sodding hide.

But I am one of Karron's brood. I've seen riches far beyond what bought the powder that's creeping ever farther up my nose. A sack of coin holds no temptation for me.

No amount of gold can buy my family back. And that is what I long for.

I've done a foolish thing, Allora. Worse than getting myself jammed into the most flammable cart in all Ilbrea.

I've lost my heart and ruined my chances with the man I adore all in one blow.

He nearly died. He's recovering, and I haven't gone to visit him.

I should have snuck out of the tunnels. I should have threatened to stab anyone who got in my way. I should have challenged the gods themselves if they dared keep me from seeing Drew.

Instead, I stayed nicely hidden in my badger den.

Until, of course, I ended up in this chivving mess.

Allora, what if he doesn't forgive me?

What if his head got smashed against that street so hard, he doesn't even remember saying he wanted me?

What if he's come to his senses and realized how tragically unworthy I am?

I'm not afraid of fighting. I'm not even particularly fussed about dying. But, by the Guilds, I need my family.

I don't know how to keep fighting this desperate war alone. And that's how I feel, even when I'm with other members of the underground.

I am so alone.

It was better when Drew was with me. But if foolishly declaring my heart drove him away, I am so chivving alone even the gods can't save me.

The wagon just went over a bump, knocking my spine against the wood and sending a fresh puff of peppery scent into my nose. You'd enjoy the faces I'm making to try and keep from sneezing.

If the gods are kind, we're nearing the city's northern gate.

Gods and stars, this much stillness and quiet feeds the demons inside me.

You understand that. Or at least you did. You're Queen of Ilbrea now. I'm not sure I have any right to claim knowing you. The woman I love so dearly might be gone.

I know it's the demons in my mind driving me to such awful thoughts, that my Allora may be dead even though you, as whatever you are, are still alive.

But if you're not my Allora anymore, then I shouldn't be writing an imagined letter to you.

I cannot bear to think I am pouring my thoughts out to a stranger, even though these thoughts will never leave the compartment of this chivving wagon.

"Cacting chivving, sodden, barren, bower-breaking misery," Kai whispered under the rumble of the carriage wheels.

He listened for the sound of soldiers coming to rip apart the wagon and discover his hiding place.

The carriage kept rumbling steadily on.

A bubble of anger, worry, and bitter resentment at the surety that he'd never be able to get the scent of black powder out of his nose shoved against the front of Kai's chest.

He needed to run. He needed to fight. He needed to climb, or have sweat-dripping sex, or sail out onto the Arion Sea until the wind swept the awful, growing, chest-smothering bubble away.

Kai took a deep breath, trading more powder up his nose for a chance of shrinking the bubble.

Drew. He could speak to Drew. Take the time to work out what he wanted to say when he finally got to see him again.

"Drew, I'm so sorry I never came to check on you while you were trapped in Lewis's cellar." Kai would hold out his hand, letting Drew know he craved physical contact without stooping to outright begging for an embrace.

Drew would look into Kai's eyes, recognizing the man who'd carried him when he was wounded, dragging him away from Death more than once. Tiny creases would form at the corners of Drew's eyes.

The wrinkles weren't from a smile, but a disgusted, incredulous frown.

"How could you think I'd want anything from you?" Drew backed away. *"How could you throw our friendship away for the hope of a chivving roll?"*

"Dudia, if you've ever cared for this wayward boy, save me from this hellish wagon." Kai scrunched his eyes shut.

Tham.

Silent Tham. Stoic Tham.

Tham, who was far wiser than he'd ever show. Tham, who watched and listened to everyone around him, learning more about his friends than most understood about themselves. Tham, who'd known Kai since he was a tiny young thing.

Dear Tham,

The world has gone to shit, my allies in the underground keep dying, and I'm not sure if we're doing any good.

You and I grew accustomed to Death as children. But even watching the terrible things the captain of our ship did...it didn't prepare me for this.

I've seen so many people die since Winter's End.

How many more will I watch fall before spring comes again?

If there's even a chance—

The rumbling of the wheels changed as the wagon slowed.

Awareness snapped through Kai's body, sharpening each jolt as the carriage trundled over ruts in the road.

He opened his eyes, gripping the hilt of his knife, squinting against the dust falling through the cracks in the wood above him.

A tiny bit of sunlight snuck through the piles of hay in the cart, giving Kai enough light to see the cracks but no hint of what might be going on outside.

The cart slowed again. Then stopped.

Hints of chatter drifted to Kai.

A woman. Another woman.

The second woman laughed.

Two different men's voices. A third woman.

The gate. We're at the chivving gate!

A wave of reckless relief swept away the terrible pressure in Kai's chest.

Whether he'd slip through the gate unnoticed or be caught and executed, at least the whole thing would be done soon.

"Go on." The driver clicked to his horse. The horse pulled the cart forward, stopping again after a few steps.

"If I had another way to earn my living, I'd stop bringing goods into Ilara altogether," a woman said.

"My task is not to discourage your entering Ilara. I am merely ensuring the safety of the city," a man said in a crisp, pompous tone that made Kai wonder if the man had a crooked nose from too many punches to the face.

"If you find a hint of danger in my carefully wrapped packet of lace, tatted for a custom order from the high and mighty Mrs. Quintrell, then I owe you a debt for discovering the perils of knotted thread," the woman said. "And could you please only touch the lace with the gloves? There's a reason I brought them, and I will gladly tell Mrs. Quintrell who ruined her lace with their dirty hands."

"You are trying my patience," the pompous slitch said.

"It is a mutual despair," the woman said. "May I please be on with it?"

"You're dismissed," the pompous slitch said.

"Well, bless the Guilds for keeping order," the woman said. "Now give the gloves back so I can protect my goods the next time we meet."

A faint clink sounded, like coin striking coin.

"Thank you for your aid, gentlemen," the woman said.

"Go on," the driver said.

The cart moved forward.

"What do you have?" the pompous slitch asked.

The distinctive sound of something sniffing came from the right side of the wagon.

Kai tightened his hold on his knife.

"Hay," the driver said.

And mining powder and a man who's supposed to be dead.

"Only hay," the driver said. "No other goods."

"Are you sure?" the pompous slitch asked.

The sniffing changed to the scratching of claws on wood.

A sharp bang came from near the driver.

"Away, you!" The driver sighed as the wagon shifted, like the man was resettling in his seat. "Sorry about that. I promise I have nothing but hay. I learned my lesson last time. My word to the gods, I have hay only."

"Your word cannot be accepted by Dudia or the Guilds," the pompous slitch said. "You'll have to be patient while we search."

"Have at it then." The front of the wagon creaked as the driver shifted in his seat again.

Thump.

Thump, thump, thump.

The wagon rocked side to side as people jumped up onto the slats right above Kai.

Dirt sprinkled onto his lips. He scrunched up his face as the need to cough scratched in his throat.

Bang. Bang.

Bang. Bang. Bang. Bang.

Something, not boots, battered the wood above Kai.

Bang. Bang.

The sound moved up and down the wagon as though it were taunting him.

Bang.

Bang, bang, bang.

More dirt fell through the cracks, coating Kai's face as the sound changed again. Scraping, like claws dragging through the hay, seemed to come from everywhere at once.

If I've earned a bit of goodwill in this life, let the story of my death be shaped into a much grander tale than being discovered in the back of a haycart.

The scraping stopped.

Boots thumped on the wood, heading toward the back of the wagon. The wagon jostled as the people jumped to the ground.

Kai held his breath, waiting for the soldiers to tear open his hiding place.

Thump, thump, thump.

Something pounded on the side of the cart.

The front of the wagon shifted as the driver's seat creaked. "I'm all set then?"

"You're dismissed," the pompous slitch said.

"Good thing, too. If I don't get frie and a biscuit in me soon, I might turn cranky. Never been one for staying cheerful when hungry," the driver said. The cart moved forward. "Suppose the gods blessed me when I was born to a fertile farm."

Kai blew out a sharp breath, puffing away the dirt in his nose.

And the gods blessed me when you grew greedy enough to risk your life for a bag of coin.

13

MARA

Never, despite all the strange journeys, deadly perils, and inexplicable ordeals Mara had endured, had she ever been so grateful for the scent of damp horse shit wafting on the southerly wind. The strength of the pungent odor gave lightness to her travel-weary legs, quickening her pace on the last few miles of road before the Dudia-blessed northern gates of Ilara.

Tham kept right by her side as she walked, never pushing her pace or arguing with her plan.

Mara reached out, brushing her fingers against the back of Tham's hand, needing to be sure he would look her way even if all she could read in his eyes was worry.

He held her gaze for longer than normal, offering her a chance to change her mind.

She chewed her lips together, trying to think of something to say that would make the path she'd set them on seem less foolish and heinous.

I won't let them separate us.

Elle bounded up the road, saving Mara from having to speak the lie.

The pup crashed into the side of Tham's legs, wriggled with

joy, then looped behind, running a circle around Elver before tearing down the road again.

"I don't think she's gotten tired of traveling yet," Elver said.

"Elle loves to run," Mara said.

Elle barked and charged back to the group, this time banging into Mara's legs before looping behind Elver.

"But we're almost done traveling," Elver said.

"We'll reach Ilara soon," Mara said. "A soft bed and something to eat. Elle will still be happy."

"Right," Elver said. "But I haven't gotten tired of traveling yet."

Mara glanced back at Elver. A line pinched between his eyebrows, adding age to his too-thin face. He tugged at the bits of his patchy beard that had grown long enough for him to grip.

"We've been walking for weeks, Elver." Mara stopped, waiting for Elver to catch up to her, but he stopped, too, keeping the same distance between them. "I know none of us are eager to face what lies ahead, but we've finally reached Ilara. We have to go into the city. We have to—"

"I know." Elver's whole body bounced as he nodded. "I know. Death prowls on the horizon. Blood will stain the north. The snow will be painted red, and we"—he yanked on his beard as though trying to tear the hair out—"we have to try to keep the red stain small. We have to make sure the blood doesn't spread and swallow everyone. Find the twist that leads to the giant white blooms that aren't spoiled by ice. No blood, no Death. That's the course set for us. I know that."

"And we've made it this far." Mara walked slowly toward Elver. "We're nearly there."

"By tonight, the weight of this mess will be on other shoulders." Elver kept nodding.

"Yes, it will." Mara lifted Elver's hands away from his beard.

"But I'm not ready to be done with the road." Tears spilled down Elver's cheeks. "What if they lock us up? What if they put a chain on me and I can't see the stars anymore?"

"That won't happen," Tham said. "They'll accept our help, or they'll execute us. Either way, you won't be put in chains."

"Oh." The line between Elver's eyebrows vanished. "If you're sure, I suppose that's all right then."

"Of course it is." Mara led Elver up to walk between her and Tham, carefully keeping her face turned away so neither of the men could see the tears brimming in her eyes.

There had to be another plan. A better plan that would keep them all safe.

An anonymous letter placed in the right hands. Mara could write down everything that needed to be said, even draw a map…

That would never be followed.

Keep him safe. Keep Tham safe.

She could go alone. Sneak away, leave the others behind, keep Tham far from danger.

He'd never let it happen. He's watching you. He knows you too well. He'll stop you if you try to run.

The rumble of a cart's wheels came up the road behind them.

Mara stepped aside, clearing the way for a farmer hauling hay to Ilara.

The farmer nodded to them as he passed, then just kept going, completely unaware that he'd driven past the Ilbreans who knew that monsters hid in the north.

Tham stepped around Elver, shifting to stand right beside Mara, placing his hand on the small of her back as they started walking again.

There's too much at stake, Mara Landil. You're out of choices.

"You should hide the ring soon," Tham said. "Before we're in view of the gate."

"Or," Mara said, "I could leave the ring with you. You could go up to the Map Master's Palace. Wait there until I come for you."

"Are you going to have this argument again?" Elver asked. "It's ended the same way the last seven times, but if you want to go for an eighth, I can walk farther back to give you privacy."

"There's no argument to be made," Tham said.

"I could go alone," Mara whispered.

Elver turned and walked back ten paces, whistling a broken tune as he pivoted to, once again, follow behind Mara and Tham.

"Where you go, I go," Tham said.

"But if you don't—"

"I won't argue this, Mara," Tham said.

"Then someone on the outside would know what happened to us," Mara said. "The truth of everything we saw in Isfol wouldn't die with us."

"With you," Tham said. "The truth wouldn't die with you."

"Tham—"

"I will follow you, Mara. I don't care what it costs. Let me walk beside you instead of leaving me to smash through ice and stone to reach you."

"And if we're all doomed?" She looked to Tham, not hiding the tears that streamed down her cheeks.

"Then we hang together."

Mara stopped, twisting away from Tham's touch. There was no hesitation in his eyes as she laced her fingers through his and kissed the back of his hand. "I think I might have doomed you the moment you fell in love with me."

"The gods have never granted such a precious doom."

"Are you done yet?" Elver asked. "Only I've found a nice boulder. Perfect place for burying a magical ring that could get a lot of people killed."

"We're done." Tham pulled a rag from his pocket and gently dried Mara's tears. "We face our fate together."

Mara wrapped her arm around Tham's waist, rising up on her toes to brush her lips against his. "I love you."

He kissed her carefully, as though he could sense how close she was to shattering.

She rested her cheek on his chest, taking comfort in his solidness. Always strong. Always there. Always hers.

The thumping of horses' hooves came up the road from Ilara.

Tham let go of Mara, but she held on, keeping her arm around him as they stepped out of the horses' path.

"Mara." Tham looked toward the approaching horse, worry furrowing his brow.

"I don't care if a traveler sees us." She reached up, smoothing the wrinkles at the corners of his eyes. "If you're going to walk into hell with me, I'm going to walk down the road with you."

She didn't look away from Tham as the horses thundered past.

"How big a hole do we need?" Elver called. "I only ask because Elle's decided to help."

"Elle." Mara took Tham's hand, locking her fingers through his as she led him through the trees to a chest-high, black boulder.

Elver peeked out from behind the rock. "I suppose you'll just have to choose which hole you like better."

"I'm sure they're both lovely," Mara said.

"Elle, don't cave in my hole," Elver snapped.

Mara pursed her lips to hide her smile as Elle kicked dirt into Elver's hole.

"That's enough, Elle," Tham said.

Elle flopped down in the loose dirt, her tongue dangling from her mouth as she stared adoringly at Tham.

"Filling in my hole." Elver knelt, clawing at the dirt to make a narrow, foot-deep hole. "Not all of us have paws, you know. Some of us have to work to dig."

"That'll be perfect." Mara reached into her pocket, feeling past the light, flint, pen, and bundle of mushrooms to find the little rag she'd wrapped the ring in.

She'd tied the fabric tight, making sure none of the silver could peep through.

For a heartbeat, the need to rip the rag away and shove the blue-stoned ring onto her finger—to let the chill of the metal sweep through her, lifting away all the aches and fatigue born of traveling for so long—shoved logic aside.

Her fingers trembled as she began untying the knot.

"We don't play with magical objects, thank you." Elver grabbed the ring from her and tossed it into the hole.

"Sorry." Mara took one of Tham's hands in both of hers, keeping herself from reaching down to stop Elver as he stomped the dirt into place. "It seems like a waste to bury it."

"Don't think of it as burying the ring. Think of it as caching a potentially deadly item we stole from a severed hand in case things become dire enough to warrant using it even though you have no actual idea how to control the magic that has the potential to kill lots of innocent people." Elver patted Mara on the back with a dirt-caked hand. "Like a squirrel."

"Right," Mara said.

"Shall we go?" Elver asked. "Now that you've said we have to doom ourselves and potentially be executed before nightfall, I think I'd rather have it done."

"Sure." Mara nodded Elver back toward the road. "The gate's not far ahead. We'll be to the tower soon."

"Good." Elver tapped each tree he passed as he made his way back onto the road. "Do you think they'll tell us if they're going to execute us right away? Or will the Lady Sorcerer make us wait to find out if they're going to kill us?"

"I don't know." Mara tightened her grip on Tham's hand as they followed Elver down the road.

"Huh." Elver nodded.

The trees on the western side of the road thinned, granting a glimpse of the Arion Sea. The sun sparkled off the waves, defying the clouds clustered on the horizon. To the south, the silhouettes of ships promised that life in Ilara had continued even though the map makers' journey to the white mountains had ended in such disaster.

Thousands upon thousands of people living in Ilara,

completely unaware of the Ice Walkers and their murderous queen.

"If the Lady Sorcerer does decide to execute us," Elver said, "do you think she'll let us choose how we're to be executed?"

"Better to put it from your mind," Tham said.

"Right," Elver said, "of course. Only, if I have a choice, I don't want to be hanged or beheaded."

Mara looked up to Tham, watching his face for any hint of fear.

"I don't think I'd like to be poisoned, either," Elver said. "I wonder what hurts the least. I suppose that could very well be beheading, if it were done swiftly, but the idea of my body and head parting ways does make me a bit queasy."

"I doubt the Lady Sorcerer would use a rope or axe," Tham said.

"Magic then," Elver said. "At least it'll be a good story for others to tell."

"I don't think anyone would ever know." Mara took a deep breath, banishing the whispers that fought to claw their way up from her deepest thoughts. "Ours would be the sort of deaths the Sorcerers Guild likes to keep quiet."

"That's good." Elver turned toward them, walking backward with a smile lighting his face. "If the sorcerers don't tell anyone they've executed us, they'll have to say we died on the journey to the white mountains. Our families will get paid for our dying in service to the Guilds."

"That's more than some get." Mara forced her lips to curve into a smile, shoving her rage beneath the weight of necessity where a stray thought couldn't make her scream. "At the very least, your family will be taken care of."

Elver skipped backward a few steps then turned around, quickening his pace as the northern gate of Ilara came into view.

A line of carts, horses, wheelbarrows, and impatient people stretched up the road. Twelve soldiers had been stationed on each side of the gate with more of them searching everyone seeking entry to the city.

An empty cart passed the line, heading north on the road.

"What's the wait for?" Mara called up to the driver.

"Wait?" The woman laughed. "You're chivving lucky so few slitches are trying to get in today. The soldiers kept me waiting for a whole day once just so they could tear through my cart searching for nothing. A pig's ass worth of waiting and not a speck of anything I shouldn't have to be found." The woman kept talking to herself as she continued down the road. "A waste of chivving time, that's what a wise man would call it."

As the line inched forward, Mara thought through everything in her pack and pockets. The clothes in her pack had been made in Isfol, but, while they were fine garments, and a woman wearing pants wasn't common in Ilbrea, the clothing gave her no cause for worry.

The coin and jewels Ture Kian had hoarded in his pack had been distributed among the three of them, tucked into hems and hidden in the ankles of their boots. And, even if the soldiers found their bounty and noticed the oddness of the coins, they still shouldn't be arrested.

Tham had a sword, but there was nothing illegal in carrying a sword.

Food. Waterskins. Sleeping rolls.

Elle ran circles around Mara and Tham, panting as though she, too, were nearing the edge of panic.

The cart in front of them reached the soldiers.

With an extra prance in front of Tham, Elle abandoned her circling and ran to the cart, distracting herself by examining the muck clinging to the wheels.

"What do you have?" A scribe stepped out from behind the soldiers, pencil and writing board in hand as he addressed the man on the cart.

"Hay," the man on the cart said. "Only hay. No other goods."

"Are you sure?" The scribe glared up at the man.

Elle clawed at the back of the cart, as though trying to dig through the wood.

The man smacked his hand against the side of his cart, twisting in his seat to glare at Elle. "Away, you!"

Tham patted his leg, calling Elle back to him.

Mara's heart hitched up into her throat as the man shifted his glare to Tham, narrowing his eyes as though preparing to shout.

But the driver only sighed as he turned back around and settled into his seat.

"Sorry about that," the man said to the scribe. "I promise I have nothing but hay. I learned my lesson last time. My word to the gods, I have hay only."

Mara's heart sank back out of her throat to hover near her collarbone.

"Your word cannot be accepted by Dudia or the Guilds," the scribe said. "You'll have to be patient while we search."

"Have at it then." The man leaned back in his seat and tipped his chin down as though ready for a nap.

Four soldiers climbed up into the back of the cart. The men used their swords, stabbing down through the hay. Once they'd proven there was nothing below the hay that could bleed, they kicked under the piles, knocking bundles of hay off the cart.

The driver kept his chin down and his arms crossed, giving no hint he'd even noticed the soldiers sullying his goods.

When the soldiers finally climbed back down, one of them pounded on the side of the cart.

The driver straightened up and rolled back his shoulders. "I'm all set, then?"

"You're dismissed," the scribe said.

"Good thing, too. If I don't get frie and a biscuit in me soon, I might turn cranky. Never been one for staying cheerful when hungry." The man clicked to his horse. "Suppose the gods blessed me when I was born to a fertile farm."

The man drove through the gates, leaving the space between the soldiers empty.

"Should we just hand you our packs?" Elver asked.

The scribe glanced up from his writing. "Where are you traveling from?"

"It's a bit complicated," Elver said.

"Whitend," Mara said.

"Didn't know people from Whitend knew how to travel this far south." One of the soldiers stepped behind Mara, jostling her as he untied the top of her pack.

"We're not from Whitend," Mara said. "I had a relation who moved up that way. Batty old getch. I got word she'd died and was told to come north to collect my inheritance."

"What inheritance did you receive?" The scribe looked up at Mara, frowning at her with a wrinkled brow.

"Not a chivving thing," Mara said. "Unless you count piss-fouled furs and a roofless hut on someone else's land. The whole thing was a waste of time and coin."

"Sorry about that," the soldier who'd searched Mara's pack said.

"It's my father who'll be sorry," Mara said. "He funded the trip north in exchange for half my inheritance. Poor man's going to have an awful night."

"You're sure you didn't inherit anything of monetary value?" the scribe asked.

"Painfully sure," Mara said.

Two soldiers planted themselves in front of Tham while a third continued rooting through his pack.

Mara's heart lurched as the men searched Tham.

But Tham's hair was unkempt, and his well-grown beard would never be allowed on a Guilded soldier.

He doesn't look like Tham. Not your Tham. Not the soldier Tham.

One of the soldiers stepped closer to him. "That's a fine sword."

"Lent by her father." Tham nodded to Mara. "I was meant to protect her on the road while she brought the riches of her inheritance home."

"If her father promised to pay you with a cut of the loot, tell him you'll keep the sword as payment," the soldier who'd spoken before said. "A blade like that will fetch decent coin from the right people."

"Thank you," Tham said. "I'll suggest it."

"You're all set." The soldier behind Tham stepped away.

"Me as well?" Elver's footing faltered as the soldier searching his pack kept digging. "I don't want to hurry you, only I've got to find out how the Lady Sorcerer's going to—"

"Hush now." Mara's words came out a bit too cheery. "These men are busy. They don't want to chat about the doings of the Sorcerers Guild. We'll hear all the news once we've faced my father."

The two soldiers in front of Tham exchanged a glance.

"Grab a bottle of frie on your way through the city," one of the soldiers said as they cleared the path to the gate.

"Frie?" Mara asked.

"Can never go wrong with a nip in times like these." The soldiers turned their attention to the next traveler in line, not offering any clue as to what news would be better greeted while drunk.

14

MARA

The streets around the Sorcerers Tower were tainted by neither people nor destruction. The fronts of the buildings hadn't crumbled, toppling stones out onto the street. The roofs hadn't been burned away, the windows hadn't been smashed, and there were no gaps between buildings where entire shops seemed to have vanished.

Despite the lack of ruin, soldiers stood in the shadows between the buildings that faced the Sorcerers Tower, watching the empty street as though waiting for an attack.

But an attack from who?

What horror had caused so much destruction in Ilara?

The lurking soldiers must know.

And if they recognize one of you, your whole doomed plan collapses like those wrecked homes.

Tham drifted away from Mara, letting go of her hand as they approached the first soldier.

Mara cut around to Tham's other side, taking Elle's lead and slipping her hand back into his. "If the soldiers realize I'm a map maker, our problems will be much worse than being spotted holding hands."

Tham didn't speak until they'd passed the soldier. "It's not safe."

"If you have to draw your sword, I promise I'll let go," Mara said. Tham tensed. "I know that's not what you meant. But if we're walking toward a demons' lair together, I want to feel your hand in mine."

"That's very nice, Mara. Quite romantic." Elver dodged around Tham and Mara to walk by her side, planting himself between Mara and Elle. He threaded his arm through Mara's, ignoring Elle's huff of displeasure, keeping his face tipped away from the soldiers as though he, out of the three of them, with his gaunt face and scraggly beard, might be recognized. "Only I've had a thought."

"What is it?" Mara kept her steps even, making the men match her pace.

"I only mention it as it seems a bit dire," Elver said.

"Do tell," Mara said.

"The Sorcerers Tower lacks a door. And a gatekeeper. And any way to actually get inside," Elver whispered.

"There are doors. We just can't see them." Mara looked up at the black tower, squinting, trying to catch a hint of the purple hue hidden deep within the dark stone.

"Right," Elver said. "I don't mean to sound unhelpful, only I don't know how hidden doors are going to help us."

Mara stopped in front of a dress shop. A gown with lace epaulets took the place of prominence in the window.

She turned her back to the gown, angling herself to cut a line between the front door of the shop and the Sorcerers Tower. Ignoring Elver's worried stare, she walked straight to the tower, stopping close enough to reach out and touch the stone.

For a heartbeat, touching the stone seemed the most important thing in the world. Her being began and ended with the need to press her palm to the dark stone.

The need vanished as worry and loathing twisted in her gut.

"I've come to request an audience with the Lady Sorcerer." Mara spoke to the stone. "We have information that shouldn't pass through other hands before reaching Lady Gwell."

Mara held her breath as she stared at the stone, unsure whether death or being admitted to the tower was more likely. Moments stretched past. Her lungs began to burn from lack of air, but still, neither had happened.

"My name is Mara Landil," she said. "I was a map maker on the journey to the white mountains. We found things that shouldn't be spoken of on the street. Danger lurks to the north. The sooner Lady Gwell understands that threat, the safer all Ilbrea will be."

"Maybe we're at the wrong part of the wall," Elver whispered.

"I've seen a door appear here," Mara said. "Right across from the dress shop. I know I'm in the right place."

"The sorcerers have guards watching the street, even if we can't see them," Tham said. "If there weren't guards on the inside ready to defend the tower, the soldiers stationed across the street would have stopped us from getting so close."

"Please," Mara said. "I'm risking my place as a map maker by coming here instead of going straight to my Guild. Do you think I would do that if I had any other choice? We need to see Lady Gwell."

The wall stayed solid.

"I can't stand out here and tell stone what we've seen," Mara said. "We can't go to the Map Makers Guild. I don't even know if we should go to the King. I promise we will not waste Lady Gwell's time."

"Don't they care that people are going to die?" Elver said. "Don't they care that there's magic in the ice?"

"Elver, don't." Mara let go of Tham to grab Elver's shoulder.

"We've nearly died, more than once." Elver knocked on the solid stone as though he could see the door. "And there's wild magic in the white mountains—"

"Elver."

"—and they won't even open a door so we can tell them about the chivving monsters who are going to destroy Ilbrea."

"Elver, stop!" Mara dug her fingers into his shoulder.

"Don't grip so hard. It already worked." Elver pointed to the tower.

The outline of a door drew itself into being, starting at the peak of the doorframe, trailing down to the street. As the lines lengthened, they widened, becoming actual slices in the stone. A handle joined the door, turning as it formed.

"I am clever, aren't I?" Elver shook free from Mara's grip, grinning at the tower as the door opened.

A man in purple robes stood in the doorway. He kept his hands tucked behind his back as he examined Elver, Elle, Mara, and finally Tham, as though he felt no whisper of a threat from the four of them combined.

"You've taken your lives in your hands by daring to disturb the Sorcerers Tower," the man said.

"The north is facing a massacre," Mara said. "Knowing thousands could die makes our lives seem petty."

The man examined each of them again. "The kind part of me hopes you're right. The practical side hopes you're fools who will be dealt the Guilds' justice for spreading lies."

"Good day for you then." Elver offered the sorcerer his hand. "The kind part of you gets to win, and that's always a nice feeling."

The sorcerer looked down at Elver's hand before stepping back, allowing them to enter the Sorcerers Tower.

Tham cut in front of Mara, crossing through the newly made door first.

Mara kept Elle beside her as she followed close behind Tham, her toes hitting the heels of his boots, her hand outstretched, ready to grab onto him if the sorcerers tried to tear him away.

The light dimmed as the sorcerer closed the newly formed door, sealing them inside the stone tower.

Whatever Mara had imagined the inside of the sorcerers' lair might look like, she'd been wrong.

Dark stone walls lined the narrow passage. Criolas had been set into the ceiling, their pale blue light raising goosebumps on Mara's arms as the man squeezed past them to the front of the group.

He led them down the passage without speaking, but there were no intersecting corridors he needed to warn them not to venture down, and no passing fellows for him to greet. Just one plain, dark, empty hall with no end in sight.

Mara watched the walls, trying to find the curve of the corridor. The passage had a slight arc, but not nearly enough to match the circular outer wall of the tower. Traveling along such a minor curve, they should have met the far side of the tower in minutes, but the passage kept going.

Magic.

The word sent a ripple of loathing down Mara's spine she'd never felt in Isfol.

Ronya is a monster.

But ice magic can't be blamed for the blood she's shed.

The sorcerers' magic shouldn't be blamed, either, a faint voice whispered in the back of Mara's mind, too soft to be properly heard over the voice that screamed for her to find a way to tear the stone walls apart.

You need their help. Your hatred cannot outweigh the fate of Ilbrea.

"You know," Elver began as the passage sloped gently upward.

"Is now the time, Elver?" Mara asked.

"I'd always assumed the inside of the Sorcerers Tower would be filled with beautiful wonders and magic bursting out of every corner." Elver spoke as though he either hadn't heard or didn't care what Mara had said. "A plain, dark, inconveniently long corridor is a bit of a disappointment."

"Elver," Mara hushed, but the sorcerer in front of them gave a soft chuckle.

"The tower is filled with more wonders than a person could get bored of in several lifetimes," the sorcerer said. "But our home isn't for people like you. The dark passage will get you where we need to go."

"And back out, too?" Elver said. "Hopefully. What I mean to say is, will this be how we leave the tower if we're not, in fact, executed?"

"Elver, please." Mara stopped and turned to face him. "You'll anger the wrong person if you speak out of turn, and I would very much like to *not* die."

"Sorry." Elver frowned.

"Just do us all a favor, and don't talk unless you have to," Mara said.

Elver opened his mouth, closed his mouth, and furrowed his brow for a moment before nodding.

"Thank you." Mara turned back to their escort. "My apologies. Please lead the way."

"There's not"—Elver began—"erm. Eiihh." He shook his head and looked down at the ground.

"This had better not be a waste of Lady Gwell's time." The sorcerer led them farther down the passage.

After another minute of walking, the angle of the floor steepened, sloping up almost like the gangplank of a large ship.

"Do not speak unless spoken to," the sorcerer said. "Do not attempt to leave the room. Follow any orders that are given, and do not touch anything that isn't handed to you."

"Understood," Tham said.

The sorcerer stopped at a patch of wall that held no mark of being special in any way. He knocked on the stone three times, then tucked his hands behind his back.

Mara squinted at the wall, trying to catch the exact moment something happened.

Much like before, the door came into being from the top down. A black stone knob carved into the shape of a rosebud grew from the door.

Elle pulled against her lead, panting as she lunged toward the door.

"Hush." Mara inched closer to Tham, soothing her own nerves by pressing her arm against his as she waited for the knob to turn.

Elver fidgeted on her other side, patting Elle's head, leaning over to stare at the knob.

Elle yanked free from Mara's grip to plant her paws on the wall, sniffing the still-emerging door.

"Get back." The sorcerer brushed Elle away and raised his hand to knock again. "I've brought three for an audience with Lady Gwell. If you know a better place for me to keep them while they wait, then you can take them there."

The rose-carved knob turned, and the door opened a crack.

A person with a wrinkled face and blue eyes peered out at them. "Does Lady Gwell know you've dragged muck into the tower?"

"Not yet," the sorcerer said. "So mind the muck while I deliver the happy news."

"Frie. A full bottle of it in my hands by sundown." The door swung fully open. A weathered woman with tufty white hair glared at them. "When was the last time they bathed?"

"Just take them, Shantene," the sorcerer said. "I'll get you your chivving frie."

"Yes, you will." Shantene backed away from the door, waving for *the muck* to enter.

"In, now," the sorcerer said. "I've got to go bother Lady Gwell."

A rough laugh came from beyond the door.

"Mock me, and it'll be a tiny bottle of frie," the sorcerer said.

"Thank you," Mara said.

"Go," the sorcerer said.

You're helping us save Ilbrea. The words balanced on the tip of Mara's tongue, but as she followed Tham through the door, the thought slipped away.

Every trace of dark stone disappeared. A worn, wooden floor and light-painted walls formed the room. Flames crackled in a wide fireplace, but the perfect warmth filling the space didn't seem to be coming from the fire. The comfort just...existed.

On the right side of the room, two doors tucked between bookshelves offered potential escape. The bookshelves took up most of the wall but held more jars and wooden boxes than actual books.

A massive window filled the left-hand wall.

Tham placed his hand on Mara's back below her pack, keeping right beside her as she walked toward the window, trying to understand the beautiful scene beyond.

Clouds dotted the bright blue sky, casting patches of shadow over a field of blue and purple flowers. A pond with deliciously clear water sat in the middle of the field, as though it had been placed specifically to lure passersby into taking the time for a swim. In the distance, a dense forest grew up the slopes of gently peaked mountains.

As Mara watched the scene, a herd of deer bounded across the field.

"Well, that's not natural," Elver said. "Sorry. I forgot, no talking."

"Where is this supposed to be?" Mara asked.

"Already done staring in wonder?" Shantene asked. "I must be losing my touch."

"Not at all." Mara leaned closer to the window, watching a raven swoop across the sky. "It's a work of art. Like a living painting."

"Not many think to describe it that way," Shantene said. "Don't usually have saelk invading my rooms, either."

"We apologize for the intrusion," Tham said.

"As well you should." Shantene thumped a tray down on the table. "Have a cup of tea, and don't dream of touching my things. That goes for the dog, too."

"Yes, ma'am." Mara removed her pack, leaning it against the table leg as she took a seat beside Tham. She patted her leg, calling Elle to sit between her and Tham.

"So"—Shantene poured tea from a pot into four plain cups—"what chivving hell landed you in my rooms?"

"It gets a bit complicated when you get to the part about the ice giving the evil queen an army and letting us escape at the same time," Elver said.

"Elver," Tham said.

"But the conflicting morality found in the ice magic doesn't *really* matter as much as the slaughter of thousands of people that could be happening any time now." Elver sipped his tea. "Could be happening as we speak, really. I don't suppose we'd know if it had begun. So we've got to keep slogging on. Lots of non-blood-ied, white snow. That's the thing we hope to find, right?"

"And Garret drops this mess on me." Shantene frowned. "Just because I'm old doesn't mean my time has no value."

"It should hold more value," Elver said. "Since you have much less of it left."

"Elver!" Mara gripped the edge of the table, waiting for some terrible magic to strike him.

Shantene's frown deepened, then her shoulders bounced as she gave a low chuckle that grew into a genuine laugh.

"Sorry." Elver shrugged. "I forgot I'm not supposed to talk. Only my mind's not good at remembering since the blue tore through it."

"Whatever happened to you, it didn't leave your mind as full of shit as most people are blessed with." Shantene winked at Elver. "Though you do smell of sweat and rancid muck."

"It was a long journey," Mara said.

"A long journey from the ice that led you to my rooms

because thousands of people are going to die?" Shantene shook her head. "With the mess you're in, I suppose it would be awful of me not to offer you cake."

Elver sat up straight, joy lighting his eyes. "It would be terrible of you."

Shantene sighed and stood, pressing her hands against the tabletop to leverage herself to her feet. "Dragging stinking strays into my rooms," she muttered as she pulled a large serving tray Mara hadn't noticed down from the shelf. "No one else would let them foul up the furniture, so they get brought to me. Trying to be a compassionate person, that's what got me roped into this mess."

Shantene set the tray of sugar-crusted cakes on the table and went back to the shelves. She reached forward and grabbed a stack of plates that had most definitely not been on the shelf a moment before.

"Every good deed comes back to bite you in the ass if you live long enough." Shantene set the plates on the table and went back to the shelves again. "If I'd have known what the gods had in store for me, I'd have become a bitter, old crone years ago."

She tossed a piece of dried meat onto the floor beside Elle.

Elle yipped and snatched up her prize, spinning in a circle three times before lying down to enjoy her bounty.

"Nice of you to give Elle a treat." Elver popped a whole cake into his mouth. "The last nice thing she had was a dead man's hand. And Mara wouldn't let her keep that."

Mara twisted in her seat and kicked Elver in the ankle.

"Well, you wouldn't." Elver took another cake.

"I should've stopped allowing visitors years ago." Shantene sank into her seat.

"We're grateful for your hospitality." Mara chose a cake from the tray.

"Gratitude won't air your stink from my room," Shantene said.

"Can you open the window?" Mara asked. "Would there be a real breeze?"

"I could have locked the door and pretended I was dead." Shantene handed Elver another cake and leaned back in her chair, glaring at the portion of the wall where the door to the dark corridor had been.

Mara bit into her cake, thinking through all the questions she wanted to ask the sorcerer if she lived long enough to have a chance.

Berry jam filled the center of the fluffy treat. If they were to be dead soon, at least their last meal was something better than wild mushrooms foraged from the forest along the road to Ilara.

Mara reached beneath the table, brushing her fingers against Tham's.

The mere act of touching him in front of someone wearing Guild robes sent an instinctual shock of fear up Mara's spine. She laced the tips of her fingers through his, batting away her panic, sinking into the comfort of feeling his skin against hers.

Three knocks pounded on the wall behind Mara. She pulled her hand from Tham's as she turned to face the noise, but there was no door behind her to have made the hollow sound that seemed like it should have come from knuckles striking wood.

"I'm too godsforsaken old for this," Shantene said.

"Would you like me to answer the door?" Mara asked. "Would that even be possible?"

Shantene planted her hands on the table and pushed herself back to her feet without answering.

Mara fixed her gaze on the wall, leaning sideways to see past the old woman as she reached the place the door had been.

Shantene gripped what looked to be nothing, but as she slid her hand sideways, a latch appeared between her fingers. She dropped her hand and huffed, as though peeved by the amount of time it took the door to create itself from the top down. Unlike the door leading in from the corridor, the inside door was wooden with an old marble knob and a coat of pale paint that matched the rest of the room.

If the room even existed as Mara saw it. The quaint space could merely have been a well-fabricated façade.

We don't belong in this place.

A second knock pounded through the door once it had fully formed.

"Better be the biggest bottle of frie I've ever seen." Shantene turned the knob and opened the door, stooping in a bow before Mara had seen who had knocked.

Lady Gwell stood in the doorway, her purple robes and bright red hair shocking against the dim light of the corridor.

Mara stood, planting herself just far enough in front of Tham he couldn't discreetly step around to stand between her and the Lady Sorcerer.

"Lady Gwell." Shantene straightened up. "If I'd have known you were coming, I would've answered the door without griping."

"And I would have assumed you were an imposter." Lady Gwell's lips curved in what she seemed to mean as a friendly smile. "May I impose upon your hospitality? I think it best to prevent any further incursion into the tower."

"Of course, Lady Gwell." Shantene waved her in. "For you, I'll even make a properly fresh pot of tea."

"I'm honored." Lady Gwell stepped into the room and closed the door behind her, giving the wall a sharp flick as the door faded back into the plain, painted wall.

"Lady Gwell." Mara bowed to the Lady Sorcerer. "Thank you for agreeing to see us. But the information we've brought, I'm not sure if you wouldn't prefer to hear it alone."

"Shall I go cower in whatever corner Garret's been banished to?" Shantene lifted a tea kettle from the shelf.

"No need." Lady Gwell reached into the corner and pulled out a finely carved wooden chair. "Any news brought to me by Karron's pets is surely fit for your ears."

"They're some of Karron's?" Shantene hung the kettle over the fire.

"Two are." Lady Gwell sat facing the table. "That one"—she pointed to Elver—"I'm not familiar with."

"I should've asked Garret for something better than frie," Shantene said.

"If you know who Tham and I are," Mara said, "then I hope you'll understand how much it means that we came to you instead of going to Lord Karron."

"Lord Karron is on a journey to the southern isles," Lady Gwell said. "Whatever news you bring couldn't have been delivered to him."

"Right." Mara turned her chair and sat facing Lady Gwell. "I'd hoped Dudia had been kind and he'd already arrived home."

"You've just returned to the city?" Lady Gwell narrowed her eyes, shifting her gaze from Mara to Elver.

"Yes, Lady Sorcerer." Elver plopped into his seat. "Came straight here from the northern gate. We've been walking for weeks, trying to bring you news."

"And the rest of your journey?" Lady Gwell said. "Did they choose not to accompany you in begging for an audience?"

"They're gone, Lady Gwell." Mara pushed the words past the pinch in her throat. "Things went wrong early on. Most of our party died. The rest of us..." The pinching in her throat got worse as cold claws pierced her lungs.

"There are people living in the ice, Lady Gwell." Tham stepped closer to Mara, standing right behind her as though he could sense her growing panic. "There's a whole city of them, living inside a mountain. Their leader plans to attack Ilbrea."

"A city's worth of violent rabble hardly seems worth a Karron coming to the Sorcerers Tower." Lady Gwell stared at Tham, her gaze fixed on him in a piercing way, as though she were studying more than his face.

"Lady Gwell—" Mara began, leaning in front of Tham, trying to steal the Lady Sorcerer's attention.

"There is magic in the ice," Tham said before Mara could form the words. "The Ice Walkers can control that magic. It's not a city of rabble that's going to attack from the north. Ilbrea faces an army, led by a queen with terrible power. She has massive beasts that fight beside her. Two of them could destroy Whitend in minutes. If the Ice Walkers' queen lets all her beasts loose, the towns north of Ilara will be massacred. If they got into the city—"

"The sorcerers would stop them," Lady Gwell said.

"Yes, Lady Sorcerer." Tham bowed. "But I can't make myself imagine how many would die in the fight."

"Please, Lady Sorcerer." Elver knelt in front of Lady Gwell. "We barely escaped that terrible place, and we came all the way here to tell you that Death is racing toward us from the north."

Mara reached for Elver. Tham gripped her shoulder, stopping her before she could pull Elver back.

"Please believe us," Elver said. "Please don't let all those people in the north get torn apart by claws or tortured by Queen Ronya. And please, please don't execute us for coming to the Sorcerers Tower with such terrible news."

"Shantene?" Lady Gwell looked past Mara.

Shantene thumped the kettle onto the table. "They smell like shit, and something terrible chiseled cracks through that poor boy's mind, but none of them are lying."

"Please," Elver whispered, "don't make everything we've endured have been for nothing."

Lady Gwell watched the steam rising from the kettle's spout.

"Please."

"You've spoken to no one else in Ilara?" Lady Gwell held Elver's gaze.

"Well, we were searched at the northern gate, and a lady laughed at us, but they were outside the gates, so—"

"Only the guard who let us into the tower," Mara said. "We've spoken to no one else. I swear it."

"Word of this cannot spread through the tower. We cannot afford rumors and worry, not now." Lady Gwell looked to Shantene. "Have them placed in the nex, then we'll start with this ice army. How many soldiers does the ice queen have? What weapons do her soldiers use in battle?"

"How far can they stretch their supplies?" Shantene added.

"I want every scrap of information written down and brought directly to me." Lady Gwell stood. "Have them fed and bathed. Danger may lurk in the north, but that's no reason to allow such an awful stench to infiltrate my tower."

"Yes, Lady Gwell," Shantene said.

Lady Gwell flicked the wall that became the door.

"Lady Gwell." Mara stood. "Thank you."

"Belief and salvation are two different things, Mara Landil. Be wary of giving your thanks too soon."

15

ADRIAL

Rows of soldiers flanked the entrance to the council chamber. Adrial studied the men as he passed, not out of fear that they might attack him, or even the vain idea that they might have been stationed to protect King Brannon from the head scribe's wrath. It was the looks in their eyes Adrial wanted to see.

Were they men? Real, living men with souls and hearts? Men who felt love and hope and fear and grief?

Or were they pure evil hiding in the forms of men, waiting for the chance to cause pain and destruction as soon as their orders gave them the opportunity?

A few of the soldiers had the decency to look away from Adrial and the wide black bands he'd had sewn onto the collar and cuffs of his white robes. A look of pity drifted across one soldier's face. Another winced, as though afraid the tragedy of Adrial's life might be catching.

The soldiers' discomfort tempered the jagged edges of Adrial's anger.

The Guilds were tainted by an evil that needed to be excised, but there were a few who had not fallen so far as to be considered worthy of the carefully cultivated hatred earned by the sorcerers, healers, and the King himself.

The scribes' guards that had traveled to the Royal Palace with Adrial and Lord Gareth were placed behind the lines of soldiers, tucked carefully out of reach should their charges need them.

"It's become the new custom," Lord Gareth said in a carrying voice. "The soldiers act as though only the sorcerers' guards are competent and all other Guilds' guards are to be brushed aside."

"There is no need for such sharp words." Lady Gwell stood behind her seat at the round council table. "We are leading Ilbrea as it faces dark and treacherous times. If an enemy should attempt to attack our council, wouldn't it be wise to have the soldiers, who have been trained to fight as one, meeting the fiends head on rather than having the guards of four different Guilds thrusting their swords about, hoping they prick the right person?"

The Lady Sorcerer looked to Adrial.

He held her gaze.

"One misplaced prick can cause such trouble." A hint of a smile lit Lady Gwell's eyes.

"Lady Gwell—" Lord Nevon shot up from his seat.

"Terrible to fear violence while inside the Royal Palace," Adrial cut across him. "But fear is the price violent rulers must pay."

"Adrial." Lord Gareth turned toward him as quickly as the old man could manage. Fear pinched his wrinkled brow.

"My apologies, Lord Gareth." Adrial bowed. "I shouldn't have spoken out of turn."

"It wasn't out of turn." Lord Nevon gave Adrial a subtle nod.

"Will you indulge in veiled threats, too, Lord Sailor?" Lady Byrd settled into her seat.

"Never," Lord Nevon said. "When I choose to make threats, I ensure they are quite clear. But the meeting has yet to begin, so our young head scribe has every right to speak. Is there anything else you'd like to add, Head Scribe?"

"The meeting shall begin at once." Lady Gwell tapped her finger on the table. A bang, like stone striking wood, pounded around the room.

Lord Nevon gave one cough of a laugh and settled into his seat.

"Come, Adrial." Lord Gareth took Adrial's arm.

The council stayed silent as the Lord Scribe led his second to the last two empty seats at the table.

Adrial sat, carefully straightening the black cuffs on his robe before looking to the King.

The King snapped his gaze away from Adrial, pinning it to the golden, seven-pointed star set into the center of the table.

"I have no taste for petty blathering today," King Brannon said.

"Your Majesty." Lord Nevon stood.

"Do not complain to me of too many goods flooding your docks." King Brannon turned his glare to the Lord Sailor. A heavy, almost pained look tainted the King's teal eyes.

"No, Your Majesty." Lord Nevon bowed. "I request a store of weapons be granted to the Sailors Guild. The violence in the city creeps ever closer to the docks. My sailors are capable of defending our ships, but if a surge of angry common folk sweeps toward us, we'll need more than the knives my sailors are issued if we're to win the fight."

"Your ships are protected by the sorcerers," Lady Gwell said. "Your men have no need for weapons."

"Your sorcerers are *protecting* Ilara as well," Lord Nevon said. "I won't have my docks ending up like the ruins of this city."

"Watch your words, Lord Sailor," Lady Gwell said. "You tread on dangerous ground."

"The truth is often dangerous." Lord Nevon shifted his shoulders ever so slightly, angling himself as though wishing he could make the foolish mistake of turning his back on the Lady Sorcerer. "Your Majesty, my men are willing to fight and die to protect the Ilbrean fleet, a fleet that would take us years to rebuild if the flames of revolt devoured it.

"Arming my men gains you fighters. Leaving them defenseless as they face an angry horde would test their devotion to the Guilds and their King during a dark and difficult time."

"They do not need weapons," Lady Gwell said. "The docks are protected."

"You can shield a child from a storm, but they still fear the thunder," Lord Gareth said. "An unused sword is a small price for the devotion of good men."

"Lord Kearney," King Brannon said, "see what can be spared for the sailors posted on the docks. Send whatever weapons the untrained are least likely to harm themselves with."

"Yes, Your Majesty," Lord Kearney said.

"Thank you, Your Majesty." Lord Nevon's jaw stayed tight as he spoke, as though he were swallowing words that were not gratitude.

"If I may." Map Maker Traim stood as soon as Lord Nevon had taken his seat.

The King waved for him to speak.

"The eastern mountains journey has returned," Traim said. "In searching their maps, there are a few paths that may indicate promising routes through the mountains to Wyrain."

"May?" The King leaned forward in his seat.

"Both map makers on the journey were lost," Traim said.

A sharp surge of grief struck the stoic shield Adrial had formed around the endless, painful hollow in his chest.

"One near the beginning of the journey, the second only a few weeks ago. An animal attack of some kind." Traim swallowed as though bile had risen into his throat. "Two soldiers were lost as well."

"What sort of animal could do such a thing?" Lady Byrd wrinkled her nose.

"I don't know," Traim said. "But the maps were recovered. The latest maps, those covering the farthest reach of the journey's progress into the eastern mountains, were damaged in the attack. We're working to remove the blood stains and restore the images well enough to make clean copies. As soon as the copies are complete and organized, I will personally deliver them to you."

"My condolences on the loss of your people," King Brannon said.

"Thank you, Your Majesty." Traim bowed.

"I want the route to Wyrain completed before my sister's wedding. Come to me with a plan to make that happen or send a more competent man in your place," King Brannon said.

Traim stared at the King for a moment before bowing. "As you wish, Your Majesty."

King Brannon looked back to the star at the center of the table. "What next?"

"The ceremony for the fallen map makers," Lady Gwell said.

"Will have to wait until copies of the maps are fit for public viewing," Traim said. "The work of a map maker should be displayed at their funeral. Hanging bloody tatters would be cruel to those who loved the fallen."

Adrial's hands started to shake.

Niko wasn't torn apart by an animal. His death wasn't that brutal.

Heat prickled in Adrial's eyes.

His death might have been worse than teeth and claws. You don't even know what killed him.

"There will be no ceremony," the King said.

"What?" Adrial said.

The King ignored him. "We will not emphasize the map makers' failure. The glory of the Guilds must be maintained. Their loss is better left in the shadows of the past."

"I'm sorry, Your Majesty," Traim said, "but Map Maker Endur and—"

"The Map Makers Guild was given a simple task, and they failed. The men you lost are an embarrassment to your Guild and Ilbrea," King Brannon said. "There will be no ceremony. I will not be swayed."

Lord Gareth reached back, planting a firm hand on Adrial's knee to keep him from standing.

"Yes, Your Majesty." Traim's shoulders rounded as he sank into his seat.

"Does anyone else wish to test my patience?" The King looked around the table, as though hoping one of the Guild Leaders might give him a reason to shout.

"I offer joyful news, Your Majesty." Lady Gwell stood and stepped forward, placing the King behind her. "A triumph in our battle against the turmoil in the city."

Adrial shifted forward in his seat as an instinctual terror begged him to flee from the Lady Sorcerer's smile.

"We have captured a leader of this so-called rebellion," Lady Gwell said. "They are, even as I speak, being questioned in the Sorcerers Tower."

A cold fear sent a shiver across Adrial's shoulders.

"Why have I been told nothing of this?" Lord Kearney stood.

"There is no need for your involvement," Lady Gwell said. "I assure you, sorcerers are quite adept at procuring information."

"I am the Lord Soldier," Kearney said. "I have the right to interrogate—"

"When, or pardon me"—Lady Gwell planted her hands on the table, leaning toward Kearney—"*if* you manage to capture any of the insurgents, you may handle them however you please. My prisoner will be dealt with as I see fit."

"Give the rebel to me when you're done questioning them," Lord Kearney said.

"No," Lady Gwell said. "Once we have finished with the rebel, they will be executed in accordance with the law."

"Your Majesty," Lord Kearney said. "If there is any chance that my interrogating them could gain valuable information, it must be done."

"Your Majesty," Lady Gwell said, "when I choose to end the questioning of the prisoner, there will be no more information to be gained. I will gather the rotta in the cathedral square to watch the rebel's execution.

"Once the people understand the power of our magic, they will embrace the futility of standing against the Sorcerers Guild. After all, a man foolish enough to defy the will of the sorcerers should expect nothing but pain and death. Do you see the wisdom in this path?"

"Of course." King Brannon stood, stepping forward, placing himself beside Lady Gwell. "The people of Ilara require a lesson in obedience. Make sure it is a lesson they will not forget."

16

MARA

Mara ran her finger over the long, curved line that cut down the center of the parchment. The path of the glacier their journey had mapped was almost right, close enough that some might not notice the flaws, but if lives depended on her work, the map had to be perfect. She shoved the parchment aside and grabbed a fresh page from the stack.

Elle huffed and flopped down on Mara's feet as though the pup could sense her frustration.

"Coming south doesn't make sense." Fergal rapped his knuckles against the table on the far side of the room. "Any angle you approach it, theirs would be a doomed advance."

Mara pushed back her shoulders and picked up her pencil, trying to block out everything around her.

"There's got to be something you're missing," Fergal said.

"There were wolves buried in the ice," Tham said. "I don't know what else might be down there."

The curve of the path, that was all Mara needed to begin. She closed her eyes, picturing the perfect map she'd created while traveling the glacier. The perfect map that had been stolen from her in Isfol.

"There's magic in the ice, for one," Elver said. "There's also frozen people, who I can only assume are going to try and kill Ilbreans."

"What does the ice demon know that we don't?" Fergal said.

Mara set her pencil down and stopped battling her mind's need to rejoin the present, regardless of how impossibly beautiful and horrifically dire the present was.

Mara, Tham, and Elver had been given quarters in the nex of the Sorcerers Tower. Despite being in a nearly abandoned section of the sorcerers' home, the rooms were more beautiful than even Allora's chambers in the Map Master's Palace.

The sitting room floor and walls were made of the same pale marble. Light curtains fluttered in the cool breeze, accentuating the stunning view beyond the balcony. Even knowing the forest, river, and brilliant blue sky outside weren't real, Mara couldn't deny their appeal.

Inside the sitting room, three worktables had been set up, giving each of them a place to sort through the mess of information demanded by the Lady Sorcerer.

Mara's table was constantly covered in parchment as she painstakingly recreated maps of Isfol and the white mountains. Tham met with sorcerers, usually Fergal, at his table, always talking through what Ronya might be planning. Elver ignored his table, instead spending his time on the softest of the three couches.

He worked through stacks of paper, his pen moving at a feverish speed, though Mara had no idea what he filled the pages with. He kept his work beside him during the day, and the papers were collected by Shantene every night.

"If the Ice Walker's army moved quickly enough," Tham said, "they could wipe out a dozen Ilbrean villages along the northern road before word reached Ilara."

"To what end?" Fergal said.

"There may not be an end you can understand." Mara's hands

shook as she pushed her chair away from her table. "I know you don't believe me, which probably means Lady Gwell doesn't believe me either, but you can't look for reason in how Ronya behaves."

"An army doesn't move without reason," Fergal said.

Mara took a breath, stilling the anger that pressed against her lungs, before standing to face Tham's table. "Not a reason that makes sense to you and me."

"Makes sense to me," Elver said, "at least a bit."

"How do you mean?" Fergal leaned back in his chair, narrowing his eyes at Elver.

Elver didn't look up or stop scribbling away on his paper. "There are people who hunt deer for food. Their reason is wanting to eat." He added the filled page to his growing stack and started on a fresh sheet. "There are people who don't need to hunt to eat, but they do it anyway so they can mount the deer's head on a wall. Their reason is pride. And then there are the people we like to pretend don't exist."

Elver shook his head. He stopped writing for a moment, frowned, and started writing again.

"You haven't finished explaining," Fergal said.

"Oh." Elver set his pen down, checked his fingers for ink, and, flattening his lips together as though swallowing his disappointment, looked to Fergal. "I thought you'd have worked it out and wouldn't need me to keep talking."

"By the Guilds." Fergal dragged his hands down his face.

"Elver, can you tell us about the people we like to pretend don't exist?" Mara sat on the arm of Elver's favored couch.

"I suppose I do have to explain for that one." Elver pointed to Fergal. "It would be easier if we could just tell the Sorcerers and Soldiers Guilds what to do."

"That will never happen." Fergal pointed back at Elver.

"Both of you take a breath." Mara spoke in a soothing tone, as though she were calming a pair of yowling cats instead of two grown men. "Elver, please explain."

"There are people who don't hunt for food or for pride," Elver said. "They hunt because they like the feel of blood on their hands. Their soul finds a release in the act of killing. So, in an overly simplistic way, you're right. The Ice Walkers don't have a normal reason to attack Ilbrea. They could never have a settlement in the barrens north of Whitend. They'd never be able to hold the land against Ilbrea's forces.

"The same goes for them gaining ground farther south. They could fight all the way down to Ilara, kill a good number of people in the city, too, but they'd be pushed back eventually and all they'd have to show for it is a smaller army on the march home. Ilbrea is too large a country. The Ice Walkers can't win a big enough victory to prevent their eventual defeat.

"But going on a bloody rampage, murdering hundreds or even thousands, painting the snow red with Ilbrean blood, and causing pain that will be remembered for centuries...*that* Queen Ronya can manage. She craves Ilbrean blood, and she'll have it, no matter the cost to her people or ours."

"Chivving cacting, chiv all demon spawn, I hate it when the madman makes sense," Fergal said.

"Glad you understand." Elver nodded to Fergal. "May I stop talking to you now? I find it exhausting."

"Please." Fergal rested his elbow on the table and pinched the bridge of his nose.

"Send soldiers and sorcerers north," Tham said. "Protect Whitend."

"One worthless village?" Fergal said. "There's not a chivving chance of my presenting that plan to the Lady Sorcerer."

"Why not?" Mara went to Tham's table, sitting in an empty chair opposite the men.

Fergal reached across the pristine, Guild-made map, tapping on the tiny marking for Whitend.

"Whitend is the northernmost point on the best road to the north Ilbrea's bothered to make," Fergal said, "but there are other ways to travel south from the white. If the Ice Walkers have giant wolves and magic on their side, it would be in their best interest not to take the road south, where the Ilbrean army, with our horses and sheer numbers, would have an advantage."

"They'd be better off coming through the forests." Tham traced a line down the map, cutting through the wilderness between Whitend and Ilara.

"And that leaves us without a chivving hope of predicting their path," Fergal said.

"You still have to protect Whitend," Mara said. "The tunnel from Isfol will lead Ronya there."

"If she chooses to take that route," Tham said.

"If the path through the ice will even open for her," Elver added.

"The tunnel aside, there are still people in Whitend," Mara said. "Ilbreans who need to be protected."

"You've said you warned the people of Whitend," Fergal said.

"Not well enough." Mara leaned back in her chair, digging her fingers into her curls. "I told them we'd found a settlement in the mountains, and the mountain people had vowed to slaughter every man, woman, and child in Whitend. I don't think they believed me. At least, none of them came south with us when I begged them to. I should have told them about Ronya."

"No." Tham's voice held an unfamiliar note of anger.

Elle whimpered and trotted over to lie on his feet.

"If they didn't believe raiders were coming, I don't think they'd have believed the bit about a bloodthirsty ice queen, either," Elver said. "Only they do believe in the legend of Kareen enough to pile rocks over the path from Isfol. So, maybe I'm wrong and telling the truth might have saved the lives of everyone in the village."

"How do you live with this man?" Fergal said.

"It's easy to overlook someone's blunt speaking when they've saved your life," Mara said.

Elver gave a pleased little humph.

"Send soldiers to Whitend," Tham said. "Whatever else needs to be done, we know Whitend is in danger."

"I can't take a plan consisting of protecting one village to Lady Gwell," Fergal said.

"Please." Mara leaned forward, touching the marking for Whitend on the map. "You at least have to ask."

Fergal narrowed his eyes as he stared at Mara.

"If the people of Whitend are murdered and you never asked Lady Gwell to protect them, the deaths of all those villagers will fall on the four people in this room," Mara said. "That is too great a weight for me to carry."

Fergal kept staring.

"If you won't ask her, then let me," Mara said. "I'm not above begging to save innocent lives."

"It doesn't matter who brings it to her. It's not enough," Fergal said. "We can't move an army to protect one village that *may* be attacked. And, if you're right about the strength of the Ice Walkers, sending even a hundred soldiers wouldn't do any good. We'd only end up with slaughtered villagers and dead soldiers."

"We've got to do something." Mara slammed her palms against the table. "People are going to die!"

"People die every day, map maker," Fergal said. "It's the tragedy of life we all must accept. My duty is to protect Ilbrea. To make sure this country survives long after all of us are gone. If we throw soldiers at the problem without having a proper plan, all we're doing is making corpses of men who are needed to protect Ilbrea."

"I can't accept that." Mara dug her nails into the wooden tabletop, refusing to let her hands shake. "There has to be a way—"

"The defenses of Ilara have been strengthened," Fergal said.

"We cannot move forces outside of Ilara until we know where to send them, and planting an army at the edge of the white will not be considered."

Tham stood and stepped away from the table. His eyes flicked to Mara before he fixed his gaze on the fabricated scene beyond the balcony. He tucked his hands behind his back, looking every bit the soldier, even in the common clothes the sorcerers had given him.

"Tham?" Mara whispered.

"Evacuate the people of Whitend," Tham said. "Send soldiers to move them south. Set them up in a camp north of Ilara, within reach of the city if they need to flee from an attack."

"It won't work," Mara said. "They won't just leave their homes."

"The soldiers can order them out," Tham said.

"They'll fight back." Mara stood. "You've met them, Tham. Even if all they have is a pile of rocks, those people will fight to stay in Whitend."

"The soldiers will win." Tham turned to Mara. He kept his gaze over her head, not meeting her eyes. "A few villagers might die in the fight, but most of them would survive. If we leave them for Ronya, no one makes it out alive."

"That would make Ilbrean soldiers the monsters." Mara sank back into her seat. "*We* would be the monsters."

"Do you want to save lives or keep your hands clean?" Elver dusted off his hands as though he'd been working with dirt rather than ink. "It would be nice to get to do both, but Death is coming, so you're going to have to choose."

"I can't." Mara stared at the marking for Whitend on the map. "What if Ronya's path doesn't lead her near Whitend? What if we set soldiers against Ilbreans for nothing? What if soldiers are killed by the people of Whitend?"

"Then we do nothing and wait to see where the Ice Walkers' army appears," Fergal said.

"We can't do that either." Tears ran down Mara's cheeks.

"There is no other path, Mara." Tham cut around the table, his steps slow, as though he were expecting Mara to shout at him to stay away. "I've been thinking through it for days while we've been reassessing every scrap of information we have. I've tried to come up with another way. But the north is too big and Ronya too unpredictable." He knelt beside Mara, holding out his hand, giving her the choice to reach for him. "I'm sorry, but if our aim is to keep as many people alive as possible, clearing out Whitend is the best option we have."

"This you'd bring to Lady Gwell?" Mara looked to Fergal.

"It's the first thing we've come up with that she might agree to," Fergal said.

Mara closed her eyes, sending fresh tears down her cheeks. "Will you ask her if it can be done peacefully?"

"I don't have to. The Lady Sorcerer will want it done without bloodshed," Fergal said. "But for your conscience, I'll ask."

"Thank you." Mara leaned toward Tham. She laid her head on his shoulder, letting him wrap her in his arms.

Tham held her close as Fergal piled up his papers and left, on his way to ask the Lady Sorcerer to draw the first blood of war.

17

———

NIKO

The clang of metal on metal sent a shiver down Niko's spine that had nothing to do with being bare-chested on the uncomfortably cold training field.

Two men, who would probably be better called boys if they weren't swinging swords at each other's throats, fought on the southern end of the field. They charged at their partner with such fury, Niko almost felt a touch of pity for whoever would face the two in battle.

If the boys weren't sent to freeze to death in the Hayes siege first.

"Niko." Danu threw her knife, letting it land tip-down in the dirt right between Niko's feet.

"Sorry." Niko pulled the blade from the ground and, like a fool, trotted to Danu to place the knife back in her hand. "Sorry."

"They'll never let you move up to sword training if you can't keep yourself alive with your hands first." Danu wiped the dirt from the blade with her sleeve.

"I have no interest in swordplay, and neither should those boys." Niko kept his voice low. "They should be dreaming about rolling beautiful women, not honing their bloodlust."

"In a kinder world, they would be. But we were born to a violent time. The best we can do for those boys is teach them how to survive. The same way I'm supposed to teach you to survive." Danu took Niko by the shoulders, turned him around, and pushed him back toward his patch of packed dirt.

The fleeting feel of her fingers against his skin almost made not wearing a shirt worth the grating chill that tensed his muscles and sent goose bumps all over his body.

"Keep an eye on the blade, Niko," Danu said.

"I'm fairly good at keeping track of things that might end my life." Niko took his place, his stance steady, his knees soft.

"Then why is it so easy for me to attack you?"

"The peak of my fighting experience is a tavern brawl of legendary proportions. You've been properly trained, and a blade in your hands is profoundly deadly. Only a slitch would bet on my surviving a fight between us." Niko paused, furrowing his brow in mock consideration. "Though, if we were both to down a bottle of frie before the fight, the odds shift considerably in my favor."

Danu bit her lips together in a failed attempt to hide her smile. "If I'm ever in a tavern brawl, I'll have to hope you're fighting on my side."

"If? Keep around me, and I promise that's a *when?*" Niko shifted his weight to his toes, preparing to lunge forward a moment too late.

Danu charged him, twisting her arm to slice her blade across his stomach.

Niko brought his fist down, hitting the hand that held her knife, knocking the blade aside as pain shot through his left shoulder and something hit the back of his ankles. He suddenly lost track of the ground, only to find it a moment later as he landed flat on his back, knocking the air from his lungs.

Rolling sideways, he kicked for Danu's ankles, but she leapt forward, planting a knee on Niko's ribs and tapping her blade against his throat.

Niko laid his cheek on the cold dirt, giving his lungs a moment to remember how breathing was meant to work.

"Better." Danu stood and reached down to help Niko up.

"Don't lie to me." Niko took her hand, letting himself stumble closer to her as she yanked him to his feet.

"I had to knock you down to kill you that time." Danu grinned. "That's improvement."

"Have I mentioned I'm a map maker, not a soldier?"

"*Were* a map maker," Danu whispered as she leaned closer to Niko, still keeping hold of his hand. "You *are* Solcha, sent to the Black Bloods by the mountain to help us fight the monsters in Ilbrea. Nothing else matters, Solcha."

"I know."

"You're one of us. You belong with us." She squeezed his hand, looking deep into his eyes with not even a foot of space between them.

The clanging of the training field fell silent.

Niko's mind went silent, too, leaving him without a witty or even foolish thing to say.

The wind picked up, fluttering through the hairs that had fallen free to frame Danu's face.

"I...Danu, everything that's happened—"

"Chivving, sodden sheep shit." Danu jerked away from Niko.

A swooping panic jammed his guts into his lungs. "I'm sorry."

She stepped farther from Niko, staring at something behind him.

Niko's panic vanished, then gave another swoop, jamming his guts *and* his lungs all the way up into his throat as he turned to find Ena striding across the training field.

Everyone on the field had stopped to watch her, even the boys who'd seemed so eager to chop each other's heads off.

Despite his fear, Niko couldn't pretend not to understand why the world froze when Ena appeared.

The rainbow of her hair had vanished, covered by a black so dark, the glinting of the sun made the strands seem to shimmer with a deep, raven-wing blue. She'd left her hair loose, letting the wind toss it behind her. The wind whipped through her cloak as well, billowing the fabric around her as though emphasizing her black clothes that so perfectly fit the tales that had swept through the valley, even creeping into the common hall where Niko downed frie to keep himself from screaming as his fellow imbibers whispered tales of the magnificent woman wrapped in darkness.

And, as though the effect of Solcha's presence weren't enough to draw awe, terror, and longing from all who beheld the raven-haired beauty, four Brien followed behind her, the same four who had been with her in Bryana's throne room. They'd dressed in black as well, the color of their clothes declaring to all that they were the acolytes of the mountain's true chosen one.

Ena didn't acknowledge the people staring at her as she made her way to the archery range. No smiling. No greetings. No attempt to endear herself to the Brien.

The master archer jogged forward to meet her, giving her a deep bow before taking her cloak.

Slowly, the sounds of the training field reemerged, but the clangs had a different feel now, as though even the weapons wanted to prove their worth to Solcha.

"She had to chivving show up now," Danu whispered.

"Because I was making such a fine show of being a warrior worthy of the mountain's love," Niko whispered back.

The worry in Danu's eyes jerked Niko's lungs and guts out of his throat, letting them settle back down into their normal positions with the additional weight of several stones. "The people have to love you, Niko. Losing you has to be too much for them to bear. I don't know how else to protect you."

"I believe I'm the one who taught you the value of adoration." Niko shook out his shoulders, trying to remember what life had felt like before the whims of a demon determined his fate. "Fortunately for us, I'm charming." He offered Danu his arm. "I think it's time we get to know the woman who claims to be married to Adrial Ayres."

"If you question the truth of her marriage, that woman may very well gut you." Danu slid her blade into the sheath at her hip and took Niko's arm.

"You may not believe it, but I have had a lesson or two in tact." Niko led Danu toward the edge of the training field. "Actual lessons, too, not just wisdom earned by angering the wrong person."

"Did your mother sit you down and teach you how to sprinkle compliments over the dreaded truth?"

Niko kept his gaze on Danu as they walked along the side of the field, heading straight toward Ena. "Worse. Allora Karron had a fit at me when I insulted some merchant woman's gown. In my defense, the gown was an awful shade of orange that should never be worn. Though my asking if she was masquerading as a squash apparently crossed the line into rudeness."

"Niko!" Danu smacked him on his bare chest. "You can't say things like that."

"Between the merchant woman's screaming and Allora spending hours making me practice things to say when honesty is dangerous, I did learn my lesson." Niko laughed. "Though, I never felt quite comfortable walking past that merchant's shop again."

Danu wrinkled her nose, refusing to join in his laughter.

Something odd prickled at the back of Niko's mind. Not relief, not sadness.

Not heartbreak, either.

Before he could sort through what the odd feeling might be, they'd reached the archery field.

Ena's four acolytes had broken off into pairs, practicing with swords while she worked with the bow the master archer had delivered to her. The archer stood off to the side, watching Ena practice, ready to collect Solcha's arrows like a pup playing fetch.

"Fine afternoon for training," Niko called from twenty feet away, giving Ena time to release her arrow before he approached her.

Her arrow struck the outer ring of the target. She took another arrow from the quiver planted in the ground.

Danu pulled on Niko's arm, but he kept walking, striding right up to Ena.

Her next arrow hit the bottom of the target.

"I've only shot a few arrows before." Niko stepped slightly in front of Ena, placing himself solidly in her line of sight. "I've asked Danu to let me try—"

"You've no place on a training field, let alone in a battle," Ena said. "If you want to kill a rabbit, use a string. If you want to survive, put on a chivving shirt before the cold seeps into your lungs."

"I'm starting to understand what Adrial sees in you," Niko said.

Ena let another arrow fly, this one landing just right of center.

Danu dug her fingers into Niko's arm.

"Unfortunately, parading around like a specter of Death won't help me win the hearts of the Brien," Niko said. "The mark the trueborn carved into my back is the best way I have of reminding the Brien why they should keep me alive, so sacrificing my shirt has become a necessity. The cold seeping into my lungs doesn't worry me nearly as much as Bryana deciding I'm of more use to the clan dead."

Ena pulled another arrow from the quiver. She trailed her fingers along the black feather fletching. "And if your death would serve the Brien?"

"It wouldn't." Danu stepped between Ena and Niko.

"Don't let Bryana forget that." Ena shot the arrow, striking just below the center of the target.

"I can help you if you like." Danu took a step toward Ena, reaching for Ena's back.

"Touch me, and I'll gut you." Ena pulled another arrow from the quiver. "Run away, little Brien. And be sure to tell your aunt of my obstinance. Loathing me brings her such joy."

"Best of luck with your practice, Solcha." Danu bowed and gripped Niko's arm, dragging him away.

"Stay, Niko." Ena's arrow struck the center of the target.

"We've bothered you long enough." Danu tightened her hold on Niko's arm.

Ena turned to them, the same dangerous smile glinting in her eyes that she'd had when facing the Brien Elder. "Don't worry. Your precious map maker is safe with me. My husband cares too much for him. I don't want his blood on my hands."

"Wonderful." Niko smiled and eased his arm away from Danu. "Perhaps you can show me a bit about archery."

"I'm chivving awful with a bow." Ena pulled another arrow from the quiver. "But training with a blade is too dangerous for the babe, and I have to do something."

The arrow struck near the top of the target.

"I'll meet you on the far side of the field." Niko placed his hand on Danu's back, giving her a soft shove and hoping he could make up for it later.

"I'll take the time to sharpen my blades." Danu strode away, her shoulders stiff and neck tense.

"I hope she doesn't sharpen her blades too well." Niko pinned a smile to his face. "She's a fierce enough teacher as it is."

"What do you want?" Ena set her bow on the stand.

"I'm sorry?"

"I've no patience for games, paun."

"Strong language from someone married to Ilara's head scribe."

"My husband's heard me say far worse."

"I find that hard to imagine."

"Adrial married? Or Adrial married to a rotta?"

"Adrial married to someone who thinks so little of the Guilds." Niko forced his smile to stay in place. "And, if I really dig into it, Adrial married to someone I've never met."

"Rather hard to introduce your wife to a corpse."

"Rather hard to believe the pregnant wife of the head scribe would run away to the eastern mountains." Niko stepped back as true anger flashed through Ena's eyes.

"If I had a chivving choice, I wouldn't be here, and I would never have left the scribe in Ilara. But this is where the gods have dragged me. There are many horrors I can be blamed for, but never say I wanted to leave Adrial behind. It was the only way to keep him alive, and I will wade through paun blood to get him back." Ena snatched her last arrow from the quiver. "Do not test me, Niko. I won't kill you myself, but I will let you stumble onto a Brien blade."

"I'm sorry," Niko said, "for whatever drove you from Ilara. But Adrial married to a woman I've never met? It doesn't seem possible."

"We did meet." Ena nocked her arrow. "On the balcony at Winter's End."

Niko looked down at the packed dirt, shifting through his chamb-blurred memories. "The mad inker. You climbed up to the balcony."

"I'd have thought the mess of colors in my hair would've given it away."

The arrow struck the center of the target.

The master archer jogged out to collect Solcha's arrows.

"Adrial, Adrial Ayres, married the girl who scaled the balcony?" Niko laughed. "Allora must've had a fit."

"She tossed coin at me, trying to get me to leave him. The babe softened her heart." Her fingers curled into fists. Niko couldn't tell if she was preparing to fight or trying not to touch her stomach. "Your turn, paun. Why did you run off into the mountains?"

"The mountain swallowed me, the Brien found me, and I can't get out." Niko shoved his hands into his pockets to keep his own fingers from curling into fists. "Even if I could escape, I don't know if I could bear going back to Ilara with Allora married to the King."

A shock of pain twisted in Niko's chest. He waited for agony to surge through him, stealing his breath and clawing at his throat. The pain clamped around his lungs, but he kept breathing.

Ena watched him, as though she could see both his pain and his confusion as to why he hadn't shattered.

"Whether you'd go back to Ilara or flee to Pamerane, if you want a chance of living to see freedom, you can't trust the Brien. Not any of them. Not even the pretty one who likes to cling to your arm, especially when she crawls into your bed." Ena raised her hand, stopping Niko's protest before he could speak. "Bryana is a monster. Her daughter was no better."

"Danu is nothing like Bryana."

"She gave her vow to Bryana. Anyone willing to swear their life to a demon can't be trusted. Your Danu bends to Bryana's will. A monster's claws are at your throat, and if you're too chivving foolish to see it, not even the gods can save you."

"It doesn't matter if claws are at my throat. A thought from Bryana, and I'm dead. I'm marked, same as Danu."

"You're not." The danger in Ena's eyes ebbed. "There is an infinite difference between choosing a monster and being trapped by one."

The master archer jogged over, bowed to Ena, and placed the arrows back in the quiver. He bowed again before trotting away, leaving the two Solchas alone.

"Are you trapped?" Niko examined the arrows, angling his

back toward the master archer as the feeling of being watched added to the chill of the growing wind.

"Until I choose not to be." Ena pulled her hair over her shoulder and began whipping it into a tight braid. She nodded to the bow. "Shoot."

"I thought a bow wouldn't help keep me alive."

"We can't let people wonder why we've been talking so long." She stepped behind Niko, clearing his path to the target.

Niko chose an arrow from the quiver. He balanced its weight on his hand, hoping it was an intelligent thing to do, then nocked the arrow and let it fly, striking the dirt two feet in front of the target. "How long do you intend to stay trapped, playing whatever vile role the demon elder has planned for you?"

"That's not your concern."

"It is if you're planning to escape the stronghold." Niko grabbed another arrow. "I could help—"

"There is no help I need from a paun."

"Then you could help me. Help Adrial's friend. I can't get out on my own, and I can't survive staying Bryana's prisoner." His second arrow struck the ground a foot away from the first. "I am begging Adrial's wife for help. If you find a way to leave, don't abandon me."

Ena looked over her shoulder to where Danu waited, knife in hand, across the field. "If you want to survive to see the outside of the stronghold, stop parading around with no shirt, and stop displaying how useless you'd be in battle."

"I've been practicing."

"Being a pretty puppet?" Ena took the bow back. "Flaunting your mark, all people see is a lost little boy who's been claimed as a pet of the Brien. A pet cannot demand freedom, and I won't risk my neck dragging Bryana's puppet along behind me. She has enough chivving playthings in Ilara. I won't be adding to her hoard."

"Her hoard?" Niko glanced to Danu, looking away before she

could meet his gaze. "I know there's at least one Brien in Ilara, but surely there can't be many."

"The Brien knew I was in Ilara. At least some of them did," Ena said. "If the Brien have enough Black Bloods in Ilara to find me and lead me here, what kind of useless slitches are in charge of their chivving mess? And how long were they watching me?"

18

―――――

THAM

The voices coming from inside Mara's room sounded cheerful. No hint of distress or anger in Mara's voice, or in the sorcerer, Torra's.

Torra laughed.

Tham couldn't make out Mara's muffled reply.

He leaned on the arm of the couch, lessening the space between his ears and her door by a few inches.

"If you really want to hear, you should get a glass and hold it to the door," Elver said.

Tham shut his eyes, trying to hear what the sorcerer was saying in such a singsong tone.

"I always thought it was just a myth," Elver said. "But a glass really does work."

"I'm not trying to spy." Tham sat up straight and opened his eyes.

"Just not pleased about Mara being alone with a sorcerer who could kill her before you'd be able to do anything to stop it?" Elver asked.

Tham pressed the heels of his hands into his thighs, trading bruises for a way to expend some of the energy surging through his body screaming that Mara was in danger.

"Tham?" Elver said.

"Something like that."

"Good." Elver emphasized the word with a flick of his pen, spattering ink across the page he'd been writing on. "If you were trying to spy and doing that awful a job of it, I'd be very concerned about your involvement in our saving Ilbrea from the demons born of ice."

Elle gave a pleased bark from inside Mara's room.

"Elle, no!" Mara shouted loud enough for Tham to properly hear.

Torra laughed as Elle barked again.

Tham relaxed his arms, took a deep breath, and willed his heart to calm.

"They wouldn't hurt her," Elver said. "Or any of us. Even you."

"How do you know?"

Elver put his pen aside and frowned at his paper. He'd filled the entire page with cramped writing except for a crooked square at the center, which, apart from stray flecks of ink, he'd left blank. "I know because Shantene said so."

"You trust her?" Tham asked.

Mara laughed. Torra joined in.

"Why wouldn't I?" Elver blotted his page. "She's never chained me up or threatened me. She's been very kind and never once poisoned my cake."

Tham didn't reply.

Mara could talk to Elver. She'd be better at explaining to the poor man that Shantene not hurting him so far didn't mean it would never happen. Being a useful guest in the Sorcerers Tower wasn't the same as being a true friend.

"Don't you dare." Torra's words became clear as she opened the bedroom door. Tham leapt to his feet. "I haven't worn anything but purple robes since I was too young to truly appreciate my fleeting chance to wear something pretty."

"But you really didn't have to go to so much trouble." Mara followed Torra through the door and into the sitting room.

"Wait." Torra held out her hands, stopping Mara. "I want to watch Tham's face."

Mara bit her bottom lip and wrinkled her nose as she looked to Tham.

"Her clothes, Tham," Elver said. "You're meant to admire her clothes."

Tham studied Mara's clothes, looking beyond the lack of bloodstains to see the garments.

The deep blue bodice cinched in at her waist and cupped the curve of her breasts, doing more than hint at the wonder beneath the fabric. Her shift hung loose at her shoulders, displaying the spatter of freckles she usually kept hidden, but had long sleeves made of fine material that looked light and soft.

Torra had given Mara pants to wear instead of forcing her into a skirt.

Mara tucked her hands into her pants pockets, wiggling her fingers to make sure Tham appreciated how deep they were. The sorcerers had replaced the boots they'd given Mara when she'd first arrived at the tower with new black ones. The leather looked pliable enough to allow her to climb.

Tham looked back to Mara's face at the sound of her swallowed laughter.

"That was disappointing." Torra huffed.

Elver poked Tham in the side. "You're supposed to tell Mara how beautiful she looks."

"It's not fun if you tell him what to say," Torra said.

Tham met Mara's eyes. He searched her gaze for any sign of warning. Her smile remained. "You look lovely, Mara."

A hint of pink touched Mara's cheeks. "Thank you."

"The two of you are impossible." Torra left Mara, going to the teapot that never cooled despite the lack of a fire to warm it. "I fully expected you to tell her she was breathtaking then sweep her back into the bedroom while Elver and I pretended to be suddenly deaf. Now the rest of my day will be tainted with bitter disappointment."

Tham shifted his weight to his toes, ready to charge the sorcerer.

"I'm sorry to disappoint you." Worry pinched the corners of Mara's mouth. "Tham and I are old friends."

Elver made a noise between a huff and a gag.

"Old friends?" Torra poured herself a cup of tea. "I've spent passionate nights with a few *old friends*, but I've never looked at them the way you two look at each other."

Tham shifted his weight again, preparing to shield Mara.

"Please, Torra," Mara said. "Tham and I care for each other—"

"Closer to the truth." Torra shrugged.

"Fine. Tham and I will find a way to live our lives together," Mara said. "But there's too much at stake right now. If the Lady Sorcerer finds out what's between Tham and me and decides not to let us help Ilbrea stand against—"

"You think Lady Gwell doesn't already know?" Torra sipped her tea.

"What do you mean?" Mara said.

"Oh dear," Elver murmured.

Giving up on subtlety, Tham placed himself next to Mara, standing just far enough in front of her to have a hope of shielding her from attack.

"Everyone knows you've been rolling each other since the night you arrived." Torra winked.

"You've been watching us?" Mara gripped Tham's wrist, anchoring him against the rage that surged through his limbs, screaming for him to protect, to attack.

"By the Guilds, no." Torra wrinkled her nose. "As much as I

enjoy a naked romp, I have no interest in watching my friends slap their bits together."

"Me either," Elver said.

"But not all work in the tower is managed by magic. Every morning, Tham's sheets are gently ruffled, and Mara's"—Torra pointed at Mara's nose—"have been rumpled in a way a person could not achieve on their own."

A different sort of heat joined the anger flushing Tham's cheeks.

"How many people know?" Mara asked.

"Does it matter?" Torra took another sip of tea.

"Very much so," Mara said. "If the wrong people find out before we've been able to plead for an exemption from the rules of the Map Makers Guild—"

"I forget how prudish saelk are." Torra frowned.

"Am I being insulted?" Elver stood.

"Of course not," Torra said. "I'm a sorcerer, you all are saelk. I understand that a good roll is an excellent bit of fun, Mara and Tham tumble each other and panic when people find out. It does seem like panic would taint the fun of sex, but I suppose if I lived under saelk rules, I'd get a bit nervous to go bed-hopping as well."

"Bed-hopping?" Mara's voice pitched unusually high.

Torra rolled her eyes and set her tea aside. "It would be wrong of me to expect you to fully understand, but I promise you, you and Tham can roll each other as much as you like and not even the Lady Sorcerer will think to care. The rules that must exist to keep the outside world from tumbling into chaos don't apply to life in the tower. Spend all your free time in bed if you like. I promise you Lady Gwell already knows what's between you two. You've nothing to fear."

"Even if you're right," Tham said, "we are saelk. When we leave the tower, we'll be ruled by Ilbrean law and the laws that govern both our Guilds. For Mara's sake, I beg for your discretion."

"The seeds have blown out of the flowerbed on that one, I'm afraid. But tower gossip never leaves our walls. History has taught us the danger of allowing whispers to leak into the outside world." Torra looked from Mara to Tham and sighed. "My word to Saint Gyntra, your secret is perfectly safe."

"Thank you." Mara slid her hand down, locking her fingers with Tham's.

The comfort of her touch muted the fear that roared she was in danger.

"As for more avoidable issues"—Torra pointed at Mara's stomach—"I'll have the kitchens add Mara to the list for the infecund tonic. Whispers of your torrid love affair are harmless inside the tower, but Mara waddling back out into the world carrying a child…even a sorcerer can't protect a saelk from those consequences."

"Thank you," Mara said. "For everything."

"You're helping protect Ilbrea from a ghastly enemy." Torra backed toward the wall. "The least the sorcerers owe you is a fine set of clothes and an opportunity to indulge in sensual delights."

Torra gave a little wave and walked through the wall, as though the rules that governed Tham's life hadn't suddenly snapped.

19

ALLORA

The clack of Gillien's boots on the marble floor sent a sharp burst of annoyance through the anxiety that already sped Allora's heart. The sorcerer kept a few steps behind Allora as they cut through the palace halls. Far enough to feign respect for the Queen. Near enough that, even if she foolishly tried to flee, Allora wouldn't be able to escape the ever-watchful eye of Lady Gwell's minion.

Allora strode past the staircase that led down to the first floor of the palace and her parlor where she usually entertained guests.

One. Two. Thr—

"Your Majesty"—Gillien's steps clacked faster as she caught up to Allora—"your parlor—"

"I know where my parlor is, Gillien," Allora said.

"Have you decided not to receive your guest?" Gillien kept the word *guest* in the same tone as the rest of her words, as though the sorcerer hadn't opened the letter Allora had dared to send Adrial—as though the sorcerer shouldn't feel horrific shame at the very thought of seeing Ilara's head scribe after the tragedy her Guild had inflicted upon him.

"My plans have not changed, only my choice of venue." Allora nodded to the two guards flanking the door that led out to the smallest balcony the palace offered. "Please tell the kitchen I've decided to have my tea outside today and have the head scribe brought to me as soon as he arrives."

"Yes, Your Majesty." One of the guards bowed and disappeared down the hall while the other opened the door.

"Allora, you will catch a chill if you sit outside," Gillien said.

Allora ignored her, stepping out into the brisk air of the cloudy afternoon.

The balcony lacked the usual gilded decorations the rest of the palace endured. A few seats and a table filled the space, allowing an air of seclusion that complemented the sweeping view of the palace grounds.

"Allora"—Gillien stepped out onto the balcony, closing the door behind her—"if you truly wish to see your guest outdoors, perhaps the terrace would be a better choice. The day is gray. It could rain at any moment."

"I don't fear rain. But you may wait inside away from the danger of a rogue storm." Allora sat in a seat facing the grounds, turning her back on the sorcerer's frown.

"Nonsense. I will stay by your side. If the sky should split open, I will shelter you from the storm myself." Gillien stepped around the table, placing herself at the corner of the balcony.

"I apologize, Gillien. I was not clear enough in my orders. You *will* wait inside while I visit with my guest. The Sorcerers Guild caused unforgivable harm to the head scribe. I will not allow one of the beasts who destroyed his life to hover over him while he grieves."

"I had no hand in the unfortunate death of the head scribe's wife."

"You serve the Lady Sorcerer. You are complicit." Allora looked up, meeting Gillien's gaze. "I share the King's bed, so I, too, am complicit. Adrial Ayres is a better, kinder, more worthy person than either of us could hope to be. I am already asking him to face the King's wife. Do not make things worse by hovering over us as though the Lady Sorcerer has ordered you to find a new way to destroy him."

"Sweet Allora." Gillien knelt beside her. "The work of ruling this country is a gruesome thing you have no part in. Do not shoulder the weight of the choices faced by the King and the Guilds Council. You are not responsible for actions decided upon entirely without you. Taking on such a terrible burden would be an unhealthy load for our Queen to attempt to bear."

"And I must stay healthy. It is my place to bear the King's heir, not the weight of his misdeeds."

"A terrible way to state a simple truth." Gillien took Allora's hand.

Allora didn't bother pulling it away.

"Your misery helps no one," Gillien said. "It will not help you conceive a child. It will not make you a better wife for the King."

"I loathe the King."

"Which does not make you a better queen for Ilbrea. It doesn't even make you a better comfort to your friend."

"Don't pretend to understand anything of comfort." Allora rallied the effort to yank her hand away from Gillien. "I will not accept a lesson on duty or caring from a merciless beast."

"Because I see you are in pain, I will tolerate your insults." Gillien stood. "But tread carefully, Your Majesty. Others will not be so forgiving."

The door opened, allowing two maids carrying heavy trays to step out onto the balcony. Both girls kept their eyes down. Still, Allora had little hope of their not noticing the chill between their Queen and the sorcerer who always stalked behind her like a beast waiting to strike.

"Bring a bottle of frie," Allora said. "The finest the palace has to offer."

"Yes, Your Majesty." The maids set their trays down and scurried away.

"I didn't know you liked frie," Gillien said.

"Please, stop," Allora said. "Just go inside and let me be."

"Very well." Gillien cut around Allora to the balcony door. "I'll be right inside, ready to protect you should a storm come."

Allora didn't respond. She couldn't even summon the will to say something cutting to the sorcerer. The only thing in her mind was a dreadful feeling that the ground might drop out from under her, leaving her to fall into an endless black, and a chilling certainty that tumbling into the black would be the better fate.

One of the maids returned, her tray laden with a bottle of frie and two glasses. She deposited her bounty and fled, leaving Allora alone to stare at the autumn-dulled grounds.

A brisk wind blew down from the north, setting goosebumps on Allora's arms and neck. She turned toward the table, ready to pour a cup of tea to warm herself.

But the frie had been placed closer to her.

Despite the cloudy sky, the etched glass bottle reflected the sunlight, giving a welcoming glimmer to the brown liquor inside.

Allora pulled the stopper and sniffed the frie, wincing at the strength of its scent. The dangerous way it stung her nose only made the liquor more appealing. She poured herself a glass and took a sip, coughing as it burned all the way down her throat.

"Positively dreadful," Allora said.

There was no one to mock her weak taste in drinks.

She took another sip, letting the frie offer her warmth against the wind as the worry in her gut twisted, pinching the bottoms of her lungs, making it more difficult to breathe.

You are the maker of your own woes, Allora Karron.

"Your Majesty." One of the soldiers stepped out onto the balcony. "The head scribe to see you."

Allora stood as her stomach shot up to pummel her heart. "Send him out, please."

"Yes, Your Majesty." The guard stepped back inside, keeping the door open for Adrial.

His face was gaunt and gray, with sunken cheeks and dark patches under his eyes. Black trim had been added to his white scribe's robes, completing his embodiment of spectral grief.

"Your Majesty." Adrial bowed. "I was honored to receive your invitation."

"I'm so grateful you came." Allora stepped toward Adrial, then rocked back on her heels, barely stopping herself from embracing him. "Please sit."

"I would prefer to stand, if you don't mind, Your Majesty," Adrial said.

"Of course." Allora looked to the guard still holding the door open. "You may go."

The guard bowed and silently closed the door, leaving Allora and Adrial alone on the balcony.

"Would you like tea?" Allora said. "There's also frie."

"Since when do you like frie?" A wrinkle creased Adrial's brow.

"I don't." Allora lifted her glass. "But Niko did. And if we're to remember him properly…" Tears pressed against her throat, stealing her words.

"We should toast with frie. I'll have a glass."

"Thank you." Allora's glass clacked on the table as she set it down. She reached for the bottle of frie, pulling the stopper out with a shaking hand.

"I can pour." Adrial moved closer to the table but kept space between himself and Allora.

"I'm fine. I can manage."

"Let me help, Your Majesty." Adrial lifted the bottle away from her and refilled Allora's glass before pouring one of his own. He took two sips, not even wrinkling his nose at the taste, as though he'd gone too numb to feel anything anymore.

"I'm so sorry," Allora whispered. "I never should have asked you here."

"If the Guilds refuse to honor Niko with a formal ceremony, his friends should at least toast his memory."

"He would have understood." Tears burned down Allora's cheeks. "You have every right to stay away from the palace after what the King did to you and Ena—"

"Don't. I won't give your sorcerer shadow the satisfaction of watching me weep."

"I'm sorry."

"You have nothing to apologize for." Adrial sipped his frie. "I've endured meetings of the Guilds Council with the King and the Lady Sorcerer."

"It's more than that and you know it. The King didn't..." Allora took a breath. "They kept what they'd done from me."

"You said as much in your letter. Your kind words were appreciated."

"You deserve so much more than kind words. If I'd known what they were planning, I swear to you I would have done everything in my power to protect you and her and the child."

Adrial looked into his glass.

"Please believe that," Allora whispered. "Even if you hate me, believe that I would have fought with everything I have to protect your family."

"I know you would. I've never doubted that. And I could never hate you."

The ache in Allora's chest sharpened. "I deserve your loathing."

"You don't."

"My choices trapped me in this wretched place. I rejected Niko's proposals. I married the King. I've made so many mistakes, and they've brought me here. The wife of a monster, constantly watched by sorcerers."

"I'm sorry, Your Majesty."

"I don't deserve your pity for the cage I've built. I only wish I could comfort my friend. I should have been there while you wept. We've lost Niko and Kai. Mara and Tham are in the north. My father is sailing through the southern storms. We're the only family we have left. We should be clinging to each other. But I can't even offer you that."

"Why not?"

Allora downed the rest of her glass, letting the liquor burn away the sharper words she longed to shout. "A close association with the Queen is laden with risks. The King knows how furious I am at what he did to you. Even asking you to visit the palace could place you in danger no matter that we're toasting the memory of a fallen friend.

"We're already too closely linked for the sorcerers to ignore our association, and I'm so sorry I've made it worse. For your sake, I must remember our ties have been severed. We are old acquaintances, nothing more."

"I don't accept that."

"You must."

"I have nothing left to lose, Allora." Adrial spoke in a carrying voice, as though daring Gillien to pretend she hadn't heard his words. "I would rather die with a blade at my throat than pretend I don't love you. You are my family. They stole my wife and the child she carried. Don't let them take my sister, too."

"Are you sure?" Allora blinked away the tears that clouded her eyes.

Adrial held his arms out to her. "We're Karrons. Karrons belong together."

Allora stepped into his embrace, gently wrapping her arms around his neck as her tears spilled onto his shoulder. He held her close, laying his cheek against her hair.

Her breath hitched, and her tears wouldn't stop.

Adrial didn't shy away as sobs battered her chest.

Lightning split the sky. Rain pounded down, blurring the palace grounds.

But the rain never touched Allora. A shimmer of purple surrounded the balcony as the sorcerer protected the King's bride from the storm that drowned the city.

20

MARA

The dim passage wasn't wide enough for Tham to walk beside her. Mara's fingers tingled, begging her to reach back and take his hand—send a thrill of delight swooping through her stomach at that simple act of affection.

She could spin around and kiss Tham. Stop following Fergal down the unnaturally long passage and kiss the man she loved. Just a quick brush of her lips against his.

She bit her bottom lip, stifling her laughter as she imagined how Tham would react.

The passage turned at a sharp angle as they came to a staircase that reached up higher than Mara could see.

Fergal continued up the stairs without looking back to make sure Mara and Tham were following, walking at the same brisk pace he'd kept to since leading them out of their room.

They'd left Elver and Elle behind to have tea with Shantene. The outing hadn't been planned, and Mara had nothing that could remotely be considered a weapon tucked into her pockets, but somehow, even as her legs began to burn from climbing the unending steps, Mara couldn't bring herself to be afraid.

Worried, yes. An army of beasts could have attacked Whitend.

Mara's joy chilled and vanished.

You're a selfish girl, Mara Landil.

She was safe. Tham was safe. But while she sat beside Tham, laughing at stories of Shantene's youthful escapades, Ronya could be murdering people, staining the ground with Ilbrean blood.

I'm a terrible getch.

What's the point in trying to survive if you don't allow yourself any fun? Kai whispered. *You don't have to be miserable to fight a beast.*

The staircase curved at a gentle angle as the passage revealed a polished, silver door at the top of the steps.

Fergal stopped in front of the door, waiting for Mara and Tham to be right behind him before pressing his palm to the silver.

For one brief moment, Mara thought she saw the metal shimmer. She leaned around Fergal, trying to get a better view of the door, but she couldn't spot any trace of magic.

Fergal shifted his feet but didn't move his hand.

Mara opened her mouth to ask what they were waiting for, but Tham touched her back, silencing her. She glanced behind.

Tham had his gaze fixed on the edge of the door, staring at the silver as though he were actually seeing something.

Mara squinted at the same spot.

A tiny shift in the metal, almost as though the reflection of the passage's lights were coming into focus, started at the edges of the door.

The glow of the criolas rounded, and the outline of Fergal's silhouette crisped. The edges of the door sank slightly away from the stone of the walls, as though the door were transforming from a barrier into an entry.

Fergal lifted his hand away from the metal. A doorknob had grown where his palm had been.

"Try to keep yourselves together," Fergal said. "I haven't the time to peel you off the floor."

"What?" Mara said as Fergal turned the doorknob.

Tham squeezed himself onto the stair beside Mara, ready to place himself in front of her as he always did when he feared danger rushed toward them. But he froze as Fergal stepped through the door, giving them a view of what lay beyond.

A brilliant blue sky with deep gray storm clouds looming on the horizon. Fruit trees growing between black stone columns. Purple flowers lining the path to a black stone railing. The Lady Sorcerer standing beside the railing, her head tipped back as though she were enjoying the chill wind that swept into the stairwell.

Fergal turned, beckoning them to follow him, widening his eyes as though begging Mara and Tham to obey.

Mara squared her shoulders, locked a pleasant expression on her face, and climbed the last few stairs. Her composure shattered as she stepped through the door and onto—no into—the sky.

Her breath caught in her throat, and her heart skipped a beat.

The path leading to the Lady Sorcerer didn't exist.

Nothing. There was nothing. Just a long stretch of nothing.

Open air. Only air. And a terrible fall, and—

Fergal tapped his toe. His boot gave a soft thump with each beat, as though his shoe truly were hitting something.

Mara struck her heel against the ground. Her foot met a solid surface. She reached her other foot forward.

Tham grabbed her arm, keeping hold of her as she patted the ground with her toe.

Fergal stepped back toward them, leaning close enough to whisper, "Don't look down. If not being able to see the path spooks you—"

Mara looked down and gasped.

"I just said not to."

She mouthed a wordless reply, clinging to Tham as she tried to make her mind understand…all of it.

Far below, farther than the height of the tower should have

allowed, was Ilara. The streets Mara had memorized as she made her first maps staring out over the city from the cliffs of the Map Master's Palace. The circular street that surrounded the Sorcerers Tower and the wider streets of the merchants' section of the city stretched out below her.

People, tiny from such a distance, hurried along the streets, trying to get home before the coming storm broke over the city.

Mara took a slow step, testing the ground beneath her front foot before shifting her weight forward.

Ruins marred the streets, just as they had when she'd returned from the white mountains. Seeing the extent of the damage from above was almost as shocking as standing on the transparent path.

"No one's going to cry or faint?" Fergal kept his voice low.

"I'm fine." Mara took another step forward. "Tham?"

He didn't answer.

She looked back.

Tham stared down at the city, sweat beading his wrinkled brow.

"Tham." She inched toward him, locked her fingers through his, and gripped his arm with her free hand. "It's all right."

Tham shook his head, his gaze locked on the ground too far below. "There are some places the gods didn't intend people to go."

"Dudia created magic," Fergal said. "Magic created the overlook."

"The gods have allowed many horrors to be created." Tham looked to Fergal. "It doesn't make those horrors any less monstrous."

"If you weren't sweating with terror, I might take offense," Fergal said.

"Perhaps we should keep to solid ground," Mara said.

"Not possible. Just keep your pace steady. I've heard it eases the dizziness." Fergal strolled down the path as though incapable of understanding the concept of fear.

"Come on." Mara took a step forward, holding Tham's arm to make him move with her. "We'll walk together."

"And if the magic beneath us gives way?" Tham let Mara lead him a few more halting steps forward.

"It won't."

"I can't save you from that kind of fall." His words rasped in his throat.

"I know." A thorny pain tightened around Mara's fear. "I love you, Tham."

"But?"

"There is no *but*." Mara lifted their joined hands to kiss the back of Tham's. "I love you."

The wind picked up as they neared the black stone rail where Fergal stood beside Lady Gwell. Both sorcerers looked north over the city, toward the Royal Palace.

"Shantene urged me not to allow you up here. Sometimes, I fear the old forget the strength of the young." The Lady Sorcerer gestured to her right, inviting Mara and Tham to join her at the rail.

Tham tightened his grip on Mara's hand, near bruising her as he clung to the woman who couldn't survive losing him.

"Shantene is wise, but she has settled into her waning years," Lady Gwell said. "The world moves on with or without her. Her actions no longer have the ability to shape Ilbrea's fate."

Mara glanced to the Lady Sorcerer, trying to judge if she was meant to reply.

"But we who stand here are not that lucky," Lady Gwell continued. "We hold the lives of multitudes in our hands. If we fail, Ilbrea falls."

"Lady Gwell"—Mara dared to speak—"has something happened?"

"Many things." Lady Gwell pointed northeast. "A settlement is being built in the woods along the eastern mountains. Far enough from the mountain road, the people of Whitend will be able to live in peace, and discreet enough, word of our clearing out the north won't reach Ilara and cause a panic. Everything will be ready before those saved from Whitend arrive.

"The emissaries I sent to remove the people of Whitend will reach the village any day. I've given orders for it to be done as peacefully as possible, offering more gold than those villagers could hope to earn in a lifetime as a token of my appreciation for their cooperating with the evacuation. A new home and wealth to build a new life. I hope the people of Whitend are wise enough to accept my generosity and allow themselves to be saved."

"Thank you, Lady Sorcerer," Tham said.

"I've placed wardens along the edge of the white." Lady Gwell pointed from northwest back to northeast, tapping her finger at intervals, as though she were pointing out where each warden had been stationed. "The Soldiers Guild has been granted a large sum for the purpose of outfitting soldiers for the deadly cold. The city walls and docks are all protected. If your ice queen does descend upon Ilbrea, we are ready for war."

The tension around Mara's lungs that had been threatening to tighten and suffocate her since she'd been pulled through the ice and trapped in Isfol eased. Not all the way—not allowing her to breathe with true freedom—just enough for a bit of real hope to surround the fear that had been threatening to drown her for so long.

"Thank you," Mara said. "For believing us."

"Your thanks have come too quickly," Lady Gwell said. "Ilbrea requires your service."

"I understand." Mara pressed her arm against Tham's side, steadying herself. "I know Ronya too well. If there's any chance my being in the north could help stop her, I will gladly go."

"I'm going with her," Tham said.

"No," Lady Gwell said.

"Lady Sorcerer, please," Tham said.

"You're both staying here," Lady Gwell said. "The greatest service you can offer Ilbrea is to hide."

"I don't understand." Mara stepped away from the rail, turning so she and Tham stood side by side, facing the Lady Sorcerer.

"Ilara has been trapped in a cycle of violence for months." Lady Gwell lowered her gaze to the city below. "Insurgents plague our streets, causing destruction under the guise of protecting the very people they end up killing. They destroy homes, end lives, and, like the rodents they are, defy all logic by continuing to avoid extermination."

"The Soldiers Guild hasn't stopped them?" Tham said.

"The soldiers catch a few rats, more appear," Lady Gwell said. "You are looking down at a city on the edge of despair."

"Then I should fight with my Guild," Tham said.

"And when your reemergence sparks questions that are best left unasked?" Lady Gwell said. "If word of an army lurking in the north reaches the city, the surge of fear will breed more violence."

"If the soldiers are preparing to move into the cold of the north—" Tham began.

"The soldiers aren't going anywhere," Lady Gwell said. "Their comfort and safety are being tended to as a token of our appreciation for their work in fighting the insurgents. Warm boots buy loyalty, Soldier Karron."

"And if the soldiers find out you knew about the Ice Walkers and didn't tell them?" Tham asked. "Do you think their loyalty will hold?"

Mara dug her fingers into Tham's arm as Lady Gwell stayed silent for a moment, still not looking their way.

"I apologize, Lady Gwell," Tham said. "I spoke out of turn."

"You spoke from knowledge," Lady Gwell said. "Lord Nevon will see my hiding the Ice Walkers from the Guilds Council as an attempt to seize power. Lord Kearney and Lord Gareth will agree. Facing their wrath is a price I am willing to pay to protect Ilara's fragile peace."

"Because you can't let them know about magic you don't control." The words leapt from Mara's mouth before she could stop them.

Lady Gwell's lips curved into a smile.

The ember of rage Mara had fought so hard to suppress brightened, singeing the layers of fear and gratitude she'd wrapped around her loathing of the Sorcerers Guild.

"You are very clever, Mara," Lady Gwell said. "But you are speaking of things you do not understand."

"Then help me to," Mara said.

Tham shifted sideways, gripping the railing as though preparing to catch Mara if the ground beneath her should disappear.

"Fear is deadly," Lady Gwell said. "Fear causes panic. Panic causes violence. Violence rips away reason, and we are reduced to our basest instincts. Protect the pack. Kill all others. If the people of Ilbrea learn there is an army lurking to the north, innocents will die even if the Ice Walkers never reach Ilara.

"The threat of magic the Sorcerers Guild does not control, that no saelk could hope to defeat, that fear ripping through Ilbrea would cast anyone born with magic in their blood as *other*. Rogue. Wild. Uncontrolled. Dangerous. My people would be attacked. My Guild would be blamed."

"But it wouldn't be your magic they're afraid of," Mara said. "Saelk need you to fight against the Ice Walkers. Their magic proves Ilbrea's need for the protection of the Sorcerers Guild in a way that hasn't been seen in centuries. The people would adore you."

"That right there is why I fear you will never understand," Lady Gwell said. "It is my duty to protect Ilbrea and the Sorcerers Guild. The least bloody path forward requires secrecy. No one can know the danger Ilbrea faces, and no one can know what you found in the north."

"So you want us to hide," Mara said.

"If you step out into the city, the only survivors returned from the journey to the white mountains, you will be forced to answer deadly questions," Lady Gwell said. "I offer you the comforts of the Sorcerers Tower as your haven."

"For how long?" Mara asked.

"Until the danger passes," Lady Gwell said.

"Our journey is due back to Ilara within the month," Tham said. "Even if we stay here, the Soldiers Guild and the Map Makers Guild will know something went wrong."

"A letter has been sent to the Map Makers Guild, begging Lord Karron's forgiveness for extending your journey without his permission. You discovered a series of caverns cutting southeast through the white mountains leading toward the eastern mountains.

"You will be spending the winter mapping the cave system in hopes of creating a permanent northern outpost between Ilbrea and Wyrain. Map Maker Traim accepted the letter in Lord Karron's absence. He is pleased with your discovery."

"If you've already sent the letter, you aren't really asking us to stay in the tower," Mara said. "You've trapped us."

"Not at all. If you agree to stay hidden, you are free to leave the safety of the Sorcerers Tower," Lady Gwell said. "But fleeing to the south or hiding in the countryside will not serve Ilbrea. If the Ice Walkers attack, you can only assist in Ilbrea's defense if you're here, where your knowledge of the foreign beasts can be used. Search your conscience before choosing your path."

Mara looked to Tham, trying to read something beyond the poorly concealed anger in his eyes.

"Return them to their rooms," Lady Gwell said. "Give them time to think."

"Yes, Lady Gwell." Fergal bowed and stepped behind the Lady

Sorcerer, ready to escort Mara and Tham back across the unseeable path.

"What about Elver?" Tham said. "If he chooses, can he leave and go into hiding with Mara and me?"

"His best chance for healing is with us," Lady Gwell said, "but if you agree to care for him, I'll allow him to leave with you."

"Thank you, Lady Gwell." Mara pulled on Tham's arm, urging him onto the path.

"You are sworn to the Guilds," Lady Gwell said, her words as clear as if she stood right beside Mara instead of facing into the northerly wind. "There is so much more you will do to help Ilbrea. Your part in her salvation has only just begun."

21

ADRIAL

The two chandeliers Adrial had ordered be hung in his office cast their light on the shelves lining the walls of the room, giving a breathtaking gleam to the rainbow of inks surrounding him.

He'd organized the inks by pigment, carefully placing each shade together, marking the shelves with how many precious jars of each color Ena had left behind.

The workers who'd hung the lights and moved the shelves had looked at Adrial as though he'd gone mad, but no one so much as whispered a harsh word. They still held too much pity for the grieving head scribe.

Overseeing the changes had taken him two days, granting him a brief reprieve from working on the vellum for Princess Illia.

The illuminated vellum should have been his masterpiece, a display of skill that marked him as a worthy heir to the Lord Scribe.

The pretty pictures and well-chosen words had lost their meaning now.

No, they were worse than meaningless.

The vellum was a monument honoring a country that abused its weak and vulnerable in the worst ways. Telling a lie-laden story romanticizing the Willoc family's rise to power and the formation of the Guilds was a vile twisting of the truth, and Adrial's duty to create.

The very act of working on the vellum pummeled Adrial's gut with nauseating self-loathing.

But hating himself was better than missing Ena. So, he continued on, arranging the office where he would create a glorious volume of lies.

After he'd sorted the inks, he'd spent days sketching out each page of the vellum, budgeting Ena's pigments, meticulously planning so her work wouldn't be tainted by his resorting to the use of inks from a lesser maker.

He'd carefully drafted the wording for each page, writing and rewriting the text six times before admitting he'd finished that work as well.

He'd run out of reasons to delay. The inks for the page were laid out in a perfect row on his desk, the jars glimmering in the too-bright light of the too-large chandeliers.

But every time he reached for his pen, his hand would start shaking.

Adrial shut his eyes, willing his heart to calm. He tried to picture the scene he needed to draw. The fifth of the Willoc Queens kneeling in the cathedral as she begged Dudia to spare Ilara from the terrible illness that had ravaged the south.

Her purity and goodness had touched Dudia's heart, and he had protected the seat of the Guilds' power from harm.

The mercy of a god granted at the will of a queen.

The Queen would need a kind face, radiant and beautiful. Soft angles and gentle hues.

The pale hair of the Queen shifted in Adrial's mind, brightening as a hundred colors consumed the strands. The pleading on her face vanished, and Ena took her place. A teasing smile lit her eyes as she reached for Adrial's hand, inviting him to join her in the perfect image.

If he could just hold her, feel the warmth of her skin against his, hear her laugh, the terrible hollow in his chest would disappear.

Hot tears rolled down Adrial's cheeks. He opened his eyes and looked down at the blank parchment.

"You can't hold a picture, Adrial Ayres," he whispered. "You can't afford to forget that, you fool. You'll slip into madness and never recover."

He opened the jar of black ink.

The dome of the cathedral at the top of the page. Easy. Manageable.

The arch of the stained-glass window that had bathed the Willoc family in otherworldly light for centuries before the cathedral was destroyed.

A pale, golden seven-pointed star on the middle of the page—the ink light enough not to interfere with the text Adrial would add once the image was finished.

The familiar feel of pen moving over parchment allowed Adrial's thoughts to blur.

"— promise, it's important." An urgent, bouncing voice pierced Adrial's thoughts.

"He has to work, Taddy," Tammin said. "Whatever you need, I'll take care of it for him."

"You can't." Taddy's voice came from closer to Adrial's door. "You're not him, and I've got to talk to him and it's important so I have to talk to him right now and I'm sorry but there really isn't time to wait and I promise he won't be angry."

Taddy burst into Adrial's office, stumbling three steps before whipping around to slam the door shut behind him.

"Taddy!" Tammin shouted through the door.

Taddy turned the lock and leapt back. "Oh, she might murder me later."

The door handle shook.

"Taddy, what are you doing?" Tammin called.

"An excellent question." Adrial set down his pen.

Taddy spun to face Adrial. "I…ooh, I'm not sure, sir."

"Not sure?" Adrial asked.

"Not sure what I'm doing." Red crept up the boy's sweat-covered face as he shifted his weight from foot to foot. "I think—well, I think I might be delivering a secret message."

"A message?"

"I'm pretty sure it's a message but not *sure* sure. That's part of the secret bit." Taddy pulled an envelope from his pocket, crinkling the edges as he thrust it toward Adrial.

Aside from the smears of Taddy's sweat, the envelope had no markings.

"Sorry for tainting the paper, sir. I've been a bit panicked."

"Take a breath, Taddy." Adrial stood and shifted his chair to behind his apprentice. "Sit and tell me where you found this."

Taddy didn't sit.

"I didn't find it, sir. I was walking down the hall, and a servant stopped me. I'd never even seen them before. But they said my name and grabbed my arm and pulled me into a doorway and I wanted to scream but they shushed me and they were gripping my arm very hard and so I stayed quiet."

"Interesting." Adrial wrinkled his brow.

"I'll have an interesting bruise, that I know." Taddy's face grew redder still. "The woman, because it was a woman, sir, and she was *very* strong, she told me to come right to you and give this envelope to you and not to open it or let anyone but you see it because she'd know if I didn't do what she said and she'd find me again and do much worse than bruise my arm."

"What?"

"Then she let go of my arm, curtsied, and walked away like nothing had ever happened." Taddy sank into the chair. "And the way she did the grabbing and threatening but most of all the curtsying, so calm, like threatening people and leaving bruises on their arm was normal for her, I really do think she meant it, sir.

So, I ran straight here and brought you the envelope and didn't read it or let anyone else see that I had it."

"Thank you, Taddy." Adrial ran his finger across the envelope. The wax seal had a pale-yellow color, as though normal candle wax had been used. He held the envelope up to the too-bright light of the chandeliers.

The heavy strokes of hastily scrawled words showed through the paper, but the letter had been folded, overlapping the lines of script, making its mysterious contents impossible to read.

"Are you going to open it, sir?" Taddy asked.

"I don't suppose I have a choice." Adrial slid his thumb beneath the seal.

Taddy held his breath, his eyes bulging, as Adrial unfolded the letter.

Adrial Ayres,

If you want the truth—

Adrial read through the letter once, his heart pounding so hard, his mind couldn't understand the words.

Adrial Ayres,

If you want the truth behind your grief, be at the fountain in the square at three today. Sit near the man in the gray hat. If you're not at the fountain, the truth of what happened to your wife on the ship to Ian Ayres will be lost to you forever.

The room swayed as Adrial read the words a third time.

—your wife on the ship to Ian Ayres —

"Sir," Taddy whispered, "you've gotten very pale."

Adrial tried to fold the letter back up, but his hands were shaking too badly. The paper fell to the floor.

"Are you all right, sir?" Taddy stared at the fallen letter as though afraid it might leap up and sting him. "Are you in danger?"

"The only danger is to the one who wrote that letter." Adrial snatched the paper up and began shredding it.

"I don't understand, sir."

"I need your help, Taddy." Adrial thrust the scraps into his pocket.

"Of course, sir." Taddy leapt to his feet.

"Collect a travel desk and meet me by the gate."

"Yes, sir." Taddy ran toward the office door. Grabbing the handle but forgetting he'd turned the lock, he slammed into the door, unfastened the lock as he stumbled, successfully opened the door, and bolted into the outer office without saying another word.

Adrial straightened his black collar and cuffs. He took deep breaths, letting the air fan the pure fury seething in his gut.

A trap. A way to lure the head scribe out of the library. A fiend ready to prey on his despair.

His rage grew, filling the hollow of his grief in a satisfying way.

Hiding his limp, Adrial strode out of his office, paying for every step with a jolt of pain that further stoked the flames devouring his reason.

Tammin leapt to her feet. "Head Scribe, are you all right?"

"Fine." Adrial didn't slow his steps. "Continue your work."

The pain in his hip grew as he cut down the corridor toward the courtyard.

A reason to go outside.

Any excuse to risk going out to the square.

With Taddy bringing a desk, he could make the excuse of writing burial papers for the common folk. It had worked before.

But now he'd condemned the slitch Travers to sit beyond the

library gates performing all the work Adrial could've used as an excuse for going to the square.

He could ask for reports of the damage from the sorcerers' raids directly from the common folk, but then he'd be mobbed. There would be too many people.

He couldn't risk the man in the gray hat fleeing into a crowd.

He could tell the scribes' guards that a fiend wished to torture him, but again, the man might flee.

You're the chivving head scribe, Adrial Ayres. Tell them you're walking to the square and be done with it.

By the time he'd reached the library gates, the pain in his hip had grown to a vicious stabbing that shot white-hot lightning from his knee to his ribs.

He made it past the first line of guards before one finally stepped into his path.

"Head Scribe." The guard bowed. "Are you waiting for a carriage?"

"No." Adrial stepped around him. "I'm walking to the square."

"I'm sorry, sir." The guard dodged back into Adrial's path. "None of the scribes are allowed to leave the library without a carriage, and all carriages must be approved by the Lord Scribe. If you'd like me to send a request—"

"I'm coming!" Taddy shouted from the far end of the court-yard. "I've got the desk!"

"Bring it here, Taddy." Adrial held the guard's gaze. "I am taking that desk and walking out to the square where I shall work for as long as I see fit. If I need your interference, I shall call for you. Then, and only then, will you interrupt me."

Taddy stumbled to a stop beside Adrial.

"Go straight back to Scribe Tammin, Taddy." Adrial took the desk from his apprentice.

"But I can carry—"

"To Scribe Tammin, Taddy," Adrial said. "You will not leave her side until I return. Am I understood?"

"Yes, sir." Worry creased Taddy's brow as he backed away.

"Do not block my path." Adrial looked back to the guard.

The guard didn't move.

"I am the second in command of this library," Adrial said. "I have no patience or caring left to offer, and making an enemy of me is not a risk a wise man should take. Move. Now."

"Yes, Head Scribe." The guard stepped aside. "We'll keep a close eye for any trouble."

Adrial gripped the desk, frantically searching for a way to order the guards to ignore him without raising further suspicion.

He couldn't think of a reason.

"Watch from a distance if you must." He walked past the guards and through the gates.

A shock jolted up his spine as he was met with more guards beside the high wall that surrounded the library. Twelve men flanked a line of people waiting in front of a small white awning.

Scribe Gend bent over a too-short desk as a common woman towered over him.

"I'm not asking for papers to build a new house." Anger creased the woman's face. "I need papers to rebuild the house your precious sorcerers burned down."

"The papers are—"

"Don't you tell me the papers are the same," the woman said as though speaking to an ill-behaved child. "I still have two walls. I'm only asking to build two more."

"I do not create the laws, only the papers," Travers said.

"Two is less than four!" The woman tapped Travers's desk.

One of Travers's guards swallowed a laugh.

The gratification Adrial should have felt at Travers's reddening face and the guard's enjoyment of the common woman's words as she dared to berate the paun didn't tinge Adrial's anger. The purity of his loathing made it easy to ignore the stares of the tilk and guards as he cut through the line and into the square.

The dull gray of the day had kept the square from filling, leaving few people crossing through the space and even fewer attempting to enjoy it. Only two people sat on the wide rim of the fountain. A younger man in worn clothes ate bread from a scrap of cloth, and—there on the far side, facing away from the library—a man in a gray hat.

Adrial's heart leapt into his throat, pounding a vicious rhythm that begged him to attack.

The younger man stood, staring wide-eyed at Adrial, giving a too-low bow before taking off down the street, still clutching his cloth-wrapped bread.

Adrial slowed his steps as he reached the far side of the fountain, his knuckles white from gripping the travel desk.

"Not too close," the man in the gray hat said. "Don't look as though you've come to meet me."

Adrial tamped his rage down just enough to keep from screaming. "Do you truly dare to give me orders?"

"Yes," the man said. "And if you want to hear what I've come to say, you'll chivving well follow those orders."

Adrial froze for a moment, letting his mind whip through every available option, before finally sitting four feet away from the man.

"Good little paun," the man said.

Adrial flipped open the top of his desk. "Say your piece, and let me be."

"So little time to spare for your wife?" Anger darkened the man's voice. "I didn't think a paun could fool Ena into thinking he cared."

"Do not speak as though you knew my wife or how deeply I cared for her." Adrial slid a sheet of parchment on top of his desk. "I loved Ena with everything I am, and, cripple or not, a grieving man is a dangerous thing."

"What can a paun know of grief?"

"They took my wife."

"And you did nothing."

"I tried." The words caught in Adrial's throat. "I begged them to punish me instead of taking her. I would give anything to change our places, but—"

"Anything?"

"To save Ena and her child, I would defy Dudia himself." Adrial unscrewed a jar of black ink. "But they are dead, and sending messages through my apprentice is an act of monstrous cruelty I will not allow."

"Even if I know the story of Ena drowning in the Arion Sea holds less truth than your Guilds' supposed honor?"

A cold horror swept through Adrial's veins.

"What happened? Did they hurt her? Did they kill her?" Adrial turned toward the man.

Burn scars crept out of the man's collar and up his cheek. Hatred burned in his dark eyes as though he were a true demon. A monster, a revenant, dragged up from the grave to torment Adrial.

"Eyes front, or I walk away."

"What did they do to her?" Adrial locked his gaze on the jar of ink. He gripped the desk as hard as he could, clinging to the wood as panic and pain tried to sweep his mind away.

"So ready to believe the worst of your fellow paun."

"Tell me who murdered my wife."

"No one. Ena's alive."

The jar of black ink tipped and fell. The glass shattered on the cobblestones.

"Calm yourself. If the guards watching from the corner come this way, I leave. And I promise you'll never see me or Ena again."

"Don't. Please don't taunt me." Tears burned in Adrial's throat. "If you want to kill me, have the kindness to use a blade."

"Ena's alive, and your babe still grows in her womb."

"Do not mock me." Adrial fought to breathe, gagging on air as pain ripped through his chest.

"Mock you? Ena swore you claimed the child as your own. Swore you'd do anything to protect your child."

The air in Adrial's lungs lifted out through his back, sealing his lungs shut.

"Did you lie to Ena, paun? Or did she lie to us?"

Adrial couldn't pull in enough air to speak.

"If you care nothing for the child, should I walk away and never come back? Tell Ena the man she's sure loves her tossed her away?"

"No." Pain spiked the rhythm of Adrial's heart as he dragged in a breath. "I love Ena. I claim the child Ena carries. Everything Ena said is true. I would do anything for my wife and child."

"Then you're to do whatever it takes to keep yourself alive. For Ena's sake."

"I will. I'll—" Adrial's chest crumpled as the pain surged to a peak he couldn't bear. "You're lying. You were sent to torture me with hope. Ena is dead. The child is dead."

"The first time you saw the bird marked on her ribs was at a waterfall. She saw the marks on your ribs that day, too."

The pain twisted, squeezing into a terrible, paralyzing void. "You can't know that."

"Such a smart little paun."

"There was no one else at the waterfall. No one to see us."

"That's the chivving point. Ena's alive."

"She told you." The ground swayed as joy seeped into the edges of the void. "She must've told you. Where is she?"

"Far away from here."

"Where?" Adrial turned toward the man.

"Eyes front."

Adrial pinned his gaze to the buildings in front of him. The stones twisted. "Tell me where she is."

"Somewhere safe. And that's where she'll be staying."

"Take me to her."

"No."

"I have to go to her."

"You'll not be going anywhere near Ena, paun."

"Please, I'll do anything. Whatever ransom you want, I'll pay it."

"Coin can't buy Ena."

"Gold, jewels. Whatever you want, however much you want, I'll pay." Tears streamed down Adrial's cheeks. "Just please don't hurt her. Don't hurt the baby."

"You're a bigger fool than I thought."

"Please, I promise you. Anything you want. Just give Ena back."

Adrial's heart thundered in his ears as the man stayed silent for a long moment.

"The weapons being delivered to the sailors. There will be errors in the records of the transfer. Fix the records so it looks like nothing's missing. You do that, I'll bring you more news of Ena." The man in the gray hat stood. "You refuse, you'll never hear from me again. Move carefully, paun. Innocent lives are at stake."

The man strode out of the square, leaving Adrial behind.

Adrial's breath roared through his ears, drowning out the thundering of his heartbeat.

A sob punctured the numb disbelief that had frozen him.

Ena alive.

The child alive.

Ena alive!

The desk slid off his lap, crashing to the ground as sobs tore through him.

"Head Scribe." An older woman sat beside him. She held a worn handkerchief in front of his face. "I'm so sorry, sir."

Adrial couldn't speak through his tears.

"We'll get this righted for you." A young girl knelt beside Adrial's spilled desk.

A boy joined the girl helping to gather the scattered papers.

"I'm so sorry, Head Scribe." The older woman pressed the handkerchief into Adrial's hand. "I'm so sorry they took your wife."

A man in common clothes sat on Adrial's other side. He laid his hand on Adrial's shoulder. "It's all right, sir. You married a tilk. You've got every right to grieve as tilk do, however the gods took her from you."

The crowd around Adrial grew as the common folk from Travers's line flocked to the head scribe. With tear-filled eyes, pats on the shoulder, and words of comfort, they surrounded the paun who'd dared to marry a tilk. They carried his desk and offered their arms as he stumbled back toward the library, surrounding him with the strength of people used to surviving the worst of pains.

He couldn't form the words to thank them as they left him at the gate. The chaos whirling through his mind allowed only one thought.

Ena is alive!

22

KAI

"Are you ill, or has Dudia swept through your heart and forbidden you from attacking the sorcerers?" Merial flicked Kai's arm without even looking his way.

"The honest truth?" Kai dared to glance toward her. Removing his gaze from his assigned slit in the Gilded Hall's curtains for even a moment felt like an awful offense. He locked his eyes back out over the cathedral square. "I have a horrible feeling of guilt rolling through my gut that's making me a bit queasy."

"You've suddenly decided our cause isn't a worthy one?" Merial knelt.

Kai followed her motion, trying to see what the smuggler had spotted.

The cathedral square had filled with people, all fools come to see why the Lady Sorcerer had bid them gather. A small platform had been erected on the landing at the top of the steps of the ruined cathedral. Soldiers flanked the sides of the steps, and more had been stationed around the edges of the square, but the sorcerers themselves had yet to appear.

"After all the pain the chivving purple-clad demons have

caused, if you've decided they deserve mercy, you'll find no agreement from me," Merial said.

"No. Sorry," Kai said. "Sorry, it's not that. I've no qualms about killing sorcerers. If we could drag them all out to sea and drown them, Ibrea would be a safer place."

"Good." Merial stood back up.

"My guilt goes entirely to the memories I've created in this room."

"This room?"

Kai took a deep breath, ignoring the stench of cheap liquor to savor the scent of wood polish, old ale, and dust. "What may seem to you like a tiny, forgotten storage room where the workers of the Gilded Hall hide the broken tables, unneeded chairs, and rags they've not bothered to clean, is a beautiful place to me. A land of wonderment where some of my finest trysts have occurred."

Merial huffed a laugh. "I don't have it in me to feign surprise."

"The first time I dabbled with men was in this room," Kai said. "My night with the two healers was up here as well. And the blond common girl who liked to bite."

"That's enough, thank you."

"None of them said that." Kai flicked Merial.

She smacked him on the chest. His ribs only gave a small throb.

"A man with my reputation happens to know a hidden entrance to the servants' stairs and how to get into the locked storage space above the Gilded Hall and you didn't guess why I'd been up here?" Kai asked.

"Guessing is a far cry from listening to you tally your conquests," Merial said.

"I'm reminiscing. We're about to do something foolish and deadly. I'd like to relive happy memories in case I've reached my last hour of life."

Another six soldiers entered from the eastern end of the square, adding to the six already guarding the cathedral steps.

"If you're so worried about the possibility of dying today" —Merial knelt again—"have you dealt with Drew yet?"

Talons clawed through Kai's stomach. "I've no idea what you mean."

The movement of the crowd changed. The people stilled, as though called to order by something Kai couldn't see or hear.

"I'm not your friend, nor do I have any desire to be," Merial said. "Even if I weren't a smuggler and you weren't a paun, I would still have no desire to seek your friendship. But you're not a total worthless chivving slitch, so I'll give you my advice whether you want it or not."

The front of the crowd shifted, causing a ripple through the horde as everyone backed away from the cathedral.

"There are very few people in this world worth loving. If you've found one, don't throw them away because you're too much of a coward to tell him you love him and want to spend the rest of your life beside him," Merial said.

"It's not that simple."

"I don't care. And neither will Death. Don't let cowardice drag regrets into your grave."

The crowd shifted again as everyone looked to the north-eastern corner of the square near the cathedral.

Eight sorcerers entered the square, walking in front of the Lady Sorcerer's carriage.

"Thank you," Kai said.

"Me? Or the Lady Sorcerer for finally showing up?"

"You."

"Good."

Another set of eight sorcerers followed the carriage.

Four of them broke away from the rest, climbing up onto the landing at the top of the stairs.

The other twelve formed two lines of six. One line went north and the other south, both cutting around the periphery of the square.

At every entrance to the square they passed, one sorcerer left their group, taking up positions surrounding the crowd, leaving the people no way to flee without passing a sorcerer.

"Chivving purple bastards." Kai scanned the perimeter of the square again, searching for an alley the sorcerers might have missed. "We've got to call it off."

"There's no signal for abandoning the plan," Merial said.

"Then we won't send any signal at all," Kai said. "We've started nothing. Our people can stay quiet and leave with the rest of the crowd."

Merial swatted Kai away, stealing his crack in the curtains. "A gathering this large is exactly what we've been waiting for."

"Did you count the sorcerers in the square?" Kai cut behind Merial to take her former place.

A sorcerers' guard opened the door of the purple carriage on the side nearest the crowd. The Lady Sorcerer stepped out, facing the people on the same level as the horde.

"She's taunting us. Taunting everyone down there," Merial said. "She thinks we can't touch her."

"She's right."

"She's not." Merial pointed to the northwestern corner of the square. "That sorcerer, right there. I'll wear the orange marker going her way." She pointed to the sorcerer on the southwestern corner of the square. "I'll send yellow to that one."

Kai peered through the glass, trying to see the faces of the two demons Merial had just condemned.

"Turn the flock toward the display," Kai said.

"And let the Lady chivving Sorcerer watch the chaos happen," Merial said.

The Lady Sorcerer's carriage left the square. The four sorcerers on the landing bowed as she climbed the cathedral steps.

"I don't like the risk," Kai said. "It's more than our people agreed to."

"If our people didn't understand that joining the underground might end with their greeting Death, it's their own chivving fault."

A second carriage, built like a wooden box with bars across the windows, entered the square and stopped in front of the cathedral steps. Two sorcerers' guards opened the door at the back of the carriage, dragging out a man with chains on his hands and feet, tossing him face first onto the cobblestones.

"Kai?" Merial said.

"Orange to the north, yellow to the south. The plan goes."

"May the gods watch over us." Merial grabbed a glass bottle from the crate at Kai's feet and headed toward the door.

"Merial," Kai said. "Be careful."

"As careful as the danger allows. But if I die down there, don't you chivving dare waste my last words of wisdom."

The door to the servants' stairs snapped shut before Kai could make himself speak, leaving him alone to stare out over the square.

"A coward in a window," Kai whispered to himself. "Such an asset to the fight against the sorcerers."

Kai moved to the center of the window, taking up more space than sharing with Merial had allowed, and knelt beside the crate. Five bottles of foul liquor with jars of mining powder fixed on the sides and rags sticking out of the tops—even knowing he could rain fire down on the front of the Gilded Hall, the weapons Kai had been left with seemed too small and useless for him to help anyone, let alone protect his people from more than a dozen sorcerers.

The prisoner's carriage left the square.

The two sorcerers' guards hauled the man to his feet and dragged him up the steps to the small platform on the landing. When they let go of the man, he crumpled to the ground, as though his injuries were far worse than having merely been thrown out of the carriage.

The sorcerers' guards walked back down the steps, positioning themselves in front of the soldiers.

"What madness have the demons planned?" Kai whispered to the empty storage room.

He couldn't even manage to imagine one of his friends replying.

A strange shimmer blossomed in front of the landing then swept to the sides, enclosing the wounded man, the Lady Sorcerer, and the four sorcerers positioned around her in whatever spell the demons had cast.

Kai glanced toward the ground closer to the Gilded Hall.

The people in the crowd stirred, but no one dared to flee.

The orange and yellow hadn't appeared.

A bright flash snapped Kai's gaze back to the landing.

A stream of light, like lightning twisted into a rope, wrapped around the man.

Even from a distance, Kai could hear the man scream as the light lifted him, placing him upright on the platform, giving the crowd a better view of his pain.

The Lady Sorcerer watched the man scream for a moment before turning to the crowd.

"People of Ilara." The Lady Sorcerer's voice radiated out over the horde, reaching Kai as though she stood just on the other side of the window. "For too long, our city has been plagued by violence. I have tried to be gentle as we excise the villains behind these atrocities, but the time for seeking a quiet end to these offenses has passed."

The light binding the man shifted from bright white to the orange of heated metal.

The man tipped his head back and screamed, his face contorting with pure agony.

Even though blood stained his face, there was something familiar about the man.

As the light brightened back to white, the man's head fell forward.

Like a receding wave, the horde drew away from the Lady Sorcerer's display, compressing the back of the crowd.

A few fought against the horde, drawn to the man's pain, plowing toward the cathedral to gain a better view.

There, in the back, Merial in a bright orange hat, shoving her way through the crowd, heading north. And Landon, wearing a yellow hat, sliding between people as though searching for someone as he headed south.

"I take no pleasure in causing pain," the Lady Sorcerer said. "But this man is a criminal. He is guilty of destroying the property of Ilaran merchants. He is guilty of inciting violence against the Guilds. He is guilty of defying the Sorcerers Guild."

The light that held the man up split in two, wrapping around him like hellish vines, slithering from his chest down to his arms. The light reached the chains on the man's wrists. With a crack, the chains fell away. But the light replaced the mundane bonds, pulling his arms out to his sides and lifting his feet off the platform.

The man kicked his still-chained legs, trying to break free.

The Lady Sorcerer waved her hand, and the man stopped moving—his legs frozen, his face front, as though he'd been trapped between two panes of glass.

Kai leaned closer to the window, squinting to better see the man's face through the shimmer of the spell protecting the Lady Sorcerer. "Arto?"

The prisoner was far thinner than Arto had been, but the color of the hair was right. The features, too.

Kai hadn't seen Arto since he and Drew had run from the Brien when they'd reached Ilara, but it hadn't been that long ago.

"This criminal has been sentenced to death," the Lady

Sorcerer said. "The city of Ilara will be safer without him. There can be no joy in such a grisly display—"

"Chivving liar," Kai whispered.

"—and no pride in ending a life. But his execution shall be a lesson to you all."

The man's shirt ripped open, exposing his bare chest.

Kai looked back to the ground, searching the crowd for the orange of Merial's hat. She stood one person away from her chosen sorcerer.

And to the south…there! Tucked into the crowd five feet from his sacrificial sorcerer, Landon in his bright yellow hat.

Kai eased the window up not even an inch.

The crowd's gasp pulled his focus back to the man he truly hoped wasn't Arto.

Even the Brien who'd plotted to kill him and Drew didn't deserve the gashes the Lady Sorcerer carved across the prisoner's chest.

She had no knife in her hand, didn't even look the man's way as the slices in his skin grew, letting blood flow down his chest.

Kai grabbed the over-polished soupspoon from his pocket and shoved the bowl through the crack below the window, tipping the bottom of the spoon to catch the sun.

A woman in the crowd screamed.

Kai glanced back toward the man.

The cuts in his chest formed a seven-pointed star. The skin within the star began to peel away.

"Come on, Merial." Kai wiggled the spoon. "Come on."

"Anyone who dares stand against the Sorcerers Guild will share this man's fate," the Lady Sorcerer said. "Anyone aiding the criminals who terrorize Ilara will share this man's fate. To all those who seek to sow—"

A wave of screams came from the northern side of the square as a burst of flames shot into the air, consuming a sorcerer. Kai looked south, away from Merial's handiwork, as three arrows flew toward the sorcerer nearest Landon.

The first arrow grazed the sorcerer's arm. The second missed. The third struck the center of his chest.

"Yes." Kai pulled the spoon inside, dropping it on the floor, grabbing the flint from his pocket. "Yes, go on."

The crowd surged away from the flames, fleeing south, making the horde turn toward the arrow-struck sorcerer, blocking aid from reaching the dying demon.

"There it is." Kai reached for one of his liquor-filled bottles. "They've seen it, now everyone, go."

Wait for the orange hat to disappear. Wait for the yellow hat to disappear. Rain fire onto the front of the Gilded Hall if his fellows needed more time to flee.

Simple. Easy. Their plan was nearly done.

Bright blue light burst from the center of the crowd, tossing people aside as though they were nothing more than flower petals.

But one person stayed on their feet.

A girl with bright red curls stood alone, facing the Lady Sorcerer.

23

KAI

Sparks flashed through the air, surrounding the red-haired girl.

"Isla." Kai whispered the name of the girl who'd saved his life.

A ball of red fire twisted into being above the Lady Sorcerer.

Isla raised her hand, and the ball fell, crashing onto the shield that protected the Lady Sorcerer and her four sorcerer guards. Fire danced along the dome of the spell, but the Guilded sorcerers' magic held.

"Run, Isla," Kai whispered.

Two forms, like black whips, lashed up from the crowd, striking the shield as another ball of flames appeared high in the air.

The panicked horde shoved away from the bases of the whips, exposing the two women casting the spells, both of them with their hands held front, anchoring the magic to their bodies.

A fresh wave of screams came from near the cathedral as the soldiers flanking the steps began to fall.

Their bodies jolted as they collapsed.

But there was no shimmer or light or fire attacking them. The men just fell, as though they'd been struck by dozens of arrows Kai couldn't see.

The second fireball crashed into the shield. The black whips struck the same spot the instant after.

A horrible screech drowned out the horde's screams as a crack split the top of the shield, tearing through the magic as though the spell itself had been wounded.

Isla stepped toward the stairs. The sparks crackling around her brightened as a streak of lightning shot down from the sky and through the already healing break in the shield.

Kai held his breath, waiting to watch the moment the Lady Sorcerer died.

But the lightning struck the prisoner.

Struck Arto.

Light pulsed through his body. He fell to the ground, free of the Lady Sorcerer's bonds, beyond her ability to ever torture again.

"I'm so sorry." Kai pressed his palm to the glass, wishing he had a better way to comfort Isla as she swayed, stumbling from the weight of something he couldn't see.

The two black whips struck the shield over and over again, pounding against the barrier even as the spell healed.

Soldiers shoved through the crowd, charging toward their fallen brethren near the stairs. Those men fell as the others had, jerking as though struck by something Kai couldn't see.

Kai scanned the crowd, trying to find where the attack was coming from, but the Lady Sorcerer stepped forward.

She walked calmly to the front of the shield, raising her hand, reaching for Isla.

The few people still near Isla knocked each other over, desperate to escape the path of the Lady Sorcerer's wrath.

Isla didn't run. She steadied her stance, as though preparing for a blow.

Kai rammed the window open and grabbed the first of his bottles.

The Lady Sorcerer tipped her head, smiling as though savoring what was to come.

The two spell-cast whips changed their aim, battering the shield right in front of the Lady Sorcerer.

Kai struck the flint, lighting the rag in the bottle.

Isla faced her palms toward the ground. Her skirts billowed around her legs, blown by a terrible wind.

Kai held the bottle out the window and dropped it straight down onto the front balcony of the Gilded Hall.

A pillar of fire blossomed as the glass shattered.

The crowd shifted, surging away from the new blaze.

Kai lit his second bottle and let it drop.

The people nearest the cathedral were shoved back by the horde fleeing Kai's flames, forcing them toward the sorcerers' battle.

The Lady Sorcerer pressed her palm to the front of her shield.

Kai tossed the third bottle beyond the balcony, striking the small bit of the street cleared by the fleeing crowd.

"Go, just go!" Kai lit the fourth bottle.

The frantic horde surrounded Isla and her two fellow sorcerers, blocking them from the Lady Sorcerer's view.

Kai lobbed his last bottle at the street and rammed the window shut, not giving himself time to watch Isla's fate.

He dodged through the discarded furniture in the storage room, bolting for the door, slamming it behind him as he raced down the servants' stairs, grateful the walls around him dampened the screams of the crowd.

The door at the bottom of the stairs had been left slightly open, just enough to give Kai a slit of light to see by. Shoving that door open, he ran across the hall, digging his fingers into the panel behind the portrait of Saint Dannach to wrench open the next door on his path.

He yanked that door shut behind him, choosing fumbling in the dark over being easily followed. The stairs to the back rooms on the main floor of the Gilded Hall were steep. Kai held his breath as he felt for each step, leaving his lungs burning by the time he reached the door at the bottom of the stairs.

He pushed the door open and stumbled out into the chaos.

Some of the crowd had managed to retreat into the Gilded Hall. The panicked people shoved their way down the corridor, looking for an exit to the far side of the building, away from the cathedral.

"This way," Kai shouted. "There's a door this way."

Keeping close to the wall, Kai barreled through the crowd, heading toward the third best private sitting room the Gilded Hall had to offer.

The door had already been opened and the panes in the window smashed, though no one but a small child could hope to fit through the crossbars.

Kai bolted to the closet in the back corner. Behind the rack for the patrons' coats, a heavy door had been set into the wall.

Someone crashed into Kai's back, sending him headfirst into the wood.

"Back up!" Kai screamed. "Step back."

Plastering himself against the door, he slid the bolt open and stumbled out onto the street, leaping to the side before he could be trampled.

He counted the people running past. Ten. Fifteen.

He joined behind the twentieth, blending into the horde as he escaped the terror in the cathedral square.

He should go back, look for Isla, make sure she'd had the sense to run.

Or head to the tunnels, make sure the others from the underground had made it to safety.

But his feet chose their own path, leading him on a winding route through the city, looping him around warehouses and burnt-out shops until he was sure he hadn't been followed.

Finally, he stopped in an alley. He leaned against the wall, panting, listening for any hint of Death racing toward him.

The streets around him had gone silent, like Ilara herself were holding her breath, waiting for the end to come.

His legs shook as he knelt and dug his fingers beneath the largest of the stones in the alley.

The pain in his hand and ribs sharpened as he lifted the stone, moving it aside just enough to squeeze into the hole beneath. He stopped four rungs down the ladder and dragged the stone back into place, shielding the sanctuary from the outside world.

He rested his forehead on the ladder, willing his lungs to keep dragging in air.

"Kai?" The most wonderful voice the gods had ever crafted came from behind him.

Kai stepped down from the ladder and turned around.

Drew.

A crutch under one arm, a knife in his hand, worried creases furrowing his brow.

"What happened?" Drew limped closer. "Are you hurt?"

"The world has gone to hell. Isla faced the Lady Sorcerer, and hundreds of people saw it. I have no idea what the sorcerers will do to stop word of the fight from spreading. They could flatten Ilara by morning."

Drew shut his eyes. "They wouldn't do that. There's no glory in reigning over ruins."

"We can't know how sorcerers think." Kai swallowed past the grating dryness in his throat. "If they're going to kill us all—"

"They won't."

"But if they do, I want to be with you when it happens." Kai dared to step forward. "If the gods are going to let the sky crumble on our heads, I want to be standing beside you when the end comes."

"Kai." The lines on Drew's brow deepened.

"I'm sorry I didn't come sooner. I'm sorry if you've entirely forgotten what was said while you were dying. And, worst of all, I'm sorry if this spoils our friendship forever. But the thing I want most in this world is to be with you, and I can't…" Kai looked down at the ground, searching for wisdom in the packed dirt.

Drew tucked his knife into his belt and held out his hand.

Kai reached forward, praying the world wouldn't end before he locked fingers with Drew.

A wave of comfort soothed Kai's heart as skin met skin. Drew's palm pressed against Kai's as he guided Kai closer.

"I'm sorry." Kai met Drew's gaze. "I'm so sorry."

Drew let go of his hand.

Kai's heart stopped then eased back into a peaceful rhythm as Drew touched his cheek, brushing his thumb across the soft skin beside Kai's eye.

"We face the sorcerers' wrath together," Drew said.

Kai stepped closer still, daring to touch Drew's hips as he carefully brushed his lips against Drew's.

An ecstatic bliss swept all thoughts of Death and horror aside as Drew wrapped his arm around Kai's waist, binding them together as one kiss became twenty and all Kai's questions became beautiful answers.

PART II

24

ENA

I have dreamt of peaceful lands, just rulers, and freedom from the tyranny of magic. Even as I fight for this hope, I know it is a future I am not meant to see.

I am forged by blood and death, buried so deep in the darkness my fate is bound to the monsters I must slay. I wish I could change my fate for you, but my path was set long before I held you in my arms.

A tiny babe with my mother's eyes and my brother's chin. Your veins carry my blood.

But you are not tethered to my tragedy.

You are untainted.

Your tiny hands should never learn to hold a sword. You should never know the pain of a blade slicing your flesh. You should never witness the kind of horror that brought you to this place.

You belong to a life of easy laughter, full bellies, and love that doesn't demand such a terrible price. You belong to a world filled with magnificent light.

I cannot follow you there.

I will not drag you into the darkness with me.

Your first cry destroyed me. Your second tethered fear to my heart.

I am grateful for the scars you've carved on my soul. They are proof that you are real. You are worth fighting for.

I will tear the Guilds apart piece by piece to protect you. I will slit every throat in Ilara and wade through seas of blood if there's even a chance of you living a life free of the monsters' rule.

I cannot belong to a world of light, sweet girl. But I will be the one to build it for you.

25

———

MARA

Faint strains of music filled the tense pause as Shantene stared down at their group.

Mara bit her lips together, clinging to Tham's hand as Shantene's silence stretched on.

"Three long, brutal, hours it took them to untie the knot the vengeful girl had twisted into his ensorcelled member. And when the bites and bruises were finally tallied, the only creature to make it out unharmed…was the original black-tailed snake!" Shantene spread her arms wide, accepting the laughter of the group sitting on the grass. "And that, young ones, is why the ban on personal acquisition of animal talents exists."

Mara tucked her face against Tham's arm in a poor attempt to hide her blush.

"I suppose all odd rules must have odd beginnings." Elver took Shantene's arm, escorting her to the lone chair at their picnic.

"And that's why ancient folk like me should be invited to more gatherings," Shantene said. "There's no written record of that debauchery. When I go, the tale goes with me."

"Not at all." Torra passed Shantene her cup of tea. "Now we know the tale and will carry it with us."

"A legacy," Shantene said dryly. "What I've always wanted."

"And you *would* be invited to more gatherings." Torra offered Shantene a plate of cakes. "But you've made it very clear you don't like people."

"She likes me," Elver said. "She came to the picnic because she likes me."

"I'll try not to be offended." Torra sat back down on her corner of the soft, oversized blanket.

"Well, I'm honored by your presence." Fergal nodded to Shantene. "Even if you're merely tolerating everyone but Elver."

Shantene shrugged, gaining another round of laughter from the group. Even Tham gave a low chuckle.

The sound of his laugh, soft as it was, washed an extra layer of joyful peace through Mara's soul.

A wonderful warmth that seemed to come from the sun in the clear blue sky kissed Mara's skin. Even knowing the sky was an illusion didn't detract from the beauty of the courtyard garden hidden deep in the passages of the nex.

Vines grew up the high stone walls, surrounding the space in green. The flowers blossoming in the beds around the edges of the garden filled the air with a luscious scent that somehow made the false sun feel brighter. A small fountain in one of the walls lent the soft rustle of water to the calm of the mysterious music whose origin Mara had yet to discover.

But it wasn't the garden, or the food, or even the company that had Mara bordering on giddy. It was the way Tham sat.

He'd watched Shantene tell her story without constantly glancing around to make sure no one could see his and Mara's fingers laced together. As they all laughed at Elle rolling in the grass, begging Fergal for attention, he rested his weight back on his free hand—a relaxed position that would cost him a heartbeat of movement if they were attacked.

Tham squeezed her hand.

Mara met his gaze, giving him a smile and a tiny shake of her head that sent a curl tumbling across her forehead.

"I wish I could meet the people in your stories." Elver sat beside Shantene, resting his head on her lap.

"I'm older than a clam." Shantene patted his cheek. "Most of my cohorts from my misspent youth are dead."

"Well, I'm glad you're not," Elver said.

"Right," Torra said in a too-bright tone. "Tales of catastrophic sex fetes entertain me, but if we're drifting toward the morose, I'd like a walk before the next course arrives."

"Next course?" Mara asked.

"Sweet, naïve Mara." Torra sighed. "When I plan a gathering, chamb and a ludicrous amount of cake are always involved. If you weren't in hiding, I'd throw a proper party instead of a picnic. Truly dazzle you with excess."

"When you've reached Shantene's"—Fergal raised his arm, blocking Elle's attempts to lick his face—"age, your stories will be worse than hers."

"Worse?" Shantene said.

"Careful, Fergal, or I'll permanently nix you from the guest list." Torra stood and reached for Mara. "Come walk with me."

Mara glanced to Tham.

He tightened his grip on Mara's hand, his posture stiffening as he sat forward.

"Don't worry, Tham," Torra said. "I promise I won't lose her."

"Of course you won't," Mara said. "There's only so far you can go in the nex."

"You would think that, wouldn't you?" Torra wrinkled her nose.

Mara twisted onto her knees and leaned close to Tham, brushing a kiss on his cheek before whispering, "I'm not going to disappear. Never again. I'll be right back."

She held his gaze as she kissed the back of his hand, making sure he'd heard her promise before letting go.

"Come along." Torra grabbed Mara's hand, yanking her to her feet. "I promise you'll love it. And, if you decide he'll like it, we can even show your stoic shadow later."

Torra winked at Tham and led Mara to the corner of the garden walls. "I do feel slightly guilty, showing you places you can't reach on your own."

"I'm a saelk in the Sorcerers Tower," Mara said. "Even if the tower would let me open doors, I still wouldn't be allowed to roam."

"I hate that for you, you know. It seems unfair for you to be trapped in the nex." Torra lifted the vines that grew up the wall aside. "That the Sorcerers Tower has a disused wing is bad enough. Restricting our guests to a glorified abandoned tunnel seems positively inhumane."

"For the good of Ilbrea." Mara waited for anger to twist in her gut, but no fury at her confinement came.

"Yes, yes, protect Ilbrea." Torra tapped on the stone wall. "Your nobility is exhausting."

"My apologies." Mara watched the stones, waiting for the moment the door would appear.

The mortar between the stones shifted, sinking away in places.

Torra rolled her eyes, as though peeved by the door's slow creation.

A long, vine-like handle grew out of the stone. By the time the handle had solidified, the mortar around the edges of the misshapen door had fully disappeared.

Torra grabbed the handle, leaning her weight back to open the door.

"Imagine the fun we'd have if you were a sorcerer," Torra said, without a hint of wonder in her voice. "You'd get to see so much more."

"It would be nice to see more of the tower than the nex and the overlook."

Mara stepped through the newly formed door and out onto a balcony. A cool wind swept around her, ruffling her curls. A mountain range, not unlike the eastern mountains, gave depth to the horizon, while a pond surrounded by reeds filled in the nearer part of the image.

"...than they ever could have managed." Torra's words crept through Mara's wonderment.

"Sorry, what did you say?"

Torra closed the door to the balcony. This side of the door matched the space—wood with cut glass windows looking in on a ballroom with a polished floor.

"Exploring the tower was one of my favorite pursuits as a child." Torra looped her arm through Mara's, leading her toward the balcony rail. "I'd wander for hours, trying to see if I'd been given permission to enter any new spaces."

"Wouldn't someone have told you?"

"Told me?" Torra frowned. "I suppose it would be harder for you to understand than the other oddities of the nex."

"Now I'm intrigued."

"Being able to roam the tower isn't a privilege granted by the Lady Sorcerer. It just sort of happens. By the will of the tower is what my mother always said, though I don't know if that biddy of a getch's word should be trusted on anything."

"How interesting." Heat rose in Mara's cheeks.

"Don't worry, I've said the same thing to her over breakfast." Torra let go of Mara and turned to perch on the balcony rail. "Mother and I have been at odds since I discovered the beauty of men. There's something about your mother flirting with the man you've just rolled that can truly turn your stomach."

"Oh." Mara's cheeks burned hotter.

"There's the blush that makes you so sweet." Torra laughed.

Mara pushed out a laugh, too, buying time to think of something to say.

"I'm done tormenting you," Torra said. "And don't worry, that lover has expertly avoided my mother since she caught me rolling him on her table in revenge."

The heat in Mara's face pushed all the way up to her forehead.

"The funniest part is, you don't know whether or not to believe me." Torra tapped Mara on the nose.

"I'm glad you find such delight in mocking me." Mara hopped up to sit on the balcony railing, twisting her legs to be over the open air, taking advantage of being able to hide her face behind her curls.

"Much to your benefit, I take more pleasure in seeing you happy than watching you blush. That's why I wanted to bring you here."

"It is a beautiful view." Mara looked down at the birds in the pond just in time to watch one dive beneath the water.

I don't even know if the birds are real.

"It's not actually the view I brought you here for," Torra said. "I've had a rather brilliant idea that I don't want Tham to hear."

A flutter of nerves raced through Mara's stomach.

"You're not going to ask me what it is?" Torra said.

"In all honesty, I'm a little afraid to."

"And that is how you know we've become true friends." Torra nudged Mara with her elbow. "Go on, ask."

"What is your brilliant idea?"

Torra twisted to face the mountains with more grace than Mara could have managed in long robes. She leaned forward, looking into Mara's eyes. "A boon."

"From me?"

"*For* you. You and Tham are so in love, it warms my shallow, jaded heart. Seeing you two together, how easy it is for you to devote yourselves to each other, it's a precious thing that shouldn't be hidden."

"It has been nice." A different sort of blush warmed Mara's cheeks. "Just being together without constantly worrying someone will see us and try to drive us apart or use him against me or have me thrown out of the Map Makers Guild…I never thought we'd have that."

"And after all you've done to protect Ilbrea—surviving the Ice Walkers, risking your lives to bring the Lady Sorcerer word of their intention to attack, staying huddled together in the absolute misery of the Sorcerers Tower, spending mornings in bed excising your nerves on Tham's—"

"Torra!"

"Fine," Torra sighed. "I only mean that after all you've done, Ilbrea and the Guilds owe you a boon. And what sort of monsters would the Guilds Council be if they didn't accept our heroes' request for an exemption from the map makers' chivving terrible rule about women map makers not being allowed to marry?"

"It's not that simple. The laws that govern the Map Makers Guild—"

"Are ridiculous?"

"Are rooted within the Map Makers Guild. And, even if Lord Karron wanted to make an exception and could gain the Guilds Council's approval, and it could be done without Lord Kearney punishing Tham for—"

"All the fabulous rolls he's given you?"

"—finding a way around the laws might not be possible. Not without Tham and me losing our places in the Guilds."

"Unless you convince the Guilds Council to grant you a boon."

"Torra—"

"With the Lady Sorcerer backing you, the council will be forced to grant your request. There's no way they could deny it without exposing themselves as heartless beasts in front of all Ilbrea."

Mara closed her eyes, allowing herself one moment to envision a proper life with Tham. A little house tucked in the Guilded section of the city. Another dog so Elle would have a companion.

"Even if it could work," Mara said, "and I'm not sure it would, we'd only have a chance if the council knew about the Ice Walkers. And the council will only find out about the Ice Walkers if they attack, which would force Lady Gwell to finally tell the rest of the council about the monsters in the north."

"Not necessarily."

"If you take away everything that's not allowed to be talked about, Tham and I haven't done anything worthy of the council granting us an audience, let alone a boon."

"So my brilliant plan only works if the Ice Walkers attack." The last of Torra's grin faded.

"I can't pin my dreams for a future with Tham on the hopes of thousands of people dying."

Torra wrapped her arm around Mara, guiding Mara's head onto her shoulder. "If the council knew how wonderful you are, they'd grant you a boon without the Ice Walkers."

"Thank you."

"Don't thank me yet. Wait until I come up with another plot to grant you and Tham the life you deserve."

A bird flew up from the pond, soaring toward the mountains on the horizon.

"Do you have an aversion to ensorcelled anatomy?"

"Torra!"

26

ADRIAL

The freezing wind whipped through Adrial's long coat, both deepening the pain in his hip and numbing the joint at the same time. Tightening his grip on the food-stuffed basket, he ducked his chin against a harsh northern gust and kept making his way across the library's courtyard.

"Are you sure you don't want me to carry the basket for you?" Tammin asked. "Or better yet, send one of the guards out to the square?"

"A little cold won't hurt me." Adrial nodded to the only other scribe crossing the courtyard, a young female apprentice whose loose hair kept wrapping around her face.

The girl stumbled into a bow then bolted for the door to the scribes' quarters.

"I am asking you not to do this," Tammin said after the door had closed behind the girl, as though Tammin had feared the apprentice hearing her over the wind.

"I have already fought both Lord Gareth and the scribes' guard. If they couldn't stop me from going to the square, you haven't a hope," Adrial said.

"The wind is too strong and too cold. No one will think less of you for staying inside in this weather."

"Tammin, I appreciate your concern more than you'll ever understand. But it is midafternoon, and I will take my walk to the square."

Tammin made a noise somewhere between a sigh and a growl. "Don't linger long. And go straight to your quarters once you've decided you're done freezing your nose off. I'll make sure there's a hot bath and tea waiting for you."

"Thank you." Adrial stopped just before the rows of scribes' guards flanking the library gates.

"Try not to lose any fingers. It would make your work on the vellum much more difficult." Tammin turned and hurried for the warmth of the library, abandoning Adrial in the courtyard.

"Going out?" Straff, a scribes' guard, stepped into Adrial's path.

"I've already been warned not to lose my fingers." Adrial smiled, cracking his wind-chafed lips. "Have your men been keeping warm enough?"

"Rotating them inside by the fires," Straff said. "Watch your step in the square, sir. There's a bit of ice."

"Thank you." Adrial nodded to Straff.

The guard backed out of Adrial's way, rejoining his fellows.

Most of the guards gave Adrial a glance as he carefully made his way through the gate, but none of them so much as muttered a word to stop him. They'd all become too accustomed to Adrial's routine.

Every afternoon, he made his way to the square. No matter the weather, no matter the wretched state of the city, the Head Scribe of Ilara would go and sit on the rim of the fountain for half an hour.

Adrial pulled his shoulders back and kept his chin up, letting the wind blast into his eyes as he passed the line of common folk waiting to deal with Scribe Gend.

Travers sat at his desk under the white awning, bundled up to a near-comical degree, with enough scarves wrapped around his neck to hide most of his scowl.

Adrial had sent two firepits out for the guards watching Travers. The added worth of placing them just far enough from Travers's desk that he couldn't feel any of the flames' warmth brought Adrial a jagged sort of satisfaction he felt no guilt for.

The line of common folk waiting for Travers's services was barely shorter than usual. Life in Ilara went on even when the wind itself seemed ready to punish the city.

Most of the common folk nodded to Adrial as he passed. A few even bowed. Not in the way they'd bow to the Lady Sorcerer, seeming to lower their heads for fear of decapitation, more as though they were greeting one of their own.

The mourning scribe who still wore black cuffs to honor the tilk wife the Guilds had stolen from him. The paun who sat among the common folk every afternoon as though they were the balm that kept him moving from one day to the next.

The man who ventured out to the square with an equal measure of terror and hope.

"Would you like an arm, sir?" A young boy, no older than twelve, trotted over. Though the child's coat was too big, and dirt stained his wind-burned cheeks, he still wore a genuine smile as he looked up at Adrial.

"I'm quite all right," Adrial said. "But, if you carry the basket to the fountain, I'll let you have first pick."

"Thank you, sir." The boy snatched the basket from Adrial, nearly knocking him over, and skipped to the fountain.

"Careful," Adrial called after him.

The boy didn't seem to hear. He was too busy digging through the treasures Adrial had brought with him.

A dozen other common folk surrounded the basket. The boy ducked free from the cluster, clutching an oversized bun to his chest.

"Thank you!" The boy waved and fled the square.

At least he'll have one meal today.

The sour taste of sick crept into Adrial's mouth.

I need to do more.

A wheelbarrow of food. He could ask one of the guards to bring it to the fountain. But more food would draw more hungry people to the square, and a horde might drive Lord Gareth to finally ban Adrial's afternoon excursions.

Lord Gareth hadn't yet hardened his heart enough to forbid the mourning husband from visiting the square, the one place Adrial found solace after the brutal loss of his wife. The scribes' guards had advised against Adrial leaving the library grounds. Even Lord Nevon had questioned the ritual.

But Lord Gareth declared that if going to sit with the common folk kept Adrial waking up every morning, then to the square he would go.

If dancing naked through the library made Adrial keep trudging onward, Lord Gareth probably would have allowed that, too.

By the time Adrial made it to the fountain, the basket was entirely empty.

"Thank you, Head Scribe," an older woman said through a mouthful of jerky.

A man with a cane bowed.

"Sir"—a little girl clutching two boiled eggs stepped into Adrial's path—"my brother's lungs haven't been right since the sickness ran through our folk in the fall, so he can't come out in the cold. May I take an egg for him and one for me? If I can only have one, I can give it to him, but I'd like to eat, too."

"Take them both," Adrial said. "And come back tomorrow. I'll bring a packet of spiced tea. It always helps my lungs feel better in the cold."

"Thank you!" The girl beamed at Adrial then ran for the

southern end of the square. She slipped on the ice, her feet flying out from under her, and landed flat on her back.

"Oh!" Before Adrial could step toward her, the girl had leapt to her feet, undamaged eggs in hand.

"She'll be fine."

A jolt of loathful relief surged through Adrial at the sound of the familiar voice.

"Children her age are hardy," the revenant said.

"Not if they're starving." Adrial glanced toward the fountain.

The revenant wore a black hat. His coat had a high collar that almost hid his scars.

Adrial sat on the fountain's rim, more than an arm's reach away from the revenant.

"Thank you for your kindness, Head Scribe." The older man with the cane reached for Adrial. His gap-toothed smile broadened as Adrial shook his hand. "Be careful of the cold. Ilara would be a sadder place without you in it."

"I promise to keep trying to do more," Adrial said.

The revenant huffed a low laugh, but didn't speak again as Adrial accepted the thanks, well wishes, and continued condolences from the common folk.

In a way, Adrial was grateful for the cold seeping into his boots, numbing his toes. The sensation distracted from the normal, blood-freezing chill the revenant always dripped into Adrial's veins.

A fickle demon, the revenant would show himself, make his demand, and disappear, like a ghost flickering in and out of being. Sometimes returning the next day. Sometimes waiting weeks to reappear, leaving Adrial with an ever-growing terror that he may never see the man again.

The revenant had disappeared for a month near the solstice. Adrial had stopped being able to hold down food from the worry churning in his stomach. After Lord Gareth had foisted a healer's care upon Adrial, the ghost flashed back into being, demanding Adrial's aid.

Once the rest of the common folk had left, hopefully going someplace warm, a young girl of no more than sixteen stepped toward Adrial, keeping her gaze pinned on his boots.

"Excuse me, Head Scribe," the girl said.

"Yes?" Adrial fought to keep his voice light, knowing the revenant was feet from him. Bearing either joy or torture, the demon was there.

"I was asked to come by the other girls in my shop." The girl bobbed a curtsy. "The shop was, well…it was raided by the sorcerers last night. The building is still there, but the shopkeeper and all the fabrics are gone."

"The building is undamaged but the supplies were taken?" Adrial asked.

"Yes, sir," the girl said. "But the trouble is we, the girls and me, we're under contract, sir. We have to work at the shop or a fine can be called against our families."

"Was that contract approved by a scribe?" Adrial said.

"I don't know, sir. But if there's no shopkeeper, and there's no fabric to sew, then there's no work, so there's no coin to be earned. None of us know what to do, and I thought, since you're the head scribe, maybe you would know."

Adrial shut his eyes, pushing down the anger-filled rant he longed to spew.

"One of you come here at this time tomorrow with a copy of this contract," Adrial said. "I'll have a look at it myself."

"Thank you, sir." The girl finally looked up at Adrial. "Truly. Thank you."

"You might want to limit your gratitude until I've read the papers," Adrial said. "But whatever they say, I'll figure out the best path forward for you and your friends."

"Thank you, sir." The girl gave a teary-eyed smile. "And I'm not being too grateful. Just the head scribe saying he'll help means the world."

She curtsied again, gave a little wave, and hurried out of the square.

"The head scribe, savior to dress shop girls," the revenant said. "Your time would be better spent with your hands around the Lady Sorcerer's neck."

"If I thought I had a chance, believe me, I'd try it." Adrial balled his gloved hands into fists before asking the dreaded question. "Where is my wife?"

"Safe."

"Safe where?" The familiar ache rose in Adrial's chest.

"Where you've no chivving chance of finding her."

Adrial leaned into the pain, rounding forward, not allowing himself to scream.

"I have more work for you," the revenant said.

"Let me see her first." Adrial squeezed the words past the tightness in his throat.

"That's not how this works. Do as I say, or I'll never come back. It's that simple."

"Please, if you'll only—"

"Do you want me to keep coming back or not?"

"Yes." Hot tears slid down Adrial's cheeks. "Of course, yes. Just tell me what you want."

"Your map makers. There's a rumor they found a path through the mountains. Is it true?"

"The eastern mountains?"

"Is it true?" Anger tinged the revenant's voice.

"Not a whole path," Adrial said. "They found a possible route, but the map maker was killed."

"And their map?"

"Brought back by the survivors of the journey. It was badly damaged, but the Map Makers Guild was able to restore most of it."

The revenant muttered something Adrial couldn't hear.

The pain in Adrial's chest wound around his heart, making it seem impossible for it to keep beating.

"Destroy the map," the revenant said.

"What?"

"Destroy the map. I'll be back to confirm it's been done." The revenant moved to stand.

"I can't." Adrial reached for the man.

"Eyes chivving front." The revenant stood and tipped forward, as though he'd slid on the ice, before thumping back down onto the rim of the fountain. "There is no can't."

"But I can't. I truly can't." Panic shook Adrial's words.

"Then you'll never hear word of your wife again."

"Please, no. You have to understand—"

"That you've decided you're better off without your rotta wife and the child she swears you've claimed?"

"Copies of the map have been made." Adrial dug his fist into his bad hip, praying the pain would keep him from slipping into an all-consuming panic. "The King, Lady Gwell, Lord Nevon, Lord Gareth—they all have a copy, and that's just to start. Even if I could get those copies back, and the original and the official record from the Map Makers' Hall, there's no way to know how many other copies have been made.

"The families of those who died on the journey, map maker apprentices, merchants favored by the King—the map has gone out into the world, and not even Dudia could steal it back. I'm sorry. I'm so sorry. You have to believe that if I could do it, I would. Give me another task, ask me for gold, but please, please don't disappear."

Adrial's lungs froze, not letting him breathe as he waited for the revenant to vanish.

The revenant finally spoke. "Four copies of the map, brought to me in two days."

Freezing air swooped back into Adrial's lungs. "Thank you."

"There's four names." The revenant tossed a paper-wrapped rock at Adrial's feet. "Add them to the list of sailors working at the docks."

"Please don't attack the sailors." The edges of Adrial's panic curled with guilt. "There are common folk on the ships and working the docks. There are innocent tilk."

"Two days, paun."

The revenant stood and walked calmly away, leaving Adrial with the growing fear that the ghost would never return and a fervent prayer to Dudia that no sailors would pay for Adrial's betrayal of the Guilds.

27

NIKO

Glyn's gasp from the far corner only brought Niko a slight surge of annoyance as Amec smashed his sword across Niko's back, sending him stumbling forward with a throb of pain that promised to be a chivving impressive bruise within the hour.

Niko let his sword droop as he pivoted back toward Amec then slashed his blade up, deflecting Amec's attack with a satisfying clang.

Glyn gasped again.

"Good!" Amec took a step back, releveling his sword.

Niko leapt to the side, dodging Amec's attack on his hip. Lunging, he drove his own blade toward Amec's stomach.

Amec knocked Niko's blade aside and leapt forward, pressing his sword to Niko's throat.

Glyn clapped.

Danu gave Glyn a sideways glare.

"Better." Amec clapped Niko on the shoulder.

"I'm still dead." Niko set his sword on the rock ledge where Danu and Glyn sat, the sole thing feigning comfort in their makeshift training room.

"But," Amec said, "I had to sweat to kill you. I'm a Guilded

Soldier. You're a map maker. Me having to work to win is impressive."

"Not impressive enough." Danu tossed Niko an already sweat-dampened rag to dry his face.

"We'll go again," Niko said.

"Such dedication." Glyn grinned, her dazzle-eyed gaze fixed on Amec.

"Even dedicated students take time to improve and need a moment to rest." Amec set down his sword and tossed Niko a waterskin.

"A moment," Danu said. "Then back to it."

Niko sank to the ground, choosing leaning against the ledge over sitting on it with the others.

The chill of the stone barely bled through the back of his leather coat, a garment which simultaneously offered a modicum of protection from Amec's sword while also making him sweat like a scribe with stained fingers.

But the purpose of the coat was neither warmth nor protection.

A bird matching the mark on his back had been stitched onto the black leather. The coat, paired with the black pants, black boots, and meticulously cut hair, completed his poor attempt at linking himself to the glory of Ena, playing the role of a worthy companion to the pinnacle of Black Blood strength—the true Solcha.

Worthy of being the second Solcha.

The Solcha who'd never win a fight.

The Solcha you'd rather follow into a tavern than into battle.

Niko glanced to the wooden door of their practice space, waiting for Ena to storm in, the perfect image of a dark warrior chosen by the mountain, come to prove Niko's unworthiness once and for all.

"Ready?" Amec said.

"Not yet." Glyn gripped his arm.

A smile devoured Amec's face as he settled in next to her.

"I'll do it if you insist on clinging to each other." Danu stood.

"One more minute," Niko said. "I want to be sure I've properly catalogued all the places Amec's left bruises before you add to the tapestry."

"Or you could be done for the day," Glyn said. "Leave these forgotten burrows and go back up to Amec's room."

Amec's face flushed.

Niko busied himself drinking from the waterskin.

"We could have some frie." Glyn kissed Amec's cheek. "Toast the happy news. Dream of the day the mountain blesses the stronghold with another babe of Ilbrean blood."

A spray of water flew from Niko's mouth. "Wh—what?" He choked on the question. "Are you two having a baby?"

"No!" Amec's spine straightened. His face lost all color. "I mean—"

"Not now, of course." Glyn giggled. "But someday. Maybe."

Glyn blushed as she batted her eyes at Amec.

Amec melted, his face losing all trace of fear as he stared into Glyn's eyes. "Someday."

Niko leaned back against the ledge, looking up at the ceiling rather than watch Amec turn into a completely witless, love-drunk getch.

Babes.

A Guilded soldier melting over tiny mewling monsters.

"Wait." Niko sat up, pushing away from the wall enough to properly look at the other three. "You said another Ilbrean babe."

"Solcha had her baby last night," Glyn said. "The servants' hall was bursting with the news."

"Ena had her baby, and no one told me?" Niko stood, rounding on Danu. "Did you know?"

"Of course," Danu said. "I didn't think to mention it."

"Why not?" Niko said.

"I didn't think you'd care," Danu said.

"Didn't think I'd care?" Niko shoved his sweat rag into his pocket and tossed the waterskin to Amec. "Did it—I mean, are they well?"

"Solcha's well, of course," Glyn said. "The mountain protected her."

"But the baby," Niko said. "What about the baby?"

"Take a breath, Niko," Amec said.

"I'm chivving well breathing!" Niko's voice bounced around the stone chamber.

"The babe is healthy." Danu stood, reaching palm up for Niko, slowly stepping toward him as though he'd been more panicked than he'd thought. "Ena and the baby both came through fine."

A stone of fear yanked out of Niko's gut, freeing a wave of joy that brought instant tears to his eyes.

"You're all right, Niko." Danu laid her hand on his cheek. "Everything's all right."

"Adrial's a father." Niko pulled Danu to his chest, holding her close as laughter joined his tears. "Adrial Ayres has a son."

"A daughter." Danu didn't try to break free as she looked up at him. "If you dare to seem disappointed—"

"Adrial has a daughter?" A fresh round of tearful laughter shook Niko's chest. "She'll be more doted on than any little girl in all Ilbrea."

"She's not in Ilbrea." Glyn stood, tugging on Amec's arm to make him stand beside her. "Solcha's daughter is a Black Blood. The baby's place is in the stronghold. Isn't it, Amec?"

Amec's face lost all its color again.

"But Adrial is in Ilbrea," Niko said.

"Solcha is beloved by the mountain." Glyn glared down her nose at Niko. "She has no need for a paun husband."

"Glyn, that's not fair," Amec said.

Ever so slowly, Glyn turned her glare on Amec.

"I just mean—"

Glyn raised her eyebrows in an impressive look of warning.

"I was born in Ilbrea." Amec took Glyn's face in his hands, softly kissing her brow. "If the mountain knows love well enough to protect the Black Bloods as her children, surely the mountain can understand that some human hearts are meant to bind together no matter where their ancestry lies."

Glyn fell into Amec's arms, viciously attacking his mouth with hers.

Niko glanced to Danu.

Wide-eyed, she bit her lips together and eased out of Niko's arms, backing toward the entrance of the chamber.

Niko crept after her, abandoning his practice sword in favor of a silent escape.

Danu made it to the worn wooden door first.

The bolt slid silently aside, moved by her magic. She pressed the door open, wincing as the hinge creaked.

"Are we done for the day?" Amec said.

Niko spun to face him, using the movement as an excuse to take another step toward escape.

Amec had his arm around Glyn's waist, facing Niko as though he hadn't been about to rip the girl's clothes off. Or skip taking her clothes off and make do with a raised skirt.

"Well"—Niko took another step back—"now that I know Ena's had the baby, I really should visit."

"You can't visit," Glyn said. "Solcha's just been through labor."

"The child is as good as my niece," Niko said. "Adrial's not here to care for his wife and daughter. What sort of beast would I be if I didn't at least check to make sure they didn't need anything?"

"Perhaps a nice letter." Danu took Niko's arm, guiding him through the doorway. "Have it delivered today and ask when she'd be up for a visit."

"That's a grand idea." Amec grabbed both swords from the ledge. "I won't lie and say I know the head scribe, but he's always seemed a good man."

"One of the very best," Niko said.

Amec stepped around Glyn to pass Niko his sword.

Glyn dug into her own pockets, pulling out the hat and wide scarf Amec had been given to wear as a condition of his being allowed to leave the confines of Paiman's rooms to help train Niko. She wrapped the scarf around Amec's neck and planted a kiss on the tip of his nose before settling the hat onto his head.

"Pity to hide such a well-made chin." Glyn sighed.

Amec's eyes crinkled as he smiled.

"May we go now?" Danu said.

"Of course." Glyn kissed Amec's nose again, then abandoned him, cutting around Niko to grab Danu's arm.

Danu's cheeks tensed into something Glyn didn't seem to notice wasn't a smile.

"Once spring comes, can you find the men a place to practice that's outside," Glyn asked. "Somewhere in the woods where we can watch while sitting in the trees. Wouldn't that be lovely?"

Niko held his breath, waiting for Danu to draw one of the knives at her hips.

"Yes, Glyn," Danu said. "I'll be sure to find the boys a nice place to practice pricking each other."

"Perfect." Glyn kept her arm through Danu's as she pulled her along, spewing a non-stop stream of prattle.

"It's nice to see them getting on so well," Amec said.

"Certainly is." Niko shoved his dulled sword through his belt, trying not to laugh at the way Danu's shoulders kept creeping closer to her ears.

"And you and Danu?" Amec slid the bolt on the door, shutting the practice room.

"What about us?" Niko asked.

"Us." Amec clapped Niko on the back. "I like to hear that from you."

"That's not what I meant." Niko glanced down the corridor.

Danu and Glyn had passed around the corner of the roughly hewn passage. "There is no *us*."

"Of course not." Amec started down the tunnel, keeping to a pace that would let the women get even farther in front of them. "But there should be."

"She's my keeper."

"And?"

"And I'm a prisoner." Niko wiped the fresh sweat from his brow.

"So am I," Amec said.

"Glad to hear you admit it."

"Who locks my door at night doesn't keep me from wanting to sleep beside Glyn. I'm in love with her, Niko."

"Amec—"

"I want to marry her."

Niko watched the shadows of the hall shift as they passed from the light of one lae stone to the next.

"You think it's madness," Amec said.

"And you're wise enough not to say that as a question," Niko said.

"I love her."

"Then you can't marry her." Niko gripped the hilt of his sword. "Break it off with her and be done."

"But she loves me, too."

"And will she love sleeping all her nights locked in your room? In bed with a husband who's not supposed to exist?" Niko stepped in front of Amec and stopped. "If she gets pregnant, who will she say is the father of her child? She couldn't tell anyone it was yours. That's no life for her, you, or a child."

"We'll find a way to get me out of that room." Amec took Niko by the shoulders. "She's already started teaching me everything I need to know to pass as a Black Blood. We can tell people I lived in the wilds of the mountains. Or left another clan to join the Brien. Or—"

"You really want to spend the rest of your life here?" Niko took a step back.

"More than I've ever wanted anything." A smile lit Amec's face. "The stronghold is beautiful. I've found a woman to love."

"And what about Ilbrea? What about your place in the Soldiers Guild and wanting to be a part of map making journeys? What about your chivving family?"

Amec's smile faltered. "My family already thinks I'm dead."

"That doesn't mean you get to stop fighting to get back to them!"

"But they'd want me to stay here. In Ilara, the best I could hope to provide a wife is a cheap set of rooms and enough coin to feed our children."

"Amec—"

"Soldiers aren't like map makers," Amec said. "There are, how many, a thousand of us for each one of you? More probably. I don't have a life of ease and glory in Ilbrea."

Niko opened his mouth to argue. A wave of guilt rolled through his gut as he found he had nothing to say.

"Glyn has good work here," Amec said. "With how many men have been hurt or lost in the Hayes siege, a healthy man can earn a fine living with the Brien. We can raise our children in a cottage in the most beautiful place I've ever seen."

"If they'll let you be anything more than a prisoner."

"It'll all work out. We fell into the black and found our way to paradise."

Niko's heart sped. Dread and terror raked down his spine as the memory of the horrible, unending darkness filled his mind.

"If we can make it out of that hell, I can find my way from a room in the cliffs to a cottage in the woods." Amec showed no hint of panic. "Whatever it takes to build a life with Glyn is worth it. Please be happy for me."

Love strong enough to dampen the nightmares of the darkness below the mountain.

A miracle born of terror.

Niko took Amec's shoulders. "You can't ask me to be happy for you until you've asked Glyn to marry you." Niko gave Amec a gentle shake as red flooded Amec's cheeks. "Get the girl to say yes, and we'll celebrate with more frie than men should ever dare consume."

"I'll ask her." Amec nodded. "I'll ask her tonight."

"Maybe not." Niko wrapped his arm around Amec's shoulders, guiding the lovesick slitch down the corridor. "The Black Bloods have godsforsaken rules for doing all sorts of things. Better to find out how you're supposed to ask her to marry you than risk mucking up your marriage before it begins."

"Then I'll ask Paiman tonight." Amec nudged Niko in the side. "And I'll pass the information on to you. In case Solcha ever gives in and realizes happiness is a dark-haired warrior with knives on her hips and stone in her blood."

28

KAI

"—and if that weren't bad enough, the only ones in Ilbrea who believe the truth are mocked." Drew took a deep breath, a rare pause in his rant. "Massive attack, hundreds of witnesses—by all measure a chivving success for the underground—toss in Isla turning up to give a display of non-Guilded magic the likes of which I've never even chivving heard of, not even from a drunken slitch telling tales in a tavern, and the only point that seems less than ideal is Arto being killed. Which I really don't view as too much of a loss as he did plan on murdering us."

"Even someone who wanted to kill us doesn't deserve that sort of death." Kai peered down both possible paths in the tunnel before going left, where the reach of his lantern showed no hint of recent travel.

"But somehow, *somehow*," Drew carried on, "the chivving Sorcerers Guild smoothed the whole chivving thing out."

"I know."

"How sodding spineless are Ilarans that when the Lady Sorcerer lies, outright chivving lies, and says even the sorcerer who took an arrow to the chest is doing just fine, as though he'd nicked his chivving finger, the common folk just nod and agree?"

"I know." Kai took a deep breath, scenting the tunnel, checking to be sure there was nothing particularly distasteful down their chosen path.

"And then Isla. Isla." Drew's voice dropped low, booming as he emphasized her name. "The chivving, demonic, hell-tainted nerve of putting out whispers that Isla is one of the Lady Sorcerer's minions digs coals through my chivving gut. I can barely think of it without wanting to breathe fire."

"Then I shan't mention it."

"And I know we've got to keep pushing onward with our fouled-up revolt, even though we've spent months spinning in circles and have yet to take a sodding step forward."

"If we give up—"

"There's no one left to fight against the chivving sorcerers."

Drew's footsteps stopped following Kai.

Kai turned around and leaned against the dirt-and-stone wall.

"I don't want to give up." Drew dragged his fingers through his beard. "I'd never suggest rolling over and handing the sorcerers control of the rest of the Guilds. But they just ignored what happened in the square. No one punished, no extra raids, so the whole thing's been played down to soldiers being killed by rebels."

"Because all soldiers are incompetent."

"And every spark of magic in the square was done at the Lady Sorcerer's will."

"Of course. Didn't you know there's no such thing as magic outside the Lady Sorcerer's control? And, since saelk can't so much as bruise a sorcerer, not even by lodging an arrow in their chest, Ilarans are still convinced it's impossible to fight the purple demons." Kai nodded for Drew to follow him farther down the tunnel.

"The things is"—Drew didn't move—"I can't think of a way to actually stand against the Sorcerers Guild."

"That's why we're here." Kai reached for Drew's hand. "A

change in our subterranean view to inspire new plots to overthrow the magical beasts."

Drew stared at Kai for a moment before stepping forward to take his hand. "How do we fight a beast we can't find?"

"We know right where the monsters are." Kai laced his fingers through Drew's and kissed the back of Drew's hand. "Though, admittedly, the fact that they've stopped stomping around, destroying buildings and killing Ilarans, and have instead chosen the route of making people disappear in the middle of the night, as though the darkness itself had swallowed them, has made our attacking the sorcerers more difficult."

Kai started down the tunnel again.

Drew took five steps before stopping…again.

"Killing a sorcerer in the square was meant to prove to the people that we can fight back," Drew said. "To rally Ilarans to join the underground's cause."

"That was the intent when we planned the thing."

"Instead, we've got people vanishing in the night. Folks are even more afraid of the sorcerers now."

"We'll stop here then." Kai let go of Drew's hand to shrug out of his pack.

"The only way I can think to prove to people that the sorcerers can be killed is to march a sorcerer into every home in Ilara and slit their chivving throat."

"While that would be enjoyable, I don't think anyone but the gods could manage it." Kai knelt and pulled the sheet of old sail canvas from his pack.

"Then what plan are we supposed to bring to Lord Nevon?" Drew pressed his palms into the dirt of the wall.

Kai unfolded the canvas.

"Not a siege on the tower. Not a direct attack. We could try to kidnap one of the sorcerers still patrolling the docks, but they're always surrounded by soldiers, and I won't propose sacrificing soldiers to try and right the sorcerers' evil."

"You're a good man." Kai spread the canvas out on the ground.

"Of all the chivving awful ideas I've had, there are only two that hold any ground."

Kai sat on the canvas, leaning back on his hands. "What's the first?"

"We move everyone out of Ilara and abandon the sorcerers to their own evil devices."

"Not the most practical, but I won't test the gods by saying we'll never fall that far." Kai reached forward and took Drew's hand, drawing him to sit. "And the second?"

"We find Isla." Drew thumped down onto the ground.

"Before or after we tell Lord Nevon we forgot to mention we met a lovely, powerful, and incredibly dangerous red-haired sorcerer while we were captured, aided, then almost killed by the Brien during our little stroll from Pamerane?"

"We should have told him before." Drew buried his face in his hands.

"No. Don't you dare." Kai twisted to kneel, pulling Drew's hands away from his face. "Telling Lord Nevon wouldn't have changed anything that's happened."

"It would if we could find Isla and convince her to help us. With her fighting for the underground, we might do some actual good instead of just hiding in the tunnels, hoping an opportunity to attack lands on our heads."

Kai froze.

"One saelk on one sorcerer—if the coins fall right, the saelk could survive. But a city of saelk against a Guild of Sorcerers? I can't think of any options but spending generations picking them off or just chivving leaving." Drew furrowed his brow, distorting his face in the lamplight. "With someone like Isla on our side, maybe we'd have a mouse's tit of a chance. Or at least some new information for us to wrap ourselves in while we spin endlessly around in circles."

"You'd have made a good ship's captain." Kai kissed Drew's palm.

Drew didn't seem to notice. "In a far-off land."

"And I don't think finding Isla is a bad plan, but I don't know how we'd do it. Not without proclaiming the existence of the Black Bloods and the sorci children the Brien have been saving from the Sorcerers Guild. If word of the Brien safe haven leaked out, we'd have endangered the lives of a few hundred innocent children. I don't know if that's a weight either of us could bear."

The wrinkles in Drew's brow deepened.

Kai leaned forward and brushed a kiss on Drew's forehead. "But at least finding Isla without involving the Brien is a new problem to stew on."

"Finding a ghost would be better than fighting a sorcerer." The wrinkles on Drew's brow grew deeper still. "Finding where the Brien are hiding without making this chivving mess worse may well be impossible, but if we could find a way to let Isla know we're hunting for her, we might be able to make her come to us."

"That could work." Kai kissed Drew's temple.

"Not here, of course. We'd have to send her somewhere else, away from the tunnels so the underground isn't exposed. But if we could get her attention, having her on our side would be better than any of Latchy's horrors."

"No one could deny that." Kai kissed Drew's other temple.

"We will have to tell Lord Nevon. Not about all of it, not yet anyway, but at least why we were trying to find someone. He might shit himself, but I don't think he'd fight us on finding Isla. She's too valuable."

"Valuable she is." Kai took Drew's hands, setting them on his hips.

"It's not a plan I like. I won't become the beast exposing the Brien's sorci children to danger, but it is something different to bring Lord Nevon, and that's better than we've managed in a long while."

"A change of scenery can work wonders for the mind."

"It's late enough there should be a runner who can go to him." Drew moved to stand up.

"Later." Kai planted his hands on Drew's shoulders, pushing him back against the wall. "Your brilliant plan can wait an hour."

Kai kissed Drew, daring him to stand up and run away.

The tension in Drew's body melted as Kai teased his lips apart.

He unbuttoned Drew's shirt, stealing access to the undeniable contours of the muscles on Drew's chest.

Drew pulled Kai closer, taking Kai's weight in his arms, balancing their strength as Kai used his lips to explore Drew's flesh, letting himself drown in ecstasy before meeting the next battle.

29

ADRIAL

Adrial dripped white wax onto the parchment, sealing the scroll.

"It's not the worst proposition I've seen." Tammin laid the poorly drawn sketch in front of Adrial. A high-arching footbridge leading up and over the city wall was the highlight of the image, with other figures marking the placement of the two existing entrances to Ilara.

A little note at the bottom of the page read, *In case of attack on city, shove bridge over.*

"Creating a path into the city solely for those on foot would lessen the strain on the soldiers at the gates," Tammin said.

A kitchen girl ducked in through the open door of Adrial's office, clutching the basket for his daily sojourn in the square.

"Smoothing the flow of goods into the city would be ideal," Adrial said, "but the hazards of an added entrance would have to be considered by Lord Kearney before I'd dare bring any hint of a footbridge to the Guilds Council."

"Shall I have the letter sent to the Lord Soldier?" Tammin asked.

The soft sounds of the girl fussing with the contents of the basket filled the moment while Adrial thought.

"Leave the letter with me," Adrial said. "I'll discuss it with Lord Gareth, make sure he agrees before sending it on."

"Yes, Head Scribe." Tammin gave Adrial a nod and stepped through the door, keeping her hand on the handle to close it behind the kitchen girl.

The girl kept fussing with the basket.

Tammin cleared her throat.

The girl jolted and looked to Tammin, who widened her eyes, tipping her head to shoo the girl from the room.

"Sorry." The girl barely spoke above a whisper. "Just need one more moment."

"Of course," Adrial said. "Take your time."

Tammin closed the door to the outer office with a sharper than normal click.

The girl jolted again.

Adrial checked his stamp on the wax seal.

"Sir." The girl turned toward Adrial, placing herself between him and the basket.

"Yes?" He watched the girl, waiting for her to speak or, from the way her eyes darted around the room as she chewed her lips together, faint from panic. He stood, readying himself to catch her. "Are you all right?"

"Yes, sir." The girl winced. "Well, I hope, sir. I know I shouldn't speak out of turn, Head Scribe, but I'm not sure what else to do."

"Well"—Adrial angled his chair, offering the girl his seat—"I can't speak for your situation exactly, but if I didn't know what to do, I'd like to think coming to me might be a good place to start muddling through."

The girl gave a strained sigh of a laugh but didn't sit.

"Are you concerned about something happening in the kitchens?" Adrial asked. "Have you been mistreated?"

"No, sir. I have a very good job at the library."

"I'm pleased to hear that."

"I'm very grateful to have work with the Scribes Guild, and I'd never want to endanger my place here. But I'm afraid to not say anything, in case…well, in case I'm not being a spooked slitch." The girl clapped her hands over her mouth, a look of pure terror in her eyes.

Adrial clenched his teeth to swallow his laugh. "My brothers by home spent their childhoods at sea. I promise, I've heard far worse before breakfast many times."

The girl lowered her hands enough to speak. "Thank you for your forgiveness, sir."

"No forgiveness needed. Just tell me what's made you wonder if you're being a spooked slitch?"

The fear on the girl's face melted just a bit. "It's, sir—I can't—well, I mean, it's nothing."

"Nonsense. Whatever your worry, I'm sure it's important."

"No, I mean truly nothing, sir." The girl stepped closer to Adrial. "I haven't seen any new burned homes or knocked-over shops in weeks."

"I'd think that would be a relief after all Ilara's suffered."

"It is. But even though there haven't been more buildings wrecked, there was still rubble. Half-burned walls and toppled stones and such."

"Inevitable scars created by wretched violence."

The girl's leg started trembling, her heel tapping against the floor. "Now, there's just nothing. Ruins cleaned away, and a coat of ice and snow filling the bare patches as though it's been that way all winter. I first noticed it a few days ago where the cobbler's shop used to be along my walk to the library. I've spotted four more empty places since."

"In just a few days?" Adrial furrowed his brow.

"Yes, sir. There are no boot prints from men dragging things away either. It's like nothing ever happened, and it feels like something scary, but I don't know who I'm supposed to tell about *nothing*."

"You're wrong." Adrial pushed his worry behind a kind smile. "You knew exactly who to bring this to, and I'm grateful you did. Do you know how to write?"

"Yes, sir." The girl gave her first true smile. "Almost all the folk working in the library are taught, no matter their position. One of the reasons I'm lucky to have my job."

Adrial tucked the information behind his still-growing worry.

"My apprentice Taddy is in the outer office. Ask him for parchment, pen, and ink. On your walk home tonight, try to memorize what ruins have been cleared. Don't go off your usual path, don't touch anything, and don't tell anyone what you're doing. Write down what you remember tonight and bring it with you when you deliver my basket tomorrow."

"Thank you, Head Scribe." The girl curtsied. "For believing me, I mean."

"Thank you for being so observant. And I promise, your work will be compensated."

The girl bit her lips together and looked at the office door. "If you think I did a good job, could I maybe keep the pen and ink? To write down anything else I notice. I don't actually have a proper pen of my own, sir."

"Of course. And as a gift, not payment."

"Thank you, sir." The girl hurried toward the door.

"And your name?" Adrial asked. "If you're to bring me information, I should be sure you're given the daily task of delivering my basket."

"Tege, sir." The girl curtsied again, then opened the door and dodged into the outer office, as though afraid Adrial would change his mind and forbid the poor child from keeping a pen.

Adrial looked down at his desk. A row of Ena's inks waited to one side and parchment of the highest quality to the other. His chosen pens were of the best make as well.

"A child thrilled to own a pen." Adrial shook his head.

He'd survived the horrors of Ian Ayres to be dropped into the wonders of the Map Master's Palace. He'd either wanted for the barest scraps of food, or nothing.

Try as he may, Adrial wasn't sure he'd ever truly understand living in the middle.

Compassion can be just as valuable as understanding, Allora whispered.

Perhaps one day I can do better.

Adrial took his heavy coat from the wall, focusing on the well-practiced routine, taking the time to put on his gloves and scarves before tucking the sealed scroll into his pocket. His heart skipped up into his throat as his fingers grazed the second, thicker, tightly rolled scroll.

Yanking his hand from his pocket as though scorched by the parchment, Adrial grabbed his basket and hurried to the outer office.

Tammin glared at him from behind her desk, seeming to count the number of scarves around his neck before leaning side-ways to be sure he'd put on both his gloves.

Adrial let his gaze slide around the office, pausing on each of his scribes, doing his best to feign boredom as he waited for Tammin to finish her examination.

With a sigh and shake of her head, Tammin went back to work, leaving Adrial to cut through the office and out into the corridor.

He anchored his focus on the weight of the basket in his hand. Heavy, grounding, tangible—a normal part of his routine. His mind drifted to the pockets of his coat.

The scent of the food in the basket.

No, that couldn't hold his mind either.

The proposal for the footbridge.

The disappearance of the rubble.

His mind snapped back to his pockets.

Dudia, grant me poise.

Adrial tightened his grip on the basket and stepped out into the courtyard.

The wind had lost some of its bite, and the sunshine gave a welcome reprieve from the cold. Even the guards at the gate, though all of them stood stoically alert, seemed to hold less visceral tension.

Relaxing his shoulders, Adrial tried to match the calm of the guards, nodding to the ones he recognized as he approached the gate.

Straff stepped out of his place to greet Adrial. "Sir, there's still ice in the square. If you'd like a guard to accompany you—"

"Thank you, but I'm fine on my own."

"It's slicker than wet marble out there."

"I'm sure one of the guards will notice if I fall." Adrial tried to give the words a humorous tone. "If the need arises, feel free to drag me back inside. I promise I won't fight you."

Straff hesitated for a moment. "Please be careful, sir."

"Thank you." Adrial stepped around Straff and continued forward, not taking a full breath until he'd passed through the gates.

The line for Travers's services stretched longer than usual, and Travers's guards still had the firepits just too far away for him to benefit from their heat.

Petty pride in Travers's discomfort distracted Adrial for all of ten steps.

"Head Scribe!" A cluster of six children charged toward Adrial with hope lighting their eyes.

"Careful on the ice!" Adrial called as three of the children skidded, somehow keeping on their feet in a very Kai-like way.

One took each of his arms, in a supposed attempt to steady him, while two more took his basket and the rest pranced in front of him like eager young pups.

Ten feet from the fountain, his two helpers abandoned him to dig into the basket before the older among the gathered had a chance.

A girl stepped around the cluster and curtsied to Adrial. "Head Scribe, I don't want to be a bother, sir, but—"

"I have the papers for you right here." Adrial pulled the sealed scroll from his pocket. "A dispensation for you and the other girls from your shop to seek work elsewhere until the shop owner to whom you're contracted returns to business."

"And if the shop doesn't ever reopen?" The girl took the parchment from Adrial and cradled it to her chest.

"Then you'll never hear any more of the contract. Though, if your employer does return, please inform me. There are several points within the contract I would like to personally discuss with them."

"Yes, sir." The girl beamed at Adrial as she curtsied. "Thank you, sir."

She ran away, departing in the same direction as the first two times she'd come to Adrial.

"Thank you, Head Scribe," a child with a mouthful of bread said.

"Thanks, sir." An older woman gave Adrial a nod.

He accepted their thanks as graciously as he could, waiting until the crowd had cleared before taking his usual seat. He pulled the basket right beside him, making himself wait a moment before looking around the square.

The revenant was nowhere to be seen.

A flicker of fear stirred sparks of panic in Adrial's chest. He shook out his shoulders and leaned his weight onto his bad hip as he studied the empty basket.

Only a few crumbs had been left behind.

Adrial moved the basket again, placing it on his other side, away from the library. He watched a man cross the square, waiting until the man was out of sight to reach into his pocket.

Another flicker of fear attacked his chest as his gloved fingers grazed the tightly rolled scroll. Keeping his gaze front, Adrial pulled the scroll from his pocket and tucked it into the empty basket.

The horrible feeling of hundreds of eyes pinned to the back of his neck sent an extra set of goosebumps to join those already born of the cold.

He looked up, watching a bird circling high over Ilara. The beauty of it—so calm, so separate from the troubles of the city—shattered when the creature swooped lower and closer to the square, as though wanting to be sure Adrial understood it to be a carrion bird.

"A bird seeking the dead," Adrial muttered. "I fear Ilara is your paradise."

"Even a flesh eater wouldn't be that foolish." The revenant spoke from just behind Adrial's line of sight.

Adrial's neck tensed. He tucked his chin into his scarves in a poor attempt to mask the fear in his voice. "Do you think Ilara could ever be paradise?"

"When it is, you won't recognize it."

"I've done everything you've asked," Adrial said. "The names you gave me were placed on the sailors' roster this morning. There are four copies of the eastern mountains map in the basket."

The revenant said nothing.

"I'm sorry for the creases in the maps," Adrial said. "I had to fold them to get the scroll small enough to fit into my pocket. But if you—"

"Marred paper doesn't concern me."

A fleeting burst of relief only strengthened Adrial's fear. "Then my task is done. Let me see my wife."

"No."

"Please." Adrial glanced toward the revenant. "I've done everything you've asked. I am begging you, let me see Ena."

"No."

Adrial glanced his way again, catching a glimpse of the revenant tucking the maps into his pocket.

"How long can you keep doing this?" Adrial gripped the rim of the fountain, fighting his need to lunge for the revenant's neck.

"As long as I want. And you'll keep following my orders." The revenant stood from his seat on the fountain's rim. "Congratulations, paun. You're a father."

A heavy, unworldly weight crashed into Adrial's gut, doubling him over. His breath caught in his throat as tears burned in his eyes.

"Ena. Is Ena safe?" Adrial gasped in air as a sob shook his lungs. He turned toward the revenant, all thoughts of secrecy gone.

The ghost had vanished.

"A baby." Adrial's tears swallowed his words.

"Head Scribe." Five guards ran toward him. "Head Scribe, are you all right?"

Adrial shut his eyes, savoring the warmth of a brief moment of joy.

"Head Scribe." A heavy hand gripped his shoulder. "Are you ill, sir?"

"I'm fine." Adrial wiped his tears on the backs of his gloves. "I've just—" He scanned the square, trying to find something that might explain his flood of tears.

Ena. If Ena's come through labor safely—

"There's nothing to explain, sir. Grief comes in waves. There's no shame in it." A guard took Adrial's elbow, helping him to his feet and leading him toward the library.

Four maps for a child.

Ena's child. The child he'd claimed.

The world blurred as terrifying joy swept through his soul.

30

ALLORA

The still air in the black stone room gave the lone candle no reason to flicker.

Allora stared at the flame, imagining the fire growing bigger. Large enough to light a torch. Large enough to burn a sorcerer. An inferno large enough to swallow the whole Royal Palace.

She reached forward, but from her seat on the floor against the wall, her arm wasn't long enough to grab one of the loose black stones on the table. She could get to her knees and crawl to the table. She could even stand up.

Neither option could be deemed worth the effort required.

"It's better that way, Allora Karron." She leaned back against the wall. "Toying with deadly things helps no one."

She closed her eyes, trying to sink into the resigned apathy of permanent entrapment. But the little voice in the back of her mind kept whispering deadly things in her ear.

If a room of black stone could destroy the palace, one black stone could surely be a worthy weapon.

Against a sorcerer. Or a king.

One stone could change so much.

"You'll drive yourself mad dreaming of such things." Not

bothering to open her eyes, she reached for the already open bottle of frie beside her.

Ignoring the terrible stench, she took a sip, letting the burn in her throat push her further toward the brink of blissful nothing.

"What a sad state in which to find Ilbrea's Queen," Gillien said, sounding as though she were nearer to Allora than the table.

Even though Allora hadn't heard Gillien enter the black stone room, she didn't bother opening her eyes. "Hiding, drinking frie, or sitting on the floor?"

"Sitting in the dark," Gillien said.

"In future, I shall attempt to bring more candles."

"And less frie."

"If you try to forbid it, I'll demand frie with every meal."

"I've no intention of forbidding anything." Gillien's voice shifted position.

Allora allowed her eyes to open and found the sorcerer sitting on the other side of the candle.

"But I would be failing in my duty as your protector if I didn't remind you that frie has not been known to aid in the conception of a child," Gillien said.

"A benefit of frie I had never considered." Allora took another, deeper drink, fighting not to cough against the burn in her chest.

"Glibness is beneath you, Allora."

"I'm sitting on the floor. Nothing is beneath me." Allora took another drink. "I used to chastise Mara for sitting on the ground. Map maker or not, she's still a woman of the Guilds and should try to follow at least the most basic rules of polite society. I never should have pushed her to be less herself."

"You were protecting her best interests as I strive to protect yours."

Allora shoved the stopper into the top of the bottle of frie. "And how, gracious sorcerer, shall you protect my interests?"

"By encouraging you to remember your duties."

"Has another round of biddies arrived to bend my ear with their complaints and gossip?"

"If you find your visitors too taxing, we will stop admitting them to the palace," Gillien said. "I will happily spread word that the decision was mine so no one dares think less of you."

"As much as I cherish my visits from Adrial and enjoy tea with Illia, if I stop accepting the women of Ilara, I may shrivel from lack of companionship."

"All the companionship you need already lies within the palace."

"If you dare forbid my visits with Adrial—"

"Depriving you of your friend is not my intention," Gillien said.

"But whipping him to death was the Lady Sorcerer's aim before she stole his wife and child. I'm sure you understand why I don't trust you or any who claim association with murderers."

"Whom you distrust is not nearly as large a concern to me as your abandoning your marriage bed."

Allora stared at Gillien, waiting for anger to rise within her, but apathy held firm.

"I have not abandoned my marriage bed," Allora said. "I endure sleeping beside the King every night."

"And when did you last pleasure your husband?"

"He is quite capable of pleasuring himself. I've watched the proceedings in our room. I found the event pathetic rather than enticing."

"The King's private habits are not my concern. Your not even attempting to conceive a child is of great concern to all Ilbrea."

"Oh yes, with all the violence running rampant in Ilara, how often the King shudders on top of me is at the front of every Ilbrean's mind."

"It is your duty to produce an heir."

"I am aware."

"An heir cannot be conceived without your coupling with the

King."

"Once again, knowledge I possess."

"Then you must open yourself to the King's pleasures."

"Have I ever once rejected him?" Allora pulled the stopper back out of the bottle. "Have I ever denied him entry to my body?"

"Not that I am aware of."

"Then perhaps your concerns are not of my making."

"The King has stopped seeking your affection."

"A wise man." Allora took a drink of frie deep enough to burn her nose.

"You are a beautiful woman. He is a virile man." Gillien laced her fingers together in her lap. The flame on the candle grew. "There is no reason for regular coupling not to occur."

"I believe you should question the King, not me." A hint of spiteful joy sent bits of life flickering through Allora's numb body.

"Explain."

"I"—Allora bit her lips together—"I was going to say I would hate to embarrass the King, but I see no reason for lying to you."

Gillien narrowed her eyes. The flame on the candle grew again.

"The King has, of late, been unable to foist his pleasure upon me. He's barely pinned me down before his lust shrivels." Allora couldn't be bothered to hide her giggle. "Quite tragic for the King. And such a temper when his lack of vigor defeats him."

"Why has he not sought the aid of a healer or sorcerer? Has he shown any other signs of ill health? What began these problems for him?"

"His troubles began when he stole Adrial's wife and caused her death. The King is a brute I hold no affection for, and the very thought of him touching me is revolting. I told the King as much. At least one part of his person has the decency to hang its head in shame for his abominable acts."

"You told the King you no longer desire his passion?"

"I told him I loathe him but would perform my duty to Ilbrea and allow him to continue writhing on top of me like a flaccid, half-decayed fish. Drink?" Allora held the bottle out to Gillien.

"That was a very foolish mistake, Allora." Gillien took the bottle and set it behind her, out of Allora's reach.

"I am aware." Allora leaned back against the wall. "Had I not the awful trait of ladylike naivety, I would have found a better way to sour Brannon's life than mocking the size and agility of his manhood. But, alas, I am naïve. And, as I am not allowed to seek vengeance by actually wounding him, stealing his joy at tossing his seed inside me was the best I could do."

"He is your husband."

"And I truly do find the thought of him touching me abhorrent in every possible way. I can make myself sweetly bear the embrace of a husband I don't love, but I will not silently offer pleasure to a murderer."

"Allor—"

"There is nothing you can say to convince me otherwise. Brannon is a monster, and I am grateful for every day he fails to bed me."

Gillien stayed quiet for a moment, as though considering her next tactic.

Allora enjoyed the silence as she waited.

"It is your duty to produce an heir," Gillien finally said. "If you continue to make coupling with you impossible for the King, you will fail in your duty to Ilbrea."

"Fail to bring an heir into a palace you could destroy at any moment." Allora knocked on the black stone wall behind her. "I can't find it in me to call that a tragedy."

"Whether you choose to believe me or not, I do want you to be happy, Allora. Not just for the good of the King or Ilbrea. For your own sake." Gillien leaned closer to the candle. "The

Sorcerers Tower does not share that sentiment. If you refuse to even try to conceive a child—"

"You'll have me killed?" Allora sighed. "Discreetly, I assume, though that doesn't imply without pain. I suppose I should leave a letter for the next Queen offering her my condolences on having tied herself to a murderer."

"Is that really what you want?"

"No. But I don't think I have it in me to save my own sorry life by betraying the principles I know to be right and ignoring the monstrosities committed by the King. Even pretending to want Brannon would shave away the bit of decency I've managed to cling to."

"I'm sorry you find your life so intolerable." Gillien picked up the bottle of frie.

"Said with so little sarcasm."

"With none at all. I am deeply sorry you're so unhappy." Gillien stood. "And while I can't change your situation, I will find a way to inspire a more enthusiastic outlook for you to carry onward."

"You will fail."

"Perhaps, but I will try." Gillien opened the door leading out to the dark staircase. "Please eat something hearty before you sleep."

The candle's flame shrank to a normal size.

"This room," Allora said, "the black stones. Whatever makes them so destructive, can it only be sparked by a sorcerer?"

"No." Gillien turned in the doorway to face Allora. She trailed her fingers down the black stones set into the wall, as though mesmerized by their texture. "A person with no magic could ignite the stones with massive effect. But that person will never be you. Tip the table, throw the stones, tear at the walls—I assure you, Allora, you will be perfectly safe."

Gillien gave Allora a sympathetic smile and left, allowing the Queen of Ilbrea to sink back into the quiet darkness.

31

NIKO

The thumping of the six guards' boots trailing behind Niko couldn't distract him from the swishing of Danu's skirt.

The fabric rustled with every step, the layers so thick, the toes of her boots barely peeked past the hem as she walked.

"Stop it," Danu whispered through clenched teeth.

"Impossible." Niko moved on to studying the thin black fabric covering her shoulders, leading down to the glorious v, which cut far lower on Danu's chest than he'd ever imagined viewing but which he forcibly deprived himself the glory of staring at. "You wearing a gown is the most astonishing thing I've ever seen."

Danu gave a tense nod to the two well-dressed men walking in the opposite direction down the endless stone tunnel, waiting until they were out of earshot to speak. "I am not the one dressed in fine clothes carrying a ridiculous doll."

Niko held the doll in front of him, not bothering to hide his grin at the sight of its green and white dress. "This doll is anything but ridiculous. I think it came out very well despite the poor description I gave the maker. I've never been able to find fault with the Brien seamstresses."

"Asking the seamstresses to make you a doll is one thing," Danu said. "Carrying it around the stronghold is quite another."

The clomping of a horse came up from behind.

Niko stepped aside, letting the horse and cart pass. "It's not as though I'm carrying it for fun. It's for my niece."

"Has Ena agreed to let you call the child that?" Danu took Niko by the arm, making him walk again.

"She hasn't even agreed to let me see her or the baby. But if whatever we're in this chivving tunnel for is important enough to have the entire keep bustling about, then Ena will be here, too."

"And if she still doesn't want to speak to you?"

Niko tugged his arm free then took Danu's hand and placed it on his elbow, walking with her as though they were strolling through the woods on a sun-filled day rather than trudging through stone to an unknown fate. "Then I'll charmingly remind her that we're family, whether she likes it or not. And I'm the only family she and the baby have in this hell, and Adrial more than anyone would want his daughter to have a reminder of how many people love her."

"If it wasn't such a sodding, heart-twisting sentiment, I'd keep mocking you."

"If you need new mockery fodder, I'm happy to provide other topics."

A hint of a suppressed smile pulled at the corner of Danu's mouth. "Just put the doll in your pocket. You can't go meet an envoy clutching a doll."

"First of all, I can't put the doll in my pocket. It would wrinkle her dress."

"And you think a baby won't do worse?" Danu's eyes began to betray her smile.

"Second, what sort of envoy are we meeting underground, and who decided making me dress in fine clothes and whisking me out of my room without telling me where I'm going was the peak decision?"

Danu's smile vanished. "I'm not sure who we're meeting, exactly. An envoy from another clan, but I don't know which."

"Peace talks with the Hayes?"

"They'd never be allowed in our passage. And Bryana wouldn't have made me wear a chivving dress if the Hayes were nearby."

"Are you trying to convince me or you?"

Danu didn't answer.

Another cart passed, heading farther down the tunnel.

Niko studied the walls of the passage. They weren't the impeccably smooth stone of the halls in the keep or the rough-ridged walls of the practice room. Rather, the stone had a gentle texture to it—smooth waves that tempted Niko to graze his fingers along them.

He tightened his hold on the doll.

Two more carts passed.

They're moving the whole keep down here.

Niko refocused his mind on the swishing of Danu's dress, tamping down his nerves.

"You're doing it again." Danu smacked him in the ribs.

"I'm sorry." Niko furrowed his brow. "But at the risk of you grabbing for one of your knives, wherever you've hidden them" —he winced as she smacked his ribs again. The tinge of pain didn't still the nerves prancing through his stomach—"you look astounding in that gown."

"I really am armed." Danu gave Niko a harder smack in the ribs. "You shouldn't mock me."

"I'm not. Dudia blessed the world when he made you a warrior. If you had fixed your aim on stealing hearts instead of stabbing them, the stronghold would be filled with broken-hearted slitches."

"But only if I wore a skirt and primped constantly. I can feel at least a dozen pins digging into my head."

"While I pity you for the pins, I regret to inform you that you are catastrophically wrong." Niko stopped, turned to Danu, turned Danu toward him, and took her hand. He looked into her eyes, and all thoughts of the tunnel and whatever Black Blood horror awaited him sank out of being. "You could steal hearts in a mud-soaked sack. No gown could make you more beautiful than you are when your hair is falling loose and you're wearing clothes suitable for charging into battle.

"But you are rather terrifying with your blades, and as I am a map maker whom you could easily kill, giving you a compliment is much easier when I can't see your weapons, even knowing you could still slay me for making you blush."

Red crept up Danu's neck and into her cheeks.

Niko's heart knocked into his throat as he kissed the back of her hand. "You've saved my life in too many ways. The least I can do is make sure you know how extraordinary you are."

Danu's blush deepened. She glanced toward the six guards waiting ten feet behind them. She stepped away from Niko, who somehow hadn't realized how very close she'd been standing.

Close enough to touch her cheek, to tip her chin up—

"Thank you, Solcha." She gave Niko a regal nod. "A compliment from you is an honor."

Niko bowed deeply, kissing Danu's hand again, allowing himself one moment to wallow in shame and self-loathing before meeting her eyes.

The clomping of horses' hooves gave Niko the excuse to step farther away, plastering his back to the wall, letting the stone prop him up as his knees considered buckling.

Three black horses walked up the tunnel, each carrying a rider.

Bryana rode the first horse, the beading of her purple gown glinting with each of the animal's steps.

Paiman rode behind her.

Then Ena. Dressed in a black gown, holding a white bundle in her arms as a groom led her horse.

"Ena." Niko stepped toward her.

She tightened her hold on the baby at the sound of her name. Her hold didn't relax when she spotted Niko.

The groom kept leading her horse on.

"Ena, please." Niko ran a few steps to catch up to her.

She looked down at the bundle, at the child, whose face Niko couldn't see.

He held up the doll. "White for the scribes and green for the map makers. I know you don't like the Guilds, but Adrial is a scribe, and he was raised by the Lord Map Maker."

Ena looked down at the doll.

"It's her family, Ena. Please," Niko said. "Adrial may not be here. But you've got to understand, to the whole Karron clan, you and your daughter are family. I only want to make sure she knows it."

Ena reached down, letting Niko hand her the doll. The faintest hint of a smile touched her lips as she studied the white-and-green dress.

"I'll keep it with her." She met Niko's gaze. "Thank you."

"You're welcome." Niko slowed his steps, letting Ena's horse get ahead of him as she turned her gaze back to Adrial's daughter.

"Walk and grin." Danu put a hand on Niko's back, making him move at her chosen pace. "If we're behind Bryana, we're late."

Beaming with joy, Niko turned to Danu, but his happiness popped and vanished at the look on her face.

He fixed his gaze front, watching Ena instead.

Her four acolytes walked two-by-two, right off her shoulders. Still the same four as when she'd arrived.

Niko would have to learn how to inspire such devotion.

A hint of the white bundle showed as Ena shifted in her saddle.

"Absolutely cruel," Danu muttered.

"What?" Niko sidestepped away from her hand, then back in to walk unherded beside her.

"The woman's just given birth, and they've put her on a horse," Danu said.

Niko glanced from Danu to the horse and back again before realizing her terrifying meaning. "Oh, by the Guilds you're right." Niko winced as Ena shifted in her saddle again. "Would it have been better for her to walk?"

"Better for her to be left up in the keep. I hope our elder had a good reason for hauling a new mother and her babe down here." Danu stiffened, turning her head as though listening to something farther down the tunnel.

Niko cocked his head, listening for impending terror.

Voices. A cluster of voices up ahead.

The light down the tunnel was brighter as well—a blue glow filling a chamber wider than the passage. The arch leading into the chamber had been carved with details Niko couldn't quite make out.

Ena's horse went right as soon as she'd passed through the arch, giving Niko a view of the strange scene that required the presence of both Solcha and Niko's sad Solcha imitation.

Tables had been laid out in the wide square. Two tiers of balconies surrounded the chamber. The doors to all the rooms above had been left open, letting each room add their light to the space.

Brien guards in their finest uniforms surrounded an arch on the far end of the square while servants scurried around the tables, preparing what looked to be a feast.

Woven rows of flowers lined a walkway leading from one arch to the other, making all the bustling workers leap over the blooms.

"What is this place?" Niko whispered, not resisting as Danu steered him to follow Ena.

"As close to the stronghold as other clans are allowed to get," Danu said. "These passages should make it feel like the clans are connected, but all they've given me is an unending fear of attack."

"This passage leads to other clans' territories?" Niko didn't let himself look to the well-armed guards blocking the archway on the far side of the chamber.

"Our passage leads to the Broinn, where all the clans' passages come together," Danu said. "Which still doesn't tell me who's coming."

"Are we the only ones who don't know?"

"I'm willing to bet the only people who do know are riding horses," Danu said.

The horses stopped.

Niko tensed, waiting for the skin on his back to tear as punishment for daring to ask questions.

The riders dismounted. The horses were led away. The skin on his back stayed whole.

Bryana cut around the side of the square, heading toward the guarded arch.

Niko kept behind Ena's acolytes, far enough from Bryana not to be noticed. Close enough to be able to see what the demon was doing.

Bryana stepped onto the flower-lined path, stopping ten feet from the arch's guards.

Ena stopped to her left, Paiman to her right.

Paiman glanced back, searching the crowd for a moment before spotting Niko and Danu. He beckoned them forward, pointing for Niko to stand behind Ena's right shoulder, as though Niko had joined her flock as chief acolyte.

Niko cut around to his assigned position, Danu staying close beside him.

Paiman nodded to them and turned to face front while Niko dared to lean forward, peeking around Ena to see the baby.

She was asleep, her lips just a bit open, her hand curled up by her perfect pink cheek.

A rumble of footsteps snapped Niko's attention back to the line of guards.

One of the guards turned and bowed to Bryana. She gave the guard a slight nod.

The guard turned back around. "Bryana, Elder of the Brien Clan, has granted safe passage."

All the guards turned sideways and filed away from the arch.

A line of people dressed in deep blue waited in the passage beyond.

Danu gave a tiny gasp.

Niko looked toward her, but she had her gaze fixed on Ena.

All the color had drained from Ena's face.

Niko leaned over to whisper in Danu's ear. "What's wrong?"

"Welcome." Bryana's voice filled the space. "You are greeted with friendship and peace, Duwead Clan."

"We are grateful for your welcome," a blond Duwead woman said. Tears streamed down the woman's pale face. "And for the friendship of the Brien Clan."

The woman ran forward.

Niko took a step back, waiting for the guards to attack the Duwead.

But none of them stopped her as she ran to Ena, wrapping Ena and the babe in her arms.

32

NIKO

Ena and the blond Duwead woman sat together at the banquet table, clinging to the other's hand as they ignored the lavish feast.

Niko had been placed right across the table from Ena, between Paiman and Danu, as though he were part of a display of dolls Bryana had created for the Duwead Clan's envoy.

The demon elder needn't have bothered. Not a single Duwead gave a sodding hint of caring about the Brien's false Solcha.

"Solcha." The murmur came from Niko's right. "Niko." Danu nudged him with her elbow.

"Sorry," Niko said.

Danu leaned in front of him, her bare shoulder coming close enough he could have kissed it as she filled his ale.

"Don't stare," Danu whispered as she retook her seat.

"Sorry." Niko switched his gaze from his slight view of the baby's face to his mug of ale while keeping his ears tuned to Ena and the Duwead woman's voices.

"Never be sorry for asking me to come here," the Duwead woman said. "You know I would cross the world to see you and this sweet, sweet girl."

"Thank you," Ena said.

A servant dished more food onto Niko's plate, giving him an excuse to look up.

Tears glistened on the Duwead woman's cheeks. "If you want to thank me, tell me you're coming home."

"Marta—" Ena began.

"You belong in Lygan Hall," the woman, Marta, said. "Your home is with the Duweads, not the Brien."

"Solcha's home is with us," Paiman said. "When she returned to the Black Bloods, she came to us."

"You may claim the stronghold as *Solcha's* home, but *Ena* belongs with her clan." Marta gave Paiman a cold glare that didn't seem to belong on her rosy, dimpled face. "Come home, Ena. The children begged me to bring you home."

Ena's breath caught in her throat. The lae stone light glistened on the unshed tears brimming in her eyes.

"Evie threw a fit when I told her she couldn't come with me," Marta said. "I've been half-afraid I'll turn around and find her stomping after me."

"So she hasn't changed too much," Ena said.

"She's just as stubborn as always." Marta smiled, putting her dimples on glorious display. "But she's so grown up. The fuss she makes if she catches me calling her a child is spectacular. Some might even call it a blaze of temper."

"What a treat for you." Ena managed a smile.

"But Evie's thriving," Marta said. "All of them are. Cinni is better than I'd ever dared hope. I promise, they're doing well."

"Good." Ena's smile faltered. "That's good."

"You could see it for yourself," Marta said. "Just come home."

"Solcha's home is with the Brien," Paiman said again.

"Did Bryana seat you there so you could try and lay claim on me?" Ena looked to Paiman. "She must be slipping if she thinks your prattle will do any chivving good."

"My apologies." Paiman gave Ena what might have passed as a reverent nod. "I had not meant to lay claim on anything, only to be sure you know you are welcome and protected in the stronghold, as is your daughter."

"As they will be in Lygan Hall," Marta said. "With their family. A mother and her newborn belong with those who love them, not carrion birds dragging Ena down the path of some legend we all know Bryana doesn't even believe."

"Not everyone here only cares for Ena and the baby because of what she means to the Black Bloods." Niko gripped the edge of the table, trying not to flinch as Marta shifted her glare to him. "She is married to my closest friend—"

"Niko, stop," Ena said.

The pink drained from the blond woman's face.

"I apologize, Ena, but I cannot listen to Black Bloods argue over the baby's home as though she's fatherless." Niko pushed away from the table and stood. "The babe's father is in Ilara. Black Bloods may only like Ilbreans they can pin the name *Solcha* on, but they might at least pretend to care about Adrial while they bicker over his daughter's fate."

"Lily." Ena met Niko's gaze. "Her name is Lily."

The simple name punched Niko in the gut, though he didn't know why.

"It's a beautiful name Adrial will love," Niko said.

Ena swallowed as though holding back either tears or sour sick surging in her throat.

"I'm sorry, Ena," Niko said. "You've every right to choose which clan you'll allow to lay claim on sheltering Solcha, and I understand you didn't want to leave Adrial. I truly do. But I can't listen to two slitches pretending he doesn't exist. If you'll excuse me."

Niko strode away from the table, heading toward the far side of the chamber.

A line of blue-clad Duwead guards had taken over for the line of purple-clad Brien guards flanking the archway of the path that led away from the stronghold.

All the Duwead guards were lightly armed with only knives at their hips and tucked into the calves of their boots.

Whether the guards were too deadly to need better weapons or hadn't been allowed anything more deadly because of some Black Blood rule, Niko wouldn't have dared guess.

One of the blue-clad Duweads nodded to the guards as she passed through the arch, walking into the dark tunnel beyond without hesitation.

Niko changed his path, arcing toward the barrels of ale along the wall. A few of the more enthusiastic imbibers had abandoned the pitchers on the tables to seek their drink straight from the tap. He headed that way, grabbing an abandoned mug from a table as he approached the barrels.

"May I?" Niko asked the girl manning the tap.

She gave Niko a coy grin, her gaze roaming from the well-tailored crest of his pants, to his chest, then finally to his face. "It would be an honor, Solcha. But I feel obliged to warn you, we've brought down a stronger batch for tonight. I can't be blamed for any mischief that might come your way."

"Mischief?" Niko handed the girl his mug. "If there's mischief to be had, I insist on finding it."

The girl passed the mug back, batting her lashes. "I'll be offering mischief all night, Solcha."

Niko bowed, winked, and cut around the barrel to the corner of the nearest table, giving himself a clean line of sight to the archway.

He'd gotten halfway through his ale before the Duwead that had left came back, again only giving the guards a nod as she passed.

As trays of cakes were carried out from one of the rooms carved into the chamber's walls, four musicians appeared, filling the hall with cheerful tunes that promised to become rollicking once the feast had finished.

More of the party drifted from their seats, going to chat with others, filling the space in the center of the tables as though waiting for the lines of flowers to be cleared away so they could dance.

Another person in Duwead blue passed through the Duwead guards without being stopped.

Niko shoved his hands into his pockets, hiding their trembling.

A coat. A chivving blue coat between him and freedom.

"Beg pardon." A wall of a man in Duwead blue bumped into Niko as he tried to squeeze behind him.

"Sorry." Niko stepped out of the man's path.

The tap girl followed the massive man, holding his hand, giggling as they reached the very corner of the chamber and slipped into the dark niche between the wall and the stairs to the first balcony.

A better night than I'll have.

Niko leaned against the wall, watching the Black Bloods roam as the servants shifted the banquet tables back.

Then the music stopped. An older woman in a purple gown walked to the center of the two lines of flowers.

Without bothering to tell the crowd something spectacular was going to happen, she raised her hands. The flowers lifted off the floor, carried by some magic. She spread her fingers as though flicking away water, sending a shower of petals sweeping around the room.

The revelers noticed the beautiful magic just enough to cheer, and the musicians began playing again.

The tap girl and her partner came back out of the shadows, her lips redder, though without any added touch of joy, the massive Duwead man grinning as he sagged into an empty chair.

The man wiped the sweat from his brow with his sleeve, unbuttoning his blue coat as though begging for someone to ask how he'd overheated.

This is a terrible plan, Mara whispered.

I haven't got a better one.

Shoving all reason aside, Niko approached the man, unbuttoning the top of his fine coat, breaking the perfection of his black Solcha costume by revealing the bright white shirt he wore beneath.

"Too chivving hot in here if you ask me." Niko plopped down in the chair beside the man, giving his remaining ale a slosh for good measure.

"Not warm enough to stop a good time." The massive Duwead man leaned back in his seat.

"Not at all." Niko finished unbuttoning his coat and shrugged it off, laying it over the back of his chair. "Of course, there are some things worth boiling for." Niko forced a chortle. "Sorry. Shouldn't have said that. Whether you take it as a brag about the fun I've had or a taunt because you can't claim such a fine night, it comes out rude."

Niko wiped the nonexistent sweat from his brow.

"You talk like you're the only one who's enjoyed themselves this evening, Ilbrean." The man took off his coat, draped it on the table, and rolled up his sleeves.

"*Ilbrean.* You're not the first one to call me that tonight. Though there was a bit more breathlessness to her tone." Niko winked. "And I know I'm not the only one who had an explosively fine time. I think my shoulder's bruised from how hard she bit me to keep the whole party from hearing our fun."

Niko lifted his mug, holding it out to cheers the man. "May more revelers enjoy the shadows' delights."

The man laughed as he knocked his mug against Niko's.

Niko took a deep drink, giving a long glance to the barrel before leaning close to the man. "I only pity the one who paired up with the barrel girl. Called the man who lifted her skirt a withered, stumpy slug."

The man stiffened in his seat.

Niko leaned closer, glancing again toward the barrel, hoping Dudia would forgive him.

"That man with the red hair"—Niko nodded toward a Brien by the barrel—"heard him promising to finish what the other slitch couldn't. Said he'd make her stars tremble twice to make up for the poor withered slug's failure."

The man's muscles tensed as red filled his face.

"I even heard the girl promise to point the poor slug out so the redhead could have a laugh while they—"

The man stood, panting like a bull as he towered over Niko.

Niko froze, steeling himself for a blow.

The man knocked his chair aside and strode toward the redhead.

Niko slid the man's blue coat from the table.

Without a word of warning, the massive man punched the redhead in the jaw, sending him stumbling into the barrel of ale. The barrel fell sideways, crashing to the ground.

The barrel girl screamed. More people began screaming.

As the barrel leaked ale onto the floor, Niko ducked down, yanked on the blue coat, popped back to his feet, and strode straight toward the Duwead guards.

Half the guards had run toward the growing brawl in the corner, but the rest stayed firmly in place.

Niko bundled the blue coat around him, doubling over to hide the mass of extra fabric, praying to Dudia, or any god willing to listen to such a fool, that it would only look like he was ill from excess.

His heart pummeled his throat as he neared the guards.

Ten feet. Five.

Niko walked through the Duwead guards and into the tunnel beyond, fighting every instinct that begged him to run.

The chaotic sounds of the fight gave way to the shouting of commands.

I truly am sorry.

The shouting stopped.

Niko picked up his pace, daring to run down the corridor into the darkness.

In the distance, the faint glow of lae stones whispered a promise of salvation.

Niko kept his gaze fixed on the lights, sprinting faster than he'd ever managed before.

Something hard crashed into the front of his ankles, and he flew forward, landing face down on the unforgiving stone floor.

33

NIKO

Niko froze, his mind begging his body to run, his body unable to do anything but wait for pain to tear through his back. Or kinder, for Bryana to rip the stone of his mark through his heart and lungs, ending his life before the torment could begin.

A heartbeat passed. Then another.

A hand wrapped around his arm, yanking him onto his side.

"No." Niko wrenched his arm free, trying to scramble to his feet. "I'm not going back to be tortured."

The hand grabbed his arm again.

"Quiet, Niko," Danu said.

He stopped fighting at the sound of her voice. He studied the shape of her silhouette, making sure his ears hadn't fooled him, before letting Danu pull him to his feet.

"What under all the stars do you think you're doing?" Danu slammed his back against the wall, gripping his shoulders, pinning him in place.

Niko moved to knock her hands away.

She grabbed his wrist, pulling his arm behind his back as she twisted him, smashing his chest against the wall.

"Let me go."

"To your chivving grave?" Danu kept her voice low, speaking close to Niko's ear.

"If I die, so be it. Let me run, and I'll at least have a chance at freedom."

"No. You won't. There's no way out of this passage."

"The Duweads came from somewhere." Niko tried to turn toward Danu, gaining himself another slam against the wall.

"It takes days to make it to the Duweads' entrance. There are two sets of Brien guards between us and the start of the Duweads' passage, and only the mountain knows how many watchers between here and the end of Brien territory. There is no path to freedom here, Niko." She loosened her hold on his wrist. "I'm sorry."

He pressed his forehead to the gentle ridges of the wall.

"We have to get back," Danu said.

He didn't move.

"Bryana can't know you tried to run." Danu took Niko's shoulder, peeling him away from the wall to face her. "Going down this passage"—she took Niko's face in her hands—"if Bryanna thinks you were trying to betray the Brien in favor of the Duwead Clan, I can't protect you, Niko. I don't want to watch you die."

Niko's head drooped forward, his chest sinking as his briefly cherished hope of freedom vanished.

Danu pressed her forehead to his, closing the tiny distance between them. "We're going to stroll back to the chamber. If anyone asks why we were down this way, we'll say you tried to leave after the fight and went the wrong way. Can you do that?"

"Yes." Niko took Danu's hands, lifting them away from his face. "A drunken, lost map maker. I'm well prepared for the role."

"We're going to be all right." Danu shoved aside the shoulders of Niko's stolen blue coat. The oversized garment fell to the ground without Niko's help. "We'll go back to the feast, have a few ales, and we'll go home."

"My home is in Ilbrea." The words cracked in Niko's throat.

"I know." Danu took his hand, pressing her palm to his, gently leading him back toward the demon's lair.

Niko walked beside her, every step taking more and more effort as his will to keep moving sapped from his body.

"You should turn me in," Niko said. "Tell Bryana I ran."

"And let her hurt you?"

"And she won't hurt you if she finds you kept my poor attempt at escape from her?"

"I'm Bryana's niece."

"No part of me believes that would protect you from the demon."

"If Bryana's anger turns my way, my punishment won't be anything I can't survive."

Niko stepped in front of Danu, tipping her chin up, trying to look into her eyes in the faint bit of light coming from the end of the passage.

"I will not let the demon torture you," Niko whispered. "Not for me. Not for anything. I'd rather let her carve down to my bones than hurt you."

"Niko—"

"I mean it." He squeezed Danu's hand, needing to be sure she heard him. "The thought of her hurting you is worse than remembering the feel of her knives. I will not let her punish you. I can't."

A tendril of Danu's hair had fallen loose.

"My soul would have shriveled up a long time ago without you." Heat burned in Niko's fingers as he trailed them across her cheek to tuck the rogue hair behind her ear. "Watching you hurt would break me for good."

She shut her eyes as she leaned her cheek against his hand.

He kissed her forehead. Her cheek.

The heat from his fingers spread up his arm and into his chest, clamping around his heart.

She opened her eyes, meeting his gaze as he leaned in to brush his lips against hers.

"Please." A voice carried through the darkness. Close. Far too close to be coming from the chamber's arch.

Danu broke away from Niko, shoving him against the wall, planting her hands on either side of him, her chest pressed against his.

"After months of letters, you beg me to come here with a wetnurse," the voice said.

Two figures hurried up the tunnel. One with dark hair, one with blond hair so pale it glinted in the faint light.

"Are you ill?" the voice asked.

Danu bowed her head.

The air around Niko chilled, setting goosebumps on his arms as the light in the tunnel shifted, blocking the glow from the chamber's arch but brightening the two figures, making them appear more dream than real.

Ena came down the passage, Lily in her arms, Marta beside her.

The furrows in Marta's brow deepened. "Is Lily ill?"

Panic shot through Niko. He tried to step forward, needing to see Lily.

"Don't." Danu leaned all her weight against him, holding him in place.

Niko rose up on his toes, gaining a view of his niece's face. Lily still seemed peaceful, healthy as she slept in her mother's arms, her new doll tucked in the blanket beside her.

"Are the Brien not feeding you? Has your milk not come?" Marta stopped right in front of Niko. "Please, Ena."

Ena stopped, too, but didn't turn away from the faint glow of the lae stones down the passage to face Marta.

"I love you, Ena," Marta said. "You know I do. And I've done everything you've asked. But now you're scaring me. Is it Bryana? Have the Brien tried to hurt you?"

"They wouldn't dare," Ena said.

Marta stayed silent, watching Ena.

Niko couldn't tell if Marta noticed Ena's shoulders shift and her chin tip up, as though something inside her had hardened.

Danu sagged toward Niko. He caught her under the arms, pulling her against his chest, gripping her by the waist to keep her on her feet.

"What's wrong?" Niko whispered.

Danu shook her head.

"I need you to take her." Ena turned toward Marta.

"Of course." Marta reached for Lily.

"Go back to your camp in the tunnels, take the guards you trust most, and ride for the Broinn," Ena said.

"What?" Marta backed away.

"How long is the ride to the Broinn?" Ena said.

"Three days, but—"

"I'll wait four to give you time, but you have to move as fast as you can. Don't let anyone stop you." Ena held her child out to Marta.

"No, Ena, I'm not taking your baby."

"You have to. She'll be safe with you."

"She's already safe with her mother."

"She can't come with me." Ena stepped closer to Marta, placing the child on Marta's chest. "You have to take her."

"Ena, no." Marta raised her arms to hold the child even as she shook her head. "Whatever you're planning, just stop. If you think Lily is safe in Lygan Hall, then that's where you should be, too."

"I can't." Ena tucked the blankets around the baby's face, blocking her pink cheeks from Niko's view. "My husband is in Ilara, surrounded by the monsters who tried to murder him. I can't abandon him to those demons. I have to get him out."

"Ena—"

"They'll kill him, Marta. The Guilds will murder my husband.

If there's even a chance I can save him…" Ena backed away, leaving Lily in Marta's arms. "I have to go. I have to try. You know you'd do the same."

"You can't—" Marta let out a shuddering breath. "You have no right to ask this of me."

"I know, but you're the only one I trust to protect my daughter. With you and Cinni, there will be no better cared for or guarded child under the stars. Please, Marta. For my brother's sake."

Both women went silent, making Danu's shallow, gasping breaths sound worse.

Niko lowered his hold on her, gripping her hips, afraid he was somehow squeezing her too hard.

"I would do anything for him." Marta bit her lips together, staring down at Lily's face. "But I won't take her unless you swear you're coming back for her."

"I'm going into Ilara," Ena said, with no trace of fear in her voice. "You and I both know I'd be lying if I promised to survive."

Marta shut her eyes, sending a fresh wave of tears down her cheeks. "Then you have to promise you will fight with everything you are to come home. Every plot, every poison, every bit of blood you spill, you will be fighting to come back to your daughter."

Ena tipped her face to the darkness above.

"Swear it, Ena Ryeland."

A shock of painful fear sped Niko's heart as Ena stayed silent.

"Swear it," Marta whispered.

"On the blood of all the ones we've lost, I swear it."

"Then I'll keep her safe until you come home."

"Thank you." The words hitched in Ena's throat. "Go now. Get as far from here as you can before you have to stop. Lily will sleep for a few more hours. You'll be well out of hearing before she starts to cry."

"Why are we running? Do the Brien want to take her?" Marta

spun to face the arch, as though ready for a hundred Brien to come charging out to steal Lily.

"If Bryana knows I'm sending Lily to the Duweads, she'll try to lay claim on Solcha's daughter. I won't give her or any of the other beasts in the shadows the chance to drag my daughter into their bloody games." Ena stepped past Marta, striding back toward the chamber. "The farther Lily is from me, the safer she'll be. Now go."

"Wait!" Marta chased after her. "You can't just walk away. You have to say goodbye."

"I'm not strong enough for that." Ena kept walking, leaving Marta and Lily alone in the dark.

Marta stared after Ena for a breath. Then another. She gasped in a stifled sob, then ran the other way, clutching Adrial's daughter to her chest.

Tears streamed down Niko's face as he watched Marta disappear into the darkness.

Lily sent away. Far from her mother. Farther from her father.

Adrial in danger. Murderers threatening a scribe.

Danu's legs gave out. Her head tipped back. Her arms went limp.

"Danu." Niko took her weight, propping her against his chest. "Danu."

"Fine." Danu tried to lift her head up. It lolled back again. "I—I'm fine."

"This isn't fine." Niko shifted his grip on her, protecting her head as he lowered her to the ground. "What happened? Are you hurt?"

He searched for any hint of a wound, running his hands across her neck and over the back of her head, feeling for any trace of blood.

"Not hurt." Danu fumbled for his hands. "Just too much."

"Too much what? Do you need a healer?" Niko checked both her arms.

"The darkness." Danu scrunched her eyes shut, her face pinching as though she were fighting some horrible pain. "For the spell. I pushed too hard."

"To hide us from Ena and Marta?"

"Just enough magic to hide us. Not enough power to maintain the spell." Danu swallowed hard. "I told you, I'm not useful as a sorcerer."

"You're the most useful person I've ever met." Niko brushed her hair away from the sweat on her brow. He kissed the back of her hand, gently holding onto her fingers, giving no resistance if she wanted to pull away. "I don't think I'd make it a day without you. So you've got to get better, or I'm thoroughly doomed."

"I told you, I'm fine. I just need rest." She held Niko's hand to her chest. "Oh, I'm going to pay for this so badly tomorrow."

"I'll be your nursemaid. I'll spoon broth into your mouth."

Danu coughed a low laugh. "Help me get home without causing a fuss, and we'll call it even."

"I'd still like to feed you broth. Just so I know you're all right."

"Don't waste your worry." Danu pushed herself to sit up.

"Careful." Niko caught her as she wobbled, wrapping his arm around her waist, holding her against him, her lips maddeningly close.

"I trust you to keep me on my feet." Danu managed a tired smile. "But I may need help getting up."

"We'll go slowly." Niko shifted his weight back, pulling her to lean against him so she could get her feet beneath her.

Danu gasped.

"I'm sorry." Niko froze.

Danu shoved him back, tipping him off balance enough he fell to the floor.

"Did I hurt—" Niko began.

Then Danu was on top of him. Her lips pressed to his.

Warm and supple and impossibly soft.

She threaded her fingers through his hair as she shifted on

top of him, laying her body against his, straddling him. The curves of her breasts pressed against him as she kissed him, betraying no hint of hesitation as she parted his lips with her tongue.

The shock that froze Niko's mind did nothing to still the heat that began throbbing through him as she gave a panted sigh. The blazing heat mounted, pulsing as her most delicate place grazed up his growing shaft.

She didn't back away.

The inferno swallowed Niko's senses, daring him to take her waist as her hips pressed against his. He trailed his hands up, finding the sides of her breasts—breasts too perfect to be hidden by fabric.

A tiny gasp interrupted the work of her lips as his thumb found the peak of her breast.

She abandoned his mouth, trailing her lips out to his ear, her hips shifted as she moved, sending more heat to the unbearable tension throbbing through him.

She stole his hand from her breast, threading her fingers through his, pushing his arm over his head, trapping him beneath her, leaving his other hand still free to explore.

Her waist. Her hip buried beneath too many layers of fabric.

The fabric masking her skin was an abomination. The fabric had to go.

He fumbled for the hem of her skirts.

She moved back to his lips, kissing him as though wanting to memorize his taste.

Past the mounds of fabric he found the soft skin of her calf. He grazed his fingers up to her thigh.

She slid lower, giving him access to the bare skin of her hip. Her back arched, the cut of her dress giving Niko a stunning view of her breasts.

He pulled her farther up him. Her breath caught as she slid

against his stiffness, the sound shifting to a throaty moan as he kissed the side of her neck.

"What under the chivving stars is going on?" The angry voice came from far too close by.

Niko tried to sit up. Danu planted a hand on his chest, keeping him down.

"Danu"—the voice got angrier—"have you lost your chivving mind?"

Niko twisted his head, trading pain in his neck for a chance to see the speaker.

Paiman stood ten feet away, fists clenched at his sides as he stared down at Niko and his sister.

Panic thrust sense back into Niko's lust-drunk mind. He tried to sit up again, but Danu tightened her thighs around him, sending another surge of pulsing need to his still-hardened member that still pressed against her.

Dudia preserve me.

"Hello, brother," Danu said.

"There is a feast in that room." Paiman jabbed his finger toward the chamber.

"Which is why we're out here," Danu said. "For a bit of privacy."

"In a tunnel?"

"A dark tunnel." Danu grinned. "Now if you don't want a show, I suggest you leave."

"Absolutely not." Paiman spoke through gritted teeth. "This chivving folly stops now. You are going back to the party."

"You cannot—" Danu began.

"As the trueborn heir of the Brien clan, I am ordering you to get off of Solcha, now."

Niko withered under Paiman's glare.

"Turn your back, brother," Danu said. "Unless you'd like to see the spectacular parts of Niko I've been enjoying."

"Chivving mountain's cursed travesty." Paiman turned around.

Danu stood, swaying as she tried to step away from Niko.

He sprang to his feet, catching her by her arms before she could crumple.

"You're supposed to be Solcha's keeper," Paiman said. "Not his plaything."

"I would never treat Danu as a plaything." Niko wrapped his arm around Danu's waist, anchoring his mind to the need to protect her rather than the want to land a punch in defense of his honor.

Danu pointed to Niko's groin and perfectly buttoned pants.

One handed, Niko loosened the top button and pulled the front of his shirt free.

"Men don't bring anything but playthings for a quick roll in a tunnel," Paiman said.

"But I'm not against luring Niko into the darkness or anywhere else I chivving well please. You'll have to blame my lust, brother. Not his," Danu said. "If you want to know the details of why I wanted a roll in a tunnel, I'm happy to share. If not, we're going back to the party."

"An excellent idea." Paiman rounded on his sister, avoiding Niko's gaze. "If you don't want the privilege of being Solcha's keeper assigned to someone who won't hop on top of the mountain's chosen Ilbrean, you'd better brand some sense into your head."

"Because I've taken up with Solcha?" Danu laughed. "The entire chivving clan would be thrilled to have Solcha linked to one of Bryana's kin."

"I'm not the entire clan. I am your brother and trueborn heir, and I'm not chivving well foolish enough to forget that, chosen or not, Niko is an Ilbrean. He is the enemy, Danu. You will not taint yourself with the paun again." Paiman strode away.

"Oh by the sodden chivving Guilds." Niko breathed the curse.

"And fix your pants," Paiman shot behind.

"You don't have time to panic," Danu whispered, "we need to follow him."

"Can you even walk?"

"If I hold your arm, I think I can get as far as my seat at the table."

"I can carry you." Niko didn't loosen his hold on her.

"Paiman's fury is bad enough." Danu shoved her hair away from her face. "I don't want people asking how I burnt myself out."

"I won't let you fall." Niko held his breath as she twisted out of his grip to take his arm. She wobbled for a moment, blinking as though trying to make the walls hold still.

"Danu?"

"I can walk."

"We'll take it slow." Niko supported her arm with his free hand, matching his steps to hers.

She kept her gaze fixed on the growing light ahead of them. Sweat slipped down the side of her neck.

"This is my fault," Niko whispered. "If I hadn't been foolish enough to think—"

Danu's stride faltered. She closed her eyes, stopping for a moment as though searching her body for the strength to keep pushing forward. She let out a slow breath and started moving again. "There's no blame to be had."

"Even if that were true, I'm still sorry."

"That I mounted you like a cat in heat?" The corner of Danu's lips twitched up. "You didn't seem very sorry."

"Of course I am."

"I'll try not to take offense."

"No, I mean the mounting was wonderful." Heat flooded Niko's cheeks and loins. "Very pleasant—much appreciated—by far the best trickery to escape certain death I've ever endured."

"Endured?"

"I meant enjoyed." The heat in Niko's loins began to pulse again. "In a very bland, very trivial sort of way."

"Trivial?" The word came out crisp.

"I'm making this worse." Niko stopped, tipping his gaze to the darkness above rather than risk plunging into greater disaster. "There is no way I could ever convince myself not to find pleasure in touching you. Quite frankly, you could slam me to the ground right now and have your way with me, and I couldn't find it in me to consider stopping you.

"But having your body and having you are two very different things. Unfortunately, the pleasure of one would only make the sting of not having the other worse. And now that I know what your lips taste like, I'll never stop wanting to kiss you. So I am very sorry for causing all this. You are my refuge in this hell, and I'm petrified of that precious relief being tainted by my own longing."

Danu took his chin, guiding his gaze down to meet hers. "If Paiman orders me away from you, I won't be able to fight it."

"And losing you would be my doom."

She laid her hand on Niko's cheek.

He closed his eyes, leaning into her touch, trying to memorize the feel of her skin against his.

She rested her head on his shoulder, letting him fold her into a proper embrace rather than just keeping her standing.

Her body fit perfectly against his.

She pressed her lips to Niko's cheek, sealing his blissful sorrow away, hiding his fleeting hopes for joy behind the easier-to-face obsessions of escape and survival.

Dudia grant me a heart of iron.

Niko pulled her arms from around his waist and placed her hand on his elbow.

They didn't speak any more. Not even to acknowledge the questioning stares of the Duwead guards or Paiman's chilling glower as they reentered the chamber.

Danu stayed on Niko's arm until they reached their place at the table.

When she finally let go to take her seat, a hollow chill settled over Niko's heart.

He grabbed a pitcher of ale from the center of the table, refilling his mug before he sat.

He took three hearty gulps before noticing Ena sitting across from him.

Her spine straight, her face placid, her hands splayed on the table in front of her as she listened to a Brien prattle on about the Hayes siege. Nodding in the right places. Speaking words of comfort and confidence.

Not a crack in the perfect armor she wore.

The living statue of Solcha played legend for the Black Bloods while her daughter raced farther and farther away.

34

———

KAI

"Is this not the rebellion you were hoping for?" Kai kept his hands planted on the crooked wooden table, barely resisting the urge to punch the cowardly slitch Barry in the face.

"What rebellion?" Barry grabbed his sack from under the bunk he'd claimed in the warren they'd been calling home for months. "If you manage to spot a rebellion, point me their way."

Merial grunted a tsk from behind Kai's shoulder.

"You're already here," Kai said. "I'm sorry if you thought you'd have killed a pack of sorcerers by now, but we're fighting against people with chivving magic! We can't run up to the Sorcerers Tower and demand a fair fight. We have to plan. We have to consider every asset we have or—"

"We have nothing. You're planning nothing." Barry shoved his spare shirt and pants into the sack.

"Enough." Drew stepped up beside Kai.

"We're helping the people of Ilara," Kai said.

"I have family in Ilara." Barry swung his sack over his shoulder. "The people I love are up in the cold right now."

"If your people are suffering from the cold, we can find a way to get them wood," Kai said.

"You don't understand!" Barry shouted. "Not all of us are lucky enough to have our lover keeping us happy in this godsforsaken chivving hell."

"Careful, Barry," Merial said.

"Aboveground, I can be with my family," Barry said. "I'll find a job in a shop the sorcerers haven't destroyed. I'll earn coin and be able to help my family, which is far better than any of us are managing down here."

"You're wrong," Kai said.

"I'm not." Barry backed away from the table.

"What happens when the sorcerers come for your family?" Drew said. "You paint a target on them the moment you go back into their house."

"If the sorcerers come, at least I'll be there to confess and beg them to only execute me." Barry's shoulders sank. "I'm sorry, all right? I agree with what the underground is fighting for. But I'm not made to hide in the shadows. If a real fight ever begins, you know where to find me."

"If you walk out now, you're done." Merial sat. She took her time as she reached forward and grabbed the bottle of frie from the center of the table, letting the glass bottom drag across the wood with an unnerving rumble. "You'll not hear from us again. You'll never be allowed in the tunnels again."

"So be it." Barry turned toward the hidden path out of the warren.

"And if the sorcerers ever raid *any* of our tunnels, you'd better hope they kill us all." Merial poured frie into a tin cup. "If even one of us survives, we'll come for you, and for your family. Every person aboveground you claim to love will end up dead, and it'll be your fault."

Barry froze.

"Give your sisters a hello from me," Merial said.

The muscles in Barry's neck tightened.

"And pray there's no need for me to pay them a visit." Merial sipped her frie.

Barry stayed frozen for a moment, as though teetering between screaming at Merial and begging to stay in the underground. The slitch chose the wise-yet-cowardly path, wrenching open the false panel in the wall and storming into the darkness, not even bothering to shut the wall behind him.

On the far side of the room the men by the fire, who'd been carefully not paying attention to Barry's tantrum, kept drinking their mugs of tea. Not even turning around to see if Barry had actually left.

"I'll close the door behind him." Drew spoke in the tea men's direction before going to the door, pushing it back into place and making sure the façade on the panel lined up with the stones of the wall.

"Sit," Merial said. "It feels like you're looming over me."

"All of Ilara is looming over us." Kai stood up straight, peeling his palms away from the table. "That sodding coward might have doomed the underground."

"He was useless to begin with." Drew pulled a chair out for Kai before sinking into his own.

"But if his leaving gives the others ideas?" Kai asked. "We've been stuck in this standstill for months."

"Sit." Merial pointed to Kai's chair.

Leaping between buildings seemed more appealing, but Kai gave in to Merial's frown.

"Would the others rather we'd all been killed?" Drew asked. "The sorcerers haven't given us anything to attack since the cathedral square."

"They sneak around, stealing people instead," Merial said.

"The lack of buildings burning in the middle of the night makes the city look safer." Kai dragged his hands down his face. "But we all know the chivving truth."

"People are smarter than you give them credit for, oh Guilded one." Merial raised her cup to Kai. "Most know what the sorcerers have been doing, they've just run out of panic. They're too exhausted to be afraid, so they plod on, ignoring the evil hiding in the Sorcerers Tower."

"Until it's their butcher, their friend, their family who've been taken," Drew said.

"That's the beauty in the sorcerers' silent terror—it's easy to ignore until it's too late," Merial said.

"And it leaves no way for us to know where the sorcerers will be. We can't plan an ambush. We can't set a trap to lure the chivving slitches to us." Kai dug his knuckles into his eyes.

Drew reached under the table, giving Kai's thigh a comforting squeeze.

If we could just topple the Sorcerers Tower and be done with it.

You can't hurt children, Kai, Allora whispered. *Even if they are sorcerers.*

They needed an army to surround the tower, make sure no sorcerer could venture out into the city without being killed.

Or, six carts of black mining power. Surround the base of the tower and—

The children, Kai, Allora whispered. *There are children in that tower.*

"Always have to be right," Kai whispered.

"I prefer the consistency of being right," Merial said.

"No, not you," Kai sighed, letting the weight of his decision settle on his soul. "Will you walk with us?" Kai raised his eyebrows toward the men still nursing their mugs of tea.

"I love going on walks I'm certain to regret." Merial downed the rest of her frie and stood.

"In that case, I promise this will be one of the best walks you've ever taken." Kai bowed Merial toward the tunnel entrance beside the fireplace.

Merial gave the same sort of grunting tsk she'd given Barry, but followed.

The tunnel Kai had selected was one of the least used the underground had. The choices in route were either abandoned after being blocked by fallen earth, led to the terrifying lads holed up at the far end of the tunnels, or butted up to the Arion Sea.

Though the underground did light the main passage, the lanterns had been placed too far apart to truly break through the shadows, leaving pools of black deep enough to hide any horror that might lurk between every godsblessed patch of light.

Each time they passed through the black, a childish fear flicked at Kai's heart, promising him something deadly hid in the shadows.

Don't become the monster in the shadows, Kai, Allora said.

"If we haven't gone far enough by now, whatever you want to say should stay between you and the gods," Merial said.

"This'll be fine," Kai said. "But I need this kept between us. Only the three of us. Not Landon. Not Lord Nevon."

"Chivving gods and stars, Kai," Drew said. "Are you sure you want to do this?"

"Is he leading me on to convince me this is something worth keeping information from the leader of the underground?" Merial frowned at Kai.

"He's trying to save me from myself," Kai said.

"Save *us*," Drew said. "If you're determined to do this, we're in it together."

"Very romantic," Merial said. "Now one of you get on with it."

"I need you to find a girl," Kai said.

"Grown discontent with each other already?" Merial glanced between Drew and Kai.

"She helped us through the southern mountains from Pamerane to Ilbrea," Kai said.

"If that's true, I might enjoy meeting her," Merial said.

"If neither of you wanted to kill the other, I'm sure you'd get along well," Kai said. "This girl, she might have information that could finally lead us in a direction where we could actually do something. A weakness in the Sorcerers Tower. A way to lure them out."

"The perfect prayer to say to the gods so they whisk the sorcerers away entirely," Merial said.

Drew's lips tensed into a thin line.

"This girl is dangerous," Kai said. "I promise she's the most dangerous person you've ever chivving met. She loathes the sorcerers. If we can give her a chance for vengeance—"

Merial held up a hand, silencing Kai. "You've already convinced me. Just tell me where to find her."

"She's somewhere in Ilara," Kai said. "But that's as much as we know. I was hoping you could help us figure out where she might be."

"I'll just roam the city looking for a girl who hates the sorcerers, then?" Merial said.

"She won't be on the streets. She'll be hiding somewhere." Kai swallowed, banishing the tightness in his throat. "She's working with a group. The other group that interfered with our plan at the cathedral square."

Merial stepped away from Kai. She rubbed her chin, staring at Kai's boots as she spoke. "It's the redhead, isn't it? The girl who stood in the middle of the chivving cathedral square and had a magical chivving brawl with the Lady chivving Sorcerer."

"That would be the one." Kai rocked back on his heels.

"Have you ever mentioned knowing this magical madwoman to Lord Nevon?" Merial asked.

"Her, yes. Her being a sorcerer, no. If the wrong people find out about her, a flock of innocent children could die."

"We should also mention that her people plotted to murder us," Drew said. "And they'd like to see the entirety of the Guilds crumble, not just the sorcerers."

"If the dangerous girl and her people want you dead, and would like to see your Sailors Guild brought down with the rest of the paun, why would you want me to find this girl if not to run her people out of this godsforsaken city?"

"Grasping onto the last shred of hope I can muster?" Kai took Merial's hands. "Having her on our side could change everything."

"Talking to her could get us killed," Drew said.

"Please, Merial," Kai said. "I just want to talk to her. If she agrees to help us, I'll bring it to Lord Nevon."

"And in the meantime keep him in the dark for his own sake while asking me to risk my neck." Merial pulled her little pencil and notebook from her pocket. "I come from a merchant family, you know. I have a house and enough coin to wait this mess out eating cake.

"I only started smuggling to give folk who'd gotten the sodding shaft from the Guilds a chance to earn decent coin. Not my fault I'm the chivving best at it. The gods gave me the talent I have, and I've learned to use it well. But my good chivving heart's gotten me wrapped up in this."

"And I thank the gods for it every hour," Kai said.

She passed the notebook to Drew. "Write down what you know about her."

"I can do it," Kai said.

"I don't want flowery language in my book," Merial said.

"Then Drew it is." Kai leaned against the wall. "The girl saved our lives. Helped us get away before her people could kill us."

"And then she carried on with the murderers." Drew glanced up from his writing.

"Would-be murderers," Kai said.

"I'm sure they've killed plenty since they've been in Ilara," Drew said.

"With all the chivving chaos in the city, who can tell which rebellion's done what anymore?" Kai said. "Other than the cathedral square, they might not have—"

A faint boom shook a dusting of dirt down from the tunnel ceiling.

"Did that come from the west?" Kai peered down the tunnel that led to the Arion Sea.

Boom.

Kai raised his hand, shielding his eyes against the fresh sprinkle of dirt.

"It sounds like it's coming from near the docks." Drew's shoulder brushed against Kai's as he leaned forward, squinting into the darkness.

Boom.

A heavier wave of dirt tumbled from the ceiling.

"If someone's attacking the docks—" Kai started forward.

"Wait!" Merial snatched the pencil and book from Drew. "Never go toward a boom you didn't cause." She turned and strode the other way down the tunnel.

"Never ignore a boom that's coming from your docks!" Kai called after her, not waiting for a response before bolting west.

It took him a moment to realize Drew had fallen behind, limping on his barely healed leg.

Kai slowed his pace, glancing back to make sure he could still see Drew passing through the patches of light.

"You go." Drew waved him on. "I can catch up on my own. Go."

Kai sprinted down the tunnel.

Distant screaming joined the sloshing of his boots as the bone-freezing, ankle-high water tried to slow him down.

The sounds of terror grew louder, the voices gaining distinction as the tunnel twisted, and the opening to the Arion Sea came into view.

The flickering of flames gleamed off the water, outshining the starlight that should have been reflected on the waves.

Kai slowed his pace as he neared the waist-high wall that stopped the Arion Sea from flooding the tunnel.

Terrified screams of panicked men drowned out the soothing rushing of the waves.

"Off the dock!" a voice called above the rest. "Everyone off the dock!"

The thunder of boots on wood shifted as the sailors surged east.

"Head for the streets!" a second voice shouted.

Kai leaned against the barrier, peering up through the slats between the dock's wooden planks, trying to spot whatever danger the sailors were fleeing.

An odd sound, almost like an unnaturally massive bee, zoomed above him. A faint, gasping scream punctuated the buzz.

A figure dressed in purple toppled from the dock, landing in the water with a back-stinging splash.

Drew grabbed Kai's wrist, yanking him away from the barrier. He wrapped his arm around Kai's chest, holding him in place as the downed sorcerer resurfaced, bobbing face up in the water.

No one from above dove in to help the sorcerer. He didn't call for help either as a wave pushed him under the dock and right up to the barrier, twisting him just enough to hit the stone wall face first.

The wave pulled back, carrying the sorcerer a few feet away. He still didn't move.

"Good riddance." Drew stepped back, dragging Kai with him.

The shouting from above changed, shifting farther from the water, morphing from fear to anger.

The waves smacked the dead sorcerer into the barrier again.

"Oh"—Kai shook his head, swallowing the words he longed to shout—"what godsforsaken hell have we come to?"

"A sorcerer's dead. That's a reason to celebrate."

"Not if his corpse bobbing at our door leads the sorcerers to the tunnels. Gods, I hate this." Kai broke free of Drew's grip and kicked off his boots.

"If the sorcerers are going to find the tunnels, the sooner we get word to the others, the better," Drew said.

"You go bring them word." Kai sat up on the barrier.

"Kai, no."

"I'm just going to swim with a corpse. I'll catch up in a moment." Kai twisted his legs over the water and dropped down into the sea.

The cold of the water shot instant pain through Kai's body, seizing up his most precious part, freezing his bones and burning his skin as though he'd tossed himself onto a bed of coals.

"Sodding demons." He gripped the side of the barrier, saving his head from going under as his teeth started to chatter.

"Kai." Drew reached for his other hand.

"No, I'm—" Kai shook his head as the cold throbbed pain across his skull. "Be a love and go get a warm blanket ready for me. This is rather terrible." Kai wrapped his arm around the dead sorcerer's waist and kicked away from the barrier.

The swimming, the actual movement in the water, felt like coming home. The sorcerer's arm floating in front of his face, blocking his view, his weight slowing Kai's strokes, made it feel like home hadn't wanted him to come back at all.

Kai pushed to swim as fast as he could, hoping the use of his muscles might lend him some heat. Still, by the time he reached the first docked ship, his breath came in shuddering gasps. Fighting to pull in more air, he tried to make his lungs expand, but the crushing cold wouldn't allow it.

He turned, treading water as he looked back toward the entrance of the tunnel. The gap in the rocks blended in with the rest of the shore in the light of the dying flames.

"Good enough." Kai twisted back, slamming the sorcerer's corpse against the nearest piling.

Trusting the tide not to whisk the dead demon away, Kai let go of the body and felt around the wooden piling, not stopping until he'd pierced his hand on a shard of torn up wood.

He grabbed the bottom of the sorcerer's purple robe and yanked it up to the man's shoulders, exposing his water-limped underclothes.

"I'm not even sorry." Kai bit the fabric just above the hem, tearing it through with his teeth. "A little humiliation in death doesn't even begin to cover the punishment you deserve."

He hooked the hole he'd made onto the sharp bit of wood, giving it a tug to make sure the sorcerer's bobbing corpse wouldn't tear free.

The movement above Kai changed. Slow footsteps moved back out to the edge of the dock.

"May the sea protect me." Kai took as big a breath as his frozen body could manage and dove deep underwater.

35

ALLORA

The change in the thundering of the carriage's wheels gave the only sign they'd crossed the palace bridge and reached the streets of Ilara.

With the starlight blocked by thick, purple curtains, and the criolas in Gillien's hand as the only source of light inside the carriage, Allora had very few choices of where to pin her gaze.

Staring at Gillien's face or light might seem like Allora was waiting for the sorcerer to explain why she'd removed the Queen of Ilbrea from the palace grounds in the middle of the night.

Looking down at her own hands would make Allora appear nervous at having been woken up and told to dress without disturbing Brannon's sleep, implying the King himself didn't know his wife was leaving their room, let alone venturing out into the city.

Fixing her gaze on the dark carriage wall behind Gillien would blatantly scream to the sorcerer that Allora was feigning calm.

Allora settled for studying the curtains, going so far as to reach over and touch them, as though entranced by the faint twisting pattern woven into the fabric.

The carriage slowed.

Sitting back in her seat, Allora straightened the shoulders of her cloak and brushed out the front of her skirt.

Gillien watched her movements, as though waiting for Allora's calm to shatter.

The carriage stopped.

Allora looked to the door.

It didn't open.

A minute stretched past. Allora gave a slight sigh, hoping to present boredom rather than annoyance.

Another minute passed.

The carriage moved slowly forward, Allora's seat tipping slightly as they traveled uphill. The sound of the road beneath the wheels held an oddly quiet and consistent rumble she didn't recognize.

Allora brushed her fingers over her hair, arranging it as well as she could after having been dragged out of bed.

"There's no need," Gillien said. "If anyone were going to see you, I would have ensured you had proper time to dress."

"We mustn't allow the people to see a disheveled queen."

"Whether or not you're joking, you're correct. The appearance of calm can be a great balm in times of worry. And the worth of presenting a gracious and tranquil queen cannot be overestimated."

"I am quite practiced at smiling in public. Perhaps you should allow me to leave the palace during the day. Let the people of Ilbrea see their poised and gracious queen instead of keeping her trapped behind palace walls."

"The danger is too great," Gillien said. "Even if walking you through the streets would cure all the unrest in the city, it couldn't be done."

"Then what could possibly be worth plucking the Queen from her gilded cage?" Allora leaned forward in her seat.

"Education."

"Intriguing. Would my new tutor not come to the palace?"

"I advise you not to jest." Gillien held Allora's gaze. "You'll regret it later."

"A blatant threat?"

"A warning from one who hates to see you hurt. Mockery in such a moment can sink guilt into the basest commoner."

A hint of true worry, or true enough Allora couldn't dismiss it, showed in Gillien's eyes.

The carriage leveled out and stopped.

Three knocks sounded on the roof.

Gillien knocked twice in return.

"Have we arrived?" Allora asked.

"We have."

Allora turned toward the carriage door.

"We'll be staying in the carriage," Gillien said.

"Such fun." Allora sat back.

"This will not be enjoyable for either of us." The worry in Gillien's eyes deepened. "Your Majesty, I've tried to explain the importance of your role as Queen. I've tried to guide you toward the path that best serves Ilbrea."

"Following the path of the snake rarely ends well for the mouse."

"I promise you, rejecting your duties as Queen will not end well. Not for you. Not for the King. Not for Ilbrea."

"My husband is a monster."

"It doesn't matter." Gillien leaned toward Allora. "You are the Queen, and your duty to Ilbrea must come before your personal opinions of the King."

"He drove a pregnant woman to her death. Brannon being a monster is not an opinion."

"Do not make me question your devotion to Ilbrea." Gillien placed her hand on Allora's knee. "If you cannot put aside your personal feelings toward the King for the good of Ilbrea, I fear you hold no love for your people at all."

"That's not true." Allora knocked Gillien's hand away. "I care very much for Ilbrea and all the people Dudia has placed in this land."

"But not enough to sacrifice your own comfort."

"My not embracing Brannon has nothing—"

"Since you cannot see how an unhappy king without an heir affects Ilbrea, a clearer example has been created for you."

Cold fear dripped down the back of Allora's neck. "What horror has my devoted companion planned?"

"Not me." Gillien reached toward the window. "Your behavior has drawn the attention of the Lady Sorcerer."

She pulled the curtains aside.

Dim light shrouded what lay beyond the glass of the carriage window.

A stone chamber with one faded criolas for light. Two figures standing in the darkness, trapped as though left as prey for some awful beast.

The smaller figure, a woman, stepped away from the taller. Her red curls caught in the light as she turned to face the carriage.

"Mara?" Speaking her name stole all the air from Allora's lungs. She dove toward the carriage door, grabbing the handle before Gillien could stop her. "Mara! Tham!"

The handle didn't turn.

"Let me out." Allora spoke through clenched teeth as she gripped the handle, twisting with all her strength.

"You can't open the door."

"Mara!" Allora pounded on the glass of the carriage window.

"They can't hear you or see the carriage, either."

"Mara. Mara!" Allora slammed her palms against the glass over and over.

Mara didn't glance her way.

"Let me go to them," Allora said.

"No."

"Please." Allora knelt, watching as Mara leaned against Tham. He wrapped his arms around her waist, as though Mara couldn't stand on her own.

"I'm not allowed," Gillien said. "Even if I wanted to open the door and let you embrace your dear friends, I couldn't."

"It doesn't matter." Allora sat back on her heels, swiping the tears from her cheeks. "It's an illusion. Mara and Tham are wintering in the white mountains. Their journey is exploring a cave system. They won't return to Ilara until after Winter's End. Maybe not even until summer."

"You were misled."

"What?" Allora glanced toward Gillien but couldn't bear to look away from the false Mara and Tham for long.

Tham brushed a curl away from Mara's face, his fingers lingering on her brow.

If she has a fever, if Mara's fallen ill, she needs me.

That's not Mara, you fool.

"Their journey to the white mountains was a catastrophic failure." Gillien slid over in her seat, placing herself right beside Allora. "Mara and Tham were the only survivors."

"You're lying." Allora leaned back enough to smash her elbow against the window.

Pain shot through her arm, but the glass stayed solid.

"Please don't do that again," Gillien said.

Allora smashed her elbow against the window a second time, paying for her defiance with another burst of pain.

"Mara and Tham are in the white mountains." Allora slammed the sides of her fists against the glass.

"When the Lady Sorcerer learned that Mara and Tham had crawled back to Ilara after such an ignominious failure, she chose another purpose for your friends."

"Liar." Allora leaned back on her elbows, raising her leg to kick the window.

"Please, Allora."

A weight clamped around Allora's ankle, forcing it back down to the floor of the carriage.

"Then let me out." Allora twisted, throwing herself at the window.

A shimmer glistened across the door as her body struck something soft.

"The love you have for Mara and Tham is known to the Lady Sorcerer. Recognizing their value to you, they were brought to the Sorcerers Tower—"

"More—chivving—lies." Allora punctuated her words with slams of her fists against the barrier.

"And they will remain here."

Allora rounded on Gillien, giving an earsplitting scream that would have cut through any non-magical barrier.

Gillien wrinkled her nose at the noise, waiting until Allora took a breath to speak. "If you cannot place your duty to Ilbrea over your feelings toward King Brannon, then perhaps you will place more value on your friends."

"They're not really here." Allora gripped the seat on either side of Gillien, leaning close to the sorcerer's face. "My friends are in the white mountains. No twisted illusion will make me forget that Brannon is a murderer."

"If you fulfill your duties as Queen of Ilbrea, your friends will remain untouched. They will be treated as guests of the Lady Sorcerer, and their comforts will be attended to. If you fail in your duties, they will be considered prisoners." Gillien pointed out the window. "They will be moved into two separate cells where they won't even be able to hear each other scream when the solitude becomes too much to bear."

"Your threats are useless." Allora pushed away from Gillien. "They're not real."

"If you openly defy the will of the Lady Sorcerer, your friends will be moved into smaller cells where they cannot stand. We will take away their light. We will limit their food to just above starving. The finest of the tower's healers will keep them well enough to survive their terrible fate, doomed to pay for every moment our Queen forgets that she is not just an unhappy wife—she is the Queen of Ilbrea, and it is her sworn duty to serve the good of our country."

"I will not tolerate the Lady Sorcerer's threats."

"Then Mara and Tham will be separated."

"More lies." Allora sat back up on the carriage seat, not allowing herself to watch the fake Mara and Tham. "Concocted by the Lady Sorcerer to make a puppet of a queen."

"If you are completely certain that I am lying and your friends are still in the north, then our journey into the city has changed nothing. Continue to be defiant in your roles as Queen and wife."

"Defiance you shall receive."

"If, however, you feel even a flicker of uncertainty, consider your actions wisely." Gillien closed the curtains and knocked twice on the carriage roof. "After all the years Mara and Tham have spent hiding their affection, it would be a pity to tear them apart. A love as devoted as theirs is a rare treasure."

"No." Panic thrummed through Allora's chest. "No. You can't know that."

"The Lady Sorcerer herself has witnessed their devotion during their time in the tower. Tham's drive to protect the woman he loves is admirable. Futile, but admirable."

"They're in the mountains. Mara and Tham aren't here." Allora forced the words past the fear that threatened to choke her.

"If you truly believe that, then the idea of our separating them, keeping Tham so far from Mara she won't even know if the man she loves is still alive, should bring you no worry. Mara won't scream for him until her throat bleeds. Tham won't end up dying in a heroic attempt to rescue Mara. Your defiance won't make you the monster that brings their love story to a tragic end."

Gillien rapped on the roof of the carriage three times. "I hope you can survive the guilt of knowing you've destroyed your closest friend."

The rumble of the carriage's wheels began again.

"No, wait." Allora tore the curtains open.

All that lay beyond the carriage window was pure darkness.

"Mara!"

36

MARA

A strange chill tingled the back of Mara's neck, waking her up just enough to be bothered by the cold. She curled closer to Tham's warmth.

Still asleep, he draped his arm over her, pulling her into the curve of his body.

His instinctive want to be near her brought a smile to Mara's lips as she faded back toward sleep.

Just as darkness embraced her mind, the lights in their room burst to full brightness.

Mara gasped and sat up, falling back against the mattress as Tham leapt to his feet, shoving her behind him. The jab of paws knocked the air out of Mara's lungs as Elle careened over her to protect Tham.

Tham crouched on the bed, facing the door, while Elle planted herself in front of him, growling, her hackles raised.

Mara scrambled free from the covers to stand on the floor behind Tham. She grabbed her glass from beside the bed, ready to hurl the poor excuse for a weapon at whoever was opening the door.

"Elle, stop being dramatic." Torra stepped into the room,

frowning down at Elle as though genuinely put out by the dog's reaction.

Tham jumped off the bed, keeping himself between Torra and Mara.

"I hope I didn't interrupt anything more interesting than sleep." Torra looked from Tham, who only wore his thin under-clothes, to Mara in her shift.

"Just sleep," Mara said. "What time is it? What's going on?"

"Good to know you're not the type to enjoy a wee-hours drop-in." Torra sighed. "Ah well. I've been sent to fetch you at the request of the Lady Sorcerer. You're to dress and follow me."

"Why?" Mara asked, even as she hurried to the wardrobe.

"It's not mine to tell," Torra said.

"Have the Ice Walkers attacked?" Mara tossed clothes to Tham.

"I've been sent to escort you." Torra pointed Mara and Tham toward the sitting room. "Leave Elle, and try not to make too much noise. It's better to let Elver keep sleeping."

Mara yanked on her pants and jammed her feet into her boots.

"The Lady Sorcerer doesn't want you to bring him?" Tham asked.

Torra shook her head. "Only you two."

Mara wriggled into her bodice, tightening the laces as she walked toward the door. "If we're not going to be back before Elver wakes up, Shantene should be here waiting for him."

"Sending him into a panic benefits no one." Torra waited for Tham to reach the sitting room before closing the bedroom door, shutting Elle in.

Elle howled and whimpered.

Torra glared at the closed door. "I'll go to Shantene as soon as I've delivered you."

"Thank you." Tension clipped Tham's words.

Mara took his hand, locking her fingers through his, as Torra reformed the door leading out of the suite the three saelk had been given.

Opening the door the moment the handle fully appeared, Torra led them into the usual dark stone corridor.

Tham shortened his stride, letting Mara walk right beside him as they followed Torra down the passage.

They'd taken the same path many times before, though what the path revealed remained as maddeningly inconsistent as the ice of Isfol.

Two branches cut off the corridor on this journey. One leading right, then a hundred paces down, another cutting to the left. The spiral staircase Mara had only seen once didn't bother reappearing. Neither did the round chamber with empty niches carved into the walls.

Another, narrower corridor crossed their path.

Torra led them down the righthand branch.

A map maker's nightmare, Niko whispered. *You and I are altogether useless in a place that refuses to stay still.*

It's magic, Mara whispered back.

All the chivving worse.

Mara pressed her arm against Tham's side, taking comfort in his solidness as their path slanted up, then led out into a square room just large enough it could have fit four blessedly soft and warm beds side by side.

Torra cut across the room, heading for the entrance to a wide tunnel that kept sloping up.

Mara's pulse quickened as their climb continued, allowing the panic she'd been ignoring to claw its way into her mind.

Something horrible had happened.

That was the only option.

People weren't pulled out of bed in the middle of the night for joyful things. It was hurt, fear, and grief that thrived in the darkest hours of the night.

You've known this was coming. You brought word of demons to the

Sorcerers Tower. You can't set yourself between two monsters and expect horrors not to find you.

The tunnel curved, gently arcing to reach a stone chamber unlike anything Mara had seen in her time within the tower.

The dark stone walls were covered in irregular ridges, giving them the look of a natural cave. Even the floor remained uneven, the texture deep enough to be felt through Mara's boots.

Two long lines cut through the center of the chamber, one white and one gray. A third, purple line crossed the chamber the other way, slicing perpendicularly through the middle of the other two.

All three lines had been inlaid with smoother stone than the floor around them, making it seem as though the lines alone had been the work of men.

Mara pressed on the compass mark on her arm, making the arrow spin to point north as she followed Torra south.

Torra led them to the southwest quarter bound between the white and purple lines.

Mara leaned sideways to peer around Torra, wanting to watch the rough stone wall transform into a new door, but Torra turned to face them instead.

"Stay inside these two lines." Torra pointed to the white and purple marks. "I'll let the Lady Sorcerer know you've arrived, but until she comes, do not cross the lines." She emphasized the warning with bobs of her chin. "You're not in the nex anymore. You're closer to the heart of the tower than you've ever been. The very fact that there are saelk here is dangerous. Wandering could cause catastrophe."

Torra held her hands forward, as though trying to get a dog to stay, as she cut around Mara and Tham and stepped out of their quarter of safety.

"How long will Lady Gwell be?" Mara asked.

"No idea." Torra backed away. "But I'll be sure Elver is looked after until you're back."

"Thank you," Mara called as Torra turned and hurried back the way they'd come.

Mara stared after her, waiting for the Lady Sorcerer to appear. The passage stayed empty. But something—a sort of faint rumbling—grated Mara's nerves.

She turned away from the northern passage to examine the wall. She trailed her fingers over the jagged texture of the stone, failing to find any hint of tools used in its carving.

Magic.

The rumble grew louder.

She looked back toward the still-empty passage, studying the shadows, searching for any hint of a change in the tower's stone—a new corridor rushing into being, or a doorway forming, leading to some new wonder.

Not even a flicker of movement disturbed the passage.

Always magic.

She leaned against Tham, letting his touch soothe her nerves as he wrapped his arms around her waist.

"It's something awful," Mara whispered.

"We don't know anything," Tham said.

"You know I'm right." Mara bit her lip, waiting for a protest that didn't come. "What if the Ice Walkers breached the city walls?"

Tham still didn't speak.

Mara turned toward him, burying her face in his chest. Tears pooled in the corners of her eyes.

What if there's been a massacre and it's my fault? How much blood is on my hands?

Horrible and honest questions she couldn't risk speaking aloud.

"We warned them," he whispered. "Whatever's happened would have been worse if we hadn't."

"Are you sure?" Mara looked up at Tham, tears sliding freely down her cheeks.

"There's no question of it." Tham held Mara's gaze.

There was no sympathy in his eyes or any hint that he was lying, only a grim worry and unbreakable resolve that added heft to the dread weighing on Mara's shoulders.

She laid her cheek against his chest, letting his arms surround her so completely, it seemed impossible for any danger to reach her. "Whatever comes, we meet it together."

And everyone will know about the Ice Walkers. The council will be told the truth of our journey's fate.

A truth worthy of a boon from the Guilds Council.

A jolt of shame sped from Mara's heart to her throat.

Dudia, forgive my selfishness.

She wrapped her arms around Tham's waist, refusing to let her own guilt deprive her of her greatest comfort.

Tham tucked an errant curl behind Mara's ear and kissed the top of her head.

She closed her eyes, listening to the thumping of Tham's heart, trying to match her heartbeat to the steady rhythm of his.

A soft wail, like a distant scream, swept through the chamber.

Mara stepped away from Tham, searching for the source of the noise.

The scream carried on and on.

Mara backed away from the crossing of the lines, grabbing Tham's arm, making him move with her.

The scream grew louder, then fell completely silent.

Mara tipped her head, listening for any hint of danger, any other sound of distress, but hearing only her own ragged breathing.

Tham slid his arm in front of Mara, pressing her back to the stone wall, placing himself between her and the empty room.

"Do you see anything?" Mara whispered.

Tham shook his head.

"Ronya can't get into the tower. Whatever else has happened, that noise couldn't have been her," Mara said.

It could be something worse, you fool.

The chamber stayed silent.

Tham didn't relax his stance.

Mara laid her hand on his lower back, offering what mute comfort she could as the silence stretched on, twisting a more piercing fear into Mara's chest than the wail had managed.

The rumble began again, muffled but close. So close, it seemed she could dodge around Tham and grab whatever made the noise. But the rumble faded, drifting away, leaving more nerve-grating silence in its wake.

Finally, the faint sound of footsteps came from the southern corridor.

Mara squeezed to the side, giving herself a clear view around the wall of Tham's shoulders.

The Lady Sorcerer stepped into the chamber, two women in plain, black dresses trailing behind her.

Lady Gwell studied Mara and Tham. She furrowed her brow, narrowing her eyes as though searching for something she couldn't quite find.

When she finally looked away, she turned her head just enough to nod to the two women behind her.

The women bowed to the Lady Sorcerer's back and retreated.

"My apologies for calling you out of bed in the middle of the night. But immediate action needed to be taken, and your participation was required," Lady Gwell said.

"Lady Gwell"—Mara bowed—"I don't understand what's going on. I will beg for information if that's what has to be done."

"No need for such things among those who fight on the same side," Lady Gwell said.

"Fight?" Tham asked.

"This way." Lady Gwell pointed them down the southern corridor.

Tham took Mara's hand, planting his feet. He met the Lady

Sorcerer's gaze, staring into her eyes for a moment before bowing deeply. "Yes, Lady Sorcerer."

Mara held her breath, waiting for magic to snatch Tham from her as punishment for his heartbeat's worth of defiance.

He led her past Lady Gwell and into the corridor. The floor didn't swallow her. No demons sprang from the stone to tear Tham away as they strode toward the total darkness looming at the end of the passage.

Mara took a tentative breath. Tham's hand stayed firmly in hers.

The darkness at the end of the corridor didn't fade as they approached. The pitch black stayed solid, as though it were a living absence of light.

"Keep walking," Lady Gwell said. "Lingering in the entryway is unwise, especially for saelk."

Mara tightened her grip on Tham until her fingers ached. She glanced back at the Lady Sorcerer.

Lady Gwell's face betrayed nothing.

Mara grabbed Tham's wrist with her free hand, anchoring herself to him as they stepped into the godsforsaken black.

37

MARA

Cold. Pressing against Mara, surrounding her, crushing the air from her lungs.

The cold dragged against her legs, trying to hold her in place.

She clutched Tham's arm to her chest.

There was no warmth in his skin, but he kept moving forward, fighting through the black, which didn't thin, didn't show any sign of stopping.

Tham's arm jerked, yanking Mara forward a step.

Dim light flashed into being as the cold vanished.

Mara gasped in a breath, sagging forward as her body struggled to understand the sudden lack of squeezing pressure. She blinked at the shadows on the stone floor, trying to make the room stop tilting.

"Mara." Tham took Mara's chin, tipping her face up so he could look into her eyes.

"Fine." Mara leaned forward, bracing her hand against Tham's chest. "Rattled, but fine. You?"

Tham gave a tense nod, then looked over Mara's shoulder.

Mara turned to follow his gaze just in time to watch the Lady Sorcerer step out of the darkness.

The Lady Sorcerer didn't acknowledge the two saelk she'd sent into the black as she walked past them, heading toward the center of the space.

Mara squared her shoulders and willed her heartbeat to slow before daring to look around the chamber they'd crossed through the darkness to reach.

The horrible black filled the archway they'd passed through. Each of the other six walls in the room were solid, leaving venturing back through the crushing cold as their only escape.

Small, carved niches covered the walls, giving the stone the look of a honeycomb.

In the center of the chamber, seven stone seats surrounded a ten-foot-tall golden statue of a woman. The woman held a young girl in her arms while two more clung to her skirts. The woman had been carved with her chin tipped up, as though she were looking to something above the horizon.

There was a certain beauty to the woman's face—the cut of her cheeks, fullness of her lips, and size of her eyes should have made her gorgeous—but something Mara couldn't have explained twisted her beauty toward monstrous.

Mara approached the wall to the right of the arch, grateful to have a reason to turn away from the statue.

She glanced back to Lady Gwell as she reached the wall, waiting for the Lady Sorcerer to forbid her from indulging her curiosity. But Lady Gwell had her gaze fixed on the statue and said nothing as Mara leaned close to the wall, studying the inside of one of the stone niches.

Words too small for Mara to read had been carved into the stone, giving the surface a rough texture. But something else about the stone didn't look quite right.

Mara tipped her head, leaning to catch different angles of the light.

She squinted, stepped back and then closer again, trying to spot what she had missed.

No, not missed. What was missing.

The normal purple hue deep within the stone wasn't there. No matter how Mara looked at it, the stone stayed pure black.

"It's a tomb," Lady Gwell said, pulling Mara's attention back to the center of the chamber. Lady Gwell stepped closer to the statue, laying her hand on the woman's stomach over what would have been her womb. "Each of these markers records the death of one our people, slain by those who have sought to eradicate our kind."

"I'm so sorry," Mara said.

Lady Gwell moved her hand to the top of one of the girls' heads. She stroked the statue as though smoothing the child's hair. "These niches were filled centuries before our time. We've had to find new ways to remember and mourn our dead."

"I'm still sorry," Mara said.

"As you should be." Lady Gwell turned away from the statue without acknowledging either of the other two girls. "As all saelk should be. If anyone else in the tower had allowed saelk into this tomb, they may well have preferred death to the punishment I would give them."

"We're honored to have been brought to such an important place." Tham bowed.

"A necessity." Lady Gwell cut around the statue, heading toward the far side of the tomb. "When I chose to allow your presence in the Sorcerers Tower, I had hoped you would feel at peace in our home and grow to consider the sorcerers friends and allies."

"We are very grateful for the safety and hospitality you've given us," Mara said. "Torra, Fergal, Shantene—they've been so kind."

"You have taken to a few of our people but still fear what we are." Lady Gwell beckoned them over her shoulder. "Your true and dedicated devotion to the safety of my people should have been carefully earned and given of your own accord, but we've run out of time."

"Why?" Tham led Mara across the room. "Has there been an attack?"

"We are always under attack. That is the horrid truth all sorcerers face and one you must understand. Every time a sorcerer leaves the tower, their life is in danger. If what I fear comes to pass, that danger will increase tenfold. And the threat to sorcerer children born to saelk mothers"—Lady Gwell trailed her fingers along the ridged edges of one of the niches—"I doubt many of them will survive long enough for us to find them."

"That can't be true," Mara said. "There are some cruel people in the world, but to harm a child?"

"They won't be seen as children." A faint blue light shimmered in the back of the niche. "They will be seen as *other*. Different. Dangerous. A creature to be exploited at best. A monster to be destroyed most often."

The blue light in the niche grew, expanding beyond the confines of the stone to create a shimmering image.

Words surrounded the face of a small girl who couldn't have been more than seven.

Name Unknown.

Killed in Merton. Gutted while alive. Intestines burned. Corpse displayed with six others.

May the child find kindness in death.

"She was so young." Mara reached out, her fingers meeting nothing but air as she tried to touch the unnamed girl's cheek.

"Her story is in no way unique," Lady Gwell said.

"But I've studied Ilbrea's history. How could I never have read or even heard about something like this happening?" Mara reread the words of the inscription.

May the child find kindness in death.

"We in the Sorcerers Tower have spent hundreds of years protecting our kind. Erasing all outside records of these tragedies was necessary. To be vulnerable is to be preyed upon. We cannot be seen as weak. It is the only way children like her can survive."

"Thank you," Tham said, "for sharing your grief with us."

"I had no choice." The Lady Sorcerer walked away from them, trailing her fingers along the wall, leaving a ribbon of blue lights blossoming in her wake. "There is a fine line between enough knowledge to forge real alliances and endangering yourself by exposing a truth that invites evil."

The blue lights grew, becoming monuments, hundreds of monuments, to slain sorcerers.

The faces of men, women, children—so many children—surrounded the room.

The lights spread, growing up and down the walls, becoming the faces of thousands.

Mara pressed her hand to her mouth, stifling her need to scream in grief and anger.

Tham wrapped his arm around her waist, pulling Mara close, as though he too were fighting the need to rage at the gods for allowing such violence.

When every niche had been filled with blue light, the Lady Sorcerer finally spoke. "This is the fate I have vowed my people will never again endure. But we are being pushed toward the brink of even darker paths."

An unreadable chill filled the sorcerer's eyes, hiding any hint of the grieving leader she'd been a moment before. "One of my wardens watching the north was killed. His manner of death could not have been caused by a person without magic."

"Ronya," Tham said.

"Or one of her people," Lady Gwell said. "Their ability to twist the ice to their will has made tracking them impossible."

"But we have to assume they're somewhere in Ilbrea." Tham switched his hold on Mara, moving to her right, freeing his dominant hand to fight.

"Foreign magic has entered our borders," Lady Gwell said. "If that magic is not stifled, it will threaten the safety of all Ilbrean sorcerers. One village being destroyed by Ice Walker magic will result in a wave of fear.

"The ones who suffer most from that fear will be the children, just like that murdered little girl. Born with powers others don't understand. Without the training to defend themselves, without the means to run for the safety of the tower, those children will die terrified and reviled."

"But if you warn people, tell them about the Ice Walkers—" Mara began.

"The saelk will see us as vulnerable, and they will attack." All trace of emotion vanished from Lady Gwell's face. "I've seen enough violence to know there are cowards in Ilara who would slay sorcerers just to see if we bleed."

"Then we find the Ice Walkers," Tham said. "Stop them before they reach any villages and drive Ronya's army back to the white. We know where they entered Ilbrea. Even if we can't track them, that narrows the area where they could be hiding. We might actually be able to find them if you send enough people to search."

"And we will try," Lady Gwell said. "But whether or not we find the invaders before they attack, we must accept one undeniable truth: battle is imminent. Blood will be spilt. I cannot allow you to face the Ice Walkers alongside my sorcerers unless you understand the threat that constantly endangers my people. Our survival cannot be taken for granted. I hope now you'll appreciate that, when the battle begins, the Sorcerers Guild will do what is necessary to protect the future of our people."

38

ALLORA

Anger and panic had twisted into a cold numbness that encased Allora's body. Sitting on the floor of the carriage as it bumped across the stone bridge and onto the palace grounds, listening for screams she'd be too far away to hear, Allora pushed against the shroud of haze filling her mind.

Mara and Tham in the tower. That could be a lie.

Mara and Tham threatened by the sorcerers. The Lady Sorcerer delighted in pain. If she had Mara and Tham, she would torment them. An undeniable truth.

Killing Allora if she didn't obey. A firm possibility.

Mara and Tham not in the north, but back home.

Mara and Tham so close by and Allora hadn't known.

Mara and Tham in danger because of Allora.

Gillien lying, tricking Allora into thinking she had Mara and Tham.

Mara and Tham tortured because Allora didn't obey.

Circles and circles and circles.

Every time coming back to the same place. If there was any chance Dudia had allowed Mara and Tham to be captured by the

Lady Sorcerer, Allora couldn't risk them suffering for her defiance.

Gillien took Allora under the arms, hoisting her back onto her seat as the carriage stopped in front of the Royal Palace.

A soldier opened the carriage door.

Revulsion crawled up Allora's arms as he bowed and offered his hand. She couldn't bring herself to touch the soldier.

She stepped down from the carriage without his aid, not looking back as she walked up the palace steps. The soldiers flanking the entrance opened the palace doors, clearing Allora's path.

Before she'd reached the stairs to the second level, Gillien's footsteps had begun tapping along behind her.

Allora unfastened her cape and let it fall, a pathetic obstacle in the sorcerer's path.

Gillien kept following.

Allora pulled out the few pins she'd used in her hair, dropping those on the floor, too.

The soldiers posted outside Princess Illia's room bowed as Allora passed.

What would they say of their Queen wandering in the middle of the night?

Allora pinched the top button on the front of her dress, willing her hands to wait until she'd reached her journey's end.

A good queen. A fertile queen. A queen that gives pleasure.

Allora pressed her hand to her heart. She couldn't feel it beating. She couldn't allow herself to hope it had stopped.

If the soldiers guarding the door to Brannon's rooms were shocked to find Allora walking toward them with her hair tumbling loosely around her shoulders, none of them dared show it.

All of the men bowed. A soldier with hair lighter than Allora's opened the door.

Shadows filled the room. Brannon still lay in bed, asleep.

The blond soldier closed the door.

Gillien hadn't followed Allora into the room, leaving Ilbrea's Queen to fulfill her duty sans watchman.

Allora approached the bed, watching Brannon sleep, trying to find something to love in the softness of his face as he slumbered. A man free from the worries of ruling Ilbrea.

Unfastening the top of her dress, Allora worked her way down the row of buttons as quickly as her trembling fingers would allow. She dropped her dress to the floor and stepped out of her shoes, leaving herself shivering in the shift she'd worn to bed.

She bit her lips together, swallowing to make sure she was capable of speech.

"Brannon." She said his name softly.

He didn't move.

"Brannon." She waited two breaths. "Brannon."

He shifted his shoulders but didn't wake up.

Allora stepped over her discarded dress, stopping just out of Brannon's reach.

"Brannon." She held her breath.

Nothing.

"Brannon." She spoke in a normal voice. "Brannon."

He bolted upright, looking to where Allora should have been sleeping, then to where she stood in her shift.

"What's wrong?" His breath rasped in his throat as though he'd been running. "Is the palace under attack?" He threw back the covers.

"There's no attack." Allora stepped right up against the bed, blocking Brannon's path. "I need to apologize."

"What?" The tension sagged from Brannon's shoulders.

"I've behaved inappropriately. I am the Queen of Ilbrea married to the King of Ilbrea. It is my duty to bear your heir. Making myself inhospitable to you was selfish and petulant. I'm sorry."

"You're sorry?" Brannon dragged his hands over his hair, digging his fingers into the back of his head.

"Yes, husband." Allora held out her hand to him, setting her jaw, bracing for the moment he would touch her.

"You're sorry you berated me with your ill-conceived accusations? That you mocked my virility? That you got your way when I left you alone?" Brannon let go of his head and leapt out of bed to stand right beside Allora. "Or is it something else, wife?"

He took her shoulders, turning her to face him.

"Brannon—"

"Are you sorry you've associated with those so disloyal to the Guilds and the laws that protect our people, they led their family to their doom?"

"No one deserves what you did to Adrial." Allora looked up into Brannon's eyes. In the darkness, she couldn't see their teal color, only his anger. "But the harm done to my friend does not absolve me of my duty as Ilbrea's Queen."

"To bed the King." He gripped her shoulders tighter. "Even if you can't feel it when he enters you?"

"I shouldn't have said that." Hateful heat pooled in Allora's eyes. "It's not true, and it was a cruel thing—"

"And why has your cruelty changed, wife?"

Allora gasped as he gripped her even harder.

"Have you decided you miss the touch of a man, or have you grown too cowardly to insult your King?"

"Why does it matter?" Allora laid her hand on his chest. "I'm here now, and I will make up for the time we've lost."

"Why?" He yanked her closer, pinning her against him.

"I am giving myself to you." The heat of tears trailed down Allora's cheeks. "However you want me, I am yours."

"Tell me why."

"Brannon—"

"Why!"

"They have Mara and Tham." Tears hitched in Allora's throat. "They're being held in the Sorcerers Tower."

Brannon let go of her, jolting away as though her skin were covered in hot coals.

"The sorcerers want a Willoc heir," Allora whispered. "I have to give them one."

Brannon slammed his fist against the bedpost.

"It's the only way I can keep Mara and Tham safe."

"So you come crawling back to me. You insult me. You mock me. You call me a murderer and a monster—"

"Please, Brannon."

"Then you expect my forgiveness, because you've finally realized life within the palace is not fueled by your wants and your petty morality."

"I'm sorry." Allora stepped toward him, reaching out to caress his cheek.

He knocked her hand aside. "You wanted to stifle my affection, and it has been done. I no longer desire you."

"You have to."

"I will not touch a woman who mocks me, degrading me to the point that the Lady Sorcerer has turned her attention to my bed."

"They will hurt Mara and Tham." Allora grabbed his hand, clinging to him as he tried to wrench free. "I'm begging you."

"Save your tears, wife. No amount of begging could induce my passion for a woman who comes crawling back to me at the sorcerers' bidding."

"Please, Brannon."

"The fate of your friends lies on your head, not mine." Brannon shoved her away, breaking free of her grip, and stormed toward the door.

"I am your wife." Allora chased after him, dodging around him to lean against the door. "I am your Queen. I have to give you an heir."

"You'll get no child from me."

"I will carry your child, Brannon. The sorcerers demand it."

"Perhaps the sorcerers will have better luck with my next queen." Pushing Allora aside, he flung open the door, striding past the soldiers and down the corridor, wearing only his underthings.

The soldier with the pale blond hair reached back to close the bedroom door. Shock filled his eyes even before he spotted Allora beside the door, tears streaming down her cheeks as she wore only a thin shift that hid nothing.

Allora shook her head, backing into the shadows.

A wrinkle appeared on the soldier's brow. He gave a tiny nod and closed the door, leaving Allora alone in the darkness.

A sob pummeled Allora's chest. She looked to the bed that held Mara and Tham's fate.

She could have woken Brannon by kissing him. Or lain naked beside him, waiting for him to wake in the morning.

"I'm so sorry." Allora pressed her hand to her mouth, stifling her sobs.

The walls of the room blurred, seeming to bend as they pressed in around her.

She bolted for the hidden door beside the bed, grabbing a doused candle, not bothering to light it until she'd slammed the panel shut behind her.

The sound of her ragged breathing filled the dark passageway. Her trembling fingers struggled to light the candle.

A flame finally caught, hissing to life, giving a wavering light to the empty corridor.

Away from the bedroom, that was Allora's intent, but instead of a spare bedroom or parlor, her feet carried her toward the black stone room.

Even as she descended the impossibly long stairs, she couldn't have explained why the deadly stones whispered of sanctuary.

A dim light flickered at the bottom of the steps. The door to the black stone room had been left all the way open, as though someone had wanted to prove its emptiness.

Allora slowed her steps, creeping toward the doorway, being sure to check every corner of the room, searching for an intruder before crossing the threshold. Her eyes didn't catch the two small objects hiding in the shadows until she'd nearly stepped on them.

She sank to the floor beside the offering.

Ripping the stopper from the bottle and filling the glass with frie, Allora downed the burning liquor before the question of why she'd been granted such a thoughtful gift grew too loud for her to ignore.

39

NIKO

Despite the undeniable magic that had gone into carving the stronghold's keep, and the magic that kept the leaves of the trees in the stone atrium a vibrant green even while they suffered a constant lack of sunlight, no Brien sorcerer or trueborn had ever bothered finding a way to block the vicious winds that swept in through the atrium's massive entryway.

While the weather's intrusion into the Brien's favored gathering place had seemed a mere oddity on the few occasions Niko had previously considered the oversight, lingering beside the archway, watching Ena walk through the frozen garden beyond as though it were a fine spring evening the gods had wrought specifically for quiet outdoor contemplation, Niko fell into complete certainty that the creator of the space had been very intentional in their design.

Whether a Black Blood or the temper-ridden mountain herself, the artificer of the atrium had chosen to make the space impossible to heat and had done so out of spite. Perhaps their intended victim of the cold hadn't been an Ilbrean spying on another Ilbrean, but the result was the same.

Niko wiggled his toes in his boots, pushing just a tiny bit of circulation through his frozen feet.

"You could invite her in for tea." Danu spoke in a low voice but didn't lean close enough to Niko to whisper.

"No." Niko kept his gaze pinned on Ena.

"Then invite her for a proper drink."

"Again, no." Niko clenched and unclenched his fingers in his pockets. They were, at least, faring better than his toes.

"Skulking behind Solcha is unwise at the best of times." Danu gave a nod to a passing pair of women wearing well-made coats.

The women slowed their pace as they passed Niko, giving themselves a moment to stare at him, until Ena and her acolytes caught one of their gazes. The gawker swatted her companion's arm and outright pointed to Ena.

The swattee gasped.

The women hurried through the archway and out onto the snowy terrace, only to slow again when they'd gotten close enough to Ena to properly ogle her.

Mountain-cursed madness.

"One Solcha openly watching the other serves no one," Danu said. "If you're worried about her—"

"Of course I'm worried about Ena. She sent her child away."

"Then talk to her." Danu cut around Niko, standing in the middle of the archway to maintain her chosen distance. "You say her marriage makes her family, then treat her like family. Go comfort her, Niko."

"She doesn't want my comfort."

A pack of children tore across the terrace, stopping to bow to Ena before scampering toward the atrium.

Danu leapt out of the herd's path just in time.

The children stumbled to a stop, giving Niko and Danu a bow and, in the case of one girl, a panicked giggle, before sprinting for the stairs leading farther up into the keep.

The panicked girl kept giggling as they ran out of sight.

"I hope I never find out what those fools are up to." Danu bit her lips together, hiding their suppleness.

She'd leapt out of the pack's path and landed right beside Niko. Close. So close, he could brush his fingers against hers, or claim her mouth…tease the tension from her lips.

Danu met his gaze, freezing for a moment, before taking two definitive steps away.

Niko looked back to Ena, pivoting his thoughts to dwelling on the cold of his toes rather than drifting into remembering the feel of Danu's body against his.

"If you're determined to keep watching her, we should move to a better place," Danu said. "There are plenty of rooms with a view of the terrace through the windows."

"I need to stay nearby."

Ena walked out of Niko's sightline, heading toward the edge of the garden.

Niko strolled to the other side of the archway, regaining his view of her.

"If people start thinking you're jealous of Ena, all your parading around in black will have been for nothing," Danu said. "Two Solchas united keeps you alive."

"Because if Bryana decides to kill one of us to keep the Brien from choosing sides, I'll be the Solcha to die. I'm aware."

Ena reached up, trailing her gloved fingers along the ice-covered branch of a tree.

"Then let's find a place to watch more discreetly," Danu said.

"I can't. Ena told Marta she'd wait four days after the feast."

"We don't know what she was waiting for."

"Whatever it is, Ena wanted to make sure Lily was safely out of the way." Niko leaned against the arch, making no attempt to hide his watching Ena as four men cut through the atrium, giving reverent nods to Niko before going out onto the terrace. "I have a distinct feeling Ena Ayres plotting something worth sending her baby away is the kind of chaos I can't afford to miss."

The four men slowed their steps as they neared Ena, cutting onto a side path that would lead them closer to her.

Niko pushed away from the arch, ready to charge the men. But they only bowed deeply to Ena before strolling away, taking a path that cut a wide circle around the terrace.

"You haven't said I'm wrong." Niko leaned back against the stone arch.

"I'm trying to convince myself you are." Danu chewed on her bottom lip as the wrinkles on her brow deepened.

"You don't have to stand with me."

"If you'd be more comfortable."

A sting flicked Niko's chest as Danu stepped back.

"No." Niko lunged toward her, fumbling as he tried to take her hand with his partially numb, gloved fingers. "I meant hovering near Ena and whatever has her loitering in a chivving freezing garden. I don't want you farther from me." He stepped back into the archway, pulling Danu with him. "I hate every breath of space between us. I understand why it's necessary, I know what happened in that tunnel was only you protecting me, but I hate it."

He let go of Danu's hand. She stayed two feet away from him. Close enough for sparks to dance through his frozen fingers at the thought of caressing her skin.

He fixed his gaze back on Ena.

She was moving again, slowly cutting around the garden, stopping to acknowledge everyone who bowed to her.

The number of people wandering the terrace had grown, as though Ena had made freezing while silently examining a snow-slaughtered garden the peak of Brien entertainment.

The flock of children who had run up the atrium's stairs bolted back the other way, their numbers seeming to have expanded as they tore through the keep. The flock stumbled to a stop, crashing into each other as they paused to bow to Niko and Danu before charging toward Ena.

"I hate it, too," Danu said.

A different, sharper kind of sting flicked Niko's heart.

"It doesn't change anything. But I promised I'd never lie to you." Danu looked above Niko, to the perfect leaves weaving up the atrium walls. "I could have just waited on top of you and given you a quick kiss for Paiman's sake. It would have turned out the same. But I was burnt out from using too much magic, and everything felt cold and empty." She took a shuddering breath. "Kissing you melted the cold, and feeling you against me shot sparks through everything, and I wanted more of you. If Paiman hadn't found us, I would have kept going as long as you let me."

A pulsing heat drove any thought of the freezing wind from Niko's mind.

"I hate that what happened has made it awkward between us and I still don't even know what your skin would feel like against mine," Danu said. "And I hate that finding out would be an even more chivving terrible idea now than it was before."

"I know."

"I never want you to think kissing you drove me away. But a few feet of distance makes not touching you easier."

The pulsing heat faded.

He studied Danu's face. Her furrowed brow. The pained worry creasing the corners of her eyes.

"Your brother's interruption may well remain one of the greatest regrets of my life," Niko said. "But if the choice is staying at arm's length or not seeing you at all, I'll ask for a larger table."

Danu cocked her head as her lips drooped into the most alluring frown.

"The table in my room is too small. Every time we sit

together, I'll be tempted to reach out and graze my fingers against yours. Even with frozen fingers in thick gloves, I want to feel your hand in mine." Niko gave the most charming smile he could manage. "A nice, six-foot wide table. Something big enough I'd have to lie chest-down on the meat platter to reach across and brush a stray tendril of hair from your cheek."

Danu gave a faint huff of a laugh.

"I'm not joking," Niko said. "Even with the promised humiliation of sloshing through soup, I will still be sorely tempted."

A glint of humor brightened Danu's eyes.

The flicking at Niko's heart surged into a soul-shattering punch to the center of his chest that drove the air from his lungs.

That tiny glint in Danu's eyes shoved aside every other accomplishment Niko had ever claimed.

To make her smile, make her laugh—that glorious quest could consume a man's life.

Danu shook her head. A tendril of hair fell across her brow.

Oh, what Niko would trade Dudia to be able to caress her cheek as he tucked that hair behind her ear.

She might lean into his touch, maybe even close her eyes as she savored the intimacy of such a simple act.

Dudia save my poor chivving soul.

Niko looked back out to the garden, praying for a disaster to snap his mind out of scrambling to find another way to bring a spark of joy to Danu's eyes.

But the snow on the terrace hadn't been coated in blood.

The clusters of Brien who'd been wandering the garden, watching Solcha enjoying freezing her toes off, had stopped, all of them staring at the far end of the terrace near the stairs that led down to the valley floor.

Niko took a step outside the arch, instinctively reaching for Danu's hand. A reverberating ache rolled through him as he shoved his hands into his pockets. "Come on."

He walked down the snow-packed paths, not stopping to see if the footsteps following behind him were Danu's.

He hadn't even reached the edge of the scattered onlookers before spotting what had captivated the peoples' attention.

Ena stood on the edge of one of the raised garden beds, looking toward the setting sun.

If her black cloak whipping around her stone-still frame weren't enough to make her seem like a warrior ready to fight the wind itself, her four acolytes standing on the edge behind her, all staring west as she did, turned the scene into something worthy of legend.

"Niko." Danu kept right on his heels as he weaved through the growing crowd. "Niko, don't go any closer."

"Why?" He didn't stop moving.

"Because we have no idea what under the chivving stars she's doing or if you would survive it." Danu dodged in front of him. "If you want to watch whatever chaos Ena has planned, fine. But we're doing it from a distance."

"You stay at a distance. I'm joining her." Niko cut around Danu.

"Niko." She grabbed his arm.

Despite the layers separating their skin, a thrill rushed through him, begging him to pull Danu into his arms.

"Whatever Ena is up to, stay out of it," Danu said. "Please."

"I can't." Niko leaned close to Danu, grateful for the wind sweeping her soul-stealing scent away as he spoke close to her ear. "I don't know what twisted force brought Adrial's wife and me to the same place. But Ena has survived the Black Bloods before. Ena is a common inker who managed to marry a scribe who will soon be one of the most powerful men in Ilbrea. I have no idea what she's planning, but if I'm going to tie my hopes of freedom to anyone, it's going to be her."

"Niko, don't—"

"This has got to be what she waited four days for."

"And if her plan doesn't involve freedom or survival?" True fear filled Danu's eyes.

"Then I'm even more grateful I know what your lips taste like." He turned away from her, running to the raised, waist-high garden bed, jumping up onto the edge without giving fear or regret a chance to creep through his resolve.

40

NIKO

Ena didn't flinch when Niko leapt up onto the stone edge, giving no sign of having even seen him as he took the place nearest her, planting himself between her and her closest acolyte.

He glanced to the acolyte, but the man gave no hint of having noticed Niko either.

Whether fool or genius, you've cast your lot now, Nikolas Endur.

He looked up in the same direction as the others, trying to mimic the proud tilt of Ena's chin and the absolute stillness of her body.

"Niko." Danu spoke from just in front of him.

He kept his gaze pinned on the last crescent of the sun setting over the peaks of the eastern mountains.

"Niko, I'm supposed to protect you," Danu said.

He'd never taken the time to appreciate the beauty of the sharp summits beyond the gentler cliffs of the stronghold. The mountains surrounding the valley had never been more than bars adding to the strength of his cage.

"Please, Niko."

Danu's voice—the pleading, her fear—slammed against Niko's resolve.

Danu should never have such worry in her voice. Not if he could prevent it.

Eyes up, Niko, Adrial whispered. *Eyes up.*

Niko bit the tip of his tongue, focusing on the pain and the metallic tang of blood in his mouth as he fought the need to glance down.

Just to see if she was there. If she'd already walked away. If her pleading had turned to anger.

Eyes up.

"You're a chivving sodding slitch of a bastard, Niko Karron." Danu moved through Niko's peripheral vision as she stepped up onto the edge of the garden bed beside him. "Shove down a bit. If I'm going to risk my neck playing along with whatever chivving nonsense you've decided to toss yourself into, I'm not standing scrunched on a corner."

Biting his cheeks to hide his smile, Niko stepped toward Ena.

"Better," Danu said. "If I have to plead with Bryana to keep us alive after this, I'll be in a foul mood until the first thaw."

Niko's grin broke free.

"Thank you," he said as quietly as the wind would allow.

"I'd prefer a promise to invest in common sense over your gratitude."

Niko puffed out a breath, relaxing his face back into a stoic mimicry of Ena's. He couldn't keep his smile from lifting the corners of his eyes.

A wave of murmurs came from the atrium side of the terrace, growing louder as they swept closer.

Watch the sunset, Adrial whispered. *Eyes on the sky.*

The red of the setting sun shimmered pink on the snow-covered peaks, giving the jagged horizon an otherworldly glow.

The murmuring surrounded Niko, then stopped.

Chivving eyes up, Kai said.

"Such a display." Bryana's voice came from right in front of Niko.

The mountains, Niko, Mara said. *Memorize the shape of the mountains.*

A cluster of three large peaks to the southwest.

"What keeps Solcha outside on this cold evening?" Poorly concealed danger laced Bryana's words.

Ena didn't answer.

Pain pierced Niko's back.

Farther north, a mountain with two summits, the taller eastern peak barely allowing Niko to see past to the western.

Niko gasped as the pain grew, spreading along the lines of his mark.

"Speak, Solcha," Bryana said.

Eyes up, Tham said.

Warm blood trickled down Niko's back.

"Your elder commands it."

The pain pressed inward toward Niko's lungs.

"I am grateful for the hospitality of your clan, Elder Bryana." Ena's voice carried over the wind. "I will be forever grateful for the shelter you've provided me as the mountain sheltered an orphan so long ago."

"As the mountain chose to shelter you, Solcha." Bryana matched Ena's volume, the loathing in her voice hidden behind the guise of poised authority.

"And now I must repay the mountain and all the Black Bloods," Ena said. "We who stand before you have witnessed our last sunset for many days."

Niko's lungs spasmed as the pain grew sharper.

"Tomorrow, we begin our journey, facing the darkness below the mountains to reach Ilara," Ena said.

"What?" Bryana hissed, too quietly for the crowd to hear.

Niko gagged on a cough as the pain pressing against his lungs spread.

"The mountain led Niko and me to the Brien," Ena said. "And

now the mountain calls upon us to join the Brien already fighting in Ilara."

The crowd's flutter of murmurs barely pierced the panic in Niko's mind.

Eyes up, Mara ordered.

"The threat the Guilds pose to the Black Bloods is worse than even I feared," Ena pressed on. "The Sorcerers Guild has stores of mountain stone, and they have learned to mold that stone into the horrible sorts of weapons the Black Bloods banned by treaty years ago."

Niko's breath came in tiny gasps. His lungs wouldn't fill any farther. They couldn't.

"I gave my oath to watch the Guilds burn, and I will see it done," Ena said. "With your elder's wisdom and the strength of the Brien clan fighting beside me, we will find a way to stop the threat of the Guilds before the demons storm through the mountains to slaughter the Black Bloods' children."

The crowd roared their love for Solcha.

The sound of it pounded against Niko's ears. The horizon began to sway.

The cheers died.

"We who stand before you have each been called by the mountain to venture into the darkness, and we will not turn away from that call," Ena said. "The Brien will have justice for your trueborn's murder."

Agony ripped through Niko's back. The heat of blood dripped down his spine.

An arm wrapped around Niko's hips, keeping him from pitching forward.

Eyes up.

"And when they tell the story of the Guilds' downfall, your elder will be remembered as the only one brave enough to face the battle ahead. The Brien will stand as heroes among the Black Bloods. For the glory of the mountain's children!"

The cheers of the horde filled the night.

Movement swept through the corner of Niko's vision.

Eyes up.

A flutter of black cloak as Ena stepped down from the edge of the garden bed.

Eyes up.

The support from Niko's hips shifted to his arm.

"Come on." Danu stepped off the edge, Niko's hand clutched in hers. "Niko."

Eyes...up.

The last of the pink glow faded from the snow-covered peaks.

"How dare you?" Bryana spoke from right in front of Niko, the demon still lurking just out of sight. "Making proclamations I have not condoned is a dangerous mistake, Solcha."

The pain in Niko's lungs surged.

He coughed, losing the last of his precious air.

"Will you tell your people I'm not seeking vengeance for Regan and a path to the Guilds' destruction, or shall I?" Ena said.

"Niko." Danu pulled on his hand.

"Your people heard me speak, Bryana. If you try to twist my words for your own sick pleasure, your people will scent out your lies," Ena said. "We are leaving in the morning. All those who stood with me will be traveling with me.

"We will join the Brien I know chivving well are already hiding in Ilara. We will fight the paun. If you want to have a tantrum because I didn't ask your permission, I wish you luck in explaining to your people how Solcha has been locked up or murdered by their elder."

His lungs couldn't reinflate. His knees buckled.

"Solcha!" A terrified cry came from the left.

Eyes up.

Hands grabbed Niko, lifting him off the edge.

He screamed as pressure hit the mark on his back.

"If you want to explain to the Brien that the hope I've just given them, the only chivving hope they've had all winter, is false, fine," Ena said. "If not, stop toying with Niko's back and send a healer to his rooms. I named him as one traveling with me, so he had better be chivving well fit to travel by morning. If you keep him or your minion niece here, it will sow doubt through your people, and their thin shred of resolve will snap."

"You will not dictate who leaves my stronghold," Bryana said.

"I already have. We're on the same side, Bryana. Or do you prefer torturing allies over avenging what we've lost?"

The pressure on Niko's lungs ebbed. He gasped in a breath.

Gentle hands laid Niko on the snow-covered ground.

Two of Ena's acolytes backed away, leaving Danu standing over him.

"You play dangerous games, Solcha," Bryana said. "I will enjoy the day you lose."

"May you learn from Regan's mistakes."

Ena stepped in front of Danu. Reaching down, she grabbed Niko's arm, yanking him to his feet.

He staggered forward.

Danu caught him by his hips, not touching his back.

"Take off your coat," Ena said.

"What?" Niko shook his head, trying to get the ground to stop twisting.

"You collapsed in front of a crowd, take off your chivving coat," Ena said.

Niko's fingers fumbled on the buttons.

Danu brushed his hands aside, making quick work of unfastening his coat.

He swallowed a scream as one of the acolytes peeled the coat away from his back.

Ena took his shoulders, turning him away from her. "Perfect."

"Wh—what is?" Niko asked.

"Thank you, Bryana." Ena smiled, bowing to the demon elder.

"Your handywork is much appreciated. Such a fine detail I couldn't have managed on my own."

Ena took Niko's arm, leading him toward the atrium.

"What is it?" Niko swallowed the bile in his throat. "What did she do to me?"

"You've got the perfect outline of a bird dripping with the blood of its enemies on your back," Ena said. "Before the night is out, half the stronghold will be certain the mountain herself made you bleed when she called you to fight."

"That's absurd," Niko said.

"That's how legends are born, Solcha"

41

MARA

A chill breeze swept in from the balcony, promising a taste of spring that didn't fit with the frozen gray muck Mara had seen filling Ilara as she'd watched the city from the lookout less than twelve hours before. But the sweet fragrance of flowers carried on the tower-made breeze seemed as real as any scent she'd ever experienced.

Don't lie, Mara Landil. Not to yourself.

The scent of fear dug deeper into the reality of life than any other. Fear from the others on the white mountains journey as they realized how badly the magic in the ice wanted them dead. Fear from the Ice Walkers as Ronya let a massive wolf murder her own people. Fear seeping from her own skin as she waited for terrible news.

She gripped the mug in her hands tighter, though its warmth did nothing against the shiver trembling up her spine. She buried herself farther into Tham's side, still watching the tower-made clouds drift across the tower-made sky.

Tham kissed her shoulder, a gentle reminder of his presence.

"Does that mean we're done being statues?" Elver whispered.

"What?" Blinking, Mara pulled her gaze from the false sky.

Elver sat on the couch across from her and Tham, Elle perched by his side, both of them staring at Mara and Tham.

"It's only that you two went very still," Elver said, "then Elle went very still, so I thought that's what we were all doing."

"Sorry. We're not playing statue. I'm just thinking." Mara took a sip of her still magically warmed tea.

"Are you thinking or worrying?" Elver said. "I'm almost certain the two are very different things."

"Then I'm worrying," Mara said.

"Because Fergal ran away from our picnic on the overlook and Torra didn't come and visit like she promised?" Elver asked

"Fergal didn't run away from the picnic," Mara said. "He was summoned."

"And Torra?" Elver furrowed his brow.

"It's not like her to not show up." Mara twisted her legs off the couch, shifting so her thigh pressed against Tham's.

"It could be sorcerer business," Tham said. "We don't know that it's anything to do with the Ice Walkers."

"Oh, I'm quite sure it is." Elver patted his lap. Elle collapsed on top of him, belly up and ready to be scratched.

"I'm afraid to ask how you're sure," Mara said.

"Does that mean I shouldn't say it?" Elver looked down, as though addressing Elle.

"I want to know," Mara said.

"Are you sure?"

"Yes," Mara said. "Please tell me."

"Because up on the overlook, the wind was coming from the north," Elver said.

"A northerly wind is common this time of year," Tham said.

"Only this wind smelled like blood." Elver wrinkled his nose. "Blood and ice."

"You can't scent blood on the wind," Mara said.

"Yes, you can," Elver said.

"Even if you could, the stench probably came from someone in Ilara butchering an animal," Mara said.

"It didn't," Elver said.

Tham shifted to the edge of his seat, moving Mara with him as though preparing them both to flee. "Then where was it? What was it?"

"North." Elver nodded. "Blood."

Tham shut his eyes, his shoulders tensing.

Mara laid a hand on his thigh. "Tham?"

"I should have been there," Tham said.

"We don't know if anything's happened," Mara said.

"It has," Elver said.

"I should be helping search for the Ice Walkers' forces," Tham said.

"You shouldn't. You're not a tracker. Mara's not a tracker. You're not magic. Mara's, well…" Elver shrugged.

"I'm a soldier," Tham said. "If Ilbrea's under attack, I should be there to fight."

Mara gripped Tham's thigh, her mind racing through a million ways to beg him to stay away from any battle that might come.

"Don't worry, Mara. You and Tham have to stay right here. That's quite important. At least for now. When the wind puffs up the big white clouds…" Elver wrinkled his nose. "It's the wrong word. I'm sure it's the wrong word."

His mouth began to move as though he were silently whispering to himself. He shook his head and chewed his lips.

They fell into silence, Elver scratching Elle's stomach and whispering while Mara fought the gnawing need to shout at Elver to explain how he knew things, if he even knew them at all.

"When you go," Elver said, "don't forget to take me with you. Shantene is nice, and I very much like our rooms, but I need to stay with you."

"If Ronya attacks, inside the tower might be the safest place in Ilbrea," Tham said.

"When the wicked queen reaches Ilara, there will be more important things than our safety. And it's going to start with—" Elver opened his mouth to say another word, snapped it shut, and frowned. "No, that's not it either."

Elle was the first to finally fall asleep. Then Elver.

The sun had started to lighten the false sky by the time Tham lifted Mara's still-warm mug from her hands. Moments later, she sank into sleep.

Strange shadows moved through her dreams. Not quite monsters, more like people so lost in the darkness they'd forgotten what they were meant to be. Threatening. Deadly. But they hadn't been born to such horror.

The shadow men crept through the streets of Ilara, unnoticed as they watched the people go about their lives.

Help them. Mara tried to speak, but she had no body, no voice. *Help them. They're people. They're not monsters. They're only lost. Help them.*

Children weaved between the shadows, laughing, playing, unaware of the dark claws reaching for their throats.

Don't hurt the children. You don't have to do this. This isn't who you are.

The shadows closed in around the children, blocking them from view.

No. You're not monsters. You're not monsters!

The screams of the children jolted Mara awake.

"…be out there." Tham's voice quelled Mara's panic. "I am capable and willing."

Mara shoved her curls away from her face, blinking at the sun streaming in from the balcony.

"I knew you and Mara would want to help," Torra said. "Fergal agreed with me. But the idea of you traveling north was presented and decided against."

"Why?" Tham said.

"What's happened?" Mara pushed herself to sit up.

Tham, Elver, and Torra sat at Tham's table, a tray of food between them, though only Elver ate.

"A village has been attacked," Torra said. "Completely sacked."

"The villagers?" Mara stood, the stinging of her numb feet barely registering against the panic stabbing at her lungs.

"Gone," Torra said. "There were a few corpses left in the road, but everyone else just vanished."

"People don't vanish," Mara said. "They escape or are taken."

Tham met Mara's gaze. His eyes held a heavy grief.

"But they couldn't have escaped Ronya." Mara sank into the seat beside Tham. "Not with wolves on her side."

"If they'd tried, they would have left an easy trail of blood and pawprints to follow." Elver tossed a bit of cheese to Elle.

"If they're not all dead and they didn't run, then Ronya must have taken the villagers. But why would she bother moving prisoners?" Mara dug her fingers into her curls. "It doesn't make sense. None of it makes sense."

"It will," Elver said. "Always does in the end."

"The Lady Sorcerer sent more of ours out this morning. They will find a way to track the Ice Walkers." Torra looked to Tham. "And as soon as they've found the would-be invaders, I promise you will know. None of us are trying to shunt you aside or pretend we know more about the Ice Walkers than you. I know you want to be out there finding the beasts, but you are an invaluable resource to the Lady Sorcerer. The best way you can help Ilbrea is by staying here."

"For now," Elver said. "Only, if you wouldn't mind, could you bring us new packs? The ones we carried here were taken from us, understandable with the blood stains, but when the wind shifts, we have to be ready to move quickly." Elver smacked his hand against the table. "Quick. Can't miss a moment. There won't be time."

"Time for what?" Torra asked.

"Doesn't matter to you." Elver pursed his lips and squinted at Torra. "Nope, not you at all. May I also have a pretty little bag for the few coins and jewels we took from Queen Ronya's father after I killed him? I've always wanted a fancy bag of coins to jingle."

42

ADRIAL

"It's the sorcerers who have brought destruction to my docks." Lord Nevon slammed his fist against the table. "The sorcerers were the target of the attack, not my sailors."

"A petty assumption," Lady Gwell said.

Lord Nevon leapt to his feet, leaning across the Guilds Council's table as though daring the Lady Sorcerer to strike. "Ten of my sailors were killed in the attack. Ten good men are dead because they were too close to your sorcerers."

"I'm sure you consider them a great loss." Lady Gwell stayed in her seat. "But your sailors died in an attack on your docks. If anything, you should be groveling and praising Dudia that my sorcerers fulfilled their duty and prevented your casualties from being drastically worse."

Adrial pressed his palms to his thighs, willing patience to stifle the embers of his anger.

"Out of the hundred men working the docks the night of the attack, ten of mine died." Lord Nevon spoke in a low voice any reasonable person would have known to fear. "All ten of my dead were near a sorcerer when they were killed. Will you really attempt to deny the intent of the attack when all five sorcerers you'd stationed on *my* docks were killed?"

"The health of my wounded—"

"Health?" Lord Nevon coughed out a rough laugh. "Wounded? My men hauled two sorcerer corpses from the water. Another of your people had a stone lodged in their head. And only a fool could believe the other two weren't mangled far past the point of survival. You don't have to be a healer to recognize when a person is dead."

"You would be wise to watch your words," Lady Gwell said.

A crackle of something like invisible sparks rolled across the table, stinging Adrial's skin as it passed.

Lord Gareth shook his head as though he'd walked through a cloud of gnats.

Lady Byrd gasped. Her second laid a comforting hand on her shoulder. Lady Byrd's breathing stayed uneven.

"We've smoothed out the inspection of goods coming into Ilara," Lord Nevon said. "My docks are no longer overrun with merchants demanding their property or hungry common folk looking for food. I thank you for the work your sorcerers contributed in such a trying time and respectfully demand their immediate removal from my docks."

"You're a fool. The docks need the protection of the Sorcerers Guild," Lady Gwell said. "And your *respectful demand* will not be met."

"The very presence of sorcerers makes my sailors a target for the kind of monsters who murdered ten of my people." Lord Nevon straightened up and looked to King Brannon. "Your Majesty, the Sorcerers Guild has earned the rage of both the common folk and the rebels through actions that have nothing to do with the Sailors Guild. The Sailors Guild has not held public executions. The Sailors Guild has not raided homes and destroyed businesses."

"Are you claiming those acts were unnecessary for the protection of Ilara?" Lady Gwell stood.

"The necessity of the sorcerers' rampage is irrelevant to the issue," Lord Nevon said. "I have endured sorcerer interference long enough. My sailors are safer without sorcerers haunting my docks. As the Lord Sailor, I have the right to run my Guild as I see fit. From this point on, only Guilded sailors and workers registered with the Sailors Guild will be allowed on my docks. There will be no exception."

"Is this where you choose to make your stand?" Lady Gwell smiled. "You will not win. My sorcerers will be placed on every Guilded ship. My sorcerers will patrol the docks."

"Actually"—Lord Gareth stood—"according to the rules of the Guilds, which the Sorcerers Guild so often ignores, Lord Nevon is correct. He does have the right to ban sorcerers from Ilara's docks. History has taught me not to expect the sorcerers to honor the sanctity of the other Guilds, and I've lived too long with that reality to expect it to change now, but fifteen lives were lost in the attack."

"My sorcerers—" Lady Gwell began.

"Are dead," Lord Nevon cut her off.

"While I'm afraid we've all become a bit too accustomed to violence over the last months, I couldn't forgive myself if we didn't honor the fifteen"—Lord Gareth held up his hands as another crackle of magic rolled across the table—"or ten lives lost, if the sorcerers have healing powers beyond normal people's imagination they've chosen to hide even from their fellow leaders of Ilbrea—or are somehow invulnerable to every attack but one very specific poison or an act of Dudia himself—by acknowledging that Lord Nevon is correct.

"The anger of Ilara's people is not directed at the Sailors Guild, just as it is not directed at the Scribes Guild. The root of the common folks' well-aimed ire is, once again, a discussion for another day, but having sorcerers on the docks provides a purple target rebels will continue to attack."

"My sorcerers have become targets while working for the good of Ilbrea," Lady Gwell said.

"Once again," Lord Gareth said, "I am not suggesting this is the moment to delve into the source of the people's anger, but it is vital we acknowledge that it does exist and that it is not aimed at the Sailors Guild or the Scribes Guild."

"Perhaps I should dress my people in white." Lady Gwell shifted her glare to Adrial. The edges of his anger sharpened, slicing through his last bits of restraint. "Send them out to picnic with the commoners while Ilara is threatened by rebels?"

"If I may, Lord Gareth?" Adrial stood.

"Keep your second in order," Lady Byrd said.

"I beg your forgiveness." Adrial bowed to the council members. "But as I am the *picnicker*, I believe was the word, Lady Gwell speaks of, I can offer the council invaluable insight. And, as Lord Gareth's second, I understand it to be my Dudia-owed duty to aid the Guilds Council, even if my speaking is unorthodox."

"Go ahead, Adrial." Lord Gareth beckoned him to stand right beside the table.

Adrial didn't allow himself to limp as he stepped forward. "I do indeed sit in the square near the library every afternoon, and I have never once been threatened by any common folk. In fact, I have received great kindness from them."

"Should we all marry rotta whores?" Lady Byrd said.

"Do not insult the dead." Lord Gareth rounded on Lady Byrd, pointing a shaking finger at her face. "The needless tragedy my head scribe endured is a stain on the Guilds that will be remembered. I have personally ensured the names of all who voted to condemn Adrial and Ena have been laid out in every record of the terrible incident. Details of this council-wrought travesty have been added to enough official records and curiosity tomes, your guilt cannot be erased."

"You have cast blame upon your King?" King Brannon said.

"No, Your Majesty." Lord Gareth bowed. "I have performed my sworn duty to the Guilds and Ilbrea by ensuring a record of the truth."

Red crept up the King's neck.

"The common folk in the square have soothed my grief," Adrial said before Lord Gareth could plow onward. "Their kindness is strengthened by the knowledge that I do not view common folk as less than Guilded. But their trust in me has grown because they know I am their ally. Giving a hungry child something to eat not only helps that child but shows others that I am not their enemy. I want to help them."

"Apples and eggs for children." Lady Gwell sneered. "You've trained them to beg from you. What will you do when your pets begin demanding coin instead of bread?"

"If they are truly in need, then I will give them coin. I've done it before," Adrial said. "While the Guilded have barely been touched, an illness has crept through the poor this winter. A horrible rattle in the lungs made worse by the cold and damp. You would be amazed at the number of tilk in desperate need of healing who were turned away by Lady Byrd's people for want of a few coins. I have gold to spare. I am happy to use it to save a life."

"And when word spreads and more come to demand coin?" Lady Gwell asked. "When they mob you with demands for your gold until you don't have enough left to buy yourself a glass of chamb?"

"Then I suppose I shall live without chamb." Adrial shrugged, carefully keeping the movement of his bad shoulder symmetrical with his good.

"And I would be happy to contribute to Adrial's works from my personal wealth," Lord Gareth said.

"Thank you, Lord Gareth," Adrial said.

Tears glinted in Lord Gareth's eyes.

"But there is a source of income great enough to ensure the poorest of Ilara's common folk have access to the care from the Healers Guild they so desperately need," Adrial said.

Lady Byrd leaned back in her seat, a pinched look on her face, as though she might be ill on the gold, seven-pointed star inlaid in the table.

Adrial pulled four scrolls from his pockets. "In the interest of record maintenance, I've been tracking the unfortunate destruction that's plagued Ilara."

Adrial held up the first scroll.

"Here is a map of all the homes and businesses that have been rendered unusable since the violence in the city began."

He laid that scroll on the table and held up the second scroll.

"This map lays out which of those buildings' rubble has been completely cleared. According to reports, the wreckage is whisked away in the middle of the night, and by morning, there's no trace a building was ever there, let alone that workers had ever tidied the tragedy away."

Lord Nevon, Lord Kearney, and Map Maker Traim all looked to the Lady Sorcerer, who kept her cold glare fixed on Adrial as he laid the second scroll on the table.

"The final map notates where citizens have simply disappeared during the night," Adrial said. "Without any reports of violence or even screams, Ilarans are simply gone. Vanished. The silence with which these people disappear has spread a new tenor of fear through the city, which cannot be discounted."

Adrial laid the third scroll down.

"But, more to the matter of paying for the healers' care" —Adrial held up the fourth scroll—"a list of shops and businesses that were emptied during the night. Not only of their owners, but also of their goods. Fabric, lace, metal-working tools, tanned leather, even items as simple as flour. I've categorized the missing goods by type with notations of the worth of the goods, using only items I could reliably confirm were missing and giving them a lower value than would be found in the market, of course.

"Even with such a diminished approximation, if those goods were sold, the profit would be more than enough to aid those suffering in the city." Adrial laid the fourth scroll down. "Though, I will admit those numbers are meaningless as the missing goods are, in fact, missing, and the only possible profit would go to the person hiding the hoard."

Lady Byrd's neck tensed as she looked to Lady Gwell.

"But the most disturbing question of all is why some businesses were raided with such stealth while others have been left untouched," Adrial said. "Very different from the chaotic destruction that has ravaged the city, these businesses seem to have been carefully targeted.

"Not the best dress maker in Ilara, but the second best. The most profitable cobbler wasn't targeted, but the finest was. Which begs the question—were these people taken to be punished and their goods destroyed in retribution? Or, as frightening as the thought may be, are the goods and workers being used for some purpose we cannot see?"

No one spoke.

"Copies of all four scrolls have been delivered to each of you," Adrial said. "Perhaps one of you will make better use of this information than a man bound to books and words can. In the meantime, I will continue to do as much as I am able for the needy in Ilara, even if it takes every last coin I have."

Adrial gave the council one more bow before stepping back to take his seat.

"You're a good man, Head Scribe," Lord Nevon said.

"Good or not, a man with useless maps fed by irresponsible speculation has no place interrupting the Guilds Council," Lady Gwell said.

"Would you rather go back to me telling you to keep your chivving sorcerers away from my docks?" Lord Nevon said. "Or would you prefer to explain what under the stars you've got your people doing with goods stolen from Ilarans?"

Lady Gwell flicked her finger. Lord Nevon flinched, his head turning to the side as though he'd been slapped.

"Would you like to start with an easier topic?" Lord Nevon tapped his unstruck cheek. "If your sorcerers have been doing something as useful as cleaning up the mess they've left all over the city, why has the great Lady Sorcerer not mentioned her peoples' good works?"

A sly smile curving her lips, Lady Gwell looked to King Brannon. "Will you indulge the council, Your Majesty? The sharing of such information must be done at the discretion of the King."

The King rubbed his hand over his mouth, staring at the star inlaid in the table. Clouds shrouded the sky, keeping the sun from streaming through the skylight to glint off the golden star.

"A Wyrainian delegate is on their way," the King said. "After our postponing their visit more than once, the King of Wyrain has become concerned about the state of Ilbrea. His implied insults have gone so far as to question the value of a marriage between Prince Dagon and Princess Illia."

The King paused, as though expecting someone to speak for him. The Lady Sorcerer did not come to his aid.

"The Wyrainian King has grown uneasy enough to force his delegate to endure the dangers of traveling the Spice Trail through the eastern mountains before spring." King Brannon didn't look up from the star. "If his journey goes well, he will arrive within the month. We will not risk any hint of rebellion endangering Princess Illia's engagement.

"The clearing of the rubble removes a wretched stain from Ilara. The secrecy has been necessary. If word of the delegate's visit reaches the rebels, we invite chaos. I will not allow violent rotta beasts to destroy an alliance that would secure prosperity for generations of Ilbreans."

"I understand the need for secrecy, Your Majesty," Lord

Kearney said, "but as the Lord Soldier, I should be included in any discussion of plans for protecting the delegate."

"In better times, you would have been," King Brannon said, "but there are too many rats in Ilara. And I am not foolish enough to believe their poison hasn't crept into the Guilds."

43

NIKO

The extra layers of padding Niko had stuffed into the back of his coat did as little to ease the pain of his torn and scabbed mark as the salve he'd carefully smeared onto the wound before dressing. And, even though the servants who'd brought him his pack had quite expertly distributed the weight of his blankets, extra clothes, and rations, the moment he pulled the pack on, stars of pain crept through his vision.

Freedom, Adrial's voice whispered. *Pain is nothing with the promise of freedom.*

The guard who opened Niko's door bowed deeply, offering to carry Niko's pack and giving no explanation as to why Danu hadn't come to fetch Niko herself.

Niko kept his pack on, afraid that replacing the weight on his back would be worse than keeping it in place.

The warmth of the blood leaking from his wound began before he'd made it to the stairs leading to the lower parts of the keep. The familiar, sickening damp of his shirt occupied his mind until he reached the atrium and realized he hadn't taken a final look around the room that had been his prison.

Not at the view that had been his solace for so long. Not at the constellation chart he'd so stubbornly carved into the ceiling above his bed, defying the stone that trapped him.

I'm never going back into that room.

The thought brought nearly as much terror as relief.

Cutting to the far side of the atrium, the guards led Niko down a steeply sloping path, plunging farther below the cliffs than Niko preferred to venture.

I'm never going back into that room.

I'm never going back into that room.

Niko repeated the phrase over and over, fixing his thoughts on that triumphant shout, fighting to ignore the fear dragging its way up from his chest to claw at his throat.

I'm never going back into that room.

The tunnel narrowed as it reached a long flight of stairs leading even farther down. Dimly glowing lae stones flanked the steps, their light seeming to stretch deeper into the earth than any man could hope to survive.

The punching of Niko's heartbeat quickened, banging through his chest, pulsing in his ears.

I'm never going back into that room.

The terror.

The terror of being so close to escape and having freedom ripped away.

That terror, he could control.

Niko pinned his gaze on the guard in front of him, watching for any hint of the man preparing to attack Niko and drag him back up into the keep.

The guard descended the stairs at a steady pace, not seeming to notice the walls narrowing, ready to entomb them in inescapable stone.

I'm never going back into that room.

Breathe, Niko, Danu whispered.

Niko glanced behind, searching for her, finding only two of his guards.

The sudden movement split the skin on his back farther open, shooting a spike of pain through him that somehow commanded the walls to hold still.

"Is everything all right, Solcha?" one of his guards asked.

"Just wondering where the rest of the travel party are." The words rasped in Niko's throat.

"I believe they'll be meeting you at the wall," the guard said.

"The wall?" Niko forced out the words as the tunnel began to collapse around him again.

"The Elder has chosen that passage for your party." The guard bowed, urging Niko farther down the stairs. "If you would, Solcha. I don't want to keep the Elder waiting."

Niko tried to make himself move, but the leaden weight of his legs was too heavy to lift.

The front guard had stopped, waiting for Niko a few steps down.

Walk down the stairs.

Niko's chivving body knew how to walk down stairs.

He tacked his gaze to the back of the front guard's head.

The man was fifty, maybe older, with thinning gray hair.

Breathe, Niko, Danu whispered again.

Niko forced his legs to move.

The gray-haired guard probably had a family. A nice family living in the open air.

A wife with gray streaked through her brown hair. Freckles from working out in the sun, tending the garden behind their little stone cottage. Two children—no, give the guard four—all with their mother's pert nose and father's height.

And grandchildren. The guard seemed nice enough, Niko gave him twelve grandchildren and another on the way. And that was without the guard's youngest having married yet.

Niko pictured the whole pack of them trying to cram into the cottage on a winter evening, mugs of ale knocked over as the children tore through the home, chasing each other around the furniture. The guard's wife sighing every time a fresh spill marred the floor that had just been scrubbed.

And a dog—the guard needed a dog—that always went after the spilled ale, making all the grownups dive to stop his imbibing, adding to the chaos.

A laugh bubbled in Niko's chest as he pictured the guard with four young children clinging to him as he tried to stop the dog from stealing the meal's roasted meat.

Brighter lights shone in front of Niko, yanking him away from his imagined domestic distraction.

A low rumble of voices sounded up ahead, far more voices than the seven Ena had named as chosen by the mountain to venture into the horrible black.

Niko's heart began racing again.

The tunnel opened into a chamber three times the size of the bedroom Niko would never go back into.

Bryana stood in the center of the space, a flock of well-dressed Brien clustered behind her, her guards lining the back wall.

Ena and her acolytes waited at the front of the room. Even though there were so few of them, the black of their clothing seemed to somehow take up more space than all the purple-clad Brien combined.

But Danu. He couldn't see Danu.

The panic in Niko's chest squeezed tighter.

"Solcha." Bryana stepped forward, loathing gleaming in the demon's eyes even as she gave him a gracious nod.

"Elder Brien." Niko gave her a low bow, letting his pack grind against his wound. He fixed his gaze on Ena as he straightened up, walking toward Adrial's wife rather than risk the demon elder seeing the panic in his eyes.

"The mountain has blessed the Brien with souls brave enough to venture into the unknown darkness beneath the mountain," Bryana said.

Chivving, cacting coward, just breathe.

"But the child. Where is Solcha's babe?" Bryana said.

An anger terrifying enough to yank Niko from his panic flashed through Ena's eyes. "My child is where the mountain wants her to be. Safely beyond reach of those who would use babes as pawns in their chivving games."

Bryana's neck stiffened.

"I appreciate your concern for my family, honored Elder Brien." The danger stayed in Ena's eyes as she bowed, holding Bryana's gaze as though daring the demon to attack. "But the mountain bids our journey begin."

"We all serve the mountain." Bryana gave Ena a nod as though the two held no desire to slit each other's throats. "May your journey be swift. And, should your lives be claimed, may your deaths be worthy of the mountain's honor. Travel well, Solchas."

"No, wait." Panic clamped around Niko's lungs. "Danu. Where's Danu?"

A smile curved Bryana's lips.

"Ena told you—" He couldn't get enough air to speak. "The mount—the mountain told Ena that Danu is coming with us."

"Of course." Bryana raised her hand, beckoning over her shoulder.

The crowd of well-dressed Brien shifted, clearing a path for Danu—a pack on her back, blades at her hips.

Niko pressed his hand to the smooth stone wall, holding himself upright.

Danu didn't meet Niko's gaze as she limped toward the group, her face set in an unreadable mask.

"Pity she caught a limp since yesterday," Ena said. "Perfect for walking through the endless black."

"A pity indeed," Bryana said.

Danu took her place beside Niko, not so much as glancing away from the wall.

"With such a difficult journey ahead, I didn't want Danu's

weakness to be a liability." Bryana beckoned over her shoulder again.

A tall man with a warrior's build stepped out of the group, the pack on his back seeming too small against the width of his shoulders.

"Trueborn Mael will be joining your journey," Bryana said.

"We don't need a trueborn," Ena said. "You can keep your war dog."

"I insist." Bryana's smile broadened. "I am allowing my niece to travel with both Solchas chosen by the mountain. I would be remiss if I didn't send someone capable of protecting your journey. And with your affinity for trueborn, Mael seemed the perfect fit."

"A gesture worthy of the Brien Elder." Ena eyed Mael. "But don't expect me to feel guilty when things go badly for your mut."

Bryana's smile tightened.

Ena turned her back to Bryana. "Well, Mael, chosen protector of our journey, open the passage and let's be off. I'd rather spend my time walking than wondering how many times someone expects me to bow."

"But Mael can't open the path, Solcha," Bryana said.

"Not trueborn enough to create a door?" Ena didn't look back at Bryana.

"You are the one the mountain called to journey through the black," Bryana said. "The mysteries below the mountain cannot be tamed. The passages through her rock are always changing. If the mountain wishes Solcha to travel through the great darkness, then having Mael create the entrance may well lead you down the wrong path. If the mountain calls Solcha, Solcha must respond."

"But she's not—" Niko began.

Danu grabbed his wrist, squeezing tight.

Gleeful malice lit the demon elder's eyes. "May the mountain ever guide your steps."

"May the mountain grant you all you deserve," Ena said.

Still beaming with delight, Bryana turned to her people. "Come. Solcha's miracles aren't wrought for lurid pageantry."

Danu kept her grip on Niko's wrist, squeezing tightly even as the guards filed out after Bryana and her minions.

The last guard in line turned on the bottom step.

He placed his hands on the walls. A faint blue glow began within the stone, right beneath his palms. The light brightened, spreading across the stone of the walls, stretching, coming together at the center of the stairs, forming one solid wall with only a six-inch gap at the top.

The light from the newly formed wall dimmed as the last of the footsteps on the stairs faded.

"Chivving demon spawn in a purple gown," Ena said.

Mael drew his shoulders back. "Elder Bryana is the honored leader of the Brien clan."

"Who's locked you in here with the rest of us." Niko turned to the smooth stretch of wall behind him, his arm crossing awkwardly in front of his chest as Danu kept hold of his wrist.

"If the mountain changes Solcha's heart and she wishes to stay in the stronghold, I will gladly clear a path back to the keep," Mael said.

"I'm not going back to the keep." Niko smacked his palm against the solid stone.

"You're really not going to open the chivving path forward?" Ena said.

"No," Mael said.

"Then go brood in the corner like the worthless slitch you are," Ena said.

Mael gave a low laugh but obeyed.

"I can't go back to the keep," Niko whispered. "I can't."

"You're not going to," Ena said.

"But—"

"I promise, you're not." Ena pressed her palms against the wall. "The path will open for us."

Danu's head snapped toward Ena. "You're a trueborn?"

"Not even a little." Ena trailed her fingers across the smooth stone, as though searching for something. "But we have an understanding, the mountain and I. She knows our journey will help protect her beloved children. She counts me among those children. The mountain has sheltered me before. Kept me alive when the gods themselves dragged me toward Death.

"She knows the promises I've made. And she'll let me keep them." Ena stopped four feet from where she'd started. She pressed her forehead to the stone as she whispered, "I can't let him down now. Not after all you and I have lost. We face an enemy with a hoard of mountain stone. We have to stop them. Please, don't let his death have been for nothing."

Niko leaned forward, waiting for the blue light to begin glowing within the stone.

Ena didn't move. She kept her forehead and palms pressed to the wall, as though savoring the touch of the unmoving stone. "For him."

Her shoulders sank.

Panic pinged through Niko's chest again, but Ena's shoulders weren't sinking in defeat.

All the tension left her body as she smiled, the first true smile Niko had seen her give.

She stepped away from the wall.

The stone in front of her vanished without any hint of the blue light, simply shifting aside as though some great beast were gathering the stone as one would pull back curtains.

Ena stepped into the gap in the wall before turning back to Mael, whose face was set in loathing-tinged shock.

"Your help is not required, trueborn," Ena said. "If you insist on tramping along behind us, the only guilt for your fate lies with you and your elder."

Mael stormed past Ena and into the darkness beyond.

Ena looked to her four acolytes. They filed into the black without a single protest.

"Danu," Ena said, "how bad is it?"

"I'm fine." Danu kept hold of Niko's wrist, leading him toward the black, but Niko couldn't make his body move.

Two feet from the opening, Danu stopped, her arm fully outstretched as she tried to pull him with her.

"If you've changed your mind and would like to stay with Bryana, I'm afraid it's too chivving late," Ena said.

"The black." The words felt jagged in Niko's throat. "How long will we be trapped in the black?"

"Until the mountain decides we've arrived. Then we'll face much worse than a bit of darkness." Ena pointed into the endless winding maze the mountain demanded they travel. "Ilbrea is through the black. Adrial is through the black. Everything you love is through the black. Does your fear mean more to you than your freedom?"

Niko tried to move, but his body had frozen, every joint locked in terror.

"Please, Niko." Danu looked at him, giving him a full view of her face.

Her eyes were hollow with no hint of anger or fear or joy at being allowed to leave the stronghold. An arc of scabs marred her bottom lip, like she'd bitten through the skin. Her jaw was tight and her neck tense, as though she were fighting to shove pain aside.

"Please," Danu whispered. She let go of his wrist as she took a step back, moving through the entrance the mountain had made for the true Solcha. Danu kept her hand out, reaching for him. Ready to touch him. To let his hand take hers. "Please."

Niko stepped into the darkness, consigning himself to the black.

44

KAI

The flickering feeling of existing in a dream poked against Kai's thoughts as he trailed his fingers down the perfectly painted wall.

He watched the people in the tavern drinking, laughing, pretending most of them wouldn't flee the tavern at dusk because reasonable Ilarans were too afraid to walk the city's streets after dark.

Years of drinks being spilled across the bar had left the scent of stale ale as the tavern's inevitable perfume, but only a light, floral scent surrounded Kai. And, while the people in the tavern eyed every stranger as though waiting for an attack, not a single soul looked up to Kai's peephole right above the bar.

Giving himself a moment of reprieve, Kai straightened up, stretching his back. He stole a sip of tea from the mug he'd placed on the shelf conveniently located at the perfect height for a watcher to reach from their post.

"Anything?" Merial asked.

"Aside from a deep yearning to visit a tavern instead of spy on one?" Kai leaned forward, peering back through the peephole.

"Give it time," Drew said. "Isla will come."

"She'd better," Merial said. "I called in too many favors for this chivving madness to come to nothing."

"Ilbrea will praise your name for the work you've done," Kai said.

A hint of red caught his eye.

Heart leaping into his throat, Kai pressed his face against the well-painted wall, trying to get a better view of…an older woman with a red scarf covering her head.

"Wrong redhead?" Drew asked.

"Scarf," Kai said. "How did you know?"

Drew gave a low chuckle.

Kai glanced back to where Drew sat in the finely upholstered chair just long enough to see his smile.

"You twitch like a startled dog when you think you've seen her," Drew said.

"I can't help it," Kai said. "I'm not made for holding still. My body will take any excuse for movement."

Kai jerked again as a girl with reddish-brown hair walked in.

Maybe Isla. If she'd darkened her hair to be harder to spot. Kai held his breath as the girl stepped up to the bar…and was a good ten years older than Isla.

"Wrong again?" Drew asked.

"Yes," Kai sighed.

"I'll take a turn," Merial said. "Watching you twitch puts my nerves on edge."

"You are more than welcome to take over." Kai turned around on the narrow platform and flipped up the board he'd been resting on.

The thoughtful perch, though only a plank of wood lying between the platform's two railings, gave Kai both a small bit of comfort and a nagging wonder as to who had spent enough hours at the peephole to warrant devising the seat.

"Your tea." Merial pointed to the shelf.

"Thanks." Kai took his mug and climbed down the stairs, clearing the platform for Merial.

Once Merial reached the top, she turned back, letting Kai pass her the little box that made her tall enough to actually see out the peephole.

The tired, impetuous part of Kai wanted to make a joke about Merial needing the box's assistance, but being locked in a room for hours on end with an angry Merial would be far worse than being locked in a room for hours on end with a perturbed Merial.

"You want to sit?" Drew stood, offering Kai the more comfortable of the two chairs the room offered.

"No, thanks."

Drew sat back down, watching as Kai paced the short path the room allowed.

Barely longer than the pub's bar, the hidden room was better appointed than anywhere else Kai had been in months.

The thick rug covering the floor muted his footsteps. The desk in the corner gleamed, so well-polished, a rogue fingerprint would be noticed. Books with fine bindings sat on two of the shelves along the back wall. The third, wider shelf had been cleared of its contents, leaving a conspicuous void where the tavern owner's records had, until recently, been kept.

"How long until sunset?" Kai asked.

"A bit over an hour," Merial said. "But I wouldn't get your hopes pinned on the redhaired beast coming today."

"Isla's not a beast," Drew said.

"I watched the girl fight the Lady Sorcerer," Merial said. "The only other word I can come up with for a person capable of what she did is *demon*, and that seemed rude."

"You could just call her Isla," Drew said.

"I prefer not to name beasts that might turn on me," Merial said.

"Why don't you think she'll come today?" Kai gave Drew a wide-eyed, warning look.

Drew frowned and leaned back in his seat.

"Do you want a list, or should I just say this is a shoddy chivving plan?" Merial asked.

"A list. It'll help pass the time." Kai cut around to stand behind Drew's chair. He laid his hands on Drew's shoulders and kissed the top of his head. A thrum of delight lifted Kai's mood as Drew's shoulders relaxed.

"To start with," Merial said, "the Tiller's Tree is a chivving terrible name for a tavern."

"But it was the name of the tavern where we met Isla," Drew said.

"I think you might have mentioned that." Merial's tone held no hint of humor. "Getting this place *temporarily* renamed the chivving Tiller's Tree cost about ten percent of the favors owed me. Ten percent gone in one chivving blow."

"The underground is grateful," Drew said.

"The underground doesn't even know what we're chivving well doing, because you want to keep this a sodding secret until you know if the beast will kill you or talk to you," Merial said. "I'd normally give it a four out of ten you'll survive the meeting. But as I've sacrificed so much personal collateral for this sodding nonsense, the gods are sure to laugh in my face and make it fail. Two out of ten you survive. At best."

"You know," Kai said, "it's your constant positivity that makes me adore you."

Merial made a sound that mixed a tsch, a grunt, and a laugh.

"The next problem is laboring under the assumption that someone in the beast's group of fouled-up, mucking fools of rebels will happen to mention the change in the tavern's name. *Oh, hello beast who took on the Lady Sorcerer in the chivving cathedral square, fancy a drink? I've heard some tavern's decided to try out a new name. The Tiller's Tree of all chivving things.*" Merial took a breath and pitched her voice higher. "*The Tiller's Tree? Gods and stars I once met two fools at the Tiller's Tree! I wonder if they'll be there.*"

"You agreed to this plan," Kai said.

"I've agreed to a great many foolish things in my life," Merial said. "Though this may creep up from foolish judgment to the thing that gets a noose around my neck."

"Is that the third reason Isla won't walk into the brilliantly renamed Tiller's Tree today?" Kai asked.

"No," Merial said. "The noose was merely an observation."

"Is there a third reason?" Drew reached up, laying his hand on top of Kai's.

Kai's knees melted.

"I've got nine reasons right now, but the list will end up being longer," Merial said.

"Then please continue." Kai laced his fingers through Drew's, savoring the bliss-driven warmth that dulled his restless nerves, soothing the itch on his soul born of having been locked in the hidden room for hours.

Drew brushed a kiss on the back of Kai's hand.

"The third reason," Merial said, "is that if the beast has managed to survive as a sorcerer free from the Guilds, she's not a chivving fool. She won't see a tavern with a familiar name and rush right in to see if it's a message for her."

"Though that would be convenient," Kai said.

Merial gave another laughing, growled tsch.

"If she even hears of the tavern, there'll be scouts sent to watch. Then they might dare to come in. Poke about. Ask questions," Merial said. "After what the beast pulled in the square, she'll have to be cautious of traps set by the Lady Sorcerer. If, *if* this girl gives the Tiller's Tree a second thought, it'll be skeptical, cautious, and take a chivving long time for her to consider acting on it."

"We don't have a long time," Kai said.

"We also don't have a better idea than this sheep's shit," Merial said. "So, learn to like it in here. Onto the fourth reason—"

45

NIKO

White flowers dripped from the willow trees, their scent filling the still air. In the glow of the lae stones, the petals seemed to gleam with their own sort of light.

Niko tucked his lae stone away, daring to pause and cup his hands around a small cluster of blooms, wanting to see if they would glow in true darkness. But the petals held no light of their own.

Plucking a well-formed flower, he ran a few steps to catch up to Danu.

He held his offering out to her. "For a weary traveler?"

"Thanks." Danu took the gift without glancing Niko's way, tucking it into her hair without so much as a flicker of joy cracking through the solemn, stone-like mask her face had been since they'd left the stronghold.

"Did you just pick a flower from the mountain's grove?" Marlo, the friendliest of Ena's acolytes, asked.

Niko turned to walk backward, staying beside Danu while looking at Marlo. "Have I just cursed us all?"

"I doubt it," Marlo said. "But maybe ask a Black Blood before making such a bold move again."

"I'll do my best to remem—"

Danu grabbed Niko's arm, yanking him toward her a heartbeat too late. His heel caught on a root. He stumbled back, crashing into the branches of a tree.

"Watch where you're going," Danu said.

"Sorry." Niko turned back around, shaking the petals from his hair in his best imitation of a dog drying itself.

Danu didn't smile.

"Your mood's improved," Marlo laughed.

"I'm attempting to ignore the all-consuming panic," Niko said.

"Usually for the best," Marlo said.

Ena's chosen path through the grove narrowed as she cut between two trees. Niko veered around one of the trees, gaining more petals in his hair as he let Danu have the clear way forward.

"And honestly"—Niko pointed to Ena at the head of the group—"someone leading you through the unending black below the mountain is much easier to stomach than stumbling through the dark lost and helpless."

"There is no one I would rather follow through the darkness," Attie, the shortest of Ena's male acolytes, said.

"Right. Absolutely." Niko trailed his fingers through the blooms, buying himself a few more moments of cheerful distraction.

Ena had been favored by the mountain more than once. Ena had been chosen by the mountain. The mountain had opened at Ena's request. The mountain would lead her to safety again.

Just follow Solcha. The real chivving Solcha.

Ena stopped, as though she'd heard Niko's thoughts and was ready to rail at him.

But she only knelt beside the path, running her fingers across the moss-covered ground, reaching toward a cluster of mushrooms. She plucked one, sniffed it, licked it, and took a tiny bite.

"We'll rest here for a bit." Ena stood, brushing her hands off on her skirt before removing her pack. "Alane, set out the stones."

The female acolyte pulled a leather bag from her pocket.

"Kace"—Ena looked to the last of her male acolytes—"gather some moss before starting on the mushrooms. It's better than you'd think for packing a wound."

"Yes, Ena," Kace said.

Niko slid off his pack, careful not to crack through the barely scabbed wound on his back.

"Come with me." Ena stepped between Danu and Niko, a well-polished wooden box in hand.

"Is everything all right?" Niko set his pack down and threaded his fingers through the nearest tree's blooms, begging whatever god would listen to a slitch trapped in the belly of a mountain for their delicate texture to be a strong enough anchor to keep him from plummeting into irredeemable panic.

"Your limp's getting worse." Ena pointed to Danu. "And from the way you move with your pack off, that's not the only thing wrong with you."

"Why didn't you tell me?" Niko looked to Danu.

"And, as there's no chivving chance I'm leaving the group's sight with only Bryana's niece"—Ena looked to Niko—"you're coming with us. I might as well have a look at your back, too."

"Thank you for the offer," Danu said, "but I'm fine."

"You're not. And I'll not risk wasting time slowing down to tend festering wounds." Ena cut through the trees heading away from the path. "Tell your chivving dog to stay behind."

Niko glanced to Mael, half-expecting the trueborn to fulfill the insult by growling.

Mael only sneered.

Danu gasped through her teeth.

"What's wrong?" Niko spun toward her, hands out, ready to catch her.

"Nothing." Danu's jaw tightened as she pulled off her pack.

"But if you're in pain—"

"We've been walking for days." Danu set her pack away from Niko's. "I'm just sore."

She cut past him, following Ena's path.

Niko watched her gait, searching for whatever growing limp Ena had noticed. Danu's stride stayed almost even, but her right heel never touched the ground.

You're a blind fool.

Niko ran to catch up, joining Danu as she reached the place Ena had chosen for her ministrations—just out of sight of the path, the faint sounds of the others' voices still drifting to Niko's ears, offering more comfort than he would ever have admitted.

"Niko first." Ena knelt on the moss and opened her wooden box. "Get your boot off, Danu. We'll start with that for you."

Niko took off his jacket, keeping his front to the others, hiding the mark Ena needed to see. He managed to pull his shirt out of his pants before his hands started to shake.

"Do you want me to do it?" Danu asked.

"Undress me?" Niko said.

"Put ointment on your mark." Danu unlaced her boot, keeping her face turned away from Niko. "If you'd rather not have Ena do it."

Ena paused her unpacking of the box, furrowing her brow at Danu. "You have your own trouble to worry over."

"Thank you." Niko yanked off his shirt, choosing cracking the scabs on his back over allowing himself to remain frozen in panic. "But I don't mind Ena doing it."

Niko sat in front of Ena, watching as Danu eased off her right boot.

"Not as bad as it could be." Ena pressed on Niko's shoulders, making him lean forward. "The wound is angry, but no signs of infection bad enough to fret over. If this starts to sting, keep breathing."

"Gah!" Niko flinched away as a sharp burn followed Ena's touch.

"And don't chivving move," Ena said.

"Right. Sorry." Niko gripped his knees, bracing himself as Ena's touch slid up his mark, following the bird's wing. "Nice to" —Niko winced as the burn deepened—"to have someone who knows about infections."

"Funny coming from a paun." Ena moved on to the other wing. "Your kind like to execute illegal healers. If you didn't already know so many things that could get me hanged, I'd have let your back fester and kill you before risking you turning me in."

"I'm sorry," Niko said, "genuinely sorry you've been made to feel any fear when you want to help someone."

Niko dug his nails into his knees as Ena moved on to the bird's head.

"If Adrial didn't care for you so much, I'd laugh at an apology from a paun," Ena said.

"If you were anyone but Adrial's wife, I don't think I could make myself walk through the darkness heading east when Ilara is west," Niko said.

"You're done." Ena tapped Niko on the shoulder. "And stop bothering with the compass mark on your arm. We follow the path the mountain lays out, no matter the direction."

Niko stood, grabbing his shirt, turning his back away from Ena. "And how do you know what path the mountain wants you to follow? Even cutting through the trees you've only been following the widest way forward."

"I can feel it." Ena tapped her chest, just below her black stone pendant. "Like a hook in my chest."

"You really are Solcha." Niko eased on his coat, grateful to have the wound on his back fully hidden.

"I know what the pull of stone magic feels like. Solcha is nothing but a fear-born myth, twisting rumors into a tale that should never have been whispered." Ena moved closer to Danu, picking Danu's foot up and placing it in her lap. "What chivving monster did this to you?"

Ena leaned sideways, her head blocking Danu's wound from Niko's view.

"It doesn't matter," Danu said. "It's nothing."

"Chivving, slitching, demon-minded Brien." Ena dragged her wooden box closer, tossing the long, wrapped bandage back in and pulling out a bottle with a cork stopper.

"It's on my own head," Danu said.

"Not even a fool would believe that lie," Ena said.

"And how foolish are your acolytes to follow you when you claim all the stories of your being Solcha are a lie?" Danu asked.

Niko inched closer before sitting down, lining himself up to get a peek at Danu's foot.

"They're not helping me because they think I'm Solcha." Ena reached into the wooden box, clearing Niko's view.

A swatch of Danu's heel had been burned a bright, shiny red.

"Sodding stars, Danu. Did they brand you?" Niko crawled closer to her.

Danu didn't look his way. "Why did they follow you below the mountain if they don't believe you're Solcha?" Danu swallowed a scream as Ena pressed a scrap of cloth to her foot.

Niko reached for her hand, but Danu pulled away.

"They're here because of my brother." Ena poured a foul-scented liquid onto the scrap.

"They've been defying their clan elder to help you because of your brother?" Danu pounded her fist against the ground as Ena touched the burn again. "Bryana could have killed them at any moment. Black Blood law wouldn't even condemn her for executing them. They are marked members of the Brien Clan."

"I know." Ena tucked the scrap away and pulled out the rolled bandage. "They know, too. But they chose honoring their debt to my brother over obeying a forced vow to Bryana."

"What did your brother do for them?" Niko asked.

"Saved their lives." Ena wrapped the bandage around Danu's heel. "Attie and Alane in the battle of the Broinn. Marlo when a run south went badly."

"And Kace?" Niko asked.

"He's never told me when my brother saved him." Ena tucked in the end of the bandage and turned back to the box. "And I don't think I want to know."

"Why not?" Niko said. "Have you asked your brother about Kace? He could be lying about having even met your bother."

"My brother's dead." Ena sat back on her heels and met Niko's eyes, holding his gaze as she hadn't before. "If you knew anything about my brother, you wouldn't question him having saved someone's life. And if you were wise, you'd understand that some of the things he did are best left to the ghosts."

"Sounds like quite the man," Niko said. "I would like to have met him."

"You would have shit yourself in terror before he killed you," Ena said. "And with that mark on your arm, it wouldn't have been an easy death."

"Oh." Niko leaned back against a tree in a poor façade of calm, which broke with a flinch as his mark touched the tree trunk.

"Your bodice and shirt." Ena nodded to Danu.

"What?" Niko said at the same time Danu said, "I have no other injuries."

"Will you choose lying to me over letting me help you?" Ena said.

"I'm not—"

"We all know Bryana's a beast," Ena said. "Are you really going to pretend that a burn on the heel and a trueborn nursemaid are all you paid for standing beside Niko when I said we were leaving?"

Danu looked up to the solid black above the trees.

"Let me help you," Ena said. "You've tossed yourself into this mess. Your chances of coming out alive don't improve by letting wounds worsen."

Shaking her head, Danu unlaced her bodice.

"Do you need help?" Ena asked.

"I can manage." Pain wrinkled Danu's brow as she eased her bodice off.

"Should I go?" Niko asked as Danu freed the bottom of her shirt from her pants.

"You're not leaving me alone with her," Ena said.

"It's fine. Only fair after what Niko's been through." Danu turned her back to Niko and Ena before pulling off her shirt.

A wave of sick surged through Niko's gut, flooding sour into his throat.

Lines, like lashes drawn in black ink, marked Danu's back, the strips so thick and deep, they seemed to have been drawn by strikes from an actual whip.

"Danu." Niko crawled toward her, taking her hand before she could pull away. "I'm sorry. I'm so sorry Bryana did this to you." He choked out the words. "I'm sorry."

"It wasn't Bryana." Ena took a jar of ointment from the box. "Mael did this."

"What?" Niko searched the trees, waiting for Mael to come charging toward them. "Why? Why would he hurt you?"

"Bryana gave me my real mark." Danu dipped her chin toward the years-old mark on the side of her ribs. "But a mark's useless with the trueborn who gave it so far away. Mael will be close enough for his mark to matter."

"That chivving demon." Niko shut his eyes as he bent down to kiss Danu's hand.

"Keep breathing," Ena said.

Danu gasped.

Niko sat back up in time to watch Ena paint ointment along the red-rimmed marks.

"He drew one of the marks on your back, too." Danu let Niko thread his fingers through hers. "That's why she chose Mael."

"We'll find a way to help you," Niko said, "make sure Mael doesn't hurt you again."

"The mark's already there," Danu said. "There's no reason for him to hurt me now."

46

ALLORA

Allora watched in horror as the maid dusted a faintly sparkling powder across the tops of her breasts.

The maid stepped back, tipping her head as she examined the exaggerated mounds of Allora's chest in the low-cut gown. She pursed her lips and tipped her head the other way, then grabbed a second jar of sparkling dust.

Allora looked away as the maid trailed the second powder between Allora's breasts, reaching into her gown to tap the brush against the bottom of the Queen of Ilbrea's breasts.

"Is this truly necessary?"

The maid stopped and stepped away, keeping hold of her brush and jar of powder as she looked to Gillien.

Gillien leaned forward in her seat. "An extra touch of allure hurts no one, Your Majesty. Add an accent to her collarbone." The sorcerer waved at the maid. "Then leave."

The maid curtsied and went back to the first jar of powder. "Your Majesty, if you wouldn't mind keeping your head front. The end result would be more pleasing."

"Certainly." Allora pinned her gaze out the window, focusing on the drab colors the end of winter had painted over the grounds. Even when the maid stopped, Allora didn't move.

"Well done," Gillien said. "Add the ornamentation to the Queen's daily ablutions."

"Yes, Sorcerer Gillien." The maid deposited the jars of powder on the dressing table and scurried across the room, disappearing into a panel in the wall.

Allora waited until the panel had clicked shut to speak. "Powdering my breasts every day would be absurd. If I walk around the palace like this, people will start to whisper, and gossip of the Queen's desperation-painted breasts will spill out into Ilara."

"A queen who embraces her sensuality to please her King would not bring the kind of gossip you fear." Gillien stood, crossing to Allora to get a better view of her breasts.

"I look like a common whore," Allora said.

"If anything, you resemble a whore with very wealthy patrons."

"That's hardly better!" Allora turned away from Gillien, skipping looking in the mirror before striding toward the door.

"Your husband currently prefers whores to his wife."

Allora froze, waiting for the pain of betrayal to carve through her chest.

Only panic came.

"The King has aimed his lust toward unacceptable shores." Gillien's footsteps moved closer to Allora. "A child born of a whore cannot continue the Willoc line." She stopped in front of the door, blocking Allora's path. "Each time the King releases his seed anywhere but inside his wife is a devastating blow to a country without a royal heir."

"I understand what you want of me." Allora spoke through gritted teeth. "I have apologized to Brannon. I have offered myself to him. I have begged—"

"Ilbrea's King can more easily refuse logic than seduction." Gillien pulled a little bottle from her pocket. "You have been appealing to his mind. It's time you demand the attention of his more vulnerable parts."

Gillien pulled the stopper from the bottle. A little glass rod extended from the cork. She brushed the glass along Allora's throat.

Allora took a breath, trying to catch the scent Gillien had added to the atrocious costume. "I can't smell anything."

"Wrists." Gillien drew the glass rod across the inside of Allora's wrists. "The scent is not for you to smell, but the King will take note."

"And if he laughs at this absurdity?" Allora's voice trembled.

"He won't." Gillien tucked the bottle into her pocket and opened the door. "Come along, Your Majesty."

Allora shut her eyes, willing her face not to flush.

For my friends.

She pushed back her shoulders, making her breasts even more prominent, then opened her eyes and stepped out into the corridor.

Gillien gave her an approving nod, waiting for Allora to reach her side before heading down the hallway.

The thump of soldiers' boots trailed behind them.

Don't blush. Don't blush.

Allora's body disobeyed, her cheeks pinking as soon as the stairs to the palace entryway came into view. "I cannot parade in front of Ilarans with my breasts plumped and polished."

"You are the Queen of Ilbrea," Gillien said. "By this time tomorrow, women in Ilara will be clawing at each other for powder to accent their breasts."

"That's atrocious."

"That's how fashions are born."

"A fashion born of a maid's skill." Allora slowed as she neared the steps, entering the view of the people below. "How did a palace maid come to have such a talent?"

"My dear Allora, the servants' uniforms have not been permanently affixed to their bodies. And young maids have been known to seek spouses of their own."

The people in the entryway stopped as Allora descended the stairs.

All of them bowed. Most of them required a lesson in how to subtly gawk at their Queen's breasts.

"If you are determined to dress me in this fashion, I suggest you have the maid train others in her skill. If her aim is to find a husband, I doubt she'll be with us long."

"Indeed." A hint of laughter bounced Gillien's breath, almost like Gillien was a friend rather than a demon in human skin.

Allora gave gracious nods as she passed through her people, hoping none of them noticed the humiliation-born heat that had crept all the way up to her temples.

A hint of relief cooled her cheeks as she turned down a corridor that offered little to the public, leaving few Ilarans for Allora to face on her trek to Brannon's private library.

"How many whores has my husband bedded since we married?" Allora whispered.

"Does it matter?" Gillien said.

"I'd like to know how many women he's chosen over me. It seems vital information for the battle ahead."

"There will be no battle." Gillien took Allora's hand.

A wave of nausea rolled through Allora at the sorcerer's touch, but she didn't dare yank her hand away as Gillien led her to the soldiers flanking the door of the King's library.

Gillien studied the soldiers for a moment before pointing to one. "You, follow us. We require no others."

A blond soldier—the one who had been so kind when Brannon had cast Allora aside, preferring to walk the palace in his underthings rather than tolerate the presence of his wife—stepped forward.

"I'm sure this is unnecessary," Allora said. "This soldier is dedicated to his duty. Let him stay near the King."

"It will take but a moment." Gillien squeezed Allora's hand, giving her no choice but to be led to a small sitting room several doors away from the King's library.

No guards had been stationed by the door of the empty room. With a flick of her finger, Gillien opened the door, though whether the magic was an act of habit or warning, Allora didn't know.

Gillien stopped in the center of the sitting room, waiting for the soldier to enter behind them before flicking her finger again to shut the door.

"What is your name?" A too-kind smile curved Gillien's lips as she beckoned the soldier forward.

"Kenrick, sorcerer." Kenrick bowed.

"Kenrick, as a soldier you have sworn to do whatever is necessary to protect the Guilds, the royal family, and Ilbrea, correct?" Gillien said.

"Yes, sorcerer." Kenrick kept his gaze solely on Gillien as though the Queen of Ilbrea weren't even in the room.

"I am pleased you understand your duty, Soldier Kenrick," Gillien said. "Approach the Queen and take in the scent on her wrist."

A wrinkle pinched between Kenrick's eyebrows, but he followed the command, stepping toward Allora.

"Your Majesty." Kenrick gave yet another bow. "If I may."

"Gillien, is this—"

"I insist," Gillien cut across Allora's protest.

Allora held out her wrist.

Kenrick tucked his hands behind his back as he bent forward. He gave a barely audible sniff, then inhaled deeply, as though wanting to devour the scent Allora couldn't even smell.

"What do you think?" Gillien asked.

Kenrick began to step back.

"Ah ah, not so quickly," Gillien said.

He steadied his stance, fixing his gaze over Allora's head.

"What do you think of the scent, Soldier Kenrick?" Gillien said.

"It"—Kenrick swallowed hard—"it's unlike anything I've ever smelled."

"And why is that?" Gillien asked.

"I feel a bit"—Kenrick furrowed his brow—"on the invigorated side of intoxicated, sorcerer."

Gillien prowled closer. "The faint shimmer on the Queen's collar bone, do you see it?"

"Yes, sorcerer," Kenrick said.

"Kiss it."

"What?" Allora stepped back. "Gillien, this has gone quite far enough."

"A warrior must know what weapons they wield," Gillien said. "Or have you forgotten what you are protecting, Your Majesty?"

Images of Mara and Tham, trapped in the darkness, separated and helpless, punished for Allora's failure, swam through her mind. She tucked the horror away, behind the numb barrier that kept her from burning with rage and fear.

"Of course not." Allora stepped toward Kenrick, stopping with only inches between them, tipping her head, giving the soldier easier access to her neck.

"Proceed, soldier," Gillien said. "Taste your Queen."

Kenrick met Allora's gaze, lingering for a moment as though trying to give her time to scream or shove him away.

She gave him a tiny nod.

Holding her gaze for as long as he could, Kenrick lowered his head, pressing a kiss to Allora's shoulder as far to the side as her gown would allow.

At the touch of his lips, a blissful warmth quivered across Allora's skin, spreading down to her breasts. Her breath caught in her throat as a faint wanting pushed against the precious numbness in her mind.

Kenrick stepped back, his breathing uneven.

Eyes wide, he stared above Allora's head as though fighting every moment to keep from looking to the sensitive place his kiss had claimed. A faint sparkle of the powder clung to his lips. He quickly licked it away, erasing the evidence with a sweep of his tongue.

"And how did that taste, Soldier Kenrick?" Gillien asked.

"Like chamb-soaked berries." Kenrick's voice came out low.

"And how did it make you feel?" Gillien asked.

"Please, sorcerer," Kenrick said.

"Answer the question."

"I feel…" Kenrick shut his eyes, keeping them closed as he spoke. "I feel a way that is inappropriate for a man to…to speak of in any way that could be"—he shook his head—"be taken to refer to the wife of the King, or even just the Queen regardless of her husband, or umm, or any woman that should be given an unbreakable barrier of respectful distance."

"Very good," Gillien whispered. "Now the fainter powder between her breasts, what does that taste like?"

Kenrick opened his eyes, his gaze immediately flicking to Allora's breasts.

"Enough." The word barely squeezed out of Allora's throat. The beautiful heat surged toward the tips of her breasts. Her breath shuddered as her body begged to be touched.

"Know your weapons, my Queen," Gillien said. "Do as you're told, soldier."

Allora raised her chin, the heat that tantalized her breasts gaining strength as Kenrick's tongue swept across his wickedly full lips again.

Kenrick leaned forward, the warmth of his breath teasing Allora's skin before his lips grazed the shadowing between her breasts.

The heat in Allora's body thundered, sinking, gaining a throbbing pulse as it found her center.

Kenrick took two steps back, ducking his chin as he wiped the shimmer from his mouth with the back of his hand.

"And this powder?" Gillien said.

Kenrick turned toward Gillien, facing her as though Allora weren't even in the room. "If midnight had a flavor, it would be that mixed with honey. I beg you, sorcerer, do not make me find a way to say how I feel in the presence of the Queen."

Gillien grinned, looking down at the stiffness intruding on the exquisite cut of Kenrick's uniform.

Allora's fingers tingled.

If she could only touch him. Explore his length.

"What under the stars is in this powder?" Allora forced her feet to move, attempting a façade of storming away instead of fleeing her swelling desire.

"A potent aphrodisiac, which complements the visual stimulation of the powder," Gillien said. "And now that you understand its efficacy, I'm sure you will find it of assistance."

"He could have licked it off a spoon," Allora snapped.

"But what good would that have done you?" Gillien said.

"What good ought I have gained from this demeaning travesty?" Allora gripped the back of the couch, letting the wooden scrollwork dig into her palms.

"Soldier Kenrick," Gillien said, "has Queen Allora's scent changed?"

"Yes. She smells…"

"Ripe with desire?" Gillien said. "Filled with a lust you long to satisfy?"

"Gillien please, stop this vulgar ridicule," Allora said.

"We've finished this demonstration," Gillien said. "Soldier Kenrick, you are free to return to your post. If you need a moment to compose yourself, please do so."

Kenrick bowed and headed for the door, reaching it in three long strides.

"And Soldier Kenrick," Gillien said, "if I hear any whisper of what's passed in this room, I will know it came from you. You will be handled accordingly."

"Yes, sorcerer." Kenrick escaped the room, closing the door behind him with a sharp thud.

Gillien sighed. "He will dream of those few moments for the rest of his days."

"That was completely unnecessary." Allora dug her nails into the scrolls of the wood, leaving halfmoon dents behind.

"You will leave this room and go straight to your husband," Gillien said. "You will place yourself close to him and allow him to catch your scent. He will taste your breasts and no amount of foolish stubbornness will diminish his wanting. I have already made his excuses for the day. The effects of the scent and powders will take hours to wear off. I suggest you make productive use of that time."

Tears burned in Allora's eyes, but the rest of her body still drowned in wanting.

"Hell must have mourned when you were born. How painful for them to lose such a prize demon." Allora pushed away from the couch. "Do not come to me again today. I will vomit at the sight of you." She stormed past Gillien and flung open the door, letting it smash against the wall with a satisfying bang.

Not allowing herself time to think, she cut down the hall to the door of Brannon's library.

Kenrick had rejoined the other guards.

Allora avoided his gaze as she knocked on Brannon's door.

The feel of a host of eyes watching her scratched down the back of her neck.

She opened the door without waiting for Brannon's response, dodging inside and slamming it shut behind her as though Gillien had deadly claws aching to slice through Allora's flesh.

Brannon looked up from the papers on his desk. He only glanced Allora's way before silently returning to his work.

"Brannon." Allora pushed away from the door, willing the

room not to spin as she approached him. "Brannon, I need to talk to you."

He didn't look up.

"I know you'd be happier if you never had to see me again, but that isn't an option." Allora reached the desk, daring to cut around to where Brannon sat. "I've been sent by Gillien. If I hadn't walked in here on my own, you and I both know she would have forced me."

Allora leaned back against the desk, placing her breasts in Brannon's line of sight.

Brannon's shoulders tensed.

"I hope you like my gown." Allora took a deep breath, arching her back ever so slightly, letting her breasts strain against the fabric.

Brannon's gaze slid up, catching on the shimmering tops of Allora's breasts.

"It was made to please you." Allora laid her hand a mere inch from his. "All of me, wrapped up like a present for Ilbrea's King."

She slid her hand closer, letting her pinky drape across his. That tiny touch renewed the heat pulsing in her center.

"The most daring part is what lies beneath the gown." She trailed her fingers up his arm, slowly working her way to his chin.

He took a shuddering breath, closing his eyes as though tumbling into bliss, not resisting as she tipped his face up.

"I've never worn undergarments cut in such a way."

Brannon's eyes flew open.

She lowered her gaze to his lips. The softness. The pleasure they could bring as they teased her most sensitive places. She leaned forward, lingering with her breasts at the perfect angle for his enjoyment before whispering in his ear.

"Will you deny your desire, my King?"

She gasped as he wrapped an arm around her waist, yanking

her toward him, sitting her on the desk. She arched into his touch, daring him not to claim her.

His lips found the powder on top of her breasts.

Allora moaned as his tongue traced through the flavor, teasing lower.

"Brannon." She widened her legs, offering him closeness as he stood.

He trailed his tongue between her breasts, devouring the powder's power.

A guttural sound rumbled in his chest as he tore open the top of Allora's gown, exposing the hardened peaks of her breasts. He nipped at their hardness, sending a tremble down Allora's spine.

She threaded her fingers through his hair, holding him in place, making him continue his work.

He yanked her forward, pressing his stiffness against the pulsing of her center.

A whimper broke free as she rubbed against him.

He froze, letting go of her, planting his hands on the desk as he broke free from her grip on his hair.

"What did that serpent do?" Brannon's voice rasped in his throat.

"What?" The flash of fear did little to quell the throbbing that begged Allora to press against him.

"Either you are an imposter, or that purple snake did something to entice enthusiasm."

"Is it wrong for a husband and wife to enjoy sensual pleasure?"

"I know my wife." Brannon backed away. "You've never been one for rampant desire. And I am a man whose anger is not dissolved by the offering of breasts, however exquisite they may be."

"Just give in to it." Allora reached for him. "Don't deny this feeling."

"The truth. Now!"

"Gillien dressed me." She met Brannon's teal eyes. "The powder and the scent—"

Brannon threw his chair, smashing it against the wall with a shout.

"I didn't know what she'd done until it was already on me," Allora said. "Gillien plotted this. She herded me to you."

"And made a whore of Ilbrea's Queen," Brannon spat.

"You seem to prefer whores." The tears in Allora's eyes spilled free. "Please, Brannon, I didn't choose this either. But whatever plot Gillien begins next will only be worse. I'm here and ready for you. Give in to your body and let it be done."

"Tell the viper I would rather fuck a pig than let the sorcerers fool with my mind." Brannon stormed to the door, flinging it open, not bothering to close it behind him, leaving the Queen of Ilbrea clutching the scraps of her gown to cover her naked breasts.

47

NIKO

The light of Kace's lae stone offered the only meager weapon in the constant battle against the darkness. He sat, keeping watch at the edge of the black stones Alane had laid out in a wide arc, enclosing their group in the safety of Black Blood magic.

Stone magic and a guard and still Niko felt as though the black were reaching into their haven, crawling across his neck, taunting him, promising to drag him so deep into the darkness not even the true Solcha could find him.

The light dimmed as Kace shifted, blocking Niko's view of the lae stone.

You've been down here for days and nothing's attacked, Mara whispered. *Sleep, Niko.*

He rolled over, turning to face the stone wall that created the back of their camp.

Shutting his eyes, he exhaled, forcing his muscles to relax.

Sleep. Just a few hours of sleep and their party would be up and moving again, traveling the winding path the mountain laid out for them.

The labyrinth under the mountain didn't allow Niko the mercy of counting each step as a step closer to home. The map maker in him wouldn't accept the foolishness of pretending traveling south brought him closer to a destination farther north. But he could almost convince himself to count each step as one step closer to the light.

Just as falling asleep would bring him one sleep closer to the light, and a bed, and a bath, and frie, and proper food, and—

Home.

A thrill wound up Niko's spine, bringing the smallest of smiles to his face as he faded into sleep.

A soft scraping came from behind him.

Niko rolled over, sitting up, preparing to flee a demon made of pure darkness.

Kace pushed himself to his feet, reaching his arms over his head, shaking his left foot in the strangest defense against a demon Niko had ever encountered.

Kace switched to shaking his right foot.

Niko grabbed the knife from under his pack.

Kace bent forward, stretching his back.

Not preparing for attack, only stretching.

Niko tucked the knife away.

If the darkness doesn't get you, your chivving fear will.

Niko dragged his hands down his face, taking a breath, willing his heart to return to a slow rhythm that might allow him to finally sleep.

His heart did not obey.

Chivving cowardly slitch.

It's not like before, a new voice whispered to Niko. *You know there's a way out.*

All he had to do was follow Solcha. Trot along behind Adrial's wife like a terrified child clinging to her apron strings and wait for their journey to end.

Better, the voice whispered. *You'll be fine.*

Amec.

Guilt joined the still-simmering fear in Niko's gut.

Amec's voice had whispered words of comfort.

Amec had kept Niko moving during the months they were trapped in the black, his companionship saving Niko from slipping into utter madness.

And Niko hadn't even fought to say goodbye to Amec before leaving the stronghold.

Requested to see Amec, yes. But seeing Amec required Niko asking for an audience with Paiman, then receiving Paiman's permission to be taken to the Ilbrean that wasn't supposed to exist.

So when the guard told Niko he wasn't to leave his room until it was time to begin the journey Ena had declared the mountain commanded, Niko didn't argue. Didn't ask for Paiman to be brought to him.

His fear of Bryana ripping his chance for freedom away had kept Niko from demanding to see his friend.

And once they'd entered the black, Danu, and the darkness, and the promise of seeing Ilbrea again, had overwhelmed all else and driven his friend from his thoughts.

You're the worst of all slitches.

The far corners of Niko's mind couldn't come up with any comforting words from his friends to absolve him of his guilt.

Flipping his blankets back, Niko turned to sit facing the wall. He pulled his waterskin from his pack, taking a drink before running his fingers across the ground, searching for a dent in the rock.

He kept one finger in the chosen dent, using it as a placeholder as he poured a trickle of water onto the ground, forming a little puddle.

The familiarity of the process soothed Niko's nerves. He corked his waterskin and began to write.

Amec,
   I'm the worst of all men.

Niko traced the words on the rock wall. He dipped his finger back into the tiny puddle before starting on the next line.

We saw each other through this horrible darkness, and I don't think I ever thanked you well enough. My spirit would have broken without you. As much as I wanted to escape the black, I don't think I could have made myself keep going for so long.

Thank you, friend. You kept me alive.

I'm sorry for abandoning you in the stronghold. I know you don't see it as abandonment. You want a life with Glyn and the Black Bloods. You wouldn't have come with me even if I'd begged and the demon elder had somehow allowed your escape. You're happy where you are.

I still should have said goodbye.

I will write my farewell on the stone and let the mountain devour my words. I'm sorry I can't send a proper letter. But I don't think a message sent through the Brien would reach you any better than a note written with water on stone.

I am sorry for the times I should have been a better friend and am so very grateful to have known you.

I wish you happiness with Glyn.

I wish you a long life filled with the joy of your children and grandchildren.

I wish you peace among the Black Bloods so you will never be called upon to fight.

I wish you—

Niko froze, his finger still pressed to the stone. He blinked away the heat pooling in his eyes.

May you never understand why your paradise was my hell.

Live well, friend,

Niko

He stared at the wall, waiting for some finality to click in his mind or an ebbing of his shame to ease the knot in his throat, anything that might calm the guilt and fear still bubbling in his gut.

By the chivving Guilds, you're a fool.

He turned away from the wall, flipping his blankets to cover his legs.

A shadow shifted in the corner of his vision. He grabbed his knife before recognizing the form.

"Danu," Niko whispered, his heart racing so fast he couldn't convince his hand to let go of the hilt of his knife. "You're really you, right?"

"I'm me," Danu said, so quietly Niko could barely hear her even though her bedroll was only five feet from his. "What were you doing?"

"Writing a letter no one will ever get," Niko said.

Danu tipped her head.

"I couldn't sleep," Niko said.

"You should keep trying. You need rest."

"So do you. I'm sorry if I woke you."

"It wasn't you."

"Is it your back? Mine can itch like a beast when I'm trying to sleep." The mere mention of Niko's mark brought a vague itching to the center of his back where scabs still covered the demon elder's handiwork. "I can try to sneak ointment from Ena's bag."

"My back's fine."

"You're sure?"

"Yes." Danu lay down, moving smoothly enough Niko almost believed her.

"If it's not your back, are you cold? You can have one of my blankets."

"Go to sleep, Niko."

"If the black is getting to you—"

"Go to sleep." Danu rolled to face away from him.

Niko watched her, waiting for her breathing to slow and her shoulders to relax. Neither happened.

He dipped his finger into the tiny puddle and twisted to face the rock wall.

P.S.

If you can think of a god who will help a pitiful fool, beg them to help me. Make me wise enough to earn Danu's forgiveness for the pain she's endured for standing with me, and make me strong enough to stand with her against whatever demons haunt her.

48

ADRIAL

The chill of the rain clung to Adrial's bones, warning him of the price he'd face for venturing out into the damp cold.

Tege had tented layers of cloth over the food in Adrial's basket, a thoughtful effort to keep the fresh-baked buns from becoming sopping mush, though Adrial had little faith in the fabric's efficacy based on the freezing drip of water that had already crept through his hood to run down his back.

Keeping his chin tucked against the rain, Adrial only gave Straff a brief wave as he plodded through the gate. He noted the idea of doing something nice for the guards who suffered in the elements—a plot for him to consider after a hot bath and strong cup of tea.

The stone of the street had that awful kind of slick that promised to be ice soon. Even the usual line of people waiting for the slitch Travers's services had dwindled to a few desperate souls.

"Head Scribe!" A familiar child's face popped up right in front of his. "Come on, sir." The child took Adrial's arm in a kind, if counterproductive, attempt at helping him.

A second child relieved him of the basket, flipping Tege's layers of fabric back, exposing the buns to the dreaded elements.

"I don't know who did it, sir," the boy clinging to Adrial's arm said. "But whoever it was seems awfully nice."

"What do you..." A white awning, covering the side of the fountain where Adrial always sat, answered his question.

Made of heavy waxed canvas, the square covering had created a patch of dry where the few tilk brave enough to come for a bit of food had all clustered together to wait for the head scribe's basket.

"Grab a bite and clear out." The child with the basket hopped into the shelter. "We have to make room for him."

"Thank you, Head Scribe," a woman called as she hurried away.

"Uuehu, ir." A girl had shoved a whole roll into her mouth.

"Careful not to choke." Adrial allowed himself a smile. Half the cluster had fled before he reached the awning.

By the time the child helping Adrial deposited him on the rim of the fountain, the rest had cleared out.

The child's face fell as he looked into the empty basket.

"Nothing left?" Adrial asked.

"But that's all right, sir. Worth it to help the head scribe." The boy bowed and turned to leave.

"Not so quickly." Adrial reached into the pocket of his cloak and pulled out two apples.

The boy's eyes widened.

"I never want someone to go hungry because they were kind enough to help me." Adrial reached into his pocket one more time.

Tege had carefully wrapped the cookie, presenting it as a gift, going so far as to sew a little paper note to the fabric.

With thanks.

   ~Friends of the Head Scribe

Utter, joyful shock filled the boy's face as he beheld the treasure.

"Don't spread word about the sweets," Adrial said in a low voice. "This had to be smuggled from the kitchens. The cooks only want practical food going into my basket."

"Yes, sir." The boy tucked the cookie up the front of his coat in a very conspicuous manner, bowed, and ran away, a huge smile radiating from his too-thin face.

Adrial moved the empty basket to sit beside him on the rim of the fountain and settled in to freeze beneath the white awning.

The nagging rain struck the canvas, punctuating every drop.

Lord Gareth must have been the one to order the covering erected, though whether it had been someone else's idea, Adrial would have to root out. Offering his sincere gratitude was the least he could do for such a kind act.

The rain strengthened, roaring against the canvas.

Adrial closed his eyes, fixing his mind on the sound rather than let it drift to darker places.

The revenant hadn't appeared in over a week. Not a horribly long time—the scarred man had vanished for much longer before.

But despite the fear and loathing, utter loathing, that curled through Adrial's being at the mere thought of the man, Adrial longed to see him again. The need thundered through his mind, joining the steady rumble of the rain.

But what if the revenant never returned?

What if Adrial never heard another word of Ena and the baby.

Patience. There is no good in panicking.

Adrial opened his eyes, looking up to watch the silhouettes of the raindrops running toward the sides of the awning.

Focus on the rain.

"It's a waste of fabric."

Equal parts terror and joy jolted through Adrial's chest at the sound of the revenant's voice.

"How is she?" Adrial asked. "How is the baby?"

The revenant stayed silent.

"Are they well?" Adrial asked.

"As well as can be expected."

"What does that mean?" Adrial glanced toward the revenant. He sat two feet away, sharing the shelter with Adrial, closer than he'd ever been before.

"I've answered a question," the revenant said. "Now you answer mine."

Panic tore through Adrial's calm. "I—"

"It's not optional." The revenant pulled a flask from his pocket and took a deep drink. "Unless you've grown tired of meeting me."

"No." Adrial tucked his hands under his cloak, hiding their shaking. "But the attack on the docks—you made me add names to the roster of workers. Are your people the ones who killed those sorcerers and sailors?"

"That's not your concern."

"It is my concern if I helped you murder innocent people."

"Innocent." The revenant's voice dripped with venom. "Did Ena marry a beast foolish enough to call a chivving sorcerer innocent?"

"The Sorcerers Guild is filled with monsters. I will not attempt to deny that. But sailors were killed in the attack."

"Paun." The revenant spat the word. "Paun died on the docks."

"Being a member of the Guilds doesn't make a person evil." Adrial leaned his weight onto his bad hip, trusting the pain to stifle his need to rage at the revenant. "Even if it did, there were unguilded sailors on the docks as well."

"Collaborators."

"Common folk doing honest work."

"Slitches who've betrayed their own people for coin."

"Ena—"

Made ink for me. Earned her coin from me.

"Ena and the baby's safety means everything to me," Adrial said. "But I beg your mercy. Please do not make me a party to murder again. The weight will crack me, and I'll be no good to you."

"No good to Ena, either." The revenant stood. "Consider her gone, Head Scribe. Our business here is done. May guilt devour your soul."

"Wait." Adrial leapt to his feet. His bad hip gave out. He fell back onto the edge of the fountain with a painful thud. "I'm sorry." He spoke through clenched teeth, pushing the words past the pain. "I shouldn't have said anything about the sailors. I'm sorry."

The revenant looked down at him.

"Tell me what you want." Adrial clasped his hands in front of him, as close to begging as he dared with the guards still in sight. "Anything. I will do anything to protect her and the baby."

"A party of fighters left through the northern gate of the city yesterday," the revenant said. "They wore no Guild's color, but there were too many of them, and they were too well-armed for them not to be on Guild business. Find out where they went."

"To the Spice Trail. There's a…" Adrial's heartbeat thundered in his ears as he fought to quell his guilt. "There's a Wyrainian delegate coming through the Spice Trail passage."

"Why?" The revenant took another drink from his flask.

"To see the state of Ilara for themselves. Whatever the Wyrainian King has heard about the troubles in the city was concerning enough for him to force a delegate to chance traveling through the eastern mountains in winter.

"The party you saw must have been the guards sent to greet the delegate when they reach Ilbrea. The Lady Sorcerer didn't even want the Guilds Council knowing the Wyrainian delegate was coming, so it makes sense to slip the guards out of the city in common clothes."

"Good work, paun." The revenant tucked the flask back into his pocket.

"Just, please try not to kill anyone." Adrial looked up, catching the revenant's gaze, meeting his eyes for a moment.

"Peace comes at a price."

"The price doesn't have to be innocent lives."

"Numb your conscience. Or you'll not make it long enough to meet your daughter."

As if by the revenant's command, Adrial's whole body went numb. "Daughter."

"Lily." The revenant strode out into the freezing rain.

"Lily." Adrial breathed the word.

A burst of radiating joy melted away the numbness and cold and pain, leaving nothing but bliss in its wake.

"Lily."

A perfect name. A beautiful name.

And lilies, such beautiful flowers. Not delicate. Bold. Stunning.

Adrial picked up the basket, walking back toward the library in a wonderful haze.

The vellum for Princess Illia didn't have a single lily in it. A terrible oversight on Adrial's part. Unforgiveable.

Lilies should coat every page, driving the beauty of the name into the tome, whether or not the royals who thumbed through the pages ever knew the meaning of the images.

The child the King and his monsters had tried to destroy, screaming her existence with every bloom.

Lily.

A shout yanked Adrial from his imaginings of the different colored lilies he might create with Ena's inks.

"Head Scribe."

Adrial looked back toward the fountain.

"Head Scribe." Movement from Travers's direction caught Adrial's eye as Travers shouted again. "Head Scribe!"

Travers had stood, but his guards gripped his arms, holding him in place, not allowing the slitch to approach Adrial.

"Head Scribe, I beg a moment of your time." Travers lowered his head, rounding his shoulders in as close to a bow as he could manage while restrained.

The few common folk gathered for Travers's services backed away, giving Adrial a clear path to the demon.

"Head Scribe," Travers said, "I did not know the harm that would be wrought by the information I—"

"Liar." The word rasped from Adrial's throat.

"I have seen the pain I have caused and regret the errors I have made. I vow to protect and serve the library and the Scribes Guild above any personal ambition or attachment. Allow me to return to my post, sir." Travers tested the hold of his guards, giving a proper bow. "All I wish is to be of service."

"You are serving your Guild, Scribe Gend." Adrial gestured to the wide-eyed tilk who had just been handed a scandal worthy of whispering to their friends. "Your position as city scribe is invaluable. I suggest you return to your work."

"Head Scribe, it is freezing out here," Travers said, "and my cot in the stables offers no relief. I am a scribe of talent with years of training. That training goes to waste if I die of a chill seeping into my lungs or lose my fingers to frostbite."

Adrial studied Travers, from the pallor of his face to the spots of ink marring his fingers.

Punish him. Ink on the fingers of a fully trained scribe. Frozen hands or not, make him write lines like an apprentice.

"Please move the fires two feet closer to Scribe Gend's desk," Adrial said, "and, if you would, request an extra blanket be added to his bedding."

The guard nearest Adrial bowed. "Yes, si—"

"You filthy, chivving bastard." Travers launched himself at Adrial.

The guards held onto his arms, ramming Travers chest-down

onto his desk, knocking him into his inkwell, spattering black across his cheek.

"Your whoring wife was a stain on the Guilds." Travers kicked at his guards. "I protected my Guild. I saved us all from having to bow to a Lord Scribe with a rotta wife and bastard child."

"Thank you, Scribe Gend. You've just absolved any guilt I might have felt at leaving you in the cold." Adrial looked to Travers's guards. "Keep the fires where they are. But do give Scribe Gend an extra blanket. His service as city scribe has only begun. We must keep him well enough to continue his work with the common folk of Ilbrea."

One of the tilk gave a low whistle as Adrial walked past them and through the library gates, his mind already back on the beauty of lilies.

49

ALLORA

The smash of the vase striking the floor did not compare to the chaos of the two soldiers chasing the barking dog through the ballroom or the flurry of the panicked maids trying to sweep away the sharp shards of crystal while protecting the rogue pup's paws from harm.

For her part, Fionnaula took great pride in fulfilling her self-proclaimed duties as royal pup by knocking over four more vases of flowers and tripping one of the soldiers, causing him to skid across the marble floor in a most spectacular tumble, before ripping the fabric swatches from the table and curling up at the Princess's feet.

Distracted from the most trying duty any woman in Ilbrea had ever faced, Illia paused her panic to scratch Fionnaula's ears, cooing that indeed Fionnaula was the best of all pups Dudia had ever created while completely ignoring the destruction around her.

"There will be treats for you as well." Illia kissed Fionnaula's nose. "But those are easy to choose. You love to eat everything, don't you?"

Fionnaula flopped onto her back, wiggling her whole body in a bid for belly scratches.

"Such a distraction." Illia laughed.

"Shall I have her sent to wait in your rooms?" Mrs. Dunne asked with a touch of hope in her voice.

"My sweet girl doesn't like being in my rooms without me," Illia said.

"Very well." Mrs. Dunne picked up the now drool-tainted fabric swatches. "If you wish to coordinate the texture of your gown with the flowers, I suggest the silk."

Illia frowned as she ran her fingers over the fabric. "What do you think, Allora?"

Allora took a sip of chamb, buying herself a moment before having to speak. "The silk is beautiful and would be beautiful on you, but with how foul the weather's been, it's impractical."

"I don't want to be practical," Illia said. "I want to be astonishing."

"Then may I suggest a change in flower choice? At this rate, Ilara will still be covered in freezing mud on Winter's End. I don't think suiting the celebration to the weather would go amiss. Perhaps rather than dahlias, orchids or dark tulips for the occasion. Add more candles and choose this fabric"—Allora pointed to a thicker fabric with an intricately stitched pattern of swirls and blooms in sparkling, silver thread that would shimmer in the light—"and you will glisten like a living jewel."

"You're brilliant." Illia clapped her hands with glee, and Fionnaula added an approving bark. "Do just as the Queen says."

"Your Highness"—Mrs. Dunne stepped back as Fionnaula growled—"while the Queen's flower suggestions would no doubt be beautiful, there's barely a week until Winter's End. There aren't enough orchids or dark tulips available to change the flowers so close to the event."

"But everything has to be perfect," Illia said.

"It will be exquisite." Allora took Illia's hand as the Princess's breathing began to quicken. "And you will have whatever flowers you choose."

"Your Majesty," Mrs. Dunne said, "I will do everything I can to have the flowers brought to Ilara, but—"

"Nonsense. Terin"—Allora looked to the sorcerer posted by the parlor door—"I'm sure you'd be pleased to use your skills to help with the flowers."

"Oh, yes! Wonderful!" Illia's distress vanished.

"I am Princess Illia's guard, not a botanist," Terin said.

"But you have to." Illia stood, sending Fionnaula on another tear around the room. "Please, I'm begging you."

"You've no reason to worry, Illia." Allora stared down Sorcerer Terin. "I'm sure there are sorcerers in the tower who *are* botanists. And, as your wedding to Prince Dagon is so vital to the future prosperity of Ilbrea, I'm sure Terin would be happy to find a sorcerer to create the perfect flowers for your party."

"Yes, Your Majesty." Terin bowed, a stony look on her face that would have frightened Allora if the blessed numbness in her chest hadn't driven away her need to care.

"In that case," Mrs. Dunne said, "may I suggest dark tulips with orchids as accents?"

"Oh, it'll be perfect!" Illia sighed. "But a change in the flowers will have to change which crystal we use."

"Of course, Your Highness." Mrs. Dunne waved to the maid in the corner.

The poor thing looked terrified as she crossed the room, bearing a tray of various crystal glasses, sweat slipping down her brow, her gaze constantly following the path of Fionnaula's rampage.

The maid reached the table unscathed, and the whole process began again, planning a party to impress a guest that might not arrive in time.

But Princess Illia's determination to host the perfect event was a better turn than her sobbing in her room, wailing that the delegate from Wyrain had been dispatched to call off her engagement to Prince Dagon.

And, while no word had come as to when exactly the delegate might arrive, the current state of the city had made the traditional gathering in the Gilded Hall impossible, and, delegate or no, a well-protected party on palace grounds would give the Guilded elite a reprieve from the wretched state of Ilara.

"Allora, I'm the most selfish beast in the world," Illia said. "You've spent all this time helping me choose fabric for my gown, and we haven't looked at a thing for you."

Allora took a breath, considering her words. "Sorcerer Gillien has taken charge of my dress."

"So kind of her to carry that burden for you," Illia said.

"Indeed." A burning hatred danced sparks across the numbness. "If you'll excuse me."

Allora stood, easing around Fionnaula, who once again lay sprawled at Illia's feet.

"Are you well?" Illia asked.

"Just a bit tired." Allora gave the best smile she could. "I've found the unending cold rain to be wearing."

"It is dreadful. And with so much work to be done." Illia turned back to Mrs. Dunne, who looked as though she, of all of them, might collapse from fatigue.

Allora strode across the ballroom, not glancing to the corner where she knew Gillien lurked, so intent on escape she nearly missed the familiar face by the door.

Kenrick stood with three other soldiers, straight-backed and unflinching, averting his eyes from his Queen's as the other guards did. But his chin tensed as she approached, as though he were clenching his jaw, biting back the terrible curses he longed to scream.

Allora slowed her steps as one of the other soldiers opened the door. She stopped just before the soldiers, tipping her head as she looked at Kenrick.

"You're normally one of the King's guards, aren't you?"

"Yes, Your Majesty." Kenrick bowed.

"Perfect." Allora pitched her tone in a mimicry of Illia's enthusiasm. "Come with me. I've been planning a Winter's End surprise for the King. The help of one of my husband's guards would make things so much easier."

Not waiting for a response, Allora walked out into the hall where her own pack of guards waited. She didn't glance behind to make sure Kenrick had joined the herd of soldiers thumping behind her as she cut along the corridor toward the largest of the palace's covered terraces.

Kenrick stepped in front of her, opening the glass-paned door before she reached it.

"Gillien, stay inside." Allora spoke over her shoulder. "I want to surprise the King without relying on sorcerer aid."

The cold damp encompassed Allora as she stepped outside, shrouding her in a chill that cut through her dress.

The door closed softly behind her.

She walked toward the edge of the terrace, savoring the abandoned view of the sodden grounds. No cheerful colors. Not even a gardener braving the weather to tend the flowerbeds.

A fitting garden for the Royal Palace.

Goosebumps covered her arms by the time she turned around.

Kenrick waited ten feet away, maintaining the stance of a guard as though Allora had never felt his lips against her skin.

Warmth blossomed in Allora's cheeks, burning against the cold air.

"I wanted to express my apologies," Allora said. "You were put in a terrible position, and I am truly sorry."

Kenrick lowered his chin, glancing behind him before he spoke. "You carry no blame, Your Majesty. You were no more willing than me. But I would be grateful for the opportunity to apologize to you."

"What for?"

Pink crept up Kenrick's neck. "Whatever was in that powder, I should have maintained better control. There is no possible excuse for that sort of behavior, especially not with my Queen."

"The effects of the powder were rather startling." Allora's mouth went dry. Her heart sped, pushing more heat to her cheeks. "Do not regret your reaction. Sorcerer Gillien wouldn't have been pleased if you'd behaved otherwise."

"You've brought me great comfort, Your Majesty." Kenrick met Allora's gaze.

There was genuine gratitude in his deep-blue eyes, and something like worry, too.

"Is there anything I can do to help you, Your Majesty?" He bowed.

"No. There is no Winter's End surprise for the King. Though, I suppose I'll have to think of something now."

Kenrick furrowed his brow. "At the risk of being too forward—"

"We're well past that." A tiny smile fought its way to Allora's lips.

The creases in his brow softened ever so slightly. "Surprise for the King or not, if there is anything you need, I am happy to serve."

Her smile faded as cold dread dripped through her veins. "Why would a queen need your aid?"

"I'm sorry, Your Majesty." Kenrick bowed, his face returning to the unreadable guard's façade. "I didn't mean to overstep."

"No, truly why? Have rumors of my disgrace finally inundated the palace?"

"I've told no one what happened between us."

"I know." Allora halved the gap between them, still keeping Kenrick out of arm's reach. "I trust you to keep our secret. But the King fleeing our bedroom. A maid rescuing me from having to expose myself walking through the palace in a torn gown. Too many people witnessed those humiliations. Avoiding whispers would be a fool's hope."

Kenrick ducked his chin again, glancing behind, checking for interlopers. "There is talk from those without the wisdom to stay quiet."

"What do they say of the King's forsaken wife?"

"Very little." Kenrick lowered his tone, speaking in a soothing voice that made it easier for Allora to swallow her tears. "The staff and soldiers appreciate your kindness. People think themselves fortunate to have you as the mistress of the house and as their Queen. If they do speak ill of your marriage to the King, the harsh words fall on him, for treating his new bride so poorly."

"Thank you." Allora didn't bother wiping away her tears.

"I am honored to aid, my Queen." He held her gaze again, a warmth filling his eyes as though he were trying to pour his caring comfort into her soul.

"You should return to your post." Allora stepped back. "Whatever I come up with to surprise the King, I'll make sure you have a hand in it. Rumors of my unnecessarily consorting with a guard would be damaging to us both."

"Yes, Your Majesty. I look forward to assisting with the surprise." Kenrick gave a final bow, turned sharply, and went back into the palace, leaving Allora alone to shiver in the unrelenting cold.

50

MARA

The tapping of Elver's pen prodded Mara from her early morning daydream of a brisk breeze sweeping across the banks of a real river, bringing the sting of cold and the earthy scent of early spring mud with it—a lovely, imperfect landscape begging her to venture out and explore.

"Eat your breakfast." Elver tapped the end of his pen on Mara's plate. "Actually—" He set his pen down on his paper, leaving an ink spot that would have set Adrial's teeth on edge, then, without so much as glancing Mara's way, added more fruit and cheese to her plate.

"I'm not that hungry," Mara said.

"It doesn't matter." Elver put more food on Tham's plate before heaping extra onto his own, then set the plate of breakfast meats on the ground. "Eat. Eat. Everyone, eat."

Elle snarfled her excitement as she tore into the meat, her tail thrashing against the table leg with a steady thump.

Mara looked to Tham. His furrowed brow mirrored her own worry.

"We'll all eat then," Mara said.

"I already said that." Elver wrote with one hand while shoving food into his mouth with the other. "I should've taken a bath last night. Didn't think of it until now."

"If you want a bath, go take a bath," Mara said between bites of fruit.

"Can't. Don't want my bits flopping about when they finally figure it out. That would be embarrassing. And a waste of time."

"Elver," Tham said, "who's figuring out what?"

"Not sure." The scratching of Elver's pen paused. "It's not like in Isfol. There's no story in my head. I'm not watching things that might be what comes next."

"Then what's wrong?" Mara reached for Elver's hand.

"Nothing." Elver resumed his frantic writing.

"Something's got you in a panic, Elver," Mara said. "Please tell me."

"It's not a story, or pictures. It's more like a whispering coming from here." Elver tapped the back of his head. "But the whisper doesn't have proper words, but I can feel it, what it's saying. You've stopped eating."

"Sorry." Mara speared another slice of fruit with her fork. "Can you tell me what the whisper is making you feel?"

"Like I need to hold my breath and close my eyes and be ready to fall into the depths of a dark frozen sea. Time's up. And I hate traveling on an empty stomach." Elver pointed his pen at Mara. "So do you. You try to hide it, but I can scent your nerves tensing when you've been too long without food.

"Tham"—Elver whipped his pen toward Tham, leaving an arc of spattered ink on the table—"is more bothered by not having a flat place to sleep than being hungry. Which is why I took the extra blankets I asked for and shoved them into our packs. They won't help with the slant of the ground, but folded up beneath us, they might at least make the rocks jabbing into our ribs a touch less annoying."

"That was very thoughtful of you," Mara said.

"I know."

"But whatever feeling the whisper in your mind gave you doesn't mean we won't be staying here," Mara said. "The Ice Walkers have already attacked once, and the Lady Sorcerer kept us here."

"Which is why we have to be ready." Elver used his sleeve to blot the ink on his paper. "Harder to say no to someone with a pack on their back."

He folded the paper up and scrawled *Shantene* across the blank side.

"And done." Elver shoved a whole roll into his mouth and rescued the meat tray from Elle's attempts to lick all remaining flavor from the metal.

Folding his hands in his lap, Elver looked out toward the balcony as though enjoying the view on a carefree morning.

Mara choked down bite after bite, not letting herself stop until her stomach felt as though it might explode. She set down her fork and leaned back in her chair. "I'm sorry, Elver. If I eat another bite, I'll make myself ill and taking the time to stuff myself will have been useless."

Elver held up a finger and tipped his head, wrinkling his brow as he held the pose.

"Elver?" Mara whispered.

Elver squinted and pursed his lips.

"Are you all right?" Mara said.

He leapt to his feet, knocking his chair back. "Perfect timing!"

Elle growled at the offending chair.

"For what?" Tham patted his leg, calling Elle back to him.

"The walls have started to move," Elver said. "Packs on, everyone. We've got to be ready."

He hurried to the place where the door to their rooms normally appeared. All three of their now-overstuffed packs rested against the wall. Elver pulled his own on before turning to where Mara and Tham still sat at the table. "No time to waste."

Mara met Tham's gaze, giving him a chance to object before going to the wall and taking the pack Elver held out for her.

"I put the prettiest of the dead regent's jewels in your pack. It seemed like the kind thing to do. Oh, my letter." Elver bolted back to the table, grabbing his letter to Shantene. "Goodbye, rooms. You've been very pretty, and my bed was very soft. Thank you for your hospitality."

He turned back to the wall just as the door began to form.

Mara reached for Tham's hand, but he'd knelt beside Elle, tying on her lead. Mara held her breath as the door's handle came back into being.

Fergal opened the door and froze, the wrinkles on his brow deepening as he took in Mara, Tham, and Elver wearing their packs while Elle strained against her lead, ready to crash into Fergal in a fervent display of affection.

"What under the blazing stars are you doing?" Fergal said.

"What did the wind bring?" Elver said.

"What?" Fergal stepped into the sitting room, moving to close the door behind him.

Elver dodged around Fergal, using his body as a barricade to keep the door from closing. "No time for that. You can answer my question while we walk."

"We're not going for a walk. And it's me who's short on time," Fergal said. "There was a troubling incident last night—"

"We already knew that," Elver said.

"We did?" Mara said.

"You can tell us why the wind screamed of trouble while we walk. It takes forever to walk anywhere in this tower, and by the time you've finished talking, we could be halfway to the way out of the tower, and I know you don't know this yet, but you're going to need us to come with you. So hurry up." Elver clapped his hands. "Can't risk missing the path chosen for us."

"Chosen?" Fergal said.

"Don't ask by whom," Elver said. "That part already confused me when there were pictures in my head. It might be the ice calling from far away. Or maybe the ice and the wind are friends so they both like to tell me things. Or maybe being in the blue broke my mind so badly everything that wants to can whisper through the cracks. The why doesn't matter, only that we have to go."

"Elver was right in Isfol," Tham said. "Listening to him is worth a wasted walk through the corridors."

"Thank you, Tham." Elver beamed. "I like that we're friends."

Fergal dragged his hand over the uncharacteristic stubble on his chin. "Fine. You can follow me while we talk. Though I'll hear no complaints when I abandon you to continue my work and you have to wait in a dark corridor until someone fetches you to lead you back."

"We're not coming back here." Elver shooed Fergal into the hall.

Fergal shook his head and strode out into the dark, setting a brisk pace. Elver went first, then Mara with Tham and Elle taking up the back.

"You may talk now," Elver said.

"Thank you," Fergal said. "Something troubling happened last night."

"Was there another attack?" Mara bit her lips together, preparing to swallow her scream of rage if more innocent blood had been spilt.

"Not an attack. A theft." Fergal turned right, cutting down a wider passage. "Five merchants' boats were stolen from the private docks."

"Boats?" Tham asked.

"Small sailing crafts," Fergal said. "A normal theft would be left to the Soldiers Guild, but all personal pleasure boats have been chained to the docks for months."

"Oh dear," Elver said.

Fergal led them through a roughly hewn, circular chamber and onto an unfamiliar, tightly spiraled ramp.

"The chains were sorcerer-forged," Fergal said. "No saelk tool could break through them."

Mara shivered as icy claws carved fear down her spine. "How were the chains broken?"

"From what we can tell, they were frozen and shattered," Fergal said.

"Ronya." Mara's steps faltered.

Elle banged against her leg as Tham placed his hand on her back, keeping her moving forward while dread tried to pin her in place.

"We think so," Fergal said. "Though taking the risk of entering Ilara to steal pleasure boats makes no sense."

"Ian Ayres," Mara said. "Ronya wants to go after Ian Ayres."

"I've read the accounts of your captivity," Fergal said. "I'm aware of her interest in the bastard's island."

"That's why she took the boats," Mara said. "She told her people she would rescue the children. She's sailing for Ian Ayres."

"It can't just be that," Fergal said. "Coming into Ilara, the seat of Ilbrean power, holds too much risk."

"Not for her," Mara said.

"There's got to be something larger at play," Fergal said. "She's spent weeks hiding her army. Even if she didn't think you'd made it back to warn us of the Ice Walkers' attack, one useless island isn't worth exposing her presence within our borders."

"Ian Ayres isn't useless to Ronya," Tham said. "She made that island a symbol of Ilbrea's evil."

"Evil?" Fergal turned around, facing them with a glint of warning in his eyes.

"If she were to rescue the children from Ian Ayres—" Tham began.

"The bastards of Ian Ayres don't need rescuing," Fergal said.

"They do," Tham said before Mara could find the right words.

"That island is a Guilds-made hell, and Ronya knows it. If she rescues the children, she's already made her invasion worth every sacrifice. Once her fighters have seen what the Guilds abandoned those children to suffer, they'll have found their battle cry. Ian Ayres is worth the risk."

Fergal stared at the black stone wall.

"The Ice Walkers are going to Ian Ayres," Mara said. "I'm sure of it."

"If that's where the fools went, we'll have an easy time handling them," Fergal said.

"And we'll be with you." Elver clapped Fergal on the back. "And don't try arguing it. Last night, the wind told me we needed to be packed. She wouldn't have done that if there weren't a reason for it."

"He's right," Mara said. "He knew exactly where we'd be and how to get us out when we escaped Isfol. I don't know what spawns these things in his mind, but for the good of Ilbrea, I don't think we can afford to ignore him."

"And I don't even have to cut off a hand this time. Though Elle did enjoy that." Elver pressed his letter to the wall. "Thank you for your hospitality. Please see that Shantene receives this."

"I am not a messenger boy," Fergal said. "And I will not…"

Fergal fell silent as the stone of the wall swallowed Elver's letter to Shantene.

"You don't have time to deliver a message, Fergal." Elver petted the wall. "We've got a few more minutes' walk before we reach the carriage to go to the docks."

Fergal shook his head.

"Aren't you grateful I made you tell us about the ships while we walked?" Elver gave the wall one more pet and shooed Fergal farther down the passage.

51

NIKO

Ena rubbed the mud between her fingers, working most of it away before adding faint filth near Niko's eyes.

Niko scrunched his eyes closed, silently accepting Ena's work. If Danu could wear a skirt while entering a city of enemies, Niko could bear a bit of dirt on his face as he finally walked back through the gates of Ilara.

Home.

A timid thrill batted at the strands of darkness their journey through the black had left wound around his mind.

The rumble of carriage wheels traveled up the mountain road, heading toward the southern gate of Ilara.

Home. Home.

Niko's leg bounced as the need to sprint through the gate and find a decent pub burned through him.

"One more moment," Ena said.

"Sorry." Niko dug his heels into the ground and his nails into his palms, just waiting for his whole body to explode.

"There." Ena brushed off her hands and stepped back, tipping her head to the side as she surveyed her work. "Keep your shoulders hunched and chin tucked."

"Not having bathed since we left the stronghold isn't enough to disguise the great map maker?" Marlo asked.

"Not when a noose is the price of failure." Ena put her pack back on before flipping up the hood of her worn cloak. She'd pulled bits of her hair free from her braid, leaving tangles around her face. She hadn't rubbed dirt on her cheeks but instead had dabbed deep purple pigment under her eyes, giving her an even more sickly look than her ever-thinning frame managed.

The chatter of voices traveled up the road.

"You four go." Ena nodded to the acolytes. "Tag on to the back of that pack."

Attie bowed to Ena. "May the mountain ever guide your steps."

Alane took Attie's arm, clinging to him like a woman in love as she dragged Attie away from Ena and through the trees. Kace and Marlo offered nods before following.

"Once we hear another group pass, Mael and Danu go next," Ena said.

"We should stay together," Niko said at the same time Mael said, "No."

"I didn't ask a question." Ena faced Mael, not even flinching as the trueborn towered over her. "If you and Danu are refused at the gate, you can walk away. If Niko or I are recognized—"

"They'll share whatever fate we face." Niko's anxious joy faded. "Ena's right. You two go ahead."

"We should stay together," Danu said. "If things go wrong, the two of you shouldn't be on your own."

"You're going ahead of us, and that's final," Ena said.

The sound of battered carriage wheels rumbled south, crossing paths with a horse traveling north.

"Did the others know about this?" Danu asked.

"Of course not," Ena said. "They agreed to go in first because they thought I'd have two people with magic protecting me. But a pet trueborn and a sorcerer with little magic in her blood won't help us if the soldiers attack. It'll only leave two more corpses to be dragged to the cathedral square, which means two less Black Bloods fighting the chivving Guilds. So go out to the chivving road and join the line at the gate. We'll either see you at the meeting place or you can come visit our corpses in the square."

Danu looked between Mael and Niko, worrying her thumbs against her fingers as though wishing she could grip the knives hidden beneath her skirts.

"Go, Danu." Niko stepped closer to her, holding his hand near hers, offering a comfort he'd learned she wouldn't accept. "If something goes wrong, it'll be easier to help us if there's not already a sword at your throat."

Danu bit her bottom lip, her gaze darting across the ground as though she were searching for something.

"Danu"—Niko dared to step closer, not hesitating to spout the comforting lie—"there's nothing to worry about."

"Of course." Danu nodded, stepping away from Niko before speaking to Mael. "We're going in first."

Mael stared silently at her for a moment before turning and striding toward the road.

"Be safe," Niko said.

Danu didn't even look his way before following the trueborn.

Niko watched until she'd disappeared through the trees, fighting his desperate need to run after her.

Will you pretend she's helpless? Mara whispered.

Niko rubbed his hand over his face.

"You're messing up my dirt," Ena said.

"Sorry." Niko shoved his hands into his pockets. "Sorry."

"They'll be fine." Pack still on her back, Ena leaned against a wide tree.

"But we might not be. Two dead Ilbreans walk up to Ilara's gate. It sounds like a tavern joke." Niko pulled his pack on, barely noticing the weight that had been his companion for so long.

Ena stayed silent.

"It's not a joke though. You and I should be terrified of going through that gate." The twisting in Niko's gut solidified, sinking a stone in his stomach as his need to run after Danu was drowned out by darker thoughts. "If either of us is recognized, all chivving hell could break loose."

Still, silence.

"I would probably survive," Niko said. "Unless, of course, the Sorcerers Guild got wind of my falling into a society built on magic that isn't supposed to exist. But you? The Guilds wanted you dead. If they find out you're alive, I don't think anything could save you from execution."

Silence.

"Ena?" Niko stepped into her line of sight. "Going back into Ilara could get you killed."

"And?"

"It's dangerous."

"Do you think I'm not aware?" Ena sidestepped, clearing her path to the road. "I'm not some puffed-up paun used to having the Guilds' protection. I've known I might die on a soldier's sword since long before you got a pretty compass on your wrist."

"And what happens to Lily if you die?"

"Lily is safe."

"You're her mother."

"And my husband is in Ilara."

The pounding of horses' hooves raced up the road toward the city.

Ena crept closer to the road, ducking low to peer through the branches as the sounds of another horse raced by.

"Ena, please, listen to me. Just for one moment." Niko grabbed her arm.

Slowly, terrifyingly slowly, she looked down at Niko's hand.

He didn't let go. "I'll take care of Adrial. I'll make sure he's safe. I'll get him out if things in Ilara go badly." Ena's gaze didn't flinch. "Please, Ena. Go back to Lily. Adrial would want you to."

Her eyes flicked up to Niko's face.

"Adrial is my family, Ena." He let go of her arm but didn't back away. "I love him. You've got to know I would do anything to keep him safe."

"How many men have you killed?"

"What?"

"How many men have you killed, paun?" Ena stepped closer to him, leaving only a breath of space between them. "If the answer is anything less than *I don't remember,* you aren't fit to protect my husband."

Niko swallowed the knot of fear in his throat. "And how many lives have you ended, Solcha?"

"I have painted valleys in blood. And my work is not done." Ena leaned closer, whispering in his ear. "Never tell me how to protect my family, map maker. You were not made to be Death's companion. You will never learn to walk by his side."

"I may have little experience with violence," Niko whispered back, "but don't blame me for wanting to protect you. Like it or not, you married one of the Karron clan, which makes you a part of a messy paun family. Things might have changed while I was gone—Adrial's married and a father, and Allora's the Queen.

"But if Allora choosing to marry the slitch of a king rather than wait for me to return from my journey hasn't turned me away from my family, then your frightening whispers won't dull my need to make sure you aren't murdered by the Guilds if I have a chivving chance of keeping you safe."

Ena stepped back, watching Niko's face for a moment before taking his shoulders. She slid her hands down to grip his elbows. "Allora didn't choose marrying the King over waiting for you. She trapped herself with the royal beast trying to flee her grief. She thought you were dead when she agreed to marry him."

52

THAM

The frigid sea spray dampened Tham's coat as the ship raced toward Ian Ayres. He stood at the bow, out of the sailors' way, letting the wind whip around him.

He rubbed his fingers over the calluses on his palms—far different calluses than the ones he'd earned during his years at sea.

The sailors chosen for the voyage worked in a seamless rhythm. Tham would be a hinderance on the ropes, though his arms burned with the instinct to help. After all the training, all the fighting, the work of a sailor still felt more familiar than that of a soldier.

Mara leaned against him, slipping herself beneath his arm to rest her head on his shoulder.

Tham shut his eyes, feeling every place her body made contact with his, leaning against him, counting on him not to let her fall. He kissed the top of her head, lingering for a moment to take in the scent of her hair, a far more intoxicating perfume than the sea could ever offer.

She rose up on her toes, brushing a kiss just below his ear.

The peace and warmth that flowed through his body from that simple touch—for that, he'd trade the sea for a battlefield.

Mara wrapped her arm behind Tham's waist, pinning herself to him as three dark shapes appeared on the horizon.

"You're not going to be trapped in that hell. Not ever again." Tham tightened his hold on her, willing the gods not to make him a liar.

They stayed bound together as the dark forms took shape.

Ian Mithe, Ian Lioche, and Ian Ayres.

"What if we're too late?" Mara said. "What if Ronya's taken the children?"

"We'll find them," Tham said.

"What if—" Mara shuddered. "What if the children are better off with her?"

He held her tighter.

"Approaching the islands!" The call rang out across the deck, then echoed from the two ships that flanked their own.

Slow footsteps approached the bow. Tham loosened his grip on Mara, moving his free hand to the hilt of his sword.

"Such small islands." Lady Gwell stepped in front of Mara, placing herself in Tham's line of sight as though she'd sensed his instinct to attack and was trying to calm him.

"If you combined all three, they would fit inside the city walls of Frason's Glenn," Mara said. "Ian Ayres would fit inside the grounds of the Royal Palace."

"An apt observation from a map maker," Lady Gwell said. "I'm afraid my perception of the size of places is a bit vague. A hazard of living in the Sorcerers Tower. I'm sure you understand."

"I do."

"Four boats spotted," a sailor called from the crow's nest. "Docked on the northern side of Ian Ayres."

"They're still there." Mara leaned forward, squinting toward the islands. "Shouldn't the Ice Walkers have run by now?"

"Pleasure crafts have neither sorcerer-made sails nor the

assistance of sorcerers on board." Lady Gwell looked to Mara, a tight grin on her lips. "The help of my people has made the Ilbrean fleet faster than ever. A fact the Sailors Guild hates to admit and the Ice Walkers will soon learn."

Tham glanced to the purple sails behind him. The sun caught on the fabric, giving a faint sparkle that seemed designed as a predator's warning—Death approaches. Flee or perish.

"There's something else around the island," the sailor in the crow's nest called. "Captain, I don't know if I'm seeing this right."

"What is it?" the captain shouted up.

"I think—I think the sea has frozen, sir," the sailor said.

Mara stilled.

A dark rumble of fear began at the back of Tham's neck, tensing his muscles, readying him for a blow.

"I know it's not possible, sir," the sailor said. "But I swear that's how it looks."

"It is very much possible." Lady Gwell turned away from the bow to face the sailors, the three other sorcerers on board, and the captain. "The enemy we face has a gift for working with ice."

"What?" the captain snapped. He waved over his shoulder, calling a sailor to him, giving the man his place at the wheel.

The captain stalked across the ship, ignoring the worried glances of his men, not saying anything until he'd reached the Lady Sorcerer. "Are you telling me that sorcerers stole those boats and bolted for Ian Ayres?"

"No," Lady Gwell said. "The thieves are gifted in working with ice. They are neither sorcerers nor my people."

"*Gifted in working with ice* seems a lot like sorcery to me," the captain said.

"Then I suggest you reframe your perception before we reach Ian Ayres," the Lady Sorcerer said. "Sail us to the edge of their ice barrier. Fergal's ship will go to the western end of the isle and Fiona's to the eastern. Remind your men that their thoughts on magic are little more than naïve bedtime stories. Though, if any of your sailors seek to prove their ignorance, I am happy to provide a lesson in what the powers of a sorcerer can do."

Sparks crackled from the Lady Sorcerer's skin, flying toward the captain. He winced as little burns peppered his face and scorch marks marred his blue Guild uniform.

"I will remind my men how little interest they have in magic." The captain bowed and strode back to his post.

"Can you melt through the ice?" Mara kept her voice low.

"Melting the ice would be simple," the Lady Sorcerer said.

"But they've probably extended the ice as far beyond the shore as they can," Tham said. "If we melt a passage through the ice and sail into it, we offer them the opportunity to trap our ships."

"Or shatter the wood of the ships as they did the sorcerer-made chains," Lady Gwell said. "You reason well, Tham."

"Thank you, Lady Gwell." Tham dipped his chin in a small bow.

The ice surrounding Ian Ayres came into view.

The waves had been frozen in place, forming an uneven field more than a thousand feet wide. The sun sparkled off the ice, casting the terrain in a dazzling glow. Even the rounded crests of the breaking waves were glassy enough to catch the light.

Tham scuffed his boot across the deck of the ship. Good enough for running on land, but the slickness of the ice would send the best of soldiers sliding.

"Can your sorcerers shield themselves while they cross the ice?" Mara asked. "Can they shield me if I travel with them?"

"You needn't worry about a shield." Lady Gwell watched the other two ships begin their paths around the island.

"I'm sorry, Lady Gwell," Mara said. "I don't mean to question you, but when you send someone to the island to talk to the Ice Walkers, shouldn't I go, too? Ronya's mind may be poisoned by the love of power, but she's not completely unreasonable."

"I care for her reason as little as for her ice," Lady Gwell said.

Mara glanced to Tham. The worry in her eyes drifted toward fear. Her fear tightened Tham's chest.

"Can you attack the Ice Walkers without being able to see them?" he asked.

"Not the way they're going to do it," Elver called. He patted Elle on the hip, herding her away from the rigging and toward Tham. "If this is the edge of the Ice Walkers' reach, the sorcerers will all stay back here and attack from a distance."

"But what about the children?" Mara said. "What if they aren't all in the children's home? Could they be hurt in the attack?"

"I don't think it matters," Elver whispered. "There are some times when being right feels very, very terrible."

"But you're not right." Mara rounded on Elver. "There are innocent children on that island. There are babies and pregnant girls."

"I am right." Elver bit his lips together and nodded toward Lady Gwell.

"No. The island can't be attacked if the children might get hurt." Mara's voice tightened.

Tham slid his arm out from behind her, taking her hand, giving her a stronger anchor.

"The residents of Ian Ayres have been taken by an enemy of Ilbrea," Lady Gwell said. "They were lost to us as soon as they fell into the Ice Walkers' clutches."

"But they didn't fall into anyone's clutches," Mara said. "Invaders took over the island. The children are still right there. We have to rescue them."

"It cannot be done," Lady Gwell said.

"It has to!" Mara shut her eyes, swallowing as though shoving down the words she longed to shout. "If we can't rescue them, then at least bargain for their safety."

"And what would you have me offer?" Lady Gwell said. "Let them keep an island so close to Ilbrea's shore? Let them run back to the ice so they can plan another intrusion into Ilbrean territory?"

"Yes," Mara said, "if that's what it takes to rescue the children."

"Crossing the ice to negotiate would put my people in danger." Lady Gwell spoke in a low voice. "Approaching the island to fight would put my people in danger."

"Then why did we come here?" Mara's voice shook.

"To stop a threat to Ilbrea," Lady Gwell said. "A threat that can and will be stopped without endangering any of my people."

"Innocent children could die," Mara said.

"An unfortunate consequence of the Ice Walkers' actions," Lady Gwell said.

"But you could cross the ice and get the children out before you attack," Mara said.

"I will do no such thing," Lady Gwell said.

"Then Fergal," Mara said. "He's a warrior. He can—"

Anger sparked in Lady Gwell's eyes. "I will not endanger even one of my people to save unwanted bastards and orphans."

Tham tightened his hold on Mara's hand, preparing to yank her behind him.

"I was one of those children, Lady Gwell," Mara said. "I spent every day hungry and alone and afraid. The children of Ian Ayres spend their lives suffering. They've already been through enough terrors. Don't give them a horrible end."

"If you go to the island to fight, you could take some of the Ice Walkers alive," Tham said. "A few stolen boats could only carry a small portion of Ronya's army, and four of her wolves at most. If we question the Ice Walkers here, we could find out where the rest of her forces are."

"We will not approach the island," Lady Gwell said. "My decision is final."

Mara yanked her hand from Tham's, stepping to the side, planting herself away from him. "You are choosing murder, Lady Sorcerer."

"You are crossing a very dangerous line, Mara Landil." Sparks crackled around Lady Gwell, flying toward Mara, singeing her skin.

Mara gasped through clenched teeth but held up a hand, asking Tham not to protect her.

Dark rage wound up Tham's spine as one of Mara's curls caught fire, but she didn't break eye contact with the Lady Sorcerer as Elver patted the fire out with his sleeve.

"I am begging you to save innocent lives, Lady Gwell," Mara said. "Please don't be the monster those children have spent their whole lives fearing."

"We have never been the monsters." Lady Gwell's sparks burned brighter as she stepped closer to Mara. "I have tried, done everything I could to make you understand how precious the lives of Ilbrea's sorcerers are. But you still cannot see it.

"My people will not be sacrificed to save those who would murder us if given the chance. We are not beasts of burden. We are not tools. We are not weapons to be forced into battle by saelk. I believed you a friend to the sorcerers. Do not prove me wrong."

Tears trailed down Mara's cheeks, sizzling in the heat of the sparks. "If you won't send sorcerers across the ice, let me go."

"Oh dear," Elver said.

"I'll try to get the children out," Mara said.

"Are you so desperate to die?" Lady Gwell said.

"I cannot stay safely on this ship wondering how fast the children will die." The words hitched in Mara's throat. "If I stay here and watch you attack Ian Ayres, I'll never breathe another full breath."

"Even after your boon has been granted?" Lady Gwell's lips lifted, twisting into a smile. "This is what you've been waiting for, Mara. The enemy has shown itself. When word of our victory over these icy demons reaches the Guilds Council, your part in alerting the Sorcerers Guild will finally be brought to light. I will tell the council to grant you a boon. They will glee-fully agree.

"You and Tham will finally be married, live whatever life you dream of. All granted by my gracious thanks to one privileged enough to call the sorcerers *friend*. I advise you to accept my generosity, Mara. You are a valuable asset. If you choose to protest the necessary actions I command, if I even so much as sense a whisper of you painting the liberation of Ian Ayres as anything but noble, Ilbrea will lose that asset. You will lose your chance at a life with Tham. Do you understand, Map Maker Landil?"

Tears shook Mara's shoulders as she looked to Tham. She held his gaze, asking a hundred questions at once.

"Your offer of a boon is kind, Lady Gwell." Tham's heart surged as he looked away from Mara to bow to the Lady Sorcerer. "We are forever grateful, but we humbly ask your permission to cross the ice on foot and beg the Ice Walkers to free the children. We understand the danger we face and gladly accept the duty of protecting the honor of the Guilds, especially the Sorcerers Guild, who have been so kind to us."

"One hour. That's all I'm asking. Let us try to convince the Ice Walkers to surrender the children. If we can't"—Mara's voice broke—"at least we'll have tried. No one will ever be able to say you didn't try. Please, Lady Gwell."

The sparks radiating from Lady Gwell changed, shifting into a faint gleam that surrounded her whole body.

"I don't want to interrupt your contemplation, Lady Sorcer-er," Elver whispered, "only I want to go to the island, too. The whispers in my head still can't find the missing word. And there's an ache in my chest and it feels like it's pulling me to the island and I think the word might be there.

"And if Tham, Mara, Elle, and I die, you already have every-thing we know about the Ice Walkers written down and the map makers and soldiers are more likely to dive fully into a war with an enemy you've hidden from them if people from their own guilds have been killed at the Ice Walkers' hands. So, really us being dead would be very useful. Quite a bit more useful than our being alive, actually."

Elver rocked back on his heels, waving for Mara to say something else.

"Let us try." Mara bowed to Lady Gwell. "I beg you. For the honor of Ilbrea and the Sorcerers Guild."

Lady Gwell reached down, placing her finger beneath Mara's chin, lifting her face so she could look Mara in the eye. She snapped her fingers, bringing a massive, glowing white sphere to life. The light inside the sphere shone in a familiar pattern, mimicking the look of a full moon. "You have one hour."

53

MARA

The ice offered no traction for Mara's boots, leaving her to slip up and down the frozen waves.

Elle scampered up a particularly tall wave, panting with delight as she slid back down on her stomach. The three traveling on two legs did not share her joy.

Mara gripped the peak of a frozen wave with both hands, pulling with her arms to leverage herself up to the top. Pivoting, she slid down the other side of the wave with her back to Ian Ayres, hoping her few seconds looking away from the Ice Walkers wouldn't doom them all.

The next few mounds were smaller, making Mara count on balance and momentum to cross, deepening her fury at the sorcerers' refusal to aid their party's approach to the island, not even to use a bit of magic to add spikes to the bottoms of their boots.

The chivving, heartless beasts.

Careful, Mara, Allora whispered. *Don't anger the wolf. You may have to stick your head right back in its mouth.*

Tham reached the far side of a steep but crestless rise. He lay against the wave, reaching back for Mara.

"Thank you." Mara took his hand, barely having to do anything as Tham pulled her over the ice.

"Me too, please!" Elver called from ten feet behind them. "I promise I'm hurrying."

We shouldn't have to hurry. There shouldn't be a spell counting down to the Lady Sorcerer sacrificing chivving children.

Allora's voice began to whisper again, but Mara shoved the soothing tone beneath the roaring of her anger.

Anger made struggling over the ice easier. Anger made nearing the place that haunted her nightmares less terrifying.

Her hands trembled with rage, but her breath stayed even.

My fault. It's all my fault.

She shoved her guilt behind the growing roar.

Monsters. She had made an alliance with monsters and forced Tham and Elver to join her.

Mara grabbed the crest of a wave, hauling herself up and over before Tham could reach for her.

Years upon years—more than half her life—she'd known what beasts the sorcerers were. Making all traces of wild magic disappear, even if that meant making people vanish, too.

Three figures came into view on the shore, two holding bows, the third with his sword unsheathed.

Mara didn't slow her pace.

The sorcerers would sacrifice children, Ilbrean children, without even trying to reason with the Ice Walkers first.

To protect their own children. To keep their own kind safe from the demons who roam outside the tower.

I did this. I brought the sorcerers into the fight against the Ice Walkers.

We will all be cursed by the blood of innocents.

Elle bolted in front of Tham, making it twenty feet before slipping onto her side.

"Elle, slow," Tham ordered.

Elle stumbled over her own paws as she made her way back to Tham.

"Stop, all of you," a voice finally called from shore.

"Don't have time," Elver called back.

"Where are the children?" Mara said. "Have you hurt the children?"

"We are not Ilbrean beasts." The man with the sword stepped in front of the other two, the gray of his beard making his fellows seem barely more than babes themselves. "Ice Walkers do not harm children."

"Thank you." Mara twisted onto her side, sliding down a chest-high wave. "Is Ronya here?"

"Queen Ronya has no time for traitors," the bearded man said.

"I think we can all admit that's not true," Elver said as Mara shouted, "Is she here!"

"Her whereabouts—"

"There are sorcerers on those ships," Mara said. "They are going to attack from a distance, and they will kill you."

One of the archers gave a low laugh.

"After all your time in Isfol, are you truly foolish enough to think us so weak?" the bearded man said. "Let them attack. We welcome battle."

"But what about the children?" Mara climbed over the last large wave before the shore and slid into place beside Tham. "If the sorcerers attack, the children will be caught in the battle."

"The children are our concern, not yours," the bearded man said.

"The Lady Sorcerer herself is on that ship." Mara pointed back over the ice. "She doesn't care if the children die."

"From the filth we found those children festering in, it's clear how little Ilbreans care for their own young," the laughing archer said. "We have claimed this island and rescued those children in the name of Queen Ronya of Isfol. We've been ordered to attempt to spare your lives if we meet you in battle. Leave before we are forced to test the boundaries of that command."

"Let us take the children across the ice," Mara said. "We can get them onto the ships, away from the fight."

"Only, from my understanding, the ships will actually be in the fight as well," Elver said. "So if the Ice Walkers fight back, the children might not be any better off either way."

"Anything is better than an attack from the Lady Sorcerer." Tham slid a careful step closer to the Ice Walkers. "All we want is to protect the children. Please help us."

"We aren't giving the children back to their tormentors. Leave now, or we will attack." A glisten of ice encased the bearded man's sword.

"Please," Mara said. "I understand why you don't want to give the children to the sorcerers or anyone in the Guilds. I survived Ian Ayres. I know the horrors that haunt this place."

"The graves." Anger added grit to the archer's voice. "A dozen bodies stacked in one grave. Mixing the bones of the dead with no honor."

"I remember," Mara said.

"Do you remember what happened to the other children? The ones who aren't here anymore?" the bearded man asked. "First, the children wanted food, then more wood for the fire, but the third thing they wanted was to know where the older children are taken. Not even the matrons knew."

Fear clawed through Mara's anger. "They're not lying?"

"We didn't grant them the option of lying," the bearded man said.

"There aren't records?" Elver said. "If you're shipping children away, there really should be records."

"We're still searching," the archer said.

"You won't have time to finish your search." Mara swallowed past the knot of unshed tears lodged in her throat. "The Lady Sorcerer gave us one hour before she begins the attack. Whatever weapons or defenses you have won't stop her. Let us help the children carry whatever records you can find and we'll get them off this demon's island. Please."

"We will not hand innocents to monsters," the bearded man said.

Mara shut her eyes.

Cold, dark, always hungry.

The screams of the mothers giving birth and wails of the babes who hadn't yet learned that no one was coming to help them.

Graves cluttered with bones. Graves reaching all the way to the southern shore.

"Don't give the children to us." Mara opened her eyes. "Create a longer section of ice to form a peninsula off the southern side of the island, stretch it as far as you can. Move the children out to the edge of the ice, away from your fighters. The eastern and western ships might catch sight of them, but the Lady Sorcerer won't be able to see the children over the island. She won't know they're so far south. It'll keep them clear of the fighting, or, at the very least, as far away as possible from the Lady Sorcerer."

"Leaving the children out in the open—" the bearded man began.

"Is a terrible idea," Elver said. "Or would be if there were a better idea. You could surrender, that would be best, but I understand your opposition to that idea."

"We will not surrender," the archer said.

"I've just said I understand," Elver said.

"If you win the battle, the children will still be in your care," Mara said. "If the Lady Sorcerer destroys you as she's said she would, at least the children would be far enough from her wrath they might have a shot at surviving."

Mara glanced over her shoulder. The false moon hovering over the Lady Sorcerer's ship had waned to a halfmoon.

"Let us help you move the children," Tham said. "If innocents die under your care, Queen Ronya will be blamed for their deaths. Hers will no longer be a just and noble fight. Do you want to be the ones who tainted the Ice Walkers' cause?"

The archers turned toward the bearded man, leaving him to make the decision that could doom hundreds.

He looked up toward the false moon, the ice on his sword crackling as though shifting with the whirling of his thoughts.

"Change our positions to face the Ilbrean ships. Ten east and west. Fifteen here," he said. "Everyone else will help me move the children to the far side of the island. Right after our prisoners lay down their weapons."

"Prisoners?" Mara said. "We came to help the children."

"And you'll be peacefully taken so we don't have to waste any time on your murdering sorcerers' clock," the sword man said.

"A prisoner is not my favorite thing to be." Elver pulled two dining knives from the ankles of his boots and threw them at the Ice Walkers' feet. "Come on, you two. The moon is ticking away, and we have to get to the other side of the island before the Lady Sorcerer rains death on us all."

Tham held the hilt of his sword, waiting for Mara, making her choose their fate.

"Fine." Mara grabbed the short dagger at her hip and tossed it toward the bearded man.

Tham unfastened his sword belt, holding it in front of him as he crossed to the Ice Walkers. "Where are the children?"

"In the children's home," the man said. "There's nowhere else on the island for hundreds of terrified little ones to go."

"Come on." Mara stepped forward, stopping short as the ice in front of her shifted, not melting away to plunge her into the sea, but smoothing out the crests of the waves and gaining just enough texture to give traction beneath her boots. "Thank you."

Holding her hand out for Tham, Mara ran back into hell.

54

MARA

The sheet of ice stopped at the edge of the Arion Sea, leaving the land beyond as mud, which dragged on Mara's boots with every step as though trying to reclaim the orphan who'd escaped the demon's island.

A foul stench of death and shit emanated from the ground, slamming into Mara's nose, clawing up memories she'd hoped had faded forever.

Mounds lined both sides of the path leading up to the children's home. Some of the mounds had been dug up, exposing the bones of the victims of Ian Ayres.

Mara tried not to look at the proof of the Guilds' horror, but two rows of skeletons had been laid out at the top of the path, as though someone had been trying to reassemble the dead for proper burial.

The bottom line were all adults, women lost in childbirth, but the skeletons in the top line were too small. Some barely more than infants, the bones were all that remained of the children who had never set foot out of the hell of Ian Ayres.

"Mara. Mara!" Tham tightened his hold on her waist.

She hadn't even noticed that he'd taken it, that he'd led her all the way to the door of the children's home.

The bearded man shoved the door open, walking through like he hadn't stepped into the worst of all places.

The stench of rot and fear surrounded Mara. She gagged as sour rolled into her throat.

"Pardon me." Elver stepped around Mara and Tham, clearing his throat as he went through the door. "Everyone up, if you please. We're going to leave here and run like the Lady Sorcerer is after us to the southern side of the island. Last one out the door has to lick the floor!"

The thumping of feet and chaos of panicked shouts covered whatever Elver said next.

"We can meet you on the other side of the building," Tham said. "Take Elle and go around."

"I'm okay." Mara pushed away from Tham and strode through the door.

Wooden benches surrounded the stained and crooked tables. Two of the benches fell with echoing crashes as their former occupants fled farther into the building.

They'd have to run past the rooms where the babies always cried, then past all the rooms packed with moldering cots for the older children. Cots crammed together so tight there was no room to stand.

"You have to go!" Tham pulled Mara with him, dragging her toward a cluster of children who'd mashed themselves into the corner rather than flee with the others. "Move. Go!"

None of the children moved.

"It's not safe in here." Mara swallowed the sour in her throat. "We're going to go wait for it to be safe out by the water. Can you come with me?"

Mara held her hand out to the girl at the front of the pack, who kept her arms stretched wide, as though shielding the ones behind her. The girl didn't move.

"I know you're scared," Mara said. "I am, too. I lived on this island once, and when someone came to help me, I didn't believe it. I thought it was a mistake or a trick. But this isn't a trick, and you really are in danger. I need you to be brave and come with us."

The girl tipped her chin up, meeting Mara's gaze. "If you hurt any of us, I'll tear out your eyes with my thumbs."

"Deal," Mara said.

"Go." The girl lowered her arms, freeing the children behind her.

The children bolted farther into the building, following the same path as the ones who'd fled before.

The girl waited until the other four had passed her before turning toward the corner.

"You need—" Mara began before catching sight of the small boy crumpled on the floor.

"Hold on tight, remember?" The girl knelt beside the boy.

"I'll carry him," Tham said.

"I can do it." The girl grabbed the boy, stumbling under the added weight as she stood.

"There's not enough time." Tham let go of Mara's hand and lifted the child out of the girl's arms. "Now run."

"I'm not leaving him," the girl said.

"We're coming, too." Mara cut around the tables, heading toward the dark, festering corridor.

Fear washed through her mind, tipping the floor as the row of doors came into view.

"Move then." The girl cut around Mara, beckoning over her shoulder for Mara to run.

Mara kept her gaze fixed on the girl. Following the girl.

A patch of red caught the corner of her eye.

She gripped the wall as she stopped, making herself look toward the red.

Fresh blood pooled on the floor in the babies' room.

"No, no, no." Mara pushed away from the wall, lurching toward the door. "No. The babies. Where are the babies?"

"Not in there." The girl grabbed Mara's arm, dragging her onward. "The ice people gave the babies back to the mothers. The blood's from one of the chivving matrons. Don't fuss about the end of one of those braidic letches."

Light fought its way into the room at the end of the corridor.

Elle darted around Mara and the girl, charging toward the light as though she too could feel the ghost of every soul lost to Ian Ayres clawing at her skin.

A smear of blood crossed the room, angling toward the open door, but part of the smear had been trampled by the fleeing children.

"Another matron?" Mara asked.

"I think so. It was a little confusing at the beginning." The girl ran faster, dragging Mara into the open air.

The stench of death surrounded her again, flowing into her lungs with the crisp sea breeze, as though reminding Mara of Death's own mercy in ending the suffering of so many tortured souls.

A steeper hill cut down to the water on the southern side of the island, but the slope hadn't stopped the matrons from covering the ground in graves. Rows upon rows leading down to the shore.

"The records." Mara looked back toward the buildings at the center of the island.

The false moon hovering just above the roofs had narrowed to a slim crescent.

"You keep going." Mara pulled against the girl's grip, changing her path to run back up the hill to the smallest and sturdiest of the buildings, where the matrons had lived.

"You said go to the water." The girl gripped Mara's arm with both hands, holding on with impressive strength, digging her heels into the mud to keep Mara anchored in place.

"If there are records of where the older children went, they'd be in the matron's house." Mara pried the girl's hands away. "Follow the other children. I'll catch up."

"There's no time," Tham said.

"But we have—"

"Mara, move." Tham balanced the little boy in one arm, using his free hand to steer Mara down the hill.

Elle bolted down the slope, turning back at the bottom to bark at Mara as though shouting her agreement.

Mara made herself move, fixing her gaze back on the living girl in front of her, ignoring the pleas of the lost children wailing at the back of her mind.

The bearded Ice Walker had been joined by a woman with ice magic. The two had smoothed the children's path across the ice, letting the children follow them at a run as they used their magic to extend the barrier into a bridge of ice reaching farther out to sea.

Elver stood where the ice met the island, waiting with the four children who'd been huddled behind the girl inside the children's home.

"I don't want to panic anyone." Elver waved his arms over his head. "Only, the moon seems to be shrinking much faster than I'd like."

"Not without Brady!" one of the children shouted right at Elver.

"They're being difficult." Elver kept waving his arms. "I'd forgotten children are like this."

Elle reached Elver and stood beside him, watching as Mara, Brady, and Tham, still carrying the little boy, weaved down the one switchback in the path then bolted across the narrow beach to the edge of the ice.

"Now we can go." The child who'd shouted at Elver turned and ran down the ice, glancing over her shoulder to make sure the others followed.

The Ice Walkers had been kind, adding enough frozen, gritty crystals to the surface of the path to allow those without magic to run.

But even without slipping, the path had gotten long, too long for half-starved children.

The massive pack ahead of them blocked Mara's view of the end of the Ice Walkers' peninsula, but the pack kept moving farther and farther south.

A few women with babes in their arms had taken places at the back of the pack, helping the children who'd fallen behind.

Brady panted, her breath coming in shuddering gasps. One of the other children began to stumble. Elver swung the boy over his shoulder without so much as a warning.

"Do you need me to carry you?" Mara asked.

"Sod—a ch—chivving—hole," Brady panted back.

Hiss.

The sound started low, barely loud enough for Mara to notice over the whooshing of her heart pounding in her ears.

"We still had a few minutes." Elver looked over his shoulder, shouting at the sky. "Filthy cheaters!"

Mara glanced back. The moon had vanished.

The whooshing in her ears thundered louder, but the hiss still cut through.

"Bad!" Elver shouted. "Very bad!"

Mara glanced back again.

A blue light spread across the ice to the east and west of the island. Dancing over the frozen sea like living flames, the light drew together, merging, blocking the children from any hope of retreating back into the hell of the children's home.

"As fast as you can." Mara grabbed the hand of another girl, dragging her and Brady forward, trying not to imagine what the living flames might do to flesh.

Up ahead, far down the path, the ice changed, rising up into a wall.

The wall grew—six, then ten feet tall—cutting off the end of the path.

"Wait." Brady screamed. "Wait!"

"No, no let them alone." Elver veered off the easy-to-travel path and onto the slick ice, cutting west.

"Elver! The flames!" Mara shouted as the dancing blue fire widened, spreading south, reaching toward them.

"Then hurry up." Elver set the boy he'd been carrying on the ice, dragging him by his ankle as he scrambled between frozen waves.

"Tham?" Mara called.

"Follow!" Tham shouted.

Mara veered off the path, pulling the two girls with her, cutting between the swells of the frozen waves, following Elver's path as he weaved toward the edge of the ice.

"Ah!" Brady slipped, crashing onto her back, banging her head against the ice, yanking Mara to her knees with the force of her fall.

"Keep going." Mara pushed the other girl forward, ignoring the pain in her knees as Tham grabbed her under the arm, yanking Mara to her feet. Mara hauled Brady up with her. Brady swayed. "Hold onto me."

Mara wrapped Brady's arm around her waist and gripped the back of Brady's filth-covered shirt, propelling the girl forward.

"I was hearing it wrong the whole time," Elver shouted over the still-growing hissing of the flames. "It wasn't a white flag I was looking for at all. Or a cloud. Or a place. The word got so fumbled by the whisper, I couldn't find the right one."

Elver reached the edge of the ice and flung the child he'd been dragging out over the water. The boy barely had time to scream before he hit the freezing water with a splash.

The three children beside Elver stared in horror. Elver shoved two of them in the back, pushing them off the edge, then grabbed the third one's wrist before she could flee.

"Stop it!" Brady screamed.

"Can't stop. I understand now." Elver jumped into the water, dragging the girl with him, disappearing for a moment before popping his head up to the surface. "Hang onto me, children. I can keep my head above water if I stand on my toes."

The children thrashed in the water, too panicked to reach Elver.

"Oh, dear." Elver grabbed one, latching the girl's arms around his neck.

"I'm not going in." Brady twisted, trying to break free from Mara's grip on her shirt. "I'm not going in!"

Dudia, let this not be a mistake.

Mara leapt into the Arion Sea, bringing Brady with her.

The burning pain of the freezing water heightened Mara's fear as the Arion Sea closed over her head. Her boots touched bottom, and she kicked back to the surface, dragging Brady up with her.

Elle landed beside Mara with a splash the moment before Tham jumped in.

Keeping her head above the waves, Mara straightened her legs, reaching for solid ground, but her feet found nothing.

"Hold onto my back." Mara tread water, moving Brady behind her. "Don't pull on my throat, and don't panic."

"If you don't know how to swim, hold still so we can grab you." Elver twisted the girl who clung to his neck onto his back and reached for another child. "Stop flailing."

Tham swam over, keeping the little boy he'd been carrying on his back while grabbing one more in each arm.

"All right, now we swim." Elver began paddling west.

"There's nowhere to swim to," a child wailed. "We're going to freeze and—"

Brady's scream covered the rest of the child's words as the hissing flames reached the edge of the ice and a boom sent waves rippling out from the island.

One of the children in Tham's arms joined Brady's screaming and kicked out of Tham's grasp.

Elle rammed her head into the child, nosing under the child's arm, letting them grip onto her fur as she dragged them forward.

The ice beneath the flames crackled, splintering apart with earsplitting shrieks.

Brady tightened her grip on Mara, as though she could sense Mara's muscles locking up from the icy sea.

"We're all right." Mara's voice shook as the cold dug into her veins, making each stroke harder than the last as she swam behind Elver.

"Almost there," Elver shouted.

Mara looked up, chancing the waves stealing her momentum for a glimpse of Elver's discovered salvation.

Boom.

Deep purple light flared across the sky.

One of the Guild's ships sailed toward them, the sailors already lowering ropes over the port side.

"Here!" Elver shouted. "And hurry, if you please."

Keep going. Keep going.

Mara's arms couldn't straighten anymore. Her breath couldn't fill her frozen lungs. She kicked as hard as she could, fighting for each inch forward.

"Tie loops for the children," Tham called up to the ship.

"Rope coming down."

A heavy rope flew out from the boat, landing two feet in front of Elver.

"You, flailing one, can go first." Elver's head went under as he stopped swimming to loop the rope under the child's arms.

"Dropping down."

A rope landed in front of Mara.

"Can you grab it?" Mara asked.

"I c—can do it." Brady pushed off Mara's back, sending both her and Mara plunging down.

Mara kicked back to the surface, gasping in breaths that gave her barely any air.

"Dropping down."

A rope landed in front of Tham.

Brady didn't resurface.

The shrieking of the breaking ice shifted to a pulsing hum.

"Brady." Mara grabbed Brady's rope. "Brady!"

Sucking in as much air as she could, Mara dove down.

The water stung her eyes, blurring her vision. Bubbles rose around her.

A hint of pale skin called her farther down.

Giving up the safety of the rope, Mara dove deeper, twisting to aim her feet down as she neared the danger of Brady's panicked thrashing.

Grabbing Brady's wrist, she launched the child toward the surface, sending herself farther under.

Air.

Air. Air.

The instinct shouted through her mind, devouring her fear of the orange flash in the sky that flared bright enough for its glare to light the water around her, as though Dudia himself had seen the horror of the Guilds and chosen to burn the world.

A hand reached down, grabbing her, yanking her up.

Something hard struck Mara's chest, knocking the rest of the air from her lungs.

"I've got you." Tham clutched her against him, one hand gripping the rope that hauled them closer to the ship.

"The children." Mara forced out the words between shivering gasps.

"On board." Tham looped the rope under Mara's arms. "Bring her up!"

Mara clung to the rope with both hands, futilely trying to use her feet to climb up the side of the ship. "Tham."

She looked down.

Tham had grabbed a rope of his own, letting the sailors bring him on board as the last of those who'd dared to enter the icy water.

Two sailors reached over the rail, grabbing Mara and lifting her the rest of the way onto the ship. They set her on the deck, one soldier gripping her arm, keeping her on her feet, while the other took the rope from around her chest.

"More blankets!" a man shouted.

"Tham." Mara's knees buckled as they dragged him over the railing.

"Keep on your feet." The sailor gripping Mara's arm shifted her weight to lean against him, propelling her toward the stern of the ship as a heavy, stale-scented blanket was draped around her shoulders.

"Just—hold—still!" The frustrated shout came from the far side of the deck. A sailor had Elle in his arms, trying to lift her as she flailed and whimpered.

"Elle," Tham called.

Elle broke free from the sailor but ran away from Tham, jumping over the jumbled strips of shimmering purple fabric on the deck, skidding toward the opposite rail. Her whimpering grew louder as she reached three purple-clad corpses. She lay down in the blood surrounding the bodies, licking the face of one of the dead.

"Stop, dog." The sailor trapped Elle in a blanket, smearing red across the fabric as he wrapped her up and carried her away.

Fergal.

Boom.

Another deep purple light flared overhead.

Fergal lay dead on the deck. His eyes open. His lifeless face damp from Elle's hopeless attempts to wake the sorcerer who'd befriended her.

"Southward course!"

"We can't." Mara stumbled toward the captain. "We have to help the other children."

"Unless you know how to break through that, we're leaving." The captain nodded over the stern and stormed back to the helm without giving Mara a chance to answer.

She had no words anyway.

The bridge between Ian Ayres and the wall of ice at the end of the peninsula had melted, leaving a barrier of sea between the blue flames devouring the island and the solid dome of ice encompassing the children.

"Sail." Elver stepped between Mara and the dome, blocking her view of the children of Ian Ayres as she abandoned them a second time. "Sail."

"Sorry, what?" Mara said.

Tham wrapped his arms around Mara from behind, adding the protection of his blanket over hers.

"That was the word I was missing." Elver pointed toward the taut, white sails carrying the ship south. "White *sails.*"

"Let's get you inside." An older sailor waved them toward the open door to the captain's cabin. "It'll be warmest in here."

Mara tucked herself under Tham's arm, staying in the haven of his blanket as the sailors coiled the strips of shimmering purple fabric and dumped them overboard, clearing her path to the captain's cabin and the few children they'd managed to save from the fires of the demon's island.

55

KAI

Kai pressed his cheek to the ground, lining up his target, hoping his skill would be enough. He held his breath and flicked the marble, shooting it to hit right on the corner of the massive book's spine.

The marble ricocheted, bouncing off the second, smaller book, then hitting the block of wood with a promising thunk, before reaching its final destination and…bouncing off the lip of the mug.

"So close." Kai rolled onto his back, digging the heels of his hands into his eyes.

"That's four to none," Merial said. "Are you finally going to surrender?"

"I name you the undisputed winner of this course," Kai said. "But I'd at least like to get the marble into the mug once."

"You're not forceful enough." Merial tossed the marble onto Kai's chest. "Give it a proper thump."

"Thanks." Kai rolled back onto his stomach.

"Crowd's starting to die down," Drew said from his place at the peephole. "But there are four men in the back who don't seem to mind that the sun's setting."

"I'm proud of them." Kai lined the marble up again. "The Guilds haven't issued a curfew, and the sorcerers scaring people enough to make them huddle in their homes is one of the offenses I plan to take up with the Lady Sorcerer when we finally flush the demons from their tower."

Kai flicked the marble. While the force of the hit was better, he'd gotten the angle wrong, missing the second book entirely.

Merial kicked the marble back to him.

"On the other hand," Kai said, "if those brave getches drink all night, defying the fear the sorcerers have spread throughout the city, we'll be stuck in this room even longer. And while our secret lair does smell better than the underground—"

"I've spent far too many hours locked in this room with the two of you and would very much like to not drag the evening out," Merial said.

"No offense," Kai said, "but the feeling is utterly mutual."

Kai flicked the marble again, getting this shot all the way to the wooden block before it veered off-course.

"There are worse places we could be," Drew said. "And far worse company to have, but I'll toast the gods when I never have to peer through this chivving peephole again."

"I'll take a turn." Kai moved to stand.

"Get the marble in the mug first," Drew said. "It'll nag you if you don't manage it."

Kai opened his mouth to protest, but a warm sort of contentment shifted his words. "Thank you."

He set the marble back at the starting place and shot again.

The force of the marble had definitely been an issue. The bindings of the books were soft, eating the marble's speed. And the steep angle needed to get the marble from the second book to the block and then to the mug was harder to manage on this course than on the previous ones they'd set up.

The sounds from the bar had faded before—

"Yes!" Kai rolled onto his back, punching the air, barely remembering to keep his victory celebration quiet. "Chivving finally did it."

"Wonderful," Merial said. "I've been as bored as a bull's tit for the last hour."

"Hour?" Kai sat up.

"I'll make the next course simpler." Merial pushed herself out of the comfortable chair.

"It'll have to wait until tomorrow." Drew came down from his perch.

"The tavern's just cleared out?" Kai took Drew's hand, letting Drew help him to his feet.

"Tavern's been clear for about five minutes," Drew said. "I just didn't want you to harp on about a marble while I was trying to sleep."

"You're a slitch," Merial said. "At some point, I'm going to demand five minutes of your life, and you'll pay it."

"A worthy trade," Drew said.

"You say that now, but have you ever scraped away the week-old carcass of a rat that died in the rancid mold bred on ale that spilled in the bottom of a damp shipping crate?"

"For the rest of my days, I will owe you for allowing my marble triumph." Kai pulled on his coat.

"It wasn't a triumph." Merial shoved on her hat. "It was a long build up to a barely accomplished event."

Kai rounded on Merial. "I will let that insult hold as it is the first and only time it shall ever apply to me."

Merial pursed her lips and shook her head in an utterly failed attempt to hide her amusement.

"Tomorrow, we up the stakes." Kai stepped in front of Merial, kneeling to open the lair's door. "Two courses, and the winner has to complete both without a failure in between."

"Do you like to frustrate yourself?" Merial asked.

"Yes," Drew answered for him.

Kai reached for the door's latch, but his fingers missed the cool metal.

"I like a challenge." Kai winked at Drew, fumbling his fingers down the door. He'd nearly reached the floor before finally looking away from the perfect small smile on Drew's face to find the…blank wall.

The latch was gone. The hinges were gone. The narrow split between the wall and the door was gone.

"Drew," Kai said, "be a dear and tell me this is where the door should be."

Drew knelt beside him, running his fingers along the wall. "Of all the chivving things."

"Move." Merial shoved the men aside. Crouching, she rapped her knuckles along the wall. The space that had been the door sounded no different from the rest. "Who has the largest knife?"

Drew pulled out his blade. "Are you going to carve through the wood?"

"I'm chivving well not staying trapped like a rat." Merial gripped the knife, angling her shoulders to make the best use of her light weight. "Whatever chivving sorcerers have trapped us in here, I'll cut our way out and then slice their chivving throats."

Sweat beaded on Merial's brow as she dragged Drew's knife across the wall.

"If it's Isla who's locked us in, please don't slit her throat." Kai crept toward the peephole. "We've spent so long waiting for her. And besides, Merial, I've grown quite fond of you. I'd hate for Isla to kill you."

"Let her try." Merial grunted as she dug deeper into the wood.

"I'd rather not." Kai pressed his eye to the peephole, peering out into the dark, abandoned tavern. "I want to talk to Isla. I've spent more hours than I want to consider locked in this room hoping the gods would lead her to us. A bit of information. That's all I'm hoping for. A chat between old friends."

The tavern stayed still and quiet.

"And the information I'd like," Kai said, "it's the sort that wouldn't hurt Isla's friends. It's the Sorcerers Guild I want to fight. And after all the pain those beasts have caused, helping us fight them would be in both our best interests."

"Under the chivving stars." Merial leapt to her feet, ramming into Drew as she backed away from where the door should have been.

Black letters formed on the wall, appearing one stroke at a time as though written by an invisible hand.

Send Kai out alone.

"All right." Kai hopped down from the peephole post.

"You're not going out there alone," Drew said.

More letters appeared on the wall.

Only Kai.

"I'll be fine," Kai said.

"How do we know it's Isla and not some other chivving sorcerer?" Drew said.

"When did you first see Drew and me naked?" Kai asked.

"What?" Merial said.

Kai pressed a finger to his lips.

"Come on, Isla," Kai said. "I'm sure you remember."

A moment passed.

Singing sea songs.

Badly.

"There we have it." Kai cut in front of Merial and Drew. "Let me out then."

The faint outline of the door began at waist height, where the top of the hidden door had always been. The lines thickened as they traced down the doorway then deepened, creating a crack between the wall and door.

It wasn't until the door had fully formed that the latch came silently back into being.

"Isla," Drew said, "if you hurt him, if you let anything happen to him—"

The latch flipped, and the door swung open.

Kai caught Drew's fingers, pressing a quick kiss to the back of his hand before ducking through the door and into the darkness.

The door swung shut behind him, blocking out the light of the lair, giving free rein to the shadows of the tavern.

He stayed frozen for a moment, listening for the soft sound of slinking footsteps, watching for any shift in the shadows. The only hints of movement came from the clouds passing in front of the moon, changing the way its silvery gleam shone through the windows.

"Would you fancy an ale?" Kai cut behind the bar and pulled two mugs down from the shelf. "If I'm supposed to keep talking to the shadows, that's fine. I'm happy to read your responses off a wall. We can even make a game of it."

Kai filled the two mugs. He stepped out from behind the bar, pausing to examine his choice in tables.

"While I'd normally choose a seat by the window, I don't think either of us cares to be spotted." Kai meandered through the tables. "The center of the room would leave both of us an escape, but we'd both be open to attack from the other's group, and neither of us likes the feeling of someone watching from behind." He headed toward a table in the corner. "I'll let you face the door while I face the bar. We'll both have two sides open. I think that's as fair as we can hope for."

He set the mugs on the table before taking his seat. "For what it's worth, I'm sorry about Arto. I was at the square that day. I watched you fight. It probably doesn't feel like it, but ending his suffering was an act of great compassion. I'm glad you were there to help him."

"Killing him didn't feel like helping." Isla's voice came from the far corner. "It felt like murder."

"I'm sorry sparing him cost you so much." Kai pushed Isla's mug toward her voice. "I hope one day you'll be able to see what happened as I do."

The shadows shifted as Isla stepped into a shaft of moonlight. "What do you want, Kai?"

"I'd like to make sure you're all right to start with."

"Don't play." Isla weaved between the tables, slowly making her way toward him. "Naming a tavern to lure me to you? Impressive, but dangerous. You wouldn't have risked such a foolish chivving thing if you'd had a better choice."

She pulled her chair out, taking a moment to study the shadows before sitting. "Talk."

Kai downed a gulp of ale.

"Now," Isla said.

"We both want the same thing," Kai said.

"The fall of the Guilds?" Isla said.

"The fall of the Sorcerers Guild. To free our home from the tyranny of the Lady Sorcerer."

"Ilbrea isn't my home anymore. Ilbrea is my enemy."

"Ilbrea isn't your enemy. The common folk aren't your enemy."

"The paun are." Isla leaned toward Kai. "And not just the ones wearing purple."

"But the purple paun are at the top of your list of demons, aren't they?" Kai chanced another sip of ale. "The sorcerers control the Guilds. If the Sorcerers Guild is destroyed, I get to save my Guild and try to salvage what's left of Ilara. If the Sorcerers Guild is destroyed, you get—"

"—to start on the rest of the paun."

"Vengeance." Kai pushed Isla's mug closer to her. "Get to take out the worst of the threats to your people. We both win."

"Until I come for your Sailors Guild."

"We'd both have to survive the Sorcerers Guild first, and I'm not fool enough to bet on that happening." Kai glanced toward the peep hole. He lowered his voice. "Both our sides are facing a battle they have shit chances of winning. The underground won't survive without your help."

"You actually call yourselves the underground?" Isla leaned back in her chair. "I thought that was only a whisper."

"Well, it's not. The underground's been doing what we can to stand against the sorcerers, but there's chiv all we can do if they keep hiding in their tower."

"Glad you figured that out."

"But there's got to be something." Kai's leg bounced as his body begged him to move. "We can't just let them hide in there, sneaking out to pick off Ilarans whenever they choose. There's got to be a way into the tower. Or, better still, a way to drive the sorcerers out."

Isla's hands shook. Her mug clacked against the table as she set it down.

"Isla, you lived inside the Sorcerers Tower. If anyone has information that might be able to help us do more than wait in the shadows, hoping the sorcerers show themselves, it's you."

"That's what you want? Information on the Sorcerers Tower?" Isla dug her nails into the tabletop.

"And anything else that might give us a godsforsaken chance against the Lady Sorcerer and her demons."

She tugged on the sleeve of her coat, yanking the material down as Kai had seen her do so many times before.

"The Sorcerers Guild are at the heart of all this evil," Kai whispered. "Help me fight them."

"Fine." Isla let go of her sleeve and met Kai's gaze. "I'll give you information to help the underground, but you have to help me first."

"How?"

"We're going to kidnap Adrial Ayres."

56

ENA

The gentle rocking of the boat soothed my impatience as the black-clad man rowed us farther out into the Arion Sea—staying south of the city walls, slipping silently past the panicked sailors patrolling the docks and the merchants' ships anchored offshore, not slowing until the few lights burning in Ilara were nothing but bright spots on the horizon, and not even the dogs on the streets would be able to hear our business.

The wind picked up, making the rocking of the boat more persistent, as though the sea herself were eager for a taste of blood.

"We've gone far enough," I said.

"A bit farther."

I looked away from the man at the oars. He was not the one that mattered. The shadow rowing the boat was a tool, the same as the knife I pulled from my boot.

The man rowed for another five minutes, both of us as silent as the unconscious monster at my feet.

He finally pulled his oars from the water, locking them in place before grabbing the pole from the bottom of the boat. He attached the pole to the bench between us, fastening it straight up and down, making our tilk version of the posts the paun place in all the town squares so they can tie common folk down while they whip us as punishment for surviving in Ilbrea.

I didn't let myself shy away as he lifted the demon from the bottom of the boat, sitting him on the bench with his back to the pole. He tied the demon's wrists behind his back and looped a second rope around the monster's waist, binding him in place.

The demon's hooded head lolled onto his chest.

I focused on the blade in my hand as the knots were checked. The feel of its familiar weight simmered through my veins, promising dark delights.

"Ready?" The question in the man's voice was larger than the word, digging deep into my chest, searching for something that should have been there.

But doubt and mercy had been carved out of my soul. There was nothing for the man to find.

"Wake him," I said.

The man pulled off the demon's hood.

A trail of blood stained Travers Gend's gaunt cheek. His mouth hung slightly open, as though he were in a true sleep, until the man held a little jar of powder beneath Travers's nose.

I counted to two before Travers gasped, jerking his chin up, cracking the back of his head against the pole he'd been bound to. His breath came in panicked pants as he looked at the sea and the boat, then finally at me.

"No." Travers strained against the ropes that bound him. "No."

"Are you trying to tell yourself this is a nightmare?" I asked.

"It—it is." Travers closed his eyes, pushing against the bottom of the boat with his feet in a pathetic attempt to break free. "She's dead. None of this is real. Wake up, Travers. Wake up!"

I flipped my blade in my hand and pressed the tip to Travers's thigh.

The paun screamed.

"It's not a nightmare." I pressed the knife in deeper, letting

Travers's scream fade back into gasps before pulling the blade free. "If you're going to try your hand at murder, you should make sure the ones you hurt are truly dead."

"I've never killed anyone! I never wanted anything to happen to you, I swear it." Sweat glistened on Travers's brow.

"You tried to have my husband murdered."

"That's not true."

"You sold a member of your own Guild to the chivving sorcerers." I tossed my knife from hand to hand. "What did the Lady Paun offer you in exchange for my husband's life? Coin? Power? The glory of being the Lord Scribe's new heir?"

"Nothing. I was offered nothing."

I drove my blade into Travers's other thigh, taking a moment to watch the stars glitter off the waves as I waited for the demon to stop screaming.

"Lies will cost you." I slowly slid my knife from Travers's flesh and wiped the blade on his filth-covered, white robes. "What did the Lady Paun offer you?"

I tapped the tip of my knife right below his kneecap.

"The position of head scribe," Travers said. "A chance to help my Guild regain a place of power in Ilbrea. The Scribes Guild has been shunted aside and manipulated for far too long."

"Just as the Lady Paun manipulated you?" I slid forward on my seat. "Tricked you into plotting my husband's murder."

"I only wanted to protect my Guild."

"Liar." I slashed my blade across his shin. "You craved power and threw yourself into a world of blood and shadows you were not made to survive." I spoke over his scream as I mirrored the cut on his other leg. "Fools should not attempt such evil. They become the builders of their own doom."

"You don't under—"

"How long after your plan to murder my husband failed did she abandon you?"

"No. Not murder."

I twisted the tip of my blade into the skin just below his kneecap.

"It's true!" Travers tried to yank his leg away from me, paying for the movement with a bloom of blood seeping into the knee of his robes. The paun panted against the pain. "I never wanted Adrial Ayres dead."

"You whispered in the Lady Demon's ear."

"I told Lady Gwell of your condition," Travers said. "I did nothing but tell the truth."

"And what did you think would come of your whispers?"

"Scribe Ayres's punishment lay in the laws of Ilbrea. I didn't write those laws. The enactment of his sentence—"

"Started with you." I tapped the side of my blade against the top of his thigh. "Your greed. Your jealousy of the head scribe. Your loathing of the rotta girl he married."

I paused, staring him in the eye, daring him to lie. But the paun had learned.

"I'm sorry." Travers swallowed as I leaned closer, sliding my blade to the dangerous place where thigh met hip. "I truly apologize for the pain I've caused you. I've spent months living in the stables, sitting with the shame of my actions. I'm not the man I was before. I've learned from my mistakes."

"Learned not to make alliances with snakes? Pity you won't be able to use that knowledge."

"Yes. Yes, I will." Travers shifted his shoulders against the pole, as though thinking he could twist away from me and find mercy from the black-clad man. "The sorcerers put you on a boat to Ian Ayres. They think you're dead. Everyone thinks you're dead. I can help you."

The man gave a low laugh.

I ignored him.

"How will you help me, paun?" I asked.

"I can make records," Travers said, "records of a whole life of a new person who's never been to Ilbrea. And I have money, too. Enough for you to build a comfortable life. You can start fresh."

"Away from my husband," I said.

"I could—" Travers's gaze darted across the waves, as though he were searching for some gods-written answer. "I'll find a way to fix this. There are holes in every law in Ilbrea. Bring me back to the library, and I'll spend every moment searching for an answer."

"You're not going back to the library, paun," I said.

"I have to go back." Hope flared through the panic in the paun's eyes. "My guards will know I'm gone by now."

"And they'll run right to the Lord Scribe, groggy, angry, and certain you slipped something into their stew to knock them out." I pulled a half-empty bottle from my pocket. "You escaped the stables and abandoned your oath to the Scribes Guild."

"No one will believe that."

"Because you're a paun of great honor?"

The man laughed again.

Travers tried again to look back at the man. "Because you kidnapped me from the library stables."

"I lived above those stables." I took my own turn to laugh. "Trapped in a paun haven. Are you fool enough to believe I didn't have a dozen ways in and out the guards wouldn't spot?"

"The Scribes Guild will look for me."

"They won't look for you. They won't even mourn you. You are a disgrace. You will always be a disgrace. Those who bother to notice you're gone will be disgusted by your cowardice in abandoning your post. And even they will soon forget you."

"You're wrong. I am an honored member of the Guilds. If you don't release me, you are dooming yourself." Spittle foamed in the corners of Travers's mouth. "The soldiers will come for me. They'll execute you in the cathedral square."

The man leaned forward, wrapping his arm around Travers's neck, squeezing until Travers's breath came in squeaking gasps.

"Don't threaten her." The man tightened his grip. "Understand?"

"Yes," Travers coughed. "Yes."

The man let go and sat back on his seat.

Travers's head fell forward as he took in shaky breaths.

I watched him, allowing time for all the fear and panic to swirl through his mind, twisting itself into vain hopes for survival.

"I have information." Travers looked up at me. "About Ilara. And the King and the Sorcerers Guild."

"You've been trapped in a stable," I said. "Your information is useless."

"I can go in front of the King and the Lady Sorcerer," Travers said. "Beg them for a posthumous pardon for your sentence to Ian Ayres. Then, once it's granted, you can come back to Ilara. They'll have to maintain the pardon even though you're alive."

"A paun's chivving pardon means nothing to me."

"Then tell me what you want!" Travers's shout carried out over the water. "I will give you whatever you want in exchange for my freedom."

"Foolish paun." I slipped my blade into the neck of his robes and pulled down, slicing through the fabric, exposing his chest. "You'll not survive the night."

"Yes. I will." Travers strained against the ropes, grazing his gut across my blade just enough for a bead of blood to trail down his pale skin. "Whatever the price for my survival, I will pay it."

"There is no bargain to be made, paun."

"There's always a deal to be made. It's the Lady Sorcerer who's at the heart of all this. It's her you're after, not me. If you wanted me dead, you would have killed me in the stables."

"But killing you isn't enough." I pressed the tip of my blade to his collarbone, freeing a fresh stream of blood. "You took my family from me. You tried to have my husband murdered. I ended up on a boat to Ian Ayres because of you."

"I'm sorry." Travers spoke through his teeth as I gently slid my knife down his chest, leaving a trail of red behind.

"I should be sleeping in bed with my husband right now, our daughter in the crib beside us." I held his gaze as I eased the blade away from his flesh. "My husband should have been with me when the birthing pains came. Joy should have radiated from his soul the first time he held our daughter. But you stole that from us. From me."

I pivoted the blade, slicing up across his chest.

Travers screamed.

"I should be exhausted from nursing my child, but she is feeding at a stranger's breast." I sliced across his chest again. "My daughter won't know my scent or my voice. I am not the one she craves when she cries. My husband has never held her in his arms, and that is because of you."

I plunged the tip of my blade into Travers's shoulder.

"I'm sorry!"

"Not yet. But you'll learn to be before the end."

"Please." Tears joined the sweat on Travers's face.

I planted the tip of my knife above Travers's heart, swiveling the blade back and forth, slowly widening the wound. "Do you know how painful it is to leave your child behind? The ache in your breasts reminding you with every heartbeat that you've torn your soul in two. Then your milk dries up and your body forgets you carried a child." My words came out calm, quiet. "And the pain of not being sure if you'd recognize her face slices deeper and deeper, carving up everything you were until there's nothing left but shattered pieces and rage."

"I'm sorry." Travers sobbed. "I'm so sorry."

"Not nearly sorry enough." I flicked the knife out of his chest. Red stained the blade. I wiped the side of the knife against Travers's forehead, marking the demon in blood.

"Please." Travers coughed through his tears. "Mercy. I beg for mercy."

"Death will be your mercy. No one will ever find your body. And the traitor scribe will never hurt anyone again."

"Dudia. Dudia, I beg for your aid." Travers's sobs sped the blood seeping from his chest.

"Not even the gods could make a demon truly understand the grief he's caused. But I will make sure you at least understand the pain before the end. And when Death draws near, I'll throw you into the Arion Sea, so even your lungs know torment before you die."

The paun screamed as I sliced deeper, letting his blood drip into the bottom of the boat.

The man waited patiently. Then helped me toss the whimpering Travers into the waves, a rock tied around the paun's neck to make sure the Arion Sea kept hold of the demon forever.

Neither of us spoke as the man rowed us back to the rocky shores just south of Ilara.

We were the same, the man and me. Meant for a world of darkness and death.

The blood that tainted us had been driven into our souls by the gods, marking us as shadows too broken and deadly to survive in the light.

I let their mark consume me.

I am blood. I am death. I am vengeance.

I am the weapon that fights for a freedom I am not meant to see.

The Guilds of Ilbrea series continues with Siege *and* Sparrow.

ESCAPE INTO ADVENTURE

Thank you for reading *Tower and Grave*. If you enjoyed the book, please consider leaving a review to help other readers find this story.

Dive deeper into the world of the Guilds on MeganORussell. com/ilbrea, where you'll find exclusive Ilbrean content, a peek behind the scenes, and updates on new books.

As always, thanks for reading,

Megan O'Russell

Never miss a moment of the magic and romance.

Join the Megan O'Russell readers community to stay up to date on all the action by visiting https://www.meganorussell.com/book-signup.

1

The crack of the whip sent the birds scattering into the sky. They cawed their displeasure at the violence of the men below as they flew over the village and to the mountains beyond.

The whip cracked again.

Aaron did well. He didn't start to moan until the fourth lash. By the seventh, he screamed in earnest.

No one had given him a belt to bite down on. There hadn't been time when the soldiers hauled him from his house and tied him to the post in the square.

I clutched the little wooden box of salve hidden in my pocket, letting the corners bite deep into my palm.

The soldier passed forty lashes, not caring that Aaron's back had already turned to pulp.

I squeezed my way to the back of the crowd, unwilling to watch Aaron's blood stain the packed dirt.

Behind the rest of the villagers, children cowered in their mother's skirts, hiding from the horrors the Guilds' soldiers brought with them.

I didn't know how many strokes Aaron had been sentenced

to. I didn't want to know. I made myself stop counting how many times the whip sliced his back.

Bida, Aaron's wife, wept on the edge of the crowd. When his screams stopped, hers grew louder.

The women around Bida held her back, keeping her out of reach of the soldiers.

My stomach stung with the urge to offer comfort as she watched her husband being beaten by the men in black uniforms. But, with the salve tucked in my pocket, hiding in the back was safest.

I couldn't give Bida the box unless Aaron survived. Spring hadn't fully arrived, and the plants Lily needed to make more salves still hadn't bloomed. The tiny portion of the stuff hidden in my pocket was worth more than someone's life, especially if that person wasn't going to survive even with Lily's help.

Lily's orders had been clear—wait and see if Aaron made it through. Give Bida the salve if he did. If he didn't, come back home and hide the wooden box under the floorboards for the next poor soul who might need it.

Aaron fell to the ground. Blood leaked from a gash under his arm.

The soldier raised his whip again.

I sank farther into the shadows, trying to comfort myself with the beautiful lie that I could never be tied to the post in the village square, though I knew the salve clutched in my hand would see me whipped at the post as quickly as whatever offense the soldiers had decided Aaron had committed.

When my fingers had gone numb from gripping the box, the soldier stopped brandishing his whip and turned to face the crowd.

"We did not come here to torment you," the soldier said. "We came here to protect Ilbrea. We came here to protect the Guilds. We are here to provide peace to all the people of this great country.

This man committed a crime, and he has been punished. Do not think me cruel for upholding the law." He wrapped the bloody whip around his hand and led the other nine soldiers out of the square.

Ten soldiers. It had only taken ten of them to walk into our village and drag Aaron from his home. Ten men to tie him to the post and leave us all helpless as they beat a man who'd lived among us all his life.

The soldiers disappeared, and the crowd shifted in toward Aaron. I couldn't hear him crying or moaning over the angry mutters of the crowd.

His wife knelt by his side, wailing.

I wound my way forward, ignoring the stench of fear that surrounded the villagers.

Aaron lay on the ground, his hands still tied around the post. His back had been flayed open by the whip. His flesh looked more like something for a butcher to deal with than an illegal healer like me.

I knelt by his side, pressing my fingers to his neck to feel for a pulse.

Nothing.

I wiped my fingers on the cleanest part of Aaron's shirt I could find and weaved my way back out of the crowd, still clutching the box of salve in my hand.

Carrion birds gathered on the rooftops near the square, scenting the fresh blood in the air. They didn't know Aaron wouldn't be food for them. The villagers of Harane had yet to fall so low as to leave our own out as a feast for the birds.

There was no joy in the spring sun as I walked toward Lily's house on the eastern edge of the village.

I passed by the tavern, which had already filled with men who didn't mind we hadn't reached midday. I didn't blame them for hiding in there. If they could find somewhere away from the torment of the soldiers, better on them for seizing it. I only hoped there weren't any soldiers laughing inside the tavern's walls.

I followed the familiar path home. Along our one, wide dirt road, past the few shops Harane had to offer, to the edge of the village where only fields and pastures stood between us and the forest that reached up the eastern mountains' slopes.

It didn't take long to reach the worn wooden house with the one giant tree towering out front. It didn't take long to reach anywhere in the tiny village of Harane.

Part of me hated knowing every person who lived nearby. Part of me wished the village were smaller. Then maybe we'd fall off the Guilds' maps entirely.

As it was, the Guilds only came when they wanted to collect our taxes, to steal our men to fight their wars, or to find some other sick pleasure in inflicting agony on people who wanted nothing more than to survive. Or if their business brought them far enough south on the mountain road they had to pass through our home on their way to torment someone else.

I allowed myself a moment to breathe before facing Lily. I blinked away the images of Aaron covered in blood and shoved them into a dark corner with the rest of the wretched things it was better not to ponder.

Lily barely glanced up as I swung open the gate and stepped into the back garden. Dirt covered her hands and skirt. Her shoulders were hunched from the hours spent planting our summer garden. She never allowed me to help with the task. Everything had to be carefully planned, keeping the vegetables toward the outermost edges. Hiding the plants she could be hanged for in the center, where soldiers were less likely to spot the things she grew to protect the people of our village. The people the soldiers were so eager to hurt.

"Did he make it?" Lily stretched her shoulders back and brushed the dirt off her weathered hands.

I held the wooden box out as my response. Blood stained the

corners. It wasn't Aaron's blood. It was mine. Cuts marked my hand where I'd squeezed the box too tightly.

Lily glared at my palm. "You'd better go in and wrap your hand. If you let it get infected, I'll have to treat you with the salve, and you know we're running out."

I tucked the box back into my pocket and went inside, not bothering to argue that I could heal from a tiny cut. I didn't want to look into Lily's wrinkled face and see the glimmer of pity in her eyes.

The inside of the house smelled of herbs and dried flowers. Their familiar scent did nothing to drive the stench of blood and fear from my nose.

A pot hung over the stove, waiting with whatever Lily had made for breakfast.

My stomach churned at the thought of eating. I needed to get out. Out of the village, away from the soldiers.

I pulled up the loose floorboard by the stove and tucked the salve in between the other boxes, tins, and vials. I grabbed my bag off the long, wooden table and shoved a piece of bread and a waterskin into it for later. I didn't bother grabbing a coat or shawl. I didn't care about getting cold.

I have to get out.

I was back through the door and in the garden a minute later. Lily didn't even look up from her work. "If you're running into the forest, you had better come back with something good."

"I will," I said. "I'll bring you back all sorts of wonderful things. Just make sure you save some dinner for me."

I didn't need to ask her to save me food. In all the years I'd lived with her, Lily had never let me go hungry. But she was afraid I would run away into the forest and never return. Or maybe it was me that feared I might disappear into the trees and never come back. Either way, I felt myself relax as I stepped out of the garden and turned my feet toward the forest.

2

The mountains rose up beyond the edge of the trees, fierce towers I could never hope to climb. No one else from the village would ever even dream of trying such a thing.

The soldiers wouldn't enter the woods. The villagers rarely dared to go near them. The forest was where darkness and solitude lay. A quiet place where the violence of the village couldn't follow me.

I skirted farmers' fields and picked my way through the pastures. No one bothered me as I climbed over the fences they built to keep in their scarce amounts of sheep and cows.

No one kept much livestock. They couldn't afford it in the first place. And besides, if the soldiers saw that one farmer had too many animals, they would take the beasts as taxes. Safer to be poor. Better for your belly to go empty than for the soldiers to think you had something to give.

I moved faster as I got past the last of the farmhouses and beyond the reach of the stench of animal dung.

When I was a very little girl, my brother had told me that the woods were ruled by ghosts. That none of the villagers dared to cut down the trees or venture into their shelter for fear of being taken by the dead and given a worse fate than even the Guilds could provide.

I'd never been afraid of ghosts, and I'd wandered through the woods often enough to be certain that no spirits roamed the eastern mountains.

When I first started going into the forest, I convinced myself I was braver than everyone else in Harane. I was an adventurer, and they were cowards.

Maybe I just knew better. Maybe I knew that no matter what ghosts did, they could never match the horrors men inflict on each other. What I'd seen them do to each other.

By the time I was a hundred feet into the trees, I could no longer see the village behind me. I couldn't smell anything but the fresh scent of damp earth as the little plants fought for survival in the fertile spring ground. I knew my way through the woods well enough I didn't need to bother worrying about which direction to go. It was more a question of which direction I wanted to chase the gentle wind.

I could go and find fungi for Lily to make into something useful, or I could climb. If I went quickly, I would have time to climb and still be able to find something worth Lily getting herself hanged for.

Smiling to myself, I headed due east toward the steepest part of the mountains near our village. Dirt soon covered the hem of my skirt, and mud squelched beneath my shoes, creeping in through the cracked leather of the soles. I didn't mind so much. What the cold could do to me was nothing more than a refreshing chance to prove I was still alive. Life existed outside the village, and there was beauty beyond our battered walls.

Bits of green peeked through the brown of the trees as new buds forced their way out of the branches.

I stopped, staring up at the sky, marveling at the beauty hidden within our woods.

Birds chirped overhead. Not the angry cawing of birds of

death, but the beautiful songs of lovebirds who had nothing more to worry about than tipping their wings up toward the sky.

A gray and blue bird burst from a tree, carrying his song deeper into the forest.

A stream gurgled to one side of me. The snap of breaking branches came from the other. I didn't change my pace as the crackling came closer.

I headed south to a steeper slope where I had to use my hands to pull myself up the rocks.

I moved faster, outpacing the one who lumbered through the trees behind me. A rock face cut through the forest, blocking my path. I dug my fingers into the cracks in the stone, pulling myself up. Careful to keep my legs from being tangled in my skirt, I found purchase on the rock with the soft toes of my boots. In a few quick movements, I pushed myself up over the top of the ledge. I leapt to my feet and ran to the nearest tree, climbing up to the highest thick branch.

I sat silently on my perch, waiting to see what sounds would come from below.

A rustle came from the base of the rock, followed by a long string of inventive curses.

I bit my lips together, not allowing myself to call out.

The cursing came again.

"Of all the slitching, vile—" the voice from below growled.

I leaned back against the tree, closing my eyes, reveling in my last few moments of solitude. Those hints of freedom were what I loved most about being able to climb. Going up a tree, out of reach of the things that would catch me.

"Ena," the voice called. "Ena."

I didn't answer.

"Ena, are you going to leave me down here?"

My lips curved into a smile as I bit back my laughter. "I didn't ask you to follow me. You can just go back the way you came."

"I don't want to go back," he said. "Let me come up. At least show me how you did it."

"If you want to chase me, you'd better learn to climb."

I let him struggle for a few more minutes until he threatened to find a pick and crack through the rock wall. I glanced down to find him three feet off the ground, his face bright red as he tried to climb.

"Jump down," I said, not wanting him to fall and break something. I could have hauled him back to the village, but I didn't fancy the effort.

"Help me get up," he said.

"Go south a bit. You'll find an easier path."

I listened to the sounds of him stomping off through the trees, enjoying the bark against my skin as I waited for him to find the way up.

It only took him a few minutes to loop back around to stand under my perch.

Looking at Cal stole my will to flee. His blond hair glistened in the sun. He shaded his bright blue eyes as he gazed up at me.

"Are you happy now?" he said. "I'm covered in dirt."

"If you wanted to be clean, you shouldn't have come into the woods. I never ask you to follow me."

"It would have been wrong of me not to. You shouldn't be coming out here by yourself."

I didn't let it bother me that he thought it was too dangerous for me to be alone in the woods. It was nice to have someone worry about me. Even if he was worried about ghosts that didn't exist.

"What do you think you'd be able to do to help me anyway?" I said.

He stared up at me, hurt twisting his perfect brow.

Cal looked like a god, or something made at the will of the Guilds themselves. His chiseled jaw held an allure to it, the rough stubble on his cheeks luring my fingers to touch its texture.

I twisted around on my seat and dropped down to the ground, reveling in his gasp as I fell.

"You really need to get more used to the woods," I said. "It's a good place to hide."

"What would I have to hide from?" Cal's eyes twinkled, offering a hint of teasing that drew me toward him.

I touched the stubble on his chin, tracing the line of his jaw.

"There are plenty of things to hide from, fool." I turned to tramp farther into the woods.

"Ena," he called after me, "you shouldn't be going so far from home."

"Then don't follow me. Go back." I knew he would follow.

I had known when I passed by his window in the tavern on my way through the village. He always wanted to be near me. That was the beauty of Cal.

I veered closer to the stream.

Cal kept up, though he despised getting his boots muddy.

I always chose the more difficult path to make sure he knew I could outpace him. It was part of our game on those trips into the forest.

I leapt across the stream to a patch of fresh moss just beginning to take advantage of spring.

"Ena." Cal jumped the water and sank down onto the moss I had sought.

I shoved him off of the green and into the dirt.

He growled.

I didn't bother trying to hide my smile. I pulled out tufts of the green moss, tucking them into my bag for Lily.

"If you don't want me to follow you," Cal said, "you can tell me not to whenever you like."

"The forest doesn't belong to me, Cal. You can go where you choose."

He grabbed both my hands and tugged me toward him. I tipped onto him and he shifted, letting me fall onto my back. I caught a glimpse of the sun peering down through the new buds of emerald leaves, and then he was kissing me.

His taste of honey and something a bit deeper filled me. And I forgot about whips and Lily and men bleeding and soldiers coming to kill us.

There was nothing but Cal and me. And the day became beautiful.

Order your copy of Ember and Stone *to continue the story.*

SIEGE
AND
SPARROW

COVER
COMING SOON

MEGAN O'RUSSELL

Megan O'Russell is the author of several Young Adult series that invite readers to escape into worlds of adventure. From *Girl of Glass*, which blends dystopian darkness with the heart-pounding danger of vampires, to *Ena of Ilbrea*, which draws readers into an epic world of magic and assassins.

With the *Girl of Glass* series, *The Tethering* series, *The Chronicles of Maggie Trent*, *The Tale of Bryant Adams*, the *Ena of Ilbrea* series, and several more projects planned, there are always exciting new books on the horizon. To be the first to hear about new releases, free short stories, and giveaways, sign up for Megan's newsletter by visiting the following:

https://www.meganorussell.com/book-signup.

Originally from Upstate New York, Megan is a professional musical theatre performer whose work has taken her across North America. Her chronic wanderlust has led her from Alaska to Thailand and many places in between. Wanting to travel has fostered Megan's love of books that allow her to visit countless new worlds from her favorite reading nook. Megan is also a lyricist and playwright. Information on her theatrical works can be found at RussellCompositions.com.

She would be thrilled to chat with you on Facebook or

Twitter @MeganORussell, elated if you'd visit her website MeganORussell.com, and over the moon if you'd like the pictures of her adventures on Instagram @ORussellMegan.

www.ingramcontent.com/pod-product-compliance
Lightning Source LLC
Chambersburg PA
CBHW030836190726
48285CB00004B/1247

9 781951 359553